JOANNA COURTNEY

IRON QUEEN

PIATKUS

PIATKUS

First published in Great Britain in 2020 by Piatkus
This paperback edition published in 2021 by Piatkus

1 3 5 7 9 10 8 6 4 2

A CIP catalogue record for this book
is available from the British Library.

ISBN 978-0-349-41956-5

Typeset in Baskerville by M Rules
Printed and bound in Great Britain by Clays Ltd, Elcograf S.p.A.

Papers used by Piatkus are from well-managed forests
and other responsible sources.

Piatkus
An imprint of
Little, Brown Book Group
Carmelite House
50 Victoria Embankment
London EC4Y 0DZ

An Hachette UK Company
www.hachette.co.uk

www.littlebrown.co.uk

To Dad – my number one reader.
With gratitude and love.

THE CELTIC CALENDAR

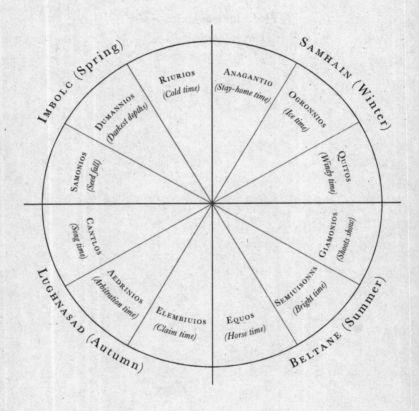

Joanna Courtney's first literary accolade was a creative writing prize at primary school and from that point on she wanted to be a novelist. She was always reading as a child

or via her website: joannacourtney.com.

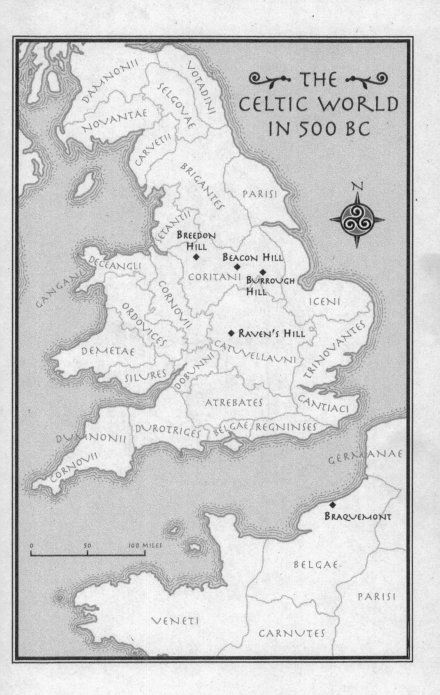

THE CELTIC WORLD IN 500 BC

N

DAMNONII
NOVANTAE
SELGOVAE
VOTADINI
CARVETII
BRIGANTES
PARISI
SETANTII
Breedon Hill
Beacon Hill
CORITANI
Burrough Hill
DECEANGLI
GANGANI
CORNOVII
ICENI
ORDOVICES
DEMETAE
Raven's Hill
CATUVELLAUNI
TRINOVANTES
SILURES
DOBUNNI
ATREBATES
CANTIACI
DUMNONII
DUROTRIGES
BELGAE
REGNINSES
CORNOVII
GERMANAE
Braquemont
BELGAE
PARISI
VENETI
CARNUTES

0   50   100 MILES

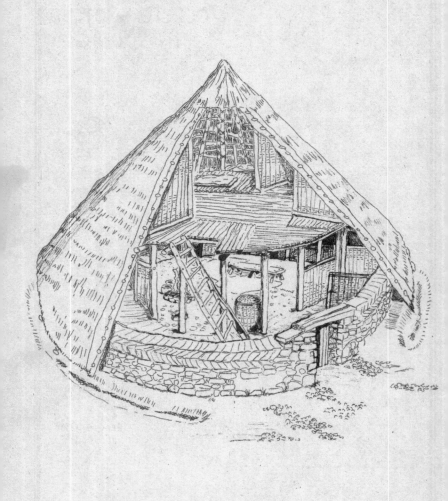

The tribal lands rang with rejoicing when Cordelia was born. A third royal daughter for the Coritani, their very own Deas Matres; the Mother Goddess in threefold form. All were proud of the sacred bloodline passed from mother to daughter – a red river of strength flowing through their people – and now there were three new wombs to carry them forward. And such a perfect three too: Goneril, eldest and fiercest with fire in her veins; Regan, second and most steadfast, with her feet firmly in the earth; and gentle Cordelia, one with the water. All different, all strong in their own ways, and together, surely, the key to the future of the Coritani tribe.

Chieftainess Mavelle called a great celebration. For three days the ancient fortress on Beacon Hill rang with lutes and pipes and joyful voices. Scented smoke from roasted boars hung sweetly across the hill and a great fire blazed from the iron beacon to call everyone to join the tribe in praising Danu for Her great blessings.

I was but a girl then, not yet into my tenth summer and still a year from beginning my studies as a druid, but the joy of those days is imprinted upon my mind in festival colours. Branwen, heiress and new mother, rested on soft cushions with the babe Cordelia at her breast. Regan played at her feet, Goneril sat at her side and her husband Leir stood guard over them all as a good consort should. It was such a pretty tableau and they were honoured like goddesses.

Branwen had amulets of triskeles – the eternal triple spiral – made for the girls, to symbolise their threefold strength. The charms were blessed before the whole tribe and she tied them around her daughters' little necks on leather cords for everyone to see, and all was well in the Coritani lands.

But the spiral of life never ceases turning and just two years later we lost Branwen trying to birth a boychild. The Goddess, it seemed, rejected the prince and he tugged the precious heiress after him to the Otherworld with his tiny, blue hands. It was three days of weeping that time and many more for Leir who loved Branwen so greatly that for a long, dark time everyone feared he would throw himself after her into the earth.

But those three girls were there still — those three precious princesses, fire, earth and water, the Deas Matres *of the Coritani — and somehow they pulled him through. He cared for them and loved them and brought them to womanhood. And now, with Chieftainess Mavelle fading, the tribe needs them to care for it in return. I can only pray they are ready to serve the Coritani as true rulers.*

IMBOLC

Spring

500 BC

Chapter One

BEACON HILL, THE LANDS OF THE CORITANI

Anagantio; Stay-home days (February)

The ice was spirit-bright on this last day before Imbolc when Cordelia stepped cautiously out into the rugged compound of Beacon Hill. It was months since she'd last been to the central fortress and she'd forgotten how craggy it was up here in the heartlands of the Coritani. She could feel the spirits pushing out of the land in the jagged rocks and twisted trees that rose relentlessly between the roundhouses, reminding all men of their place in the world.

Heading past the sacred oak at the centre of the compound, she made for the great iron beacon at its peak. The fort was enclosed by earthen ramparts higher than the tallest man, but the hill rose above them, making it easy to see out across the Coritani lands on all sides. It was dark yet and no one else was stirring in either the roundhouses within the ramparts, or the byres and workshops just outside them. To the west, however, a line of burnished bronze

5

was spreading across the lowest reaches of the skies, making the white lands glow. It was as if the embers of the night were being stirred into life ready for a new day and Cordelia was glad to see it being birthed.

She shivered and tied her heavy plaid cloak more tightly across her chest, wishing she'd put on a second tunic. It had been hot in the royal house last night, with the hearth-fire burning high and so many people crammed in that they'd been sleeping on top of each other like puppies. Cordelia swore she could still feel the imprint of her sisters' elbows in her sides, as she so often had when they were girls, and stretched herself out gladly.

Her eyes drifted inexorably east, trying to see across the plains to her own fortress on Burrough Hill, but the shadow of the night was still upon the land and she was forced to fall back on her mind's eye to picture her hound, Keira.

Stay there, she willed the pups inside the hound's blessed belly. *Stay warm inside for just a few more days until I can return to see you safely into the world.*

She bent down and placed both hands flat upon the sacred ground, sending her love through the soil. Her fingers numbed but when she drew back, the grass beneath her touch was green and she smiled. The spirits had heard her. They would guard Keira until the tribe had welcomed the first Imbolc moon and Cordelia could ride back to her side.

'Dee? Dee, is that you?'

Cordelia squinted into the gloom.

'Father?'

Leir's greying hair was wild from sleep and his eyes were still half closed, though they looked at her with their usual sharpness.

'Pining for your pups, Daughter?'

'Praying they are still safe inside their dam, Father.'

Leir placed a large hand on her shoulder.

'You said they were not due for another seven days.'

Cordelia shifted.

'That would be usual, yes, but the Imbolc moon may draw them out early.'

'And if it does, their dam will care for them, sweet one, and Solinus besides.'

Cordelia grunted.

'That's true but Solinus does not understand as I do, Father. He does not have the same *feel*.'

Leir patted her shoulder again.

'I know it. You have a talent with the animals – as your mother had before you.'

Cordelia saw Leir's whole body tighten against the lightening sky and leaned back in to hug him again. She'd been just two years old when Branwen had died, leaving him in charge of their new fort at Burrough and their three girls. Memories of her were mere wisps of mist across Cordelia's mind but she felt the loss keenly through her father.

'She would be proud of you, Dee,' Leir said now. 'Of Goneril and Regan too, but you, I think, most closely carry her spirit.'

Cordelia swallowed back tears.

'My sisters are like you, Father.'

'Ambitious, impetuous and ever restless for more?'

'Active, bold and born to lead.'

He laughed softly.

'You are too kind, sweet one. And perhaps in Goneril you speak true. She is keen to rule.'

'As she should be. She is the heiress so holds the fire of the Coritani in her veins.'

'And longs to tug it to her own ends. But the tribe will not be hers until her grandmother departs this earth and I pray that will not be for some time.'

'I pray so too, Father,' Cordelia agreed hastily. Mavelle was a strong chieftainess but she grew old. Next year would be her fiftieth, a fine count for any soul, and when the ice-moon had claimed her beloved consort, Bladdud, this Samhain it seemed maybe it had

7

stolen her spirit too. For a long time she had drawn in on herself but the new shoots of Imbolc were perhaps growing inside her too for these past few days she had seemed more animated.

'Last night Grandmother was more like herself,' Cordelia said cautiously.

Leir gave a small smile.

'She was, my sweet one. When she talks of the birds, she comes alive again.'

They were silent a moment, remembering. The tribe had eaten in the ceremonial house together, bringing food from their own hearths to share. The fire had been stoked high, the steam and noise of a hundred happy people had filled the great circle of a room, and Chieftainess Mavelle had leaped up, as if infused with the energy of her tribe. She had always been a small woman, but age had shrunk her further, and with her thin limbs and white hair, she had looked almost like a spirit dancing before the fire.

'We are close,' she'd told them. 'Truly, we are close to taking to the skies, to being one with the birds.'

'You will fly, Grandmother?' Regan had asked excitedly, for she loved any physical challenge.

'I will fly, Regan. Before I leave this life, I swear I will fly.'

'Perhaps immediately before,' Leir had said fearfully and Mavelle had laughed and clapped her son-by-marriage surprisingly strongly on the back.

'Have faith, Leir. Bladdud always did. And he will be up there waiting to support me, I know it.'

All eyes had turned upwards, though there had been only the smoky thatch to see. Chieftain Bladdud, Mavelle's consort, had loved the birds even more passionately than she and had had more time to pursue experiments with flight. Since his death she had taken up his passion with even greater enthusiasm – and even greater urgency, as if his passing to the Otherworld had alerted her to the shortness of her own time left on earth.

'We have been making great strides with our experiments, have we not, Olwen?' she'd said last night, turning to her high druidess and fellow seeker into the ways of birds.

'We're excited by the possibilities,' Olwen had agreed with a sideways smile that could have been joy or could have been a sneer or could have been a thousand emotions in between. You could never tell with the druidess.

Mavelle, however, had been less enigmatic.

'I have wings.' She'd danced suddenly around the astonished tribe, flapping her thin arms. 'I have big wings, constructed feather by feather upon a frame of wood, sliced as thin as it is possible to achieve. They are modelled on my own dear hawk, as fine a flyer as any in the skies, and once we balance them against the weight of a human they will work.'

'Can we see them?' Regan had asked, her dark eyes alight.

'Soon,' she'd promised. 'Very soon.'

'Not that soon,' the high druidess had said sternly. 'We have not yet tested them in the air. The ratio of feather to wood is not perfected and—'

'Soon,' Mavelle had repeated firmly, and then she'd flapped her way back onto her fur-covered stool and sunk back into lethargy as quickly as she had shrugged it off.

'We can only hope,' Leir said softly now, 'that the festival will restore dear Mavelle's spirit in a similar way.'

Cordelia nodded and looked around the compound. Others were waking and smoke was snaking out of the thatched roofs of the ten roundhouses amongst the rocks of Beacon Hill, as well as the many travelling tents housing those who had journeyed here to welcome the first moon of fertile Imbolc.

It was Cordelia's favourite of the four great festivals that quartered the year. It had none of the wanton joy of moon-bright Beltane, the gluttonous richness of earthy Lughnasad, or the dark wildness of fiery Samhain, but water-blessed Cordelia liked its quietness. She liked the soft relief of the first flowers unfolding and the promise of the ewes' bellies swelling. She liked the gentle happiness of green shoots shaking off the last of the snows and the waters gurgling free of their ice prison. Imbolc was, perhaps, the shyest of the celebrations but Cordelia was the shyest of the Coritani's royal daughters so she had taken it to her heart.

'It will be a good day,' she said to her father, gesturing to where Lugh, the great sun, was raising his golden head above the earth.

He nodded but his blue eyes, fully awake now, scanned the horizon for more than just Lugh's light. There had been rumblings from the Setantii tribe on their western borders recently. Last Beltane their heiress had married an ambitious young man who was keen to gift his bride new lands – Coritani lands. Mavelle had troops out on regular patrol to repel raiders but Leir feared a more concerted attack. Cordelia put a hand on his arm.

'No one would attack under the Imbolc moon, Father, for they would be cursed by the Goddess if they did so.'

'Maybe they would think that curse a fair price to pay for Coritani riches?'

'Father!'

He shook his head.

'Sorry, Dee. You're right. Danu would punish anyone daring to break the peace of her sacred day. I will think no more of threats, but of the blessings of Imbolc. Shall we break our fast?'

Cordelia shook her head at him.

'Today you should be more spirit and less stomach.'

Leir laughed heartily and patted at his belly.

'But a stomach like mine is so demanding.'

'You are perfectly lean, Father.'

'I am perfectly fit, Daughter, fret you not, but life is bulging beneath my skin a little, especially around the middle.'

Cordelia tried to laugh but her stomach lurched and she turned for home to cover her confusion. He spoke true, she knew; it happened to everyone. Even dogs thickened as they trod the latter paths of their current time on earth, but with Mavelle growing frail and Leir admitting to the effects of age, everything seemed so uncertain. It was as if one age of the Coritani was sinking into the waters of the past and a new one was bubbling to the surface. Its shape was not yet clear and that made Cordelia as nervous as if the ground beneath her feet was shaking.

'You are *sure* you are well, Father?' she asked, and was rewarded by another laugh.

'I am very well, sweet one. See!' He caught her around the waist and flung her up over his shoulder as he had often done when she was small. 'Strong as an ox.'

'Father!' She banged on his back with her fists but made little impression. 'Father, put me down.'

'Am I well?'

'You are well,' she giggled, despite herself. 'You are very well. Now put me—'

'What on earth?' demanded a furious voice. Cordelia twisted in Leir's grip to see her eldest sister standing squarely in the doorway of the royal house, hands on shapely hips. 'What are you doing, Father? Cordelia is a woman now and a royal woman besides. What of dignity?'

Cordelia felt Leir shrug beneath her.

'What of joy, Goneril?'

Goneril's wrinkled nose revealed exactly what she thought of joy and slowly Leir lowered Cordelia to the ground.

'Good morning, Sister,' she said, hastily rearranging her plaited belt and settling her blue plaid tunic in place. Goneril had clearly risen on the dark side of their shared pallet today and it would not do to rile her.

'Is it? It seems a *cold* morning to me.'

'But a bright one.'

Cordelia indicated Lugh, shining thinly down on the compound as people began to emerge and call greetings to one another. Goneril grunted.

'I hope it's bright enough to melt the sacred brook or it will be a sorry ceremony indeed.'

Cordelia took a slow breath, hoping to suck patience in with it. In truth they had all been worried about the brook. The festival of Imbolc celebrated the release of the Goddess Danu's lifegiving waters from the grip of Samhain but until a few days ago it had been solid.

'The brook flows free,' she assured Goneril. 'I visited it when we arrived yesterday.'

'Did you?'

'It seemed wise to check.'

Goneril tossed the auburn hair that so proudly marked her out from her darker sisters.

'Yes, well, maybe it froze again overnight with the rest of the land?' She stamped on the earth and sparks of frost flew obligingly upwards, revealing the warm earth beneath. Cordelia looked at the ground but said nothing and Goneril tossed her hair again. 'I suppose you want to eat?'

'Yes, please,' Leir agreed, making for the door. 'And perhaps you should too, dear girl. It might . . . cheer you.'

He threw Cordelia a wink and she hastily ducked in after him to hide another smile. Everyone was up now and it was busy around the hearth. Mavelle had ordered a magnificent new roundhouse for her family last Beltane, constructed in the latest way, with the outer bedrooms shut off with willow walls, leaving a contained space in the middle in which to eat, work and live. She had even designated the higher floor as her and Bladdud's own bedroom, rather than using it for storage, and it was a beautiful space. Being in here was Cordelia's favourite thing about coming to Beacon and she went gladly towards the central fire, feeling sensation already returning to her frozen fingers.

Chieftainess Mavelle sat with Olwen, supping pottage from a bowl and talking intently to the druidess. Cordelia caught the words "feathers" and "flight path" and moved to the other side of the hearth. She truly hoped her grandmother would achieve her aim of flying but had no wish to learn the mechanics of it.

'Morning, Regan.'

'Cordelia.'

Regan saluted her from the floor where she was contorted in a peculiar position, one leg out front and one behind as she stretched to grab her own foot. It looked most uncomfortable, not to mention putting a strain on the knitted trews she was wearing beneath the short earth-brown tunic she always favoured for ease of movement.

'What are you doing?' Cordelia asked, bending down to her sister's level.

'Lengthening my spine.'

'Really?'

'Hopefully.'

'Why do you want a longer spine?'

'Why?' Regan sat up abruptly, her head almost clattering into Cordelia's chin. 'Because then I will be taller and will fight better.'

'Ah. Of course.'

Most things Cordelia's earth-blessed middle sister did were to enable her to fight better. She was forever running or practising swordplay or lifting rocks to harden her flesh. Mavelle had often tried to explain to her that a woman's strength lay in her mind, not her arm, but Regan wanted both.

'You look taller already, Ree,' Cordelia told her.

'I do?' Hope sparked in Regan's eyes.

'Of course you don't,' Goneril snapped. It died instantly.

'I'm told it takes time,' she mumbled and pulled herself up off the ground, plucking at the tight plaits she always wore to keep her hair out of her face, and looking a little desperately towards the older sister whose good opinion she ever sought. Goneril, thank Danu, relented.

'You do not need to be taller, Ree. You are a fierce fighter just as you are.'

Regan beamed and Cordelia thanked the fire spirits for Goneril's rare praise. She put a hand to the amulet around her neck and saw her sisters do the same. They all wore the triskele, the triple spiral, to symbolise that as the three elemental royal daughters of the Coritani they were eternally joined together – however much they might quarrel.

'Shall we eat?' she suggested and, with a nod, they took stools side by side.

Cordelia's mind wandered to Keira and her pups but she forced it back to the hearth. She might be away from her precious hound but she was with her family for her favourite festival and must keep her mind tuned to the joys of the Mother Goddess' blessed day.

The tribe gathered at dusk, preparations made and all dressed in their finest – and warmest – clothes. Those who had them wore furs over their tunics, trews and long woollen cloaks, and all heads were covered with knitted hats and thick shawls. Cordelia had pulled her own coverings on with reluctance as she'd been hot all day, sweeping the roundhouses clear of the dust and dirt of Samhain to be fresh and ready for Imbolc, but now the temperature was dropping fast and she was glad of them. The Coritani huddled close as the first Imbolc moon began to rise, fat and full, and a thousand stars picked up its light and flung it around so that Beacon Hill was bathed in silver.

All the inhabitants of the heartland fort and those on the homesteads nearby were here to keep vigil, plus those fit enough to have made the full day's tramp from Leir's second fortress at Burrough. Nigh on one hundred men, women and children stood around the sacred oak as Chieftainess Mavelle stepped up before them. She was finely dressed in her ceremonial robes but Cordelia saw how her white hair blew thinly in the breeze and noticed a rip in her chequered red cloak and prayed that age was not stealing her grandmother from them. As she raised her old head to the moon, however, Mavelle's eyes took on the light of all the stars and she seemed to grow before them.

'Hail, Danu, Mother, Bringer of Life. We ask for your blessings on this wakening Imbolc that we may revel in the bounty of this your earth and dance beneath the moon in prosperity and joy.' Her voice echoed around the hilltop and seemed to bounce off the skies and ripple back to them three times over. Cordelia closed her eyes and gave herself to the ceremony. 'We thank you for restoring life to the earth and we reach out to the spirits of the rocks and of the ground, of the trees and the flowers, of fire and of air and of lifegiving water, to come with us into the swelling season of fruitfulness.'

The earth seemed to thrum as the spirits rose to Mavelle's call and threaded between the crowd. Cordelia stretched out her hands to feel the pulse of the dead beating through the tribe, tethering them to their past so they could stand strong in the face of whatever the future might bring.

A ewe, fat with lamb, was brought forward, bleating. She had been selected first at the tupping and been separated from the herd ever since. Kept in splendour, fed the sweetest hay and given a place near the fire with the family, she would now go to Danu in triumph. Mavelle raised her knife – a fine blade, beaten out beneath the previous year's Samhain moon, to fill it with the spirits of the ancestors. The ewe looked up and in one merciful stroke, it was done. The druids lifted her onto the heartstone set beneath the oak and, just as deftly, slit her open to pull the lamb from her womb.

Cordelia held her breath, fighting to stay in the sacred moment and not think of Keira and her wombful of pups. Almost instantly the little creature bleated and the crowd sucked in this sign of favour for if the lamb lived, the year would be prosperous. Olwen swiftly cut the cord and wrapped the creature in a blanket before putting it to its dead mother's teat to suckle as her blood ran into the heartstone, to fill it with new life. Tomorrow the mother's fleece would be flayed for the lamb's bed and the high druidess would nurse it as her own special charge. All being well, they would feast on its flesh with the year's harvest at Lughnasad, but for now it was as fragile as all new life and Cordelia's heart went out to it.

Suddenly unnerved, she looked to her sisters, but both of them were intent on the ceremony. Goneril had her green-gold eyes fixed on Olwen with awe and something sharper – admiration perhaps, or even longing. Cordelia glanced back at the druidess and saw her eyes flicker to Goneril and darken with a predatory sparkle. Was Olwen bedding Cordelia's sister? It would be little surprise. Olwen had sworn her soul to the Goddess but invited many to her bed, male and female alike. Was Goneril the latest to feel her pull? Cordelia leaned towards Regan to whisper then reminded herself that this was a sacred moment and tore her mind away from gossip.

'Come,' Mavelle called, drawing them back to her. 'Take light and follow.'

Leir lit a brand from the small fire burning below the heartstone and, stretching up, set it to the kindling in the ancient beacon stand. Well coated in fat, the wood roared to life, to shine out the tribe's commitment to Danu the Mother and Lugh the sun, her blessed consort. All stared upwards in joy as the chieftainess nodded to the three royal daughters to take torches from the druids and lead the procession down the hill to the sacred spring.

Goneril went first, with Regan in her wake and Cordelia last. She felt her feet turn numb within her leather boots as the frost settled around them and willed herself not to stumble, but thankfully all eyes were on Goneril who walked tall, head back to show off the golden heiress' torque around her slim neck. The firelight danced in her auburn hair so that it seemed a second beacon for the people to follow and as she passed Olwen, she brushed so close that the lamb in the druidess' arms bleated anew.

Two steps behind, Regan stood heavily on the stately druidess' foot so that she had to bite back an undignified yelp of pain and her sister's display of jealousy told Cordelia all she needed. For the first time, someone else was closer to the royal daughters than they were to each other and she nervously touched her amulet, but this was no time to worry at the inevitabilities of growing up so, looking again to her numb feet, she followed her sisters as the rest of the Coritani fell into line behind.

The tribe twisted in a serpent of torchlight out of the great gates of the fort and down the slope to the spring below. Their path took them past the Guardian, the great man-shaped rock who kept lookout over the rolling plains, and all paused to bow to him before moving on into the woodland below. Cordelia's sharp ears picked up the gurgle of the water long before they saw it spilling merrily into the great stone trough beneath and she glanced triumphantly at Goneril. Her sister, however, did not even deign to look her way, and now Olwen was stepping up and inviting everyone to ask for the Goddess' personal favour.

People began fumbling in the pockets at their belts for the strips of cloth they had brought to run in the new-flowing water, to absorb the blessing of Danu. Regan had a strip from her rough brown training tunic. She would be asking, as she did every year, for skill with her sword but, as Cordelia felt for the piece she had brought from Keira's bedding, she suspected she was becoming every bit as predictable. Over the last few years she had experimented with matching different hounds and bitches to bring out certain traits in their offspring and was making excellent progress. If all went well, she would have many new hound pups needing Danu's safe-guarding over the next years and it was with excitement as well as reverence that she dipped Keira's cloth in the lifewaters and selected a branch before standing back to let others take their turn.

Goneril, unusually, hung back and Cordelia could not help but notice the cloth her elder sister held. It was a rich, chequered red and looked, if she was not very much mistaken, just like Mavelle's glorious cloak. Cordelia remembered the rip she'd noticed in it earlier and looked around for her grandmother, but she was nowhere to be seen and now Goneril was bending to dip the fabric in the spring's flow and the colour darkened too much for Cordelia to be sure.

She took a few steps back down the path and so it was that she noticed movement in the trees before anyone else. Her heart lurched. Had the Setantii chosen to break the Imbolc taboo and attack? She looked for Leir but could not make him out amongst the crowd and before she could cry a more general warning something launched itself from the branches and filled the sky above the grove. All eyes turned upwards and people cried out in alarm but now the torches lit up the astonishing figure of Chieftainess Mavelle, clad in nothing but a plain white tunic and a giant pair of wings.

For a moment she hovered above them, half woman, half bird.

She's done it! Cordelia thought, but barely had she framed the words in her head than her grandmother was plummeting earthwards, wings flapping wildly and catching in the torches of those too slow to scramble aside. She landed, ablaze, and it was only Olwen quickly scooping Danu's water onto her feathers that saved them all from being set alight. The crowd stood gazing dumbstruck at their chieftainess as she sat up, white hair sodden and wings charred and steaming in a mist around her.

'I did it,' she pronounced. 'Danu be praised, I did it. I flew.'

Chapter Two

The next day

Olwen kicked helplessly at the charred and broken remnants of
the precious wings, trying not to see in them the equally broken
remnants of all their dreams. So long they'd been working on this
project, so much time and energy they'd put into the studies and
the tests and the calculations, and Mavelle had dashed it all to the
ground in one ill-judged swoop. It was all the druidess could do
not to rage and swear at her, but Mavelle was her chieftainess and
her mother-in-science and it was not Olwen's place to question her
decisions. She was still raging inside though.

She'd always been a seeker. Even as a small child she'd been
eager to probe the workings of the world. She'd heard the spirits of
everything chattering in her ears at all hours – leaves whispering,
bark rasping, water gurgling, and all saying: *We have secrets, intricate,
sacred secrets. Come, Olwen, come and find out what they are.* How could
she have resisted?

She'd cut open her first creature at five – a hare caught in a trap
that she'd begged her mother to let her look inside before she con-
signed it to the pot. With a sigh the poor woman had agreed and,
oh, it had been like the universe opening up to her in the innards

of that one wonderful creature. Hours she'd spent working out how the maze of glossy organs fitted together. Her mother, despairing of dinner, had eventually joined her and together they'd traced how the beautiful little thing might turn food into life in an everyday miracle. Olwen had been hooked.

She'd had to wait until she was nine to see inside her first human – a raider caught stealing corn from the tribe and hung outside Beacon's great gates. She'd pleaded with Chieftainess Mavelle to be allowed the corpse and that was the first time she'd heard the order that was to change her life: *You, child, are to go to the druids and receive their instruction.* Two years later she'd been bundled up in blankets and ridden across frost-bitten lands to join a carefully chosen community of others keen to see inside the heart of the things that move the earth. For Olwen, those two years of learning had been Elysium on earth.

She *was* a natural seeker, the druids had confirmed within weeks. She was not a singer, for her voice slid off the notes making all around wince. And she was not an augur, for she examined the sacrifices more for how they had worked in their living past than for what they told her of the future. It was her destiny, she'd known, to study the world, and when she'd returned to the Coritani bringing with her the wisdom of the druids, she'd sought to listen to the secrets of the spirits and work with them to improve the lot of man. And so far she had been blessed by having royal patrons who shared that aim. The chieftainess had promoted Olwen to high druidess last Beltane and given her autonomy in all her endeavours – until now.

'You're cross, Olwen,' Mavelle said as Lugh's first rays slanted in through the door and across the ruined wings.

Olwen shrugged.

'It seems they did not work anyway.'

That was the heart of it. If she was cross, it was not truly with Mavelle for testing the wings but with the wings for failing.

'Not yet.'

Olwen had to smile; the chieftainess was a woman of eternal optimism. Not to mention eternal carelessness. The druidess lifted the edge of her cloak to examine a nasty rip.

'What have you done here, Mavelle?'

She looked down.

'No idea. Must have caught it on something.'

'It looks more as if you've cut a piece out.'

She laughed.

'Why would I do that, Olwen?'

'Because you needed it for something, I'd imagine, and cared less about your appearance than your invention.'

The chieftainess smiled.

'You know me too well, but in this case ... '

She stopped as a knock sounded out on the door. The guards hurried to unthread the laces holding the leather curtain closed and Cordelia's bright young face appeared around its edge. Olwen's heart picked up a beat. Was she alone? No. As she slid inside, she was followed by her royal sisters, first Regan and then Goneril. Olwen's Goneril.

The druidess had taken the flame of the Coritani to her bed in the cold depths of Samhain and, Danu knew, the young woman burned bright. She had an energy unlike any Olwen had known – a fierce, restless passion that it had been her joy to ignite and that had ignited something in herself in return. She had missed Goneril more than she cared to admit when she'd had to return to her father's fort at Burrough and Olwen's very skin sang to have her back and close for the Imbolc celebrations.

Never, in all her twenty-five years on Danu's earth, had anyone made Olwen feel both beautifully powerful and utterly helpless and she could almost see why people spoke of love. It was not a concept she cared for, not being traceable even within a dissected heart, but the eldest royal daughter was intoxicating and Olwen couldn't prevent herself from following the young woman's languid movements with her eyes as Cordelia ran forward ahead of her.

'Oh, Grandmother – this place is magnificent! Look at your beautiful birds!'

Her eyes were darting all over the open roundhouse, following the flight of the creatures swooping above. It was vital, when trying to mimic birds, to study them as closely as possible and Olwen and Mavelle had gathered every species they could into their workshop. Ollocus, the old blacksmith, had crafted over thirty cages but usually they only kept the chieftainess' precious hawk shut up and Cordelia had to duck as a pair of sparrows swooped past her and landed on Mavelle's knee.

'They trust you,' she said.

'Why should they not? I'd do nothing to hurt them. Come in, come in.'

The three girls approached their grandmother, their matching amulets winking in the sunlight sneaking through the thatch. Goneril brushed past Olwen and she could have sworn she actually felt the heat of her, but Mavelle's eyes were on the royal daughters and Olwen had to let her pass untouched.

'Are you well, Grandmother?' she heard Cordelia ask over the pulse of her own damned blood.

'Well? I'm very well. Why wouldn't I be well?'

'After your, er . . . flight.'

'My fall, you mean. I'm unharmed. No damage done at all.'

'You've ripped your beautiful cloak,' Regan pointed out.

'Oh, no,' Cordelia said, 'it was ripped before. I noticed it in the procession.'

Olwen looked curiously at her but there was no chance to ask more for Mavelle had whisked it crossly away.

'The only thing I ripped was my pride,' she insisted. 'Tell me, girls, is everyone laughing at me?'

'No!' Cordelia said. 'Not at all. They're excited. You hovered, Grandmother. We distinctly saw you hover. Not for long, perhaps, but it's a start, is it not?'

Mavelle leaped up and grabbed for her hands.

'It *is*, my little Dee-Dee. It *is* a start.'

'And an end,' Olwen reminded her. They all looked towards what was left of the wings.

Mavelle kicked at the side nearest her and blackened feathers fell off and crumbled into dust beneath the exposed wooden frame.

'We'll just need more feathers,' she grunted.

'A *lot* more.'

She waved her hand.

'The bees will be producing again soon. We can bribe the children with honey to collect them for us, like we did last year. '

Olwen sighed. Their chieftainess spoke true but it would take time and what good would it do to repeat the same mistakes?

'I think we need to find a new way,' she said, 'though Danu knows how.'

Suddenly Goneril was beside her, so close Olwen felt the enticing curve of a hip against her own.

'I'm sure *you* know how, High Druidess.'

'Truly, Goneril, I do not.'

Cordelia was eyeing them closely, too closely. Olwen tried to step away but the heat of the heiress was fusing them together and she had to force herself to bend and touch the blackened wood to break the connection. Goneril knelt beside her, a smile playing on her lips.

'But you'll work it out. I know it.'

Olwen so wanted to believe her but they'd been working on this for years; surely a new way would have come to them if there was one? Now, though, Regan walked slowly around the sorry structure, nudging at it with her sword.

'Have you considered iron, Grandmother?'

'Iron? Would it not be too heavy?'

'Perhaps but it would be more malleable than wood and the smiths, you know, can beat it very fine these days. My new shield is wonderfully easy to lift and you would only need iron for the outer frame. You could have leather within.'

'Leather! Iron!' Mavelle took Regan's face in her wizened hands and kissed her forehead. 'How clever my granddaughters are. I knew my Branwen was blessed to produce three royal daughters for the tribe, but to have produced three such clever ones was a double gift. Leather and iron, Olwen, is it not worth a try?'

Her mind was already busy exploring the possibilities.

'It would certainly be more resilient,' she allowed, 'and perhaps more flexible too. As it would need to be.'

'Why?' Regan asked.

Olwen reached up and lifted one of her most prized possessions carefully down from the centre rafter – the skeleton of a long-dead bird, preserved by the druid who first taught her the art and gifted her this specimen on their parting. Gently lifting one wing, she showed the royal daughters the astonishingly delicate pattern of tiny, almost translucent bones. It moved as perfectly as it had always done, each bone folding into the next as it closed up before opening out again with fluid ease. Olwen never tired of studying it and was glad to see the girls mesmerised too.

'It's so intricate,' Cordelia said.

She nodded.

'Too intricate for us to recreate.'

'For us to recreate *yet*,' Mavelle corrected firmly. 'But maybe Regan is on to something. Leather and iron, Olwen. It's worth a try, is it not?'

'It is,' she agreed. 'I have a very clever new apprentice, Caireen, who knows much about fabrics and could help us there, but I'm not sure Ollocus is up to the ironwork. He's a skilled smith.' She paused to indicate the birdcages over their heads. 'But he grows old.'

'Has he no apprentice?'

Olwen thought of the coarse lad who'd come into the smithy last summer. He'd seemed strong and keen but that wasn't always enough.

'He does but the fire spirits do not like him.'

In truth, the fire spirits liked the poor boy so little that they frequently burned his fingers. It was a sign from the goddess and they had to listen but ironwork was a pure craft and successful practitioners hard to come by.

'We must just find another one,' Mavelle said impatiently.

Olwen tried not to scream.

'I am trying, Chieftainess, believe me, but the spirits have not yet indicated anyone more promising.'

Mavelle threw herself back into her chair.

'Then Ollocus will just have to try harder. I don't have time to mess around. I am old.'

Cordelia shivered but Goneril flung herself forward and took her hands.

'Not that old, Grandmother. The earth is not yet ready to release you, I know it.'

'You *know* it? You have had visions?'

Goneril peeked up at her.

'Not visions, Grandmother, not yet. More ... feelings. A sense of certain truths permeating me.'

'And one of those truths is my continued health?'

Goneril bent her head, still on her knees. Olwen's flesh sang at the sight of her in supplication but she was nervous too. Goneril had spoken to her of a plan last night but she'd thought they had agreed to keep it between themselves.

'It *is*, Grandmother, though it is dark around the edges, telling me ...'

Her voice tailed off and she looked to the ceiling where the birds swooped and twittered.

'Telling you what, girl?'

'Telling me that you must be looked after.'

'Well, of course.'

'Looked after by the *right* people.'

'Goneril,' Olwen started to say, but her voice came out strangely hoarse and Goneril ignored her easily.

'I think it best, Grandmother, if I move here to Beacon, where I can be tireless in pursuit of your wellbeing.'

Regan gave a disbelieving grunt but before anyone could ask more a horn sounded out.

'Messengers!' she cried. 'This can't be good news.'

She darted to the door but the curtain was bound at many points to keep the birds inside and she twitched furiously as guards fumbled at the ties whilst the sound of hooves thundered up the road beyond. At last one side was loose and she was able to squeeze through, Goneril and Cordelia tight behind her. Not that their haste did them any good as they were forced to wait for Mavelle to reach them before the messenger could deliver his news. The chieftainess leaned heavily on Olwen's arm as she laboured up the hill and into the compound, but drew herself up in her usual stately way when the man bowed low before her.

'Chieftainess, we have ridden from Breedon at all speed.'

'Breedon?' Mavelle asked, eyes sharp. 'What news? Not the Setantii?'

Olwen heard the concern in her voice. Breedon was a hilly outpost on the far western edge of the Coritani lands and forever threatened by the Setantii tribe beyond. Mavelle had talked with the elders of building a border fort there but their labour had seemed better employed in expanding Burrough so the hill fort had remained as a lone guardhouse.

'We think they are massing, Chieftainess.'

'How many?' she demanded. 'And where?'

'A small band but they look well trained. As you know, the new bridegroom Martius is looking to prove himself and seems to feel stealing Coritani lands is the best way to do so. They paused for the Imbolc moon but set out again this morning. We came as fast as we could.'

'You did right,' Mavelle told him. 'We must act fast.' She looked around. The tribal elders had all come out at the fuss and stood attentively in a circle. 'Who believes we should ride out to find this band?'

Most arms went up. Mavelle looked to an older soldier who had not given his assent.

'Calgacus – you do not like the idea?'

'The Goddess does not condone attack, Chieftainess.'

'You speak true,' Mavelle agreed. 'And wisely. We should not engage with this band unless they encroach on Coritani land – then it is not attack but defence. Agreed, Calgacus?'

The older man nodded solemnly.

'Agreed, Chieftainess. We should ride out to the borderlands in readiness.'

Everyone else was nodding too so Mavelle turned to Leir.

'Can you muster a band?'

Her underchief saluted.

'Of course, though it is your granddaughter who commands our troops now. Regan?'

Regan sprang to his side and bowed to Mavelle.

'I will summon all fit fighters, Chieftainess. With so many here for the celebrations we can gather a fine band fast. Martius will not take one foot of Coritani land.'

She rushed off, her mind already fixed on the battle ahead, and Leir turned to follow her. Panicked, Cordelia stepped forward and put a hand on his arm to halt him.

'Father, please may I go back to Burrough? Keira's pups are due any day and I must be there for the birthing.'

Leir frowned.

'I cannot spare men to guard you, sweet one.'

'You need not. I'll go with the people when they walk back tomorrow. I'll be quite safe.'

But at that Mavelle shook her head.

'The people will not walk back tomorrow, Dee. I cannot have their lives at risk whilst there are enemies abroad. All will stay safely here.'

'But I could . . .'

Leir put up his hand.

'You are a daughter of the Coritani, Cordelia, so precious to us all. You cannot ride about the countryside unguarded. You must do as our chieftainess says and wait here in safety.'

'Keira—'

'Keira will do well enough with Solinus.' Leir's voice was hard as iron. 'She is but a hound. Her safety is worth ten times less than your own.'

'Not to me.'

Olwen saw his eyes narrow.

'Then you are clearly not as mature as I thought. You will stay at Beacon until we return, your continued safety assured, however long that takes. Is that clear?'

Cordelia hung her head.

'It is clear.'

'Good.' He patted her arm awkwardly. 'And it will not, you know, take long to dispatch the Setantii. You may yet return for the birth.'

Then he was gone again, striding off to join Regan in the muster. Cordelia looked longingly to the east then knelt on the earth, placing her hand flat upon it. Olwen, moved by the simple gesture, went to her side.

'Danu will look after Keira, Cordelia, as she looks after all mothers.'

Cordelia turned cornflower blue eyes to her.

'Not mine.'

Olwen swallowed and placed her hands on the earth beside the youngest royal daughter.

'Then let us ask for her blessing.'

Cordelia nodded gratefully and they knelt there together as the compound turned around them.

'What are you doing?' Mavelle asked.

'Asking the Mother to keep Cordelia's hound safe,' Olwen told her.

'Wise,' the chieftainess agreed, then she tilted her head to one side. 'And whilst you're there could you ask Her to find me a smith? And fast.'

'Yes, Mavelle,' Olwen agreed, though in truth she feared Danu was far too busy for that.

Chapter Three

Anagantio; Stay-home days (February)

Taran pumped the bellows into the heart of the fire and felt the heat flare across his face as if Lugh himself were breathing upon him. He tugged on the linen bindings around his hands to be sure they were secure and lifted his hammer. For a moment he paused to admire the tool. It had been an Imbolc gift from Vindilus the Smith, to signify Taran's promotion from simple apprentice to undersmith, and he treasured it.

Vindilus had etched Taran's name into the handle, binding the fire spirits into a pact that should last his whole life. The forge was where he belonged. He'd known it from the moment he'd stepped inside four years ago as a young man of just thirteen years and seen the old smith bent over the fire, heating and re-heating a length of iron to twist it into a beautiful pattern. The dull grey metal had come to life beneath the smith's tools, pulsing in the dark air of the forge as if blood flowed through it, and Taran had come to life with it.

Hours he'd sat in that doorway, watching the smith work his magic. He'd seen him pull the ore from the bog, a lump of crude, worthless-looking dirt, and heat it to such glorious temperatures that the slag fell away and the iron was born from within. He'd watched his master hammer it out on a hot stone over and over, every blow breaking a little of the hard core of the metal until finally it bowed to his will and became like clay in his big, fire-gnarled hands. Taran had seen him fight the stuff, wrestling it into submission, pinning it down in his tongs and beating it flat with his hammer. And in the end, he'd seen the grubby substance lovingly fashioned into gleaming knives and swords, ploughs and pails, handles and cages, and returned, at last, to the dark grey that all thought dull, and all – bar the smiths – underestimated.

The people loved iron for its strength and its flexibility, for the way you could sharpen it into an edge so perfect it could cut a man's throat in one smooth motion. They thought it solid, useful, practical, but they had not seen it dance as Taran had and did not know that its true power rested in the way it could shift shapes. A smith could prise an old handle off a coffer and, with skill and patience, re-fashion it as an eating knife worthy of the greatest feast. A smith could take a sword, blunted and chipped from battle, and bathe it in his fires to bring it forth reborn, to fight again. That was what Taran loved about iron and it was why, when finally the smith had invited him closer, he had sworn his life to its service.

A smile on his face, Taran took the slim blade from the coals with pincers, laid it carefully across the block and brought his hammer down, swift and true. The force of the blow rippled up his arm but he was strong from continual work and barely noticed it. He turned the blade, struck again, and plunged it mercilessly back into the fire. It reddened instantly and he forced himself to hold it there for a count of two, three, four – always that bit more than was comfortable on his hands, to truly kindle the spirits of the metal.

Again he lifted it to the block, again he struck. It would take all morning but he had to be patient for he intended this knife for Chieftainess Enica and it must be his finest work. Most of the other young people of Raven's Hill had ridden out to hunt but Taran was far happier here. Indeed, so keen was his focus that he didn't notice two people enter the forge until their shadows cut across the blade. He looked up reluctantly but then his face broke into a broad smile.

'Gleva! Map! You're back.'

Taking the blade from the fire, he plunged it into the pail to his right. It hissed furiously and the air between him and the newcomers filled with steam.

'Still working your magic then,' Gleva said, stepping into the fierce little cloud to wrap her arms around him.

'It's not magic, Gleva, it's—'

'Hard work. I know, I know. You've told me many times but it still looks like magic to me. Smiths dance with the fire spirits, and you, young Taran, are learning the steps faster than most.'

'You're too kind,' he mumbled, turning hastily to Map to hide his confusion.

'She's right, you know, lad,' he said, clapping him on the back. 'And dammed proud of you we are for it.'

'And proud of ourselves besides, for finding you,' Gleva added, sparing him any further confusion.

Taran led them to the bench at the far side of the forge and poured ale from the jug that Vindilus always kept on the side. As they clinked cups, he looked fondly at the pair of travelling traders he'd first seen in a rough market five years ago. He'd been lost and miserable, his mother taken to the air at his birthing and his beloved father gone after her when a ferocious fever had swept through their homestead. His aunt would have cared for him but Taran believed himself too old and had headed off to the Equos horse-fairs to sell himself into service. He'd had visions of training as a fighter and had pictured some upright leader plucking him from the crowd, but the fair had been crowded and dirty, full of horses, chickens, sacks of grain, and men and women shouting and prodding. He'd cowered behind a cage of fowls but a burly man had yanked him from his hidey-hole and set him on a stone.

'What have we here then? A young lad looking for work?'

'No, sir,' he'd stammered for the man had stunk of liquor and his eyes had been piggy-small and so tight together they'd seemed to drill into the top of his nose. 'I'm just here to buy ... ' he'd cast fearfully around ' ... to buy spoons for my aunt.'

'Spoons? I see. And what, pray, will you barter for these spoons?' Taran had had no goods and no answer. But the man had. 'Your work, correct?' He'd paced around him. 'There's not much on you but you're shapely enough. I'll take you, I guess. You'll be good for something.'

He'd bent closer then, his ruddy face so tight against Taran's that his spittle had hit his cheeks. His piggy eyes had glinted wickedly and Taran had hated him even before he'd suddenly stuck out a meaty hand and clasped his most private parts. His skin flared even now at the memory of it and the thought of what might have become of him if he had not at that moment spotted Gleva. She'd been sternly assessing a ball of twine but he'd seen a kindness in her eyes. If he'd known his mother, he'd suddenly been certain, she'd have had eyes just like this. Acting on instinct he'd pointed to her and said loudly, 'You'll have to ask my mistress.'

'Mistress?' The man's eyes had narrowed even further. 'I didn't know Gleva dealt in men.'

She'd looked up on hearing her name and Taran had prayed to every spirit he'd ever known that she would take his side. She'd eyed him up and down and, returning the twine to the disappointed seller, stepped up to the big man who had withered and, praise Danu, released his hold on all that Taran held dear.

'Only in *good* men,' Gleva had said, her voice like iron. Map joined her.

'Trouble, my love?'

'Catto here was asking the price of our boy.'

'Our ... ?'

'Our boy, here, yes.' Her voice had rung with conviction and, glancing at Taran cowering behind her, Map had given a nod.

'I see. Well, I'm afraid we're not selling him today.'

The man's tiny eyes had been pinpricks.

'And why not?'

'Because he's on order for Chieftainess Enica at Raven's Hill. You know Enica? Of course you do. Well, she asked for our boy 'specially.'

'Why? What's he got that's so desirable? He looks like a runt to me.'

'In which case he won't be much of a loss to you. And you wouldn't want to upset the chieftainess, would you?'

'No.' Catto had backed off hastily. 'No, I wouldn't want that at all. Well, good day to you and I hope he proves pleasing to her.'

He'd disappeared into the crowd surprisingly fast for such a large man and Taran had started to stammer his thanks before Gleva had cut him off.

'You look half starved, lad. Let's get you some food, shall we?'

And so it had been that over a bowl of delicious stew Taran had told the couple his story and they, in turn, had explained that they travelled lands far and wide trading in whatever caught their eye. They bought rich oil and fruity wine and elixirs that fired the tongue. They traded beautiful pottery for elaborate board games. They picked up cooking pots and amphorae of all shapes and materials, as well as jewels and decorative pieces of high quality. Taran, they'd assured him, was their finest treasure yet and they'd offered him lodging with them until he found a place to set his feet.

'Do you have children?' he'd asked.

Gleva had looked towards Map and even at thirteen Taran had seen a wealth of sorrow pass between them, but Map had squeezed his wife's hand and she'd smiled.

'We do now,' she'd said, and called for a second bowl of stew.

Now Taran eyed the traders carefully, relieved to see them back after what had felt like far too long.

'Where have you been this time?' he asked. 'In the bright lands?'

They usually spent the Samhain months in the southerly lands where Lugh shone throughout. Gleva's bones ached in the cold, and when Gleva's bones ached, Map's heart ached with them, so whilst the snows were on the ground they headed over the seas.

Taran had no idea what the 'seas' were and though he'd asked his dear friends over and over to describe them, all they could tell him was that they were like a thousand rivers laid side by side. Once launched into their centre, a man could see no land in either direction and must trust to the stability of his boat to hold his life safe. There were waves, they had told him, where the sea spirits threw their salty water up far above a man's head and sent the boat cresting high one moment and then crashing down the next, until they either sucked their prey into the depths or cast them, exhausted, onto the far shores. The seas sounded monstrous to Taran and he could only pray they would not come to Raven's Hill, but Gleva and Map seemed quite enraptured by them.

'You can move so fast, Taran, if the winds fill the sails. It is almost like flying and far, far more comfortable than the bumps and ruts of even the finest roads at Burrough.'

They talked a lot of Burrough – a fort some miles north of Raven's Hill, established less than a lifetime back by the lost Coritani heiress Branwen and her consort Leir. It was smaller than Raven's Hill, they'd told him, but built with every convenience, including roads of such perfect cobbles that they held firm in even the worst rains. The forge, run by a gruff but talented smith called Dubus, was apparently the largest they'd ever encountered and Taran longed to see it.

'We've been all the way to the Lake-sea,' Map told him now, eyes shining. 'Truly, Taran, it is beautiful.'

'It is,' Gleva agreed. 'And so calm. The spirits there must be very indolent, for the highest waves barely even came up to my knees.'

'It's the heat,' Map said. 'It makes everything move slowly. Even in the depths of Samhain it was warm enough to go without a cloak in the daytime.'

Gleva stretched out her arms as if reaching again for the feel of Lugh's heat upon her skin. She and Map always wore the brightest weaves and most elaborately patterned belts and ties but they were no substitute for sunshine.

'It's a wonder you came back,' Taran said as lightly as he could.

Gleva and Map were all the parents he had these days and, though he saw them only occasionally, those visits warmed his heart enough to carry him through. The thought of a year empty of their cheery faces felt dismal indeed. Gleva, however, just wrapped her arms around him and kissed him.

'I'd travel through Baltic snows to see you, my Taran.'

My Taran! The simple words tingled through him and he hugged her close to hide his emotion. Gleva and Map had saved him. They'd kept him close and they'd brought him here to Raven's Hill and sold him to Enica because they'd seen how much he liked it.

'You will stay a while?' he asked them. 'Chieftainess Enica will be glad to see you, I am sure.'

'She will,' Gleva agreed. 'For we have fine goods for her. Beautiful pottery, painted with the most astounding colours and patterns. You should see—'

Map put his hand on her arm.

'I'm not sure the lad cares much for pots, my love, though I bet he'd like to examine the sword I picked up from Chieftainess Sophia of the Belgae. It has a pattern etched into the blade, Taran, that I know you will love.'

Taran leaned forward eagerly at the mention of swords but Map's words were drowned out by a shout from beyond the forge. He leaped up and ran to the door to see four men from the latest hunting party coming in through the vast gates, bearing a rough-hewn litter on their shoulders.

'Who is it?' Gleva asked, sidling out beside him. 'Who's dead?'

The men looked sombre and for a moment Taran feared that

it was Chieftain Dias gone to the Otherworld but then saw him walking behind the litter, his brow dark.

'Not Catia?' Map gasped, but, no, the heiress was just behind her father, leading two horses, and at her side walked her brother Aledus. Who, then, had inspired such sorrow?

Taran, Gleva and Map watched with trepidation as the men carried the litter past them and laid it gently on the ground in the centre of the compound. They all looked down at the corpse.

''Tis just a hound,' Map said.

Taran shushed him.

''Tis not *just* a hound, Map. That is Corio, Dias' favourite. He's made more kills than any other.'

'And now he has made his last.'

They all took in the red gash across the animal's throat where a boar must have finally bested him.

'I fear Dias will not be wanting pottery today,' Map whispered to his wife.

Gleva looked at him, eyes alight.

'No,' she whispered back, 'but he will be in need of a new hound and we know just where we can find him one, do we not?'

'Burrough,' Map said, and his own eyes gleamed.

The hound was sent to the Otherworld that night, burned on the litter in which he had been brought home, with the druids chanting and Dias standing tall before the pyre, fighting to keep his eyes dry. Corio's spirit rose on the smoke and the chieftain stepped up to catch it on his clothes in the hope that it would linger long enough to enter the next hound he took to his side.

Taran watched Gleva and Map hovering, waiting respectfully for their moment, and was close by when Map finally slid up to Dias after they had all feasted in the dog's memory.

'He was a great hound, Chief.'

'There will never be a greater.'

'Perhaps not. But if you hold fast to his spirit, we can find you a fine beast to carry it once more.'

Dias looked at him, a spark of hope entering his red-rimmed eyes. 'You can?'

'There is a girl at Burrough, one of Chieftainess Mavelle's grand-daughters, who is breeding fine hounds. We sold the last litter to Prince Lucius of the Belgae. He is much taken with them and is begging us for more, but we could, I'm sure, reserve one for you first, if you so wished.'

'Hunting hounds?'

'Of course. Strong and swift. Cordelia has an eye for the best combination of sire and dam and the pups she breeds are rare creatures indeed.'

'Not as rare as Corio.'

'No. But with his spirit . . . '

Dias tugged at his smoke-thick cloak and Taran saw his hand twitch to his side where Corio had ever been wont to sit. But Dias was a strong-minded man and practical besides.

'Well, I'll need another hound, it's true, and we can see how well it shapes up. You are travelling on to Burrough?'

'We can do, Chief, for you.'

Dias gave a hoarse laugh.

'And will ask your price accordingly, I am sure. Are you a good judge of canines, Map?'

'I claim no expertise, Chief, but I trust Princess Cordelia to pick me the finest.'

Dias frowned and looked to his wife.

'No. No, that will not do. A purchase like this needs more per-sonal direction.' Again his hand twitched to his side but he brought it quickly to the table, drumming his fingers against the wood as his eyes roved over their household. Enica put her own hand over his and rose.

'Aledus!'

Taran, seated next to the prince, felt him jump at the call.

'Mother?'

'We have an important task for you. You must travel to Burrough with the traders, to choose your father a new hound.'

Aledus' eyes lit up. He was a young man of eighteen years, the same age as Taran, and they had talked together often. His sister Catia stood as heiress, leaving Aledus champing at the restrictions of his position and now he leaped up and bowed low.

'It would be my honour, Mother. I will go at once. Well, tomorrow morning. As soon as it suits. Truly, I am happy to serve.'

'So it seems.' Enica smiled at him and Dias stepped forward and clasped his son's hand.

'I thank you, Aledus. You must take men to protect you. Pick a band of six.'

'Yes, Father. Thank you, Father.'

Aledus looked even more delighted at the chance to command men of his own. His eyes met Taran's and he grinned.

'Can I take Taran?' he asked Dias.

'The apprentice smith?'

'Undersmith,' Taran muttered beneath his breath.

'I hear they have a strong forge at Burrough, Father. It will be a chance for him to expand his learning and he is one of the strongest men we have. He will keep me safe on the road, will you not, Taran?'

'Gladly, Prince,' he said, bowing low. 'And I would be honoured, Chieftain, if—'

'Fine, fine,' Dias interrupted him. 'No need to fawn. Off you go and get ready for you will leave at dawn.'

Bowing again, Taran excused himself and made eagerly for the forge to gather his hammer, his apron and his other tools. He was going to Burrough and he couldn't wait.

Chapter Four

Seven days later

'My lady! She's called you back.'

'Who has?' Cordelia swung down from her horse and looked at the sentry. 'Keira?'

'Yes, Princess. Of course, Princess.'

'She is whelping?'

'Just started panting this morning, Princess, as if she knew you were on your way.'

Cordelia ran for the royal house, grateful to be back in her orderly home at last. Although Burrough was set on an imposing hill, its summit was far less craggy than Beacon's. When it had been established twelve years ago, her parents had set people working for a whole moon-turn to remove rocks and even out the land. As a result, sheltered within great earthen ramparts was a wonderfully flat compound, dissected by two perfect stone roads, one running south to north from the grand main gates to the single back one,

39

and the other east to west. Both ran to the side of the sacred oak, set dead centre to safeguard the souls of those within, and a narrow third road created a perfect triangle around it. When they were young, Cordelia, Goneril and Regan had each claimed a side as their own but Goneril had swiftly tired of this equality between them and taken to climbing the oak instead.

Living accommodation was equally carefully organised, with the forge, weaving sheds and other workshops in the northerly quarter at the back, the animal byres and all-important grain pits in the west, and living accommodation in the south and east. Leir was fastidious about ensuring repairs were made every Lughnasad so all the great thatched roofs, stretching down almost to the ground at the back and curving elegantly up over the doors at the front, were thick and moss-free.

The ceremonial house sat to the left of the main entrance road and the royal house to the right, both slightly bigger than the other buildings so that in times of celebration or extreme cold everyone could be fitted into them together. Cordelia made straight for the royal house, bursting through the porchway and turning left into the bedchambers. Those rooms ran around the outside of the roundhouse with Leir's at the farthest point of the curve, for privacy. Goneril and Regan occupied rooms to either side of him and Cordelia's was nearest the door. Usually she complained bitterly about the endless traffic this brought through her sleeping space but today she was grateful.

Keira was lying in her whelping box, breathing in short bursts whilst Solinus stroked her head and murmured softly to her. Cordelia flung herself down at his side and the older man gave her a quiet nod and moved aside. The hound lifted her head and nuzzled it into Cordelia's hand with a soft whimper of recognition that turned rapidly into something more urgent.

'The first one is coming,' Solinus said and he moved down the box to help ease the pup into the world.

It came out easily enough, small and wet but mewling strongly as the cold air hit its little body. Cordelia took it from Solinus and nudged it in next to Keira who lifted her head to lick away the birthing mucus. The pup squirmed beneath her ministrations, his little face curling up so crossly that Cordelia had to laugh and once she'd started, she couldn't stop. She'd made it. She was here and by the sound of Keira's ragged breaths, the second pup was already on the way. She was blessed indeed.

It had been an anxious few days pacing Beacon waiting for permission to travel. Every morning she had crouched with her hands flat on the earth, to send her love out across the tribal plains. Everyone else had been looking to the west, fearful of Setantii incursions, but not Cordelia. Leir, Regan and their band would do their job, she'd been sure, but she could not do hers and it had pained her so greatly that on the third morning she'd almost broken her father's command and taken a horse for home. Luckily, before the ice had released its night-hold on the ground, a messenger had ridden in trumpeting victory for Leir and she'd been spared disobedience.

It had been further agony waiting for the main party to return and sitting through Mavelle's victory feast, but it had been made bearable by two things: Leir's promise that they would leave the next day, and the fury sparking the golden flecks in Goneril's green eyes as she'd had to sit through tales of Regan's heroism. Their middle sister, it seemed, had sniffed out the Setantii camp the moment it had made incursions onto Coritani land and led the charge into its midst at first light, scattering the enemy and personally wounding their leader.

Leir had left half of their band at the outpost at Breedon with instructions to start pacing out a new fort and all had declared the mission an unqualified success. Goneril had been forced to proclaim herself delighted by the valour of her stolid middle sister and the pain of this had shown in the sharp lines of her face. Cordelia had very much enjoyed seeing Regan getting everyone's attention for once, though she'd been less pleased with her fighter sister when she'd been slow out of bed the next day. But they had eventually dragged her forth and now they were back at Burrough at last, minus Goneril, but with new lives rapidly arriving.

The second pup came nearly as easily as the first and four others followed in quick succession. Lugh dipped beneath the earth but Leir ordered the fire banked high in the central area and Cordelia sat listening to the rest of her family around the hearth on the other side of the willow walls whilst she tended to her precious hound. She could see their shadows crossing the gaps in the weave and hear them talking but only like a hum from the Otherworld. One more pup came and then, after a gap, the last. Eight pups – a goodly litter.

Cordelia was stashing the placentas carefully to one side for Keira's food tomorrow when Leir poked his head in.

'All well, sweet one?'

'All is very well, Father. Eight healthy pups and Keira seems content.'

'We are blessed.'

Leir smiled down at her but just then Keira started panting again and suddenly pushed herself up, causing her babies to squeal indignantly. She circled in the bed and Cordelia leaped to her feet.

'Keira? Keira, what is it?'

'She'll be wanting to void herself,' Solinus said sagely.

'Of course. I'll take her out.'

Cordelia led Keira outside but although she did void herself in the icy grass, it did not seem to bring her any relief and Cordelia only just caught her collar in time to stop her bolting off across the compound.

'Keira! Here, sweetheart. All is well. I have you safe.'

She held the dog's head in both hands and looked into her eyes and Keira stilled enough to allow herself to be led back to the box. Still, though, she wouldn't settle but turned uneasy circles whilst the pups chirruped like birds beneath her.

'Reckon there's a ninth on the way,' Solinus said. 'A lucky pup.'

'Not lucky for Keira,' Cordelia said drily, but she doubled her efforts to soothe the poor dog until she lay down at last and the panting began again. 'Easy there,' Cordelia murmured. 'Good girl, Keira. You're a good girl, a clever girl.' The words felt useless but they were all she had. 'Where's this last pup then? Let's have it out and you can rest.'

Keira gave a little yelp of agreement and then a low moan and Cordelia moved to her rear to see the last pup emerging. Gently she took hold of its emerging body and tugged. It came in a sucking rush and Keira gave a gasp of relief but the pup lay in Cordelia's hands, apparently lifeless in its birthing sac.

'Breathe on it,' Solinus urged her.

Cordelia lifted the tiny thing up to her face and blew gently. Nothing. Desperately she pulled apart the sac, cleared a trail of mucus from the pup's mouth, then blew again.

'Wake up, little one,' she crooned. 'It's a good world, I promise.'

A third time she breathed and now the pup gave a tiny twitch, sucked in a breath and spluttered it back out. Its legs kicked, strong and sure against her hands, and it began rootling into her fingers.

'Yes!' Cordelia gasped. 'He lives. Look, Solinus, his spirit is awakened and he lives.'

She began laughing, half joy, half tears, but now Keira was reaching round, keen to meet her lucky ninth pup, and Cordelia held him out for her to lick. When he was clean, she placed him amongst his brothers and sisters and, though he was the smallest by some margin, he trod unashamedly over them all to edge one of his sisters off a teat and lustily suck in nourishment.

Keira gave another soft sigh, laid her head down, and slept. Cordelia knew how she felt but these were precious moments at the start of these nine tiny lives and she would keep vigil for as long as she could. The ninth pup had drunk his fill and fallen asleep, teat hanging half out of his pink mouth as if he were guarding it against future hunger. Cordelia stroked his head and felt him nuzzle against her.

'I think I will keep this one for my own,' she said.

'You should, my lady,' Solinus agreed, 'for it was you who breathed life into him so he will ever hold a little part of you.'

She smiled.

'I shall call him Anghus – strong – and if I'm lucky, he will go on to sire many more such brave pups.'

The pup wriggled and the teat fell out of his mouth, making him wrinkle up his nose and rootle to find it again. He gave a few desultory sucks and fell asleep once more. Cordelia and Solinus laughed. The thought of this tiny creature one day siring anything seemed ludicrous, but then, life was ludicrous at times and all you could do was enjoy its twists and turns.

Cordelia sent Solinus to bed with her thanks and lay down next to the box, to watch the pups and praise the earth spirits for keeping them safe for her return.

'All well?' asked Regan, creeping past on her way to bed.

'All well,' Cordelia agreed sleepily.

'Your own little victory, Dee.'

With Goneril Cordelia would have detected a sneer but Regan seemed genuine.

'It's not quite sword-fighting,' she said.

'So? We all have our own talents. And maybe one of these hounds will ride into battle with me one day and you will have done your part in defending the tribe that way.'

Cordelia shivered at the dark thought but Regan spoke true. She bred these hounds for hunting and for fighting and their spirits would turn gladly to the task once they were grown.

'Would you like a hound?' she asked her sister.

Regan shifted from foot to foot.

'May I, Dee?'

'Of course, as long as Father permits it, and I cannot see why he would not. A hound knows what is important – loyalty, love and trust. Every good fighter needs one.'

'They do. And I would like the company.'

'Company?' Cordelia squinted at her sister and even in the low light of the guttering candles she saw her flush. 'Are you missing Goneril?'

'No!'

Regan turned to move on to her own room.

'I am,' Cordelia said softly. 'I mean, she can be a pain but it is strange not having the three of us all together, as if the elements are out of balance.'

Regan turned back. Cordelia saw her hand go to the amulet at her neck and felt for her own.

'I suppose it had to happen,' her sister said sadly. 'Goneril is destined to rule.'

'And we to support her. We will be together again soon enough, but for now, a hound is good company – gentle and uncritical.'

Regan gave a low laugh.

'How refreshing.'

The two sisters' eyes met and for the first time Cordelia felt Regan's spirit call to her. She'd always been so busy looking up to Goneril that she'd had little time for her middle sister, but perhaps with Goneril now living on Beacon Hill that would change.

'Would you want a dog or a bitch, Ree?'

Regan did not hesitate.

'A bitch. A girl – to fight as fiercely as this girl fights.'

Cordelia smiled.

'Then I shall pick you the fiercest of them.'

Regan almost smiled back but it seemed the strangeness of this new intimacy hit her and with a crisp nod and sharp 'Night then', she sidled past to her own chamber. Cordelia lay listening to her clattering around, putting ointment on her wounds and groaning gently as she threw herself onto her straw mattress and then, as if someone had blown out her flame, fall instantly silent.

All around she could hear others doing the same. Peat was chucked on the fire and Magunna, their longstanding helpmeet, laid out her bed beside it. Leir retreated to his chamber and silence settled where Goneril would usually have been, fussing for water and combs and herbs for her pillow. Now it would be Mavelle she was bothering. Or Olwen. Cordelia lay next to Keira as everything hunkered into the warm hum of communal sleep and watched the new pups squirm and nuzzle. She was home at Burrough and all, thank Danu, was peace and quiet.

Chapter Five

The next day

'Visitors! Visitors approaching!'

The camp was jolted from its everyday activities by shouts from the guardhouse and Cordelia reluctantly prised herself away from the whelping box to go and see what was happening. Regan shot past her, sword at the ready, but the guard had called 'Visitors!' and sure enough, as the gates swung open, a little troop rode up the entrance road beneath a green branch of friendship. Regan dropped her sword and Cordelia saw her reach self-consciously to straighten her hair as the first of the band dismounted.

Instantly Cordelia could see why. The earth spirits had crafted this young man well. Tall and muscular, his shoulders were straight and his legs strong. It was his face, though, that truly caught the eye – chiselled like rock with a fine, high brow and eyes so dark they were almost as black as his thick hair. He took a step forward and, spotting Regan, bowed low.

'Princess?' he hazarded.

'Princess,' she confirmed. 'Eldest of Mavelle's granddaughters here at Burrough.'

It was cleverly done. The young man bowed lower.

'Prince Aledus of the Catuvellauni at your service.' Regan held out her hand and he took it and kissed it, then asked, 'Are you the breeder of hounds of whom I have heard so much?'

'I am not.'

She pulled her hand from his so fast he almost stumbled, but he collected himself with style.

'You must, then, be the one who fights so well?'

Regan gave a modest little cough.

'I have a little skill in that area, yes.'

'I hear tell that you saw off Martius of the Setantii.'

'You heard that already?'

'Oh, yes. A bold victory, I believe.'

A smile was creeping inexorably over Regan's face.

'It was an effective campaign.'

'I'm sure. Perhaps, Princess, we may train together whilst I am here?'

'Perhaps,' Regan said with a little shrug, though standing behind her, Cordelia saw her neck flush. 'If you can take a beating.'

Aledus smiled and looked about to answer but Leir was striding across the compound towards them and he was forced to turn his attention that way.

'Chieftain Leir! May the Goddess bless you. I come to offer the hand of friendship from my mother, Chieftainess Enica of the Catuvellauni.'

'Welcome indeed.' Leir clasped Aledus' hand and shook it hard.

'We have been escorted by Gleva and Map, whom I believe you know?'

He gestured to the two traders and Leir turned to them with open arms.

'Of course. They are dear friends to the Coritani.'

Cordelia was delighted to see the pair, for they were dear friends to her too. As Leir led Aledus towards the ceremonial house, she sidled towards them, dying to ask how the pups had been received by Prince Lucius of the Belgae. She pulled up short, however, as Gleva drew a young man in between them. He looked very comfortable, laughing when Map stamped his feet on the road and smiling down at Gleva as she tucked her arm under his, and Cordelia felt a twinge inside her at their easy familiarity.

She had long thought of Gleva and Map as her own special friends but it seemed this lad had an equal claim on their attention and she realised with a start that they may well have similar friends in every place they visited – and they visited many places. The world beyond the tribal lands was, by their account, vast, and for the first time in her sixteen years Cordelia felt its magnitude pressing in upon her homeland, in a way that seemed far more threatening than any marauding Setantii raiding party. She held back to let the group pass but Gleva waved and she had to go over.

'Gleva, Map – good to see you.'

If Gleva spotted that her greeting was less effusive than usual, she didn't comment.

'You look well, Cordelia. How is Keira?'

Despite herself, Cordelia beamed.

'Very well. She birthed nine pups last night.'

'Nine? That's marvellous. All healthy?'

'So far. We will know more when they open their eyes to look upon this world.'

'You will be selling them?'

Cordelia smiled.

'I hope, Gleva, that *you* will be selling them.'

Gleva looked to Map and laughed.

'Maybe sooner than you think, Dee. Prince Aledus is here looking for a new hound for Chieftain Dias.'

Cordelia jumped.

'He cannot have one yet. They are but newborn.'

'Steady, Dee. No one will take them until you say so. But it is good, is it not, that your reputation has travelled as far as Raven's Hill?' That, Cordelia had to admit, gave her a small thrill but now Gleva was pulling the damned lad forward, saying, 'Let me introduce you to my dear Taran.'

Cordelia looked at him.

'I have not heard you speak of *your* Taran before,' she said stiffly.

'Have you not? I apologise. Map and I rescued him from a market five years ago. He was about to be bought by a man who had ideas for his employment that did not meet with our approval.'

Cordelia saw Taran shiver, his large frame suddenly appearing far less solid, and looked curiously at him. His face hadn't the striking lines of Aledus' but he was nice-looking with unruly brown curls and hazel-coloured eyes. He was taller than the prince and his shoulders were broader, but he held himself more shyly and Cordelia found herself wondering how he had ended up in that market.

'You are a trader?' she asked him.

'No. I have not the skill to sell.'

'Taran is a smith,' Map told her.

'Apprentice smith,' Taran said.

'Undersmith,' Gleva corrected him. She looked to Cordelia. 'He has just been promoted.'

Her voice glowed with pride and Cordelia felt herself tighten again.

'Congratulations,' she muttered.

'Thank you.' He looked to the little group around Aledus as it moved towards the roundhouse. 'We should perhaps catch up? I do not wish to appear remiss.'

Gleva glanced over.

'You're right, Taran. You will come with us, Cordelia?'

She looked at the three of them and shook her head.

'I must check on Keira.'

'Will your father not want you in the hall?'

'He'll understand. This is a critical time for the pups.'

'Can no one else tend them?' Taran asked.

'Do you let others work your forge?' she shot back, and he visibly jumped.

'Er, no.'

'Well then.'

'Of course. I apologise.'

His voice was as warm as glowing embers and his eyes richer than hazel now that she saw them closer up. More like sweet chestnut . . . not that it mattered to her.

'Yes, well, enjoy your meal.'

They had reached the triangle at the centre of the compound and as Leir steered his guests left to the ceremonial house, Cordelia turned determinedly right to the royal one and her precious hound. Something inside tugged at her as the others moved off and she almost ran after them, but then Gleva tucked her arm through Taran's again and she spun crossly away. Who was this damned undersmith with his chestnut eyes and his mild manners and his special place beside Gleva and Map?

'Who cares?' she muttered to herself and stomped off to Keira's bedside, fighting to ignore the sounds of chatter and laughter already rising from the hall.

Cordelia woke up the next morning feeling as fuggy and out of sorts as only someone who'd barely slept could. Or perhaps someone who'd supped too deeply at their chieftain's best ale, which meant everyone in the compound would be equally grumpy today. She fumbled for the edge of the whelping box in the thin light of a reluctant dawn and her hand met the reassuring warmth of Keira, her breathing slow and relaxed. In the safe curve of her big body Cordelia felt the pups squirming and ran her hand gently along until she counted to nine, though she could have counted one twice, so tightly were they packed in.

Pushing herself up from her makeshift bed and taking the blanket with her over her nightgown, she padded into the central area. Magunna was already up, coaxing the fire back to life, and Cordelia took a candle and taper and lit it from the flaring edges.

Making her way back to Keira, she shone the light across the pups, making certain they were all there and alive. Imbolc was a hard time of year to be born and these pups would have to be tough. Her brow knitted again as she recalled the party that had come visiting her late last night, bellies full of food and ale.

'Finest hounds in the world,' Leir had asserted, leading the group noisily into Cordelia's chamber just as she was dozing off.

She'd leaped up, terrified one of them would trip and fall on the fragile creatures. She loved her father dearly and he was an excellent underchief, but at the end of the day he was just a man and at times like this she almost wished she were at Beacon under Mavelle's civilising rule; the chieftainess would never allow such uncouth behaviour.

'Can you stay back, please?' she'd begged. 'They are very young.'

'And very small,' the visiting prince had said, peering at them in the light of his dangerously wavering torch. 'My father wants a big hound.'

'They are but one day old,' Cordelia had growled at him. 'Given time and space and *peace with their mother*, they will grow.'

'I hope so.' He'd leaned closer in. 'Where are their eyes?'

Cordelia had rolled her own towards the low roof.

'They do not open until later.'

'Why?'

'So they are spared the sight of drunkards ogling them?'

Aledus had blinked at her and someone had slid forward at his side.

'There's no need to be rude, Dee. The prince is here to honour you with his custom.'

'In which case, Regan, he will understand the need for me to protect his goods.'

This had met with a few low whistles but Leir, at least, had seen her distress and had the sense to lead his guests away, all bar one – the quiet undersmith, Taran.

'Yes?' she'd snapped at him, and he'd jumped.

'I ... No matter. Sorry to have disturbed you.' He'd given a funny little bow and, with a nod to the pups, added, 'They're beautiful,' then melted into the night before she could find a reply to his sudden softness.

She wondered why he'd lingered. He'd stood very still, unlike the others, and there'd been something compelling about his steady presence. Cordelia shook herself. Steady presence! What nonsense. He'd only been less bother than the rest, which wasn't saying much. If he'd been properly considerate, he'd have stayed well away as Gleva and Map had done. No doubt they would not approve at all.

She smiled down at the pups, delighted to see Anghus in the midst of them all, suckling hard. Keira looked up at her with a slow thump of her tail.

'You must be hungry, girl?'

She swore the creature's eyes lit up and was glad when Solinus slid into her chamber, leaving her free to head out again. Her own stomach growled and she went to see what Magunna was cooking up. To her delight it was a hearty beef broth and she persuaded the woman who had stood as mother to her and her sisters all these years since Branwen's sad death to fish out several chunks of meat to take to Keira. Returning to accept a bowl of broth for herself, Cordelia took it outside, away from the stench of ale-sour breath and sweat.

'Cordelia!'

Gleva and Map were coming towards her with, she was pleased to see, no dammed undersmith in tow.

'How are your heads?' she asked.

'Clear as the sky,' Gleva replied cheerily. 'We were worn out from the road and retired early last night.'

'If only everyone else had. Did you hear, they all came in breathing ale over my pups?'

Map smiled as he and his wife settled down beside her on the grass.

'We didn't but does it really matter?'

'They could have crushed them.'

'Did they?'

'No, but that's not the point.' Cordelia knew she sounded churlish but didn't seem able to stop herself. 'Your boy was there.'

'Taran?'

'Do you have others?'

Gleva put an arm around her. Cordelia resisted but the older woman was strong.

'Taran is to us like one of your pups is to you, Dee. We rescued him when he was young and vulnerable so of course we will always take an interest in him. Does that bother you?'

'No! Of course not. That would be silly.'

'We're all silly from time to time.'

'Well, we shouldn't be. I shouldn't be. It's not like I'm a child anymore, is it?'

Gleva hugged her tight.

'If you don't mind, Dee, I'll always think of you a bit as my child.'

'You will?'

Cordelia felt tears sting at the back of her eyes and supped hastily at her broth.

'Of course,' Gleva assured her. 'We've known you since you were a babe in your mother's arms. Since just a few moon-turns after we married.'

'Hey – did I ever tell you how I met Gleva?' Map asked, nudging her.

Cordelia groaned.

'Once or twice, Map, though I always like to hear it.'

He grinned and reached for his wife's hand.

'I was gathering grain with my tribe, as usual, and suddenly this mysterious girl was at my side, bringing me water, as if she had been drawn there by the Beltane moon. Her smile was so soft and her eyes so kind and her breasts so ripe that I knew immediately I must make her mine.'

'Map!' Gleva objected but she did not pull away.

'It turned out she was visiting her aunt to help with the harvest. She had an eye for travel, it seemed, and I was already making treasure selling my mother's basketwork to people passing by on the road, dreaming of where it might take me if I was brave enough to tread it.'

He looked fondly at his wife.

'I took the cup of water from her and drained it. When she reached out to take the cup back, I seized her hand in mine and said, "I want to spend the rest of my life with you." And I did.'

Cordelia smiled as she always did at the simple tale, but as she caught the pair exchange knowing glances, she felt the strange crossness rise inside her again. She thought of Regan fawning over Aledus yesterday, and the lingering looks she'd caught between Goneril and Olwen, and felt her whole body prickle, as if she'd fallen in a patch of unknown plants and found that they stung. She leaped up and away.

'I need more food. Have you eaten?'

'Yes, thank you. We ate early and came to find you. We travel on today.'

'Already?'

They rose at her side, brushing themselves down and nodding.

'I'm afraid so, Dee. We have a cartful of goods we must sell to make room, I hope, for some lively pups by the time the moon turns. Map has been asking everyone he meets what they look for in a hound. He is making himself quite the expert.'

'Really?' Cordelia looked keenly to him. 'And what do they say? What particular traits do they seek?'

'It varies depending on the terrain of the tribe. Those hunting on the plains required different hounds from those more used to woodland.'

'Of course.' Cordelia considered this as they set out across the compound. 'So with care, we could breed different litters for different customers?'

'Could we? I mean – you could do that?'

55

'Oh, yes. We just have to find the right sires and dams. If I select two animals with short legs, we are likely to produce short-legged pups – long-legged similarly. It takes time, obviously, and it won't always work but we can at least try.'

'Special orders!' Map's eyes gleamed. 'Cordelia, you are a gem.'

'A gem?'

'A jewel. Like amber or amethyst but even brighter and clearer. I shall conduct more research and then I am sure we can do great business together. And we will treat you fairly on price, Princess, I swear it.'

'I know you will, Map.' They'd reached the royal house now and she waved them in. 'Would you like to see the pups?'

'Just a quick peek perhaps.'

They crept in, cooed delightedly and soon rose to leave again. Perfect guests.

'You'll need more space,' Gleva commented, 'if you and Map are to create all these new breeds.'

'They will not all birth at once,' Cordelia said, looking around her little chamber. 'And with Goneril at Beacon now we could use her chamber.'

'Use it for what?' someone grunted and they all looked up as Leir came blearily out of his bed.

They followed him into the communal area where Aledus' men were gathering, heads low as they tried to force a little food into their groaning stomachs. Cordelia tried not to smile and failed miserably.

'Map and I are going to breed hounds to order,' she told her father as he waved a bowl of stew away and asked for spring water.

'And you wish to do so in your sister's chamber?'

'She doesn't need it anymore.'

'She doesn't, perhaps, but our guest might not wish to share his bed with your pups.'

He gestured to where Aledus was emerging, looking ridiculously bright-eyed and every bit as handsome as yesterday.

Cordelia heard rustling behind the willow walls and moments later Regan appeared on the far side of the communal space. Cordelia watched her closely and saw her eyes, also mightily bright, meet Aledus' the moment she emerged. Goodness – had her sister taken the prince last night? The Imbolc moon was truly exerting her pull this year.

'Gleva and Map are leaving,' she said abruptly.

Leir turned to them.

'Already?'

'Some time today, Chief, but there's no hurry. We have some goods you might like to see before we depart. Some innovative whittling tools that might suit you.'

'Whittling tools?' Leir perked up instantly. He was very fond of woodwork and always on the hunt for ways of improving his skills. 'Excellent. Let's take a little of Mags' fine stew and then maybe I can lighten your cart before you take to the road.'

'No road is as fine as yours, Leir. Taran was most eager to see it and is very impressed.'

'The smith? Will he travel on with you?'

Despite herself, Cordelia froze, listening far too intently for the answer.

'No.' It was Aledus who answered. 'Taran stays here with me.'

'Here?' Cordelia squeaked, so quietly that thankfully no one heard her, save perhaps Gleva. 'You will stay, Prince?' she asked hastily.

Aledus nodded.

'Chieftain Leir has kindly invited me to remain at Burrough as his guest until the pups are ready to leave their dam in a moon-turn.'

'A moon-turn and a half,' Cordelia said.

'At least,' Regan added. Leir looked sideways at her. 'We do not wish to send Dias a weak pup, Father.'

'Indeed, Daughter. I did not realise you knew so much about it but I'm sure the prince will be glad of your expertise.'

Regan flushed but stood her ground.

'I would be happy to serve our guest.'

Leir's blue eyes twinkled but he kept himself to a quiet reply: 'Good. Our two tribes should work together.'

He knew, then, exactly what was going on and it suited him. Breeding men was much, Cordelia supposed, like breeding dogs – you shaped them to suit your needs. The Catuvellauni held all the lands to the south of the Coritani so good relations would be hugely beneficial to both tribes. And relations, judging by the glow in both Aledus' and Regan's eyes, were very good. The prince would be here for the weeks ahead and his smith with him. Burrough would not be the quiet place Cordelia had been craving but, then again, quiet could be overrated and the pups, at least, would have plenty of people to play with as they grew. Cordelia took a second bowl of stew and ate eagerly. It was doing its work – she felt decidedly less cross already.

Chapter Six

BURROUGH HILL

Ogronnios; Ice days (March)

Cordelia marched up to the forge. She wanted a means of marking her puppies and hoped Dubus might fashion something for her. She reached up to knock at the open door but the sight of the two smiths working together made her hesitate. The fire burned brightly and Dubus stood so close to it that Cordelia could not believe his skin was not fried from his bones. At his side was Taran, staring intently at the piece of iron he was twisting with a complicated set of tongs. Cordelia looked at the metal and, seeing it flexing in the heat like a living serpent, was momentarily mesmerised.

Taran too was concentrating deeply, so deeply that he hadn't noticed the smudge of soot on his cheek or even the soft brown curl that had flopped almost into his eye. Cordelia felt a sudden urge to reach out and smooth it away. Her fingers twitched but met only the wood of the doorframe and cried out at the sharp pain as a splinter bit cruelly into her skin.

'Who's there?' Dubus called. Cordelia sucked at her finger and turned to flee. 'Princess Cordelia?'

Damnation! Taking her finger hastily out of her mouth, she held her head high and marched into the forge.

'That's right, Dubus. I've come to ask if it would be possible to craft me some small metal discs.'

'Discs?' The smith squinted at her and she forced herself to focus on him and not the young man at his side, muscled forearms lit by the dancing flames.

'To tag the puppies,' she said. Still he frowned. 'Sorry, you're obviously busy. I'll, er, leave you to it.'

'No rush.' It was Taran who spoke and now she did look at him and saw he'd pushed the stray curl back, though the soot remained. 'That is, don't let me keep you from your business.'

Was he blushing? It was impossible to tell with the fire turning everyone's skin scarlet. Cordelia felt the heat of it prickle her own temples and took a couple of steps back. It wouldn't do to get all sweaty.

'Perhaps,' Dubus suggested, 'I could ask young Taran here to make them. He has an eye for detail and it would be a good task for him. What do you think, Taran?'

'Of course. Absolutely. If the princess would like me to. That is, if you think it would be good experience for me, Dubus.'

'I do,' Dubus said, turning back to his hammering.

Taran edged around the fire to join Cordelia in the doorway. 'Tell me what you need.'

'Some markers for the puppies, so I can identify which one is which. The leather-worker is making me plaited collars and I thought that if I hung a disc from each, I could give them all a, a . . .'

'A name?'

'No, not that. Well, apart from Anghus.'

'Anghus?'

'He's mine. That is, I'm keeping him, to breed from.'

'I see. Then the first tag shall say Anghus.'

'Oh, no. I don't need to identify Anghus.' Taran's face fell so she quickly added, 'But for the others that would be perfect. Not names, though, because that's for their future owners to give them, so that they bond.'

She was babbling. She put a hand to her mouth and, catching the splinter against her lip, gave a little gasp.

'Are you well, Princess?'

'Call me Cordelia, please. And I'm fine. I just caught the doorframe.'

'Oh no.' He glared gratifyingly at the wood. 'Can I see?'

She held out her hand and he took it gently in his own, holding it to the last of the sunlight. His hands were red from the fire but curiously smooth and she felt the strength of them as they held hers steady.

'I see it. It's a big one. One moment.'

He let go of her to turn to his tool bench and she felt the lack of his touch instantly.

'Please don't trouble yourself,' she said awkwardly. 'I can do it.'

But he was back with a tiny pair of pincers and, with a precision she wouldn't have believed his strong hands capable of, grabbed the end of the sliver of wood and pulled it swiftly from her flesh. A bead of blood followed it out and he lifted her finger towards his mouth then visibly jumped at his own audacity and stepped back.

'You should suck it, Princess.'

'Cordelia.'

'Cordelia, yes. It will heal better that way.'

She put her finger in her mouth, grateful for the excuse not to speak as she seemed to be finding little of any merit to say.

'Thank you,' she mumbled.

'My pleasure. I get them all the time, although mainly iron filings.' Cordelia winced and he shuffled his feet. 'So I'll, er, have a go at making the tags for your dogs, shall I? And you can see what you think.'

'Thank you.' Dubus coughed loudly and Taran glanced awkwardly over at him. 'I'll look forward to seeing them,' Cordelia said quickly and spun away, feeling strangely foolish, although really all she had done was to place an order. Wasn't it?

She hurried back to her dogs but was stopped halfway by a shout.

'Oi, Cordelia! What have you been up to?'

'Regan! Hush.' Her earth-blessed sister was lying in the dirt of the training area – a fenced off section in the southern quarter – curling up and down in an endless cycle of what Cordelia could only presume was another of her strange exercises. She hurried over. 'I've been up to nothing. What would I have been up to?'

'I don't know but you look very pink for someone who's been up to nothing.' Regan grinned up at her. 'Was that the forge you were coming from?'

Cordelia turned to the poor girl holding her sister's feet.

'Shall I do that?' she suggested and the girl willingly relinquished her post and scuttled off. Cordelia didn't blame her. 'You stink, Ree. Whatever are you doing?'

'Strengthening my stomach,' Regan said, hitting it hard. 'But what about what *you've* been doing, Dee-Dee?'

'I told you—'

'Nothing! Right.'

She started her strange exercise again and Cordelia frowned.

'Is that good for you?'

'Of course.'

'What if you're with child?'

Regan stopped dead and looked around, aghast.

'Cordelia! Shhh.'

'But what if you are?'

'Then my muscles would protect it. Like armour. Anyway, I'm not. I'm bleeding.'

'Right.'

'Not that it's any of your business.'

'True.'

'And not that I'd want to be fat with child.'

Cordelia shrugged.

'They're not in there long, Ree. Look at Keira, running around already.'

'Keira is a hound.'

'And you are a wolf!'

Regan resumed her curls, faster now.

'What do you know of getting pregnant anyway, little sis?'

Cordelia deliberately let go of her sister's feet as she was on the rise. Regan toppled sideways into the dirt and glared at her.

'I know nothing,' Cordelia said, unruffled, 'save what I've learned from watching you.'

Regan shot her a dirty look.

'Very clever.' She shoved her feet at Cordelia again. 'Hold on tighter this time.'

'You've done enough, Ree.'

'Never.' She started up again then suddenly said, 'I'm going to ask him to marry me.'

Cordelia almost let her sister go again.

'Aledus?'

'Yes, of course Aledus. Who else?'

'Sorry. That's good news, Regan.'

'He hasn't said yes yet.'

'He will. He's clearly mad about you.' Regan moved even faster. 'You'll be the first of us three to marry.'

Her sister paused, mid-curl.

'Not sure Goneril will like that much.'

Cordelia giggled.

'She'll hate it!'

Regan reached out and gave her a playful shove. Cordelia tipped sideways and Regan flopped back onto the ground, pulling her down next to her. Cordelia tried to resist but Regan was strong and determined and, besides, her tunic was already filthy from the pups so she gave up and lay back with her sister.

'I'm very happy for you, Ree.'

Regan groaned.

'No need to be mushy. It makes sense, doesn't it? He's from the Catuvellauni. An alliance with them will protect our southern borders nicely.'

'It will. And Aledus' handsome face has nothing to do with it?'

Regan gave Cordelia a wicked grin.

'It doesn't hurt, I admit. You should consider marriage yourself, Sister.'

'Ree!' Cordelia protested, looking determinedly up at the clouds rushing past overhead. One of them formed itself inexorably into the shape of a smith, hammer raised, forearms rippling, curl of hair flopping over one chestnut eye. Heat flushed across her body and she closed her eyes but the image was still there, stronger than ever, and after all she was a woman now, and a princess besides. She was free to choose a consort if she so wished.

She just had no idea how on earth to go about approaching him.

Chapter Seven

Seven days later

Taran leaned over to tap his hammer as hard as he dared on the stamp for the eighth disc he'd made for Princess Cordelia's dogs. Dubus had honoured him with the commission and Taran was determined to prove that he could do it well. Already he had learned so much here but it was nothing to what remained to be mastered before he could become a real craftsman; he only wished he could craft a wedge to stop time and prevent his days at Burrough from passing too quickly.

Lifting the disc, he gently filed the edges. It would not do to have them sharp. Princess Cordelia would be very upset to see the puppies' soft skin cut and he did not want that. She was so good with them. Every so often his tasks for Dubus took him past the royal house and, with the whelping box being so close to the door, he couldn't help but see inside. Just to look at the dogs, of course, not at the beautiful girl tending them. He wouldn't begin to presume to stare at a princess, even such a kind, friendly one.

The pups were growing fast – far too fast. They were trying to escape their box and just yesterday he'd seen one of them wedged on the top, forelegs out but hindlegs kicking helplessly behind.

He'd looked so comical hanging there that Cordelia had been laughing at him, her cornflower blue eyes shining and her long dark curls falling forward over the struggling pup as she bent to help. Standing watching, Taran hadn't realised he was laughing himself until someone had marched past and stared reprovingly at him for lingering too close to one of the princesses. He'd hurried away swiftly but had smiled all day at the recollection of the girl and her pup.

He must get on with his work for she would come asking for the discs soon and he did not want to disappoint her. She'd been so pleased when he'd dared to take the first one for her approval. He'd battled to work it into a perfect full moon of a circle and marked it with a tiny leaf pattern. He had been gratified when she'd run her hands over it again and again.

'It's so pretty, Taran. How did you do it?'

'Just something Dubus showed me,' he'd muttered. 'It's not so hard when you know how.'

'Well, I think it's fine work,' she'd said, and he'd glowed from her praise.

Now he went to the door to check the pattern on this penultimate disc – a small hawk. Getting it right had taken him three torturous attempts but he was quietly pleased with it now. As he turned the disc to the sun, however, he noticed a slight figure heading past the forge towards the back gate with a pail in her hand. Swiftly he turned back into the forge.

'You need water, Dubus.'

'Do I?'

The big smith frowned and leaned over to look but Taran had already lifted the pail away.

'I'll fetch it for you.'

'Are you sure?'

But Taran was gone already, making for the back gate. He tumbled down the winding path into the grove below, where he could just see the princess bending to fill her pail. She'd pushed up the sleeves of her chequered blue tunic and her forearms were tantalisingly pale.

'Oh, Princess Cordelia – what a surprise.'

It sounded so false he feared the mischievous water spirits might jump out and splash him but they made no move and she turned and smiled at him.

'Oh, Taran. I'm in your way.'

'Not at all. Here, shall I do that for you?'

'Thank you.'

He went forward to take the pail from her. Their hands brushed on the handle and water splashed across them both. She gasped.

'I'm sorry,' he said.

'It's fine. Really. It's a hot day.'

Taran looked up to Lugh, shining clearly if rather weakly down on them.

'Isn't it?' he agreed. 'Why don't you take a, er, seat and dry out?'

He indicated the large rock next to the brook and she perched on it and watched while he filled the pails. But all too soon they were both up to their brims and Taran had to take them from under the stream and set them down.

'Is this for the puppies, Princess?' he asked.

'Call me Cordelia, Taran, please. And that's right. It's a warm day. They'll get thirsty.'

'They will. We all will. Are you?'

'Am I what?'

'Thirsty?'

'No, I . . . well, yes, actually, I am a bit.'

'I have a cup. If you don't mind sharing?'

He lifted the leather cup clipped to his belt.

'Not at all.'

He held it beneath the spring, then brought it over to Cordelia.

'It's not much of a drink to offer a princess,' he said awkwardly but she just laughed.

'It's perfect. Do rest.'

She shuffled up on the rock to make space for him and he sat at her side as she sipped delicately at the spring water.

'Are the pups well?' he asked.

'Very well,' she agreed. 'They're so lively now. You should come and see them.'

'I'd like that.'

'Any time. They, er, they love having anyone to play with. Well, not just anyone but, you know . . . '

'I'll come next time I'm free.'

'Lovely.'

'I could bring you the tags perhaps?'

'Are they finished?'

'All eight, yes.'

'Eight?'

'You didn't want one for Anghus.'

'Ah. No. That is, I might now. Just in case he, maybe, got lost or something.'

'Got lost?'

She blushed prettily.

'And because they're so lovely. He'd be sad to miss out. His brothers and sisters might tease him.'

'Well, we can't have that.'

Taran dared to nudge his leg against hers and felt it soft and firm as she nudged him back. She slid a little on the stone and he shot out an arm to hold her safe. They sat there, his arm around her shoulders, their thighs pressed against each other, and he felt a warmth hotter than any Lugh's Imbolc glory could muster. He stared down at her and suddenly she was turning her head towards him and looking up at him from her beautiful blue eyes and he saw the whole world reflected in them. Hardly able to believe it, he dared to dip his own lips towards hers but just then a voice from up above bellowed, 'Taran, where's my bloody water?!' and he leaped away.

'Sorry, Dubus! Coming, Dubus!'

He scrambled for his pail and Cordelia made a grab for hers, dropping the cup. They both moved to pick it up and their fingers collided. Water sloshed, splashing them both again, and Taran wondered if the spring spirits were finally punishing him for his audacity.

'I'm so sorry, Princess.'

'Cordelia. And don't be. Here.'

She lifted the cup and handed it to him.

'Thank you.' He clipped it to his belt. 'We should get back.'

'We should.'

Still they stood there but then Dubus roared again and Taran snatched up both pails, sloshing more water over them both in his confusion.

'Good job Lugh is shining on us,' Cordelia said.

'He'll dry us in no time.'

'Probably before we're back up the hill.'

They were so conscious of each other on the narrow path through the budding woods, however, that they spilled more than they kept and finally made it into the compound red-faced and soggy. Even so, Taran felt foolishly happy, or happily foolish – either, both. He found he didn't much care.

'I'll make Anghus a tag then,' he said to her as they stepped onto the path across the compound and saw thickset Dubus tapping his foot in the doorway of the forge. 'What mark do you want on it?'

Cordelia looked to the skies, considering, and Taran fought to control the impulses of his body at the sight of her pretty face turned to Lugh's light. *She's a princess*, he reminded himself. *A royal daughter of the Coritani.*

'A hammer, please,' she said, and her smile as she met his eyes was dazzling.

He blinked at her.

'A fine mark.'

'Taran!' Dubus' voice echoed around the compound and several people looked up from their tasks to stare at him.

'Well, I'll, er, bring them over later, Princess.'

'Cordelia!'

'Cordelia.'

It took all Taran's control to turn away from her but Dubus was standing, hands on hips, in the forge doorway and he loped towards him, trying not to spill any more of the precious water onto the cobbles.

'I had to help Princess Cordelia,' he puffed.

'Did you indeed?' Dubus grunted. 'How nice for you. But now – back to work!'

Taran went willingly. He had a ninth tag to make, marked with the sign of his own hammer, and it would be the best one of all.

Chapter Eight

BEACON HILL

Quitos; Windy days (April)

Olwen lay naked and sated, glorying in the energy of her royal lover. She'd feared that her interest in the Coritani heiress might fade once Goneril was at Beacon all the time, but it seemed that proximity only increased the hunger between them. Goneril had come to her at dawn with two fine horses and all morning they had roamed the great plains below the fort. The heiress had ridden fast, easily jumping the fallen trees and ditches that obstructed their race across the open lands, and Olwen had delighted in following her, both on horseback and later when, sweaty and invigorated, Goneril had tumbled her into bed.

Now she stretched out, looking lazily around Goneril's new bedchamber on the raised floor of the royal house. It was richly furnished with carved wooden chests and tables. Scented oil burned in a bronze bowl, casting flickering patterns across rafters twined with purple vines, and the bed on which they were lying was a glorious heap of mattresses and pillows, all in russets and golds. It was a room fit for a fire princess and it set Olwen alight every time she was invited into it.

It had not taken Goneril long to make it her own. She had slept down below for her first nights at Beacon but when Mavelle had stumbled on the ladder up to the eyrie one day, she had pounced. It had taken little persuasion for the chieftainess to admit that her legs shook on the upper rungs and that she feared falling if she was feeling bleary in the mornings. And from then on it had become a matter of extreme tribal importance to create her a new, safe chamber below.

For two days Goneril had personally supervised the building of a magnificent bed, sourcing the softest mattresses, the warmest furs and prettiest blankets. She'd done a truly wonderful job for her grandmother and then, once she was ensconced, had looked around casually, said, 'I suppose I'd better sleep in the upper chamber then,' and that had been that. And it *was* best for Mavelle, there was no denying it. But it was even better for Goneril.

'And for you,' she'd told Olwen when she'd pointed it out, then showed her all the ways in which it was very much better for her. And, really, if all benefited, what was there to complain about?

Now, Olwen rolled over and reached for Goneril but for once the girl did not respond. Olwen propped herself up to see her lying frozen, staring at the thatch above.

'Goneril? Is all well?'

Goneril looked sideways at her.

'I need a man.' The words chilled Olwen's glowing skin as if she'd been thrown into an icy pool. She heard herself make an odd squeak and Goneril laughed and finally turned to her, running her fingers lightly up her body. 'Not like *that*, Olwen. You are more than enough for me like that.'

Olwen already feared that wasn't true. Goneril was a woman who liked to dominate and who, she suspected, liked even more to be dominated. Olwen had not the weaponry. And though she loved exploring the curves and hollows of the heiress' body, she had no desire to impose herself upon it. She said nothing; that always made her lover uneasy.

'Truly, Olwen, I adore you.' Goneril kissed her. 'But I cannot make you my consort, can I?'

'Neither would I want you to.'

Goneril looked pleased that she'd provoked her into speech but Olwen spoke a simple truth. She had no more desire to rule a tribe than to rule a person. Every part of the Mother's world had its own spirit. She wished to tease them out, to know more of them, to work with them, but not to shape them for they were perfectly shaped already.

'I need a man,' Goneril said again. It sounded no better the second time and Olwen pulled the covers up and over herself. 'You know it's true.'

'Am I denying it?'

'You're not endorsing it.'

'You do not need me for that.'

'I do!' Goneril's green eyes widened all too appealingly and she lay closer to her lover. 'I do, Olwen. It's hard being heiress. I need your strength and your wisdom and your support. I can't do it without you.'

They were sweet words. Were they true? Maybe. Goneril certainly believed them. Olwen lifted an arm and held her close.

'There's no rush, Gee.'

Goneril huffed in disgust.

'It's not a rush, my flame, so much as spotting an opportunity.'

Olwen sat up.

'What opportunity?'

'Messengers arrived from Burrough today. Prince Aledus of the Catuvellauni is staying there. That would be a useful alliance for us, would it not?'

There was no point in denying it. The Catuvellauni were a strong tribe and their lands very well placed.

'Why is their prince in Burrough?' Olwen asked instead.

Goneril leaped out of bed, perfectly naked save for the triskele around her shapely neck.

'He's gone to see Cordelia apparently. Something about a hound?'

'Of course. Keira must have whelped. It will be another fine litter, I'm sure. Your sister has a good eye for matching sires and dams.'

'Has she indeed?'

'You know she has. Gleva and Map say her pups command high prices.' Goneril looked furious. She hated anyone else excelling but Olwen wasn't going to let her get away with that. Cordelia's dog breeding was truly fascinating, and besides, if Goneril were to be a good ruler one day, she had to learn to value others. Olwen reached for her loose white robe, pulling it over her head and looking around for the belt. 'And they bring the Coritani into good repute abroad too,' she pushed. 'I've heard that the Belgae love them and are keen to know more and that—'

'They're puppies, Olwen.'

'But puppies grow into great hounds – as princesses grow into great rulers.'

'Yes, well, great rulers need strong husbands to back them.' Goneril flung the words petulantly at her and Olwen rose and began carefully tying her belt in crossed loops across her hips. 'Where are you going? Olwen?'

'You will need your rest, Gee, if you are to woo a prince.'

Panic flashed into the green eyes.

'I can rest with you.'

Olwen looked pointedly to where she paced, naked, around the bed.

'It seems not.'

'Don't go.'

Goneril came over, wrapping herself around her. Her hair tickled Olwen's face, her fingers ran sensuously down her back, and the pure fire of her flared across Olwen's skin and straight

74

to her groin. She groaned. Goneril smiled and knelt to lift the hem of her robe. Slowly she lifted it up, her tongue following in a tantalising line: up her calf, over her knee and across her thigh. Olwen's groan turned to a moan of need and she let the belt drop to the floorboards.

'No rush, Olwen,' Goneril teased.

Olwen looked down at her.

'You really want to go to this prince?'

'Not *go to* him, Olwen, but it can't hurt to take a peek can it? Assess him for . . . potential. He won't come between us, you know.'

Her tongue travelled higher. Olwen was fast losing rational thought and it wouldn't do. Not yet. She tangled her fingers in the heiress' fiery hair and forced herself to tug her back.

'What if he's ugly, Gee?'

'Then he will come nowhere near me. There are plenty of princes out there. The messengers, however, say he is very well formed.' Olwen stiffened and Goneril looked up at her with a sudden glint in her eye. 'They also say that he has in his retinue a young smith.'

'A smith?' That caught her. 'A good one?'

'I'm assured that he shows promise, yes. He has made Cordelia some stupid discs to tag her damned puppies that are apparently as thin as the finest wool.'

'Truly?' Olwen pulled Goneril up. Her groin protested but this was more important than mere pleasure. She and Mavelle had been trying to work with Ollocus on an iron wing-frame but it was so heavy they couldn't drag it out of the workshop, let alone get it into the air. 'You think he might be able to help us with the wings?'

Goneril smiled.

'I think it's worth a try, don't you?'

'I do,' Olwen agreed. She had to. If Danu, in Her wisdom, had provided a smith then she must honour Her gift. And if he came with a prince suitable for Goneril then that was the price Olwen must pay. Mastering the skies was worth more than any passing intimacy, however damned sweet.

'Good.' Goneril looked smug. 'Grandmother can come too. We'll go tomorrow.'

'Tomorrow, Gee?'

'Why not? We'll take the chariot. You like the chariot.'

Olwen did. It had been brought from the Ethiops a year ago and was a marvel of science. It ran on just two wheels and was so fleet, riding it felt almost like flying. But did she want to fly Goneril to this damned prince?

'Why rush?'

Goneril winked.

'Why wait?'

And then she was on her knees again and Olwen could do nothing but submit to the fiery royal daughter.

Chapter Nine

BURROUGH HILL

Quitos; Windy days (April)

The first Cordelia knew of the new arrivals at Burrough were the
gasps and calls from people in the compound. She came around
from the puppy pen she'd had commandeered among the animal
byres to see everyone scrambling onto the earthen ramparts.
Hurrying to join them, she instinctively looked for Taran's big
figure and saw him emerging from the forge. He was wiping
his brow on his sleeve and looking bemusedly around as if he'd
emerged from a dream, which maybe he had.

Cordelia had watched him often at his work in these last weeks
and had seen the almost trance-like state he entered while fully
absorbed in it. It was sometimes as if he danced in the mists
between the spirit world and the world of men. His face, veiled in
smoke and lit by the flames, seemed to glow as brightly as the iron
he worked with such dedication, and it both awed and scared her.
The fire sprits must truly dance with this young man and she found

herself increasingly glad that Gleva and Map had rescued him from some oaf's base lust. Increasingly aware, too, of her own.

Her conversation about marriage with Regan had run around and around in her head ever since her sister had dragged her down into the dirt of the training area, and Cordelia kicked herself for the missed opportunity at the brook. If anything were to happen with Taran, the first move had to come from her. She was the woman, she was the princess, so it was up to her. But Danu help her, it felt so difficult.

She threaded her way towards him as the crowd surged upwards to see what all the fuss was about. The precious Beacon chariot – a sleek, lightweight vehicle on two large wheels – was being pulled up the road by two fine horses. Painted in swirling colours and with an elaborate cross-bar system, it carried Mavelle, beaming from a seat at the back, with all the natural rhythm and grace of the horses that powered it. Surely, Cordelia thought, if craftsmen could make a vehicle that so clearly mimicked the horses, they could find a way to match the movement of birds too? And maybe the chieftainess was thinking the same for as she saw the watching crowd, she spread her arms wide, letting her rich robe flutter out like wings. Cordelia almost clapped.

It was not, however, Mavelle who truly caught the eye. For in front of her, standing tall to control the horses, were Olwen and Goneril, both in short tunics and long cloaks. Olwen's tunic was the colour of new bark and her cloak a dark green to match the leaves she wore woven into her hair so that she resembled a fresh young tree. Goneril wore a red tunic and a bronze-coloured cloak to match the auburn tresses that streamed behind her in the lively winds. Her golden torc shone magnificently around her neck and all eyes followed her as she drove the chariot, still at some speed, up the rise in the road and through the gates of the fort where she drew it skilfully to a halt. Goneril and Olwen's cloaks settled around them but still they stood there, well aware of the spectacle they made.

'Goneril looks like a goddess,' a voice said at Cordelia's side and she turned to see Taran.

Her body gave its usual pulse, as if he had set his hammer to her skin.

'She looks like a chieftainess,' she replied.

'Ah. Yes.'

They stood together watching as Olwen leaped lightly to the ground then held up her hand to guide Goneril down. Both women then turned to escort Mavelle out of what was ostensibly her chariot, though her wobbly, hunch-backed climb down from the high platform left no doubt as to who was truly commanding this particular show.

'She's very beautiful,' Cordelia said, gazing at her elder sister.

Had Goneril always looked this stunning? She couldn't remember. When she'd been permanently around, Cordelia had noticed little more than her sister's bad temper in the mornings or her grumblings about lack of light or combs or new tunics, but seeing her anew she recognised Goneril's radiance. It might just be her clothes or the way her hair had been combed out into a sheet of pure bronze, but it seemed to Cordelia that her sister looked purposeful, precious, powerful.

'Beautiful?' Taran queried as they watched her lead Mavelle through the crowd. 'She looks sort of cold to me.'

'Cold? Taran, she shines like one of your fires.'

'No, not like that. More like water at sunset – glorious on the surface but dark beneath.' Cordelia looked at him curiously and he shook himself. 'Sorry. I don't know why I said that. She is beautiful. I just like women who look more real.'

His eyes seemed to be fixed on hers and in his steady gaze Cordelia felt very, very real – far too much so – and found herself longing for even a little of Goneril's poise.

'We should follow them,' she said. 'My father will expect it.'

'He will expect *you*, Princess.'

She grimaced at him.

'And I will need an escort down this slope or I will surely fall and cover myself in mud splatters.'

She looked ruefully down at her pale grey tunic and Taran laughed.

'It would be my honour.'

He held out an arm and she took it gladly for though Lugh shone down, it had rained yesterday and the grass was wet. It would be just like her to slip and land at Goneril's feet – an entrance, for sure, but not an elegant one.

Leir came out of the royal house, resplendent in his own ceremonial cloak, with his silver torc around his neck and his almost-as-silver hair combed out behind him. Cordelia caught Goneril glancing back at her chariot, perhaps annoyed that her father had missed her arrival, but Leir clearly knew the tricks of a good show himself for he threw his arms wide and let a shower of white petals fall from each hand. They whipped around in the swirling breeze as he spoke: 'Welcome, Mavelle – chieftainess, mother, honoured guest. Lugh shines upon this happy day.'

He went down on one knee amongst the scattered blossom to kiss his mother-by-marriage's hand, drawing her forward and leaving Goneril standing behind. She stiffened with annoyance but Cordelia saw Olwen place a hand on her arm and, as if her touch contained magic, Goneril relaxed again and the smile returned in time for Leir to welcome her forward also. Cordelia held a little tighter to Taran. He had called Goneril "water at sunset" and she could see now what he meant, but water at sunset was still beautiful.

Now Regan was embracing Goneril and Cordelia saw her father look around for his third daughter and had to let go of Taran's arm and move forward to join her family. Her fingers went instinctively to the triskele around her neck as the three of them came together again after their longest ever time apart. Cordelia brushed shyly at her grey tunic and saw Regan pull down on her own brown one as Goneril stood proudly before them in immaculate bronze. Fire, their older sister seemed to be saying, was the most worthy of their elements, but Cordelia shook the mean thought away; Goneril shone brightest today simply because she was more prepared.

'Goneril, welcome.'

Her sister looked at her for a split moment too long, as if she had forgotten who she was, then drew her into a lavish embrace.

'Cordelia, sweetness. You look so . . . natural.'

Real? Cordelia wondered.

'I didn't realise you were coming,' she apologised, 'or I'd have changed. I've been with the hounds.'

'Hounds? Oh, your little puppies. How sweet.'

Goneril looked away, bored, but Mavelle reached for Cordelia's hands.

'I hear they are marvellous creatures, Cordelia. May I see them?'

'Of course, Grandmother. I'd love to show you, if there is time?' She glanced at Leir but he waved her on.

'Please go, Cordelia. We must summon up a feast for our guests so there is time enough.'

His voice was light but it was clear the new arrivals were a surprise to him and not an entirely welcome one. There was much work to be done in the fields at this time of the year and Leir, as a good ruler, liked to be involved. A feast would keep everyone to their hearths for today and slow their movements tomorrow, but the royal daughters were back together and the occasion had to be marked.

'Can I come too?' asked Olwen.

Cordelia blinked. She wasn't used to attention from the stately druidess.

'Of course,' she agreed. 'I'd be honoured.'

She thought she saw Goneril glaring at her but already her sister was turning to Leir. 'I hear you have guests, Father – royal guests.'

'I do,' he agreed and Cordelia found herself hurried away by Olwen.

'Tell me how you match a sire to a dam,' she demanded.

It was very much her favourite topic, so Cordelia happily let herself be drawn. Olwen was an intelligent and interested audience and they reached the byres before Cordelia had even realised it. Mavelle had been trailing behind but as they drew close to the puppy pen she quickened her pace.

'Oh, look at them! So full of life. May I go in?'

'Of course, Grandmother. Here.'

Cordelia carefully opened the little door at the side of the pen, keeping any alert puppies back with her foot, and ushered Mavelle in amongst them. The pups sprung forward, clawing and yelping excitedly, but she sank down amongst them seemingly without noticing the nips and tears in her old skin and gathered them in a great, hairy heap into her lap where they fell over each other to lick her face.

'Oh, hello there,' she said to each one. 'Hello, hello, hello. Aren't you funny little things? Aren't you gorgeous?' They responded with little yelps, as if trying to reply, and Mavelle threw back her head and laughed and laughed. 'Oh, Cordelia, this is doing me good. They're so energetic.'

'That they are,' she agreed ruefully. 'Even this pen is too small to contain them now. They are ready for their own homes.'

Her voice caught and her grandmother looked sharply at her.

'You will miss them?' She nodded. 'It is always the way. Parents suffer when their children go out into the world.'

'Do they?' Cordelia considered this. 'Does my father miss Goneril, do you think?'

Mavelle laughed again.

'I'm sure he does in some ways, but that one is definitely too energetic to be kept in a pen.'

Cordelia looked more closely at her.

'Is she looking after you well, Grandmother?'

Mavelle glanced towards Olwen, standing outside the pen.

'She looks after Beacon well,' she said eventually, 'and that leaves me free to spend time with Olwen on my birds and experiments so I am content.'

'You are ruler still.'

'Oh, I am, I am. But I grow old, Cordelia. This is my forty-ninth year and a woman has only so much life in her before she must return to the earth to be refashioned.'

'Grandmother!'

'It is not something to be afraid of, Dee, but rather to be embraced. And who knows? If I am granted passage on to Elysium, I may find my precious Bladdud again. I should like that, you know, very much, for he was half of me and sometimes I feel lost without him.'

Her voice was steady and her hands firm as they tussled with the pups but Cordelia felt her sadness and hated it.

'Grandfather was an excellent consort, Grandmother, but you are a worthy ruler alone.'

Mavelle smiled softly at her.

'And you are a very kind-hearted young lady. You remind me of your mother, Danu bless her. Mayhap I will meet my Branwen in Elysium too and if I do, Cordelia, I will tell her of you.'

Cordelia felt tears rising in her throat, like spring water behind Samhain ice.

'Grandmother, don't, I—'

'And I will tell her of your hounds. She will be very proud, I know it. And very jealous. She spoke of breeding dogs sometimes but never had the chance.'

Still the tears dammed in Cordelia's throat and she grabbed Anghus in an effort to keep them inside. She could not remember her mother, so did not truly feel grief for her but she sometimes felt the hole where Branwen would have been like a sacrificial pit waiting to swallow her up. She saw other mothers sitting in the sunshine, plaiting their daughters' hair or guiding them at the loom, and wondered how that felt. Then she touched her fingers to her amulet to remind herself of her sisters. How could she feel alone with them at her side? Not to mention her grandmother and her father, Magunna, Gleva and Map, and the whole tribe, all there to care for her and teach her and chat to her. It was foolish and self-indulgent to let herself feel sad.

'Here, Grandmother, you must meet Anghus.'

'Anghus?'

Cordelia pointed to the big puppy who had escaped her grasp and was throwing himself against the walls of the pen.

'I'm keeping him. I think he will make a fine sire.'

They both watched as he flung himself high against the wall, bounced off it and landed on his back, kicking his legs helplessly at the air before righting himself and trotting off as if it was exactly what he'd intended to do all along.

'In time, perhaps,' Mavelle said. 'We all need time to grow up and then more to grow down again.' She gave her a mischievous grin. 'Some days, Cordelia, I feel a girl once more and it's marvellous. Let Goneril have the dull running of the compound – I'm going to fly.'

Cordelia felt the waters of emotion recede from her throat and swallowed gratefully.

'How are your new wings?'

Mavelle tipped her white head on one side and looked again towards Olwen.

'The idea of an iron frame is promising,' the druidess said carefully. 'But it is too heavy. We need to make it thinner but the smith says that is impossible to achieve.'

'Does he? How thin?' Cordelia picked up the nearest pup and reached for the tag dangling from her collar. Taran had presented them all to her two days ago and she thought no puppies had ever looked finer. 'This thin?'

Mavelle reached out a hand and touched it. She looked to Olwen who stepped over the pen wall and bent down between them, examining the beaten metal closely.

'This thin would be marvellous,' she said eagerly. 'Who made this, Dee?'

'Taran,' she said proudly.

'Taran?' Mavelle asked.

'He's a—'

'Smith from Raven's Hill,' Olwen supplied.

Cordelia looked at her in amazement.

'How do you know?'

'Word travels fast. He came here with the Catuvellauni prince, yes?'

'That's right.'

'I'm told he is very promising.'

Cordelia pictured Taran at the forge, deep in his work, and looked down to hide the flush that rose to her cheeks. 'Dubus says the fire spirits like him,' she managed.

'That's very good,' Olwen said, excitement clear in her voice.

'And he is here?' Mavelle demanded. 'This smith, this . . . ?'

'Taran. Yes, he is in Burrough, Grandmother. Would you like to meet him?'

'I would.'

'Shall I fetch him?'

But at that Olwen intervened.

'No. We should see him at the forge where he works his magic, should we not, Mavelle?'

'We should.'

Mavelle pushed herself up and Cordelia rushed to help her to her feet.

'Now?'

'Why not? Olwen can take me if you are busy with the pups.'

Again, Cordelia saw Taran at his forge fires.

'No, no. I'll come with you. Let the puppies play together for tomorrow they will be separated.'

'If you're sure?'

'I'm sure.'

Taran looked so surprised when Chieftainess Mavelle limped into the forge on Cordelia's arm that he almost dropped his precious hammer into the fire. He caught it just in time, juggling it precariously above the flames before grasping it tight and coming forward, bowing low. Dubus lumbered away from his work too and Mavelle allowed them to kiss her hands before waving them impatiently to rise.

'Wings,' she said.

Taran and Dubus blinked.

'Wings, Chieftainess?'

'That's right. Iron wings.'

'For a bird?'

'No, no, no. For me. So I can fly.'

Taran, who had not met the Coritani ruler before, looked astonished, but Dubus was catching on fast.

'Of course, Chieftainess, I see. We'd be honoured to make some but . . . iron? They would be very heavy.'

Mavelle waved this away.

'Not all iron. Just a frame.'

Olwen stepped forward and Cordelia saw Taran's eyes widen further. A chieftainess and a high druidess – an honour indeed. Olwen did not, however, stand on ceremony but spoke to them both as equals.

'Ollocus, the smith at Beacon, has made a pair but they are not, as you rightly say, light enough. We need them thin.'

'As thin as the puppies' tags,' Mavelle added. 'I believe you made them, young man?'

She looked straight at Taran, with not a trace of the bewildered old woman who had arrived in Goneril's sparkling wake. Taran stood up straight.

'I did, Chieftainess.'

'They are very thin.'

'They are very small, Chieftainess. You are talking of something large?'

'I am.'

'Strips of iron maybe as long as you are tall?'

86

'Precisely.'

Taran was looking upwards, as if seeing possibilities in the air, and Cordelia watched him, fascinated.

'Tapering towards the base?'

'Yes.'

'Would they need to move? To fold up?'

'Could they?' Olwen demanded.

'I'm not sure. With the right joints, perhaps, though that would add weight, of course.'

'Of course. At the moment they are a little like this.'

Mavelle hitched up her robe and crouched to draw in the dirt. Olwen and Taran sank down at her side and Cordelia looked over to Dubus as the three of them began pointing and sketching and talking.

'As mad as each other,' Dubus mouthed and Cordelia laughed, though in truth she did not know if it was madness or genius. Or both.

She moved to the doorway, looking out across the compound as it bustled around the ceremonial roundhouse near the centre. Smoke was billowing from the roof on the rising winds as Leir set his people to cooking up a feast. Magunna was rallying a group to carry boards and cups and Cordelia could smell fresh bread baking and the tang of ale as a barrel was broached by Nairina, the tribe's most skilled brewer.

Goneril had been escorted to a carved stool set beneath a canopy to keep her from the worst of the gales and was entertaining a crowd of ladies and not a few eager young men. Regan was not with her, Cordelia noticed, but then she saw movement by the entryway to the stables and spotted her coming out with Leir, flushed and bouncing on her toes as if she wasn't sure where to put herself. Leir had his arm around her shoulders and was beaming at her and now Aledus came out behind them and Leir turned back to draw him in too.

Cordelia smiled. It seemed her earth-blessed sister had been quick to take the opportunity of having Mavelle here to propose to Aledus. He had clearly said yes and they would be heading this way to ask the permission of the chieftainess. Cordelia turned back into the forge where Taran was still talking animatedly with Mavelle and Olwen. He looked up and caught her eye.

'All well, Princess?'

His lopsided smile was wide, his habitual curl flopping over his left eye.

'All is very well, thank you.'

If Aledus was staying at Burrough then perhaps Taran could too, especially if the chieftainess was keen to use his skills. Cordelia's stomach rumbled and she smiled – it would be a happy feast tonight she was sure.

With Regan collaring Mavelle for "a quick word", the scientists were forced to abandon their discussions in the forge and Cordelia was free to take the pups back to the royal house for the night and prepare herself for the feast. Delving into the wooden chest that held her clothes, she picked out a blue tunic she had talked Magunna into embroidering with rich knot-work and dug out matching cords to tie into her dark curls.

Regan soon came in. She'd changed her brown training tunic for a smart dark green one and even let her hair loose from their usual tight plaits. Cordelia watched, amused, as she tried to sit elegantly still but within moments she was up again, bouncing around like a hare out of hibernation and setting the puppies yapping wildly in their box. Aledus sat himself quietly to one side but he, too, looked like a pot whose lid was only just staying on. Mavelle and Leir took some time to join the rest of the royals around their hearth, but came in smiling genially as the rest of the tribe could be heard gathering across the way in the ceremonial house. Only Goneril, it seemed, was unhappy.

'I'd forgotten how cramped it is in here,' she said. 'Why on earth don't you have your chamber upstairs like Mavelle, Father?'

'Like *Mavelle*?' their grandmother echoed, one eyebrow raised at Goneril.

Goneril flushed a little.

'You said you couldn't manage the ladder anymore, Grandmother.'

'I cannot. I am far more comfortable in the lower chambers. And you, I think, are happier up above.'

'It was the most sensible solution,' Goneril said stiffly.

Mavelle caught Cordelia's eye and winked.

'Well, for tonight, Gee, I'm afraid you will have to sleep below again.'

'But where?' She spun around, arms thrown wide. 'I hate sleeping with Regan because she squirms so, Cordelia's chamber is overrun with hounds, and my room has Aledus in it.'

'Our guest, Sister,' Cordelia reminded her.

'*I* am a guest now.'

'And may have that room with pleasure,' Aledus said, standing up to bow before her.

'I may? Oh.' She looked him up and down and moved a step closer, her voice dipping. 'Aledus, Prince of the Catuvellauni, I believe?'

'At your service, Heiress.'

Goneril blushed prettily.

'Such a pleasure to meet you. And, of course, you are welcome to my bed.'

Her voice was low, intimate even. Cordelia squinted at her eldest sister. Was she propositioning Aledus, right here in front of them all? If so, she had badly miscalculated. He was backing hastily away and now Leir stepped between them.

'Fret not, Gee. Aledus will not need his bed tonight, for he has found a better one.'

'What?' All Goneril's poise left her. She looked around uncertainly. 'What's going on? What better bed?'

Leir beamed.

'It's very good that you brought the chieftainess here, Goneril, for she now has a happy announcement to make to the tribe.'

'Announcement? Tonight?'

'Your dear sister Regan is to marry.'

'Marry! Marry whom?'

For a clever woman, Cordelia thought, Goneril could be remarkably stupid at times, perhaps because she found it hard to see past her own concerns.

'Why, marry Aledus, of course. We will be united with the Catuvellauni and our southern borders will be secure. Is that not marvellous news?'

Cordelia watched Goneril intently and saw anger ripple through her like the Quitos winds. But then Olwen was at her side, a calming hand on her arm, and just as swiftly she smoothed the ripple away.

'Marvellous,' she agreed, too loudly, then she leaped across to Regan and clasped her to her bosom. 'Truly marvellous. Haven't you been busy in my absence, Sister?'

Regan flushed.

'It just . . . we . . .'

Aledus stepped up to join them.

'Your sister does me great honour, Heiress.'

Goneril's eyes, when she looked at him, were coldest green, with none of the warm invitation of moments earlier.

'She does.' She looked across to Regan and then suddenly reached out and yanked both her and Cordelia close to her side. 'We three royal daughters are very close, you know, Prince. I hope you will not come between us?'

Aledus quailed.

'I would not dream of it, Heiress.'

Goneril sniffed and put an ostentatious hand to her triskele amulet.

'Good, for that would be very bad for the tribe.' She spun away to speak to Mavelle: 'You will announce this tonight?'

'We will. The people will be delighted.' Mavelle looked over to Regan. 'Are we all ready? Then you, my dear, should lead the way.'

'*She* should?' Goneril shrieked.

'Yes.'

'But I am the heiress.'

'And she is the bride.'

'Not yet. And it will, surely, spoil the surprise of the announcement?'

Mavelle pretended to consider this then shook her head.

'I think it will, rather, enhance our people's anticipation.'

And it did. There was a buzz of excited speculation the moment Regan and Aledus led the royal family into the ceremonial house, a dark-browed Goneril in their wake.

'My sister is cross,' Cordelia said quietly as she followed with Mavelle and Olwen.

'Goneril likes being cross,' Mavelle said.

'And it is good for her not always to be the centre of attention,' Olwen added calmly.

Cordelia bit back a smile and took her place on the royal benches closest to the hearth. She could feel the people pressing in, eager for news, and Mavelle did not make them speculate for long. She stood by the fire as the royal party was seated and then smiled around at the tribe circling out to the far edges of the ceremonial house.

'I thank you, good people of the Coritani, for welcoming myself and your dear heiress to Burrough.' She gave a little nod to Goneril who sighed. 'And I am pleased to announce that we have someone else to welcome on this fine night for my beloved granddaughter Princess Regan is to take as husband Prince Aledus of the Catuvellauni and bring a fine alliance to this, our most blessed tribe.'

Cheers rang out instantly. No one was surprised and why would they be? It was almost impossible to do anything in the compound without everyone seeing. Cordelia glanced awkwardly to Taran to find him looking straight at her and wondered how many had whispered about them on their pillows at night? She looked hastily away. There was nothing to whisper about and, besides, tonight was not about her.

Mavelle raised a hand.

'I have gifts for the couple.' She looked to Aledus. 'First, Prince, you must take your pick of the pups that, praise Danu, brought you to us in the first place.' Aledus bowed low and looked over to Cordelia. He had been in earlier to pick a solid, steady pup he had named Oak and she was delighted one of her hounds had brought him to Regan. 'And second . . . ' Mavelle paused again. She looked very pleased with herself and Cordelia fought to think what the surprise could be. 'The second, Granddaughter, is guardianship of our new fortress at Breedon.'

Regan's hands flew to her face. She looked in astonishment from Mavelle to Aledus to Leir.

'Breedon, Grandmother? As our own?'

'Your father and I can think of no one better equipped to protect our troublesome eastern border, Princess. The Coritani will sleep safer in their beds with you and Aledus in charge of its care.'

Then Regan was hugging her and Aledus was bowing over and over and everyone was cheering again. Everyone bar one. Goneril sat frozen, her eyes as dark as water beneath a sunset. She had ridden into Burrough this morning as the gleaming centre of attention but now she was just one in the crowd surrounding her younger sister and she clearly did not like it. She did not like it at all. Cordelia touched her fingers to her amulet and could swear she felt it uncurl just a little. But that was not possible. The iron was fixed into an eternal, linked spiral and the royal daughters were too. Goneril would find her own husband soon enough and then all would be well once more.

BELTANE

Summer

Chapter Ten

BREEDON HILL

Giamonios; Shoots-show days (May)

Cordelia paced the raised perimeter of the new compound at Breedon. She'd arrived six days ago with her father to prepare for Regan's forthcoming wedding and been fascinated to see the new fortress being moulded from the willing earth. The area on top of the hill here at Breedon was not quite as big as Burrough and more oval than circular but it was clear from the foundations marked out on the rough earth that Regan planned to set it out along similar lines to her home fort. Only the ceremonial and royal roundhouses had been built so far, but with the wedding just two days away many of Regan's new subjects had erected travel tents where permanent roundhouses would soon stand and there was a tangible excitement about the place.

Most importantly, the royal party of the Catuvellauni was due any moment and Cordelia could focus on little else. She was trying to train Anghus but could not stop herself glancing constantly to the rising grasses of the south meadows. Would Taran be in Chieftainess Enica's train? If not, she might never see him again.

Her hopes were pinned on Olwen. The high druidess wanted her wings and she saw Taran as the man to make them so, in the wake of Regan's announcement, she had spoken to Aledus about bringing him to join the Coritani. Olwen could, it turned out, be very persuasive when she put her mind to it, especially when backed by an equally eager chieftainess. Leir had not been slow either, putting up a considerable amount in treasure to purchase Taran's apprenticeship. Aledus had ridden back to his parents with little Oak, news of his impending marriage, and the promise of a fortress, so Cordelia could only pray they would be amenable to such a small matter as selling the services of an undersmith.

She looked again towards the road, willing the royal party to arrive and Taran to be with them, but Anghus, sensing her preoccupation, was leaping and pulling and tying himself in overexcited knots on the end of his lead so in the end she had to give herself a stern talking to. Her looks, however longing, would not draw the Catuvellauni to Breedon any faster, but they could teach Anghus to behave like a proper hound and he needed all the help he could get.

The puppy had grown even faster since Gleva and Map had taken his siblings off to trade and he'd been able to command the entire food bowl. Only Hawksheart, the bitch Regan had chosen for her own, had remained to keep him company. At the first moon of Beltane, however, she had gone with her new mistress to join Aledus in overseeing the works at Breedon. Cordelia had arrived at the new fortress half a moon-turn later to find the young bitch far calmer and more obedient than Anghus and had been ashamed of herself.

'Come on, boy, heel!' She picked up her feet to head along the earthen rampart and Anghus leaped forward but his paws all seemed to go in opposing directions and he tumbled over himself. 'Heel, Anghus – heel!'

She yanked him back and he looked up at her contritely, trotted at her side for a few paces and then, as he caught the scent of something tasty, shot off again. Cordelia scrabbled to keep her footing as he dragged her down the new-dug rampart. Taran was used to seeing her look a mess but after these long weeks apart she'd rather keep her tunic clean for once.

'Anghus, stop!'

But he had charged down into the compound and was heading determinedly for the centre so Cordelia had little choice but to chase after. She followed the markings of the new paths between the tents, trying to avoid the worst of the mud, and caught him up at the edge of the sacrificial pit in the centre. Reluctantly, she followed her hound's eager gaze, trying to reprove him though in truth the pit fascinated her too.

It was one large stride across and deep enough to knock on the door of the Otherworld. A pile of rich earth lay heaped at its side, waiting for the young oak to be planted where it could grow and watch over the new community, but for now the pit lay open. Cordelia could see down the central stake to the body tied to it, decaying in the heat and shrouded in greedily buzzing flies. It stank and the putrid flesh bore no resemblance to the man who had been sacrificed to ensure the prosperity of those dwelling here, but his spirit, at least, was gone to the Otherworld in glory.

The ceremony had been on the first day of their arrival here at Breedon. As a royal daughter Cordelia had been at the front of the crowd to see the man, a long-held Setantii prisoner who had volunteered for his death and been feasted in preparation. His wits had, she suspected, been wandering before he put up his hand to be guardian of Breedon and two weeks of rich food and the druids' most sacred herbs had scattered them to the winds so that he had already been halfway to the Otherworld when he'd been tied to the stake.

It had been Olwen, as High Druidess, who had plunged the sacred dagger into the victim's heart. She had done it with both drama and, thankfully, precision and the man had died with a cry of ecstasy on his lips, his hazed eyes already fixed on his next life. Cordelia, however, had still had to close her own at the final strike and Goneril had laughed at her.

'You can bring lives into this world, little sister, but not dispatch them onwards? Where is the strength in that?'

'I never said I was strong,' Cordelia had retorted, but her voice hadn't had quite the ring she'd intended.

She was a daughter of the Coritani so she was meant to be strong. She had visited and revisited the pit, trying to see the glory in it. She was too sentimental, she knew. The man was gone to the Otherworld to rest and, one day, return in a new form. Everyone carried within themself the spirit of a life that had gone before, and if no one moved on, no one could return. It was a cycle as clear and immutable as the moon's and the seasons' and she owed it to the tribe to respect it.

Anghus, bored of her stillness, edged closer to the tantalising bones within the pit, bringing her back to the present. Danu knew whose spirit her dog carried but it was a lively one and needed taming. Fast. She must be sterner with him.

'Anghus, sit,' she told him. He cocked his head on one side. 'Sit!' she commanded more firmly, and, to her surprise, he did.

She caught back a cry of triumph just in time and resisted the urge to hug him. 'Good dog,' she said instead, but then a sound caught her attention and she turned to see the guards calling, 'Men on the road!'

They were here! The Catuvellauni were here and it was time to find out if Taran was with them.

People came flooding out of the temporary shelters and Cordelia ran back up the ramparts with them all, squinting into the hazy sunshine to make out the particulars of Enica's considerable retinue. She swore that the man behind the shining royals was larger than average, and the hair spilling from beneath his travelling helmet was surely curly enough to burst free from the metal. Before she could consider him more closely, however, Aledus came rushing past her, heading out to welcome his father with Regan hot on his tail and Hawksheart loping eagerly in her wake.

'Mother!' he called. 'Father! Catia!'

They reached the party and began saying their hellos. Hawkshead was leaping around with Dias' hound and Cordelia realised with a start that this was young Oak, already growing into a fine-looking creature, but for once her eyes were not for the dogs. She watched Aledus clasp arms with the tall figure and saw the two men laughing together. It was someone he was familiar with then, someone he might want to have as part of his new tribe. Cordelia hugged Anghus tighter and he squirmed but now the new arrivals drew close and she must join the royal party to greet them. Releasing her hound to shoot off to his brother and sister, she moved to where Chieftainess Mavelle was sitting on a high-backed chair to welcome their guests.

'What a fuss,' Goneril muttered as she slotted in at her grandmother's side, careful to place herself to Mavelle's right.

'It's a wedding, Gee, an alliance. There's *meant* to be a fuss,' Cordelia told her.

'Even so.' Goneril kicked at the bare earth with her sandal. 'Regan is only a second daughter and this is only a minor fortress and one that isn't even built.'

'I think they've made amazing progress.'

'You would. Two houses and a dead man's pit – it's hardly triumphant.'

'It's not meant to be, Gee. It's new-born. It has to be given time to grow.'

'Like your damned pup?'

They both looked over to see Anghus rolling on the ground with Oak and Hawksheart. Cordelia considered calling him over but feared he would not listen and, anyway, the guests were dismounting and he was here, Taran, taking off his helmet so that his curls sprang free, a little damp from the ride but as wild as she remembered them. His eyes flew straight to her and her heart leaped.

'Just be nice, Goneril,' she said firmly.

'Nice?'

'For Regan's sake.' She leaned over and lightly touched Goneril's triskele amulet. 'Surely you are strong enough to do that?'

Goneril flinched away.

'There is no strength in being "nice", Dee.'

'Oh, I think there is. Try it.'

Goneril snorted but Cordelia didn't care for Taran drew close. Bound into the formal greeting, she took her turn in the royal line to shake the hands of Chieftainess Enica, Chieftain Dias and their beautiful daughter, Heiress Catia. She spoke graciously, she hoped, despite the fact that they seemed to linger forever, and then finally the smith was bowing before them. Leir, to Cordelia's left, clasped his hand first as Cordelia battled to hide her jealousy at this precious contact with him.

'Taran! Welcome back. You are here to stay?'

Cordelia held her breath so tightly she felt her chest straining with the pressure of it. Taran was still bowed low but as he rose she could have sworn he shot her a quick grin.

'Chieftainess Enica has been kind enough to agree to your purchasing my apprenticeship, Leir, thank you.'

Cordelia's breath came out in a loud burst and everyone looked her way. Danu help her, she was as badly behaved as Anghus! But she didn't care. Taran was back and he was staying. This would be a glorious wedding indeed.

Cordelia had never thought of Regan as beautiful but standing at Aledus' side beneath the new oak, planted in the thankfully filled-in pit to suck life from the dead man's bones, she shone. Both wore thigh-length tunics of richest soil-brown and shining amber bands on their heads and they glowed in the soft light of Lugh setting behind them. Three times the two of them circled the oak, following the path of the sun, before Olwen bound their hands with fine cloth and bade them kneel together whilst she called on all the spirits of the natural world to infuse them with their blessing.

One by one she beckoned her druids forward to bring offerings symbolising all the couple would need: water for health and wine for joy, bread for sustenance and meat for strength, wood for protection and flowers for beauty. All the gifts were gathered in a circle around the pair and Regan bent to commit them into the pit with the sacred oak to ask the earth, her own special element, to offer them back to her throughout her married life. She paused a moment, head bent in private prayer, then the poet-druids set up a haunting song and she returned to her groom's side. Olwen chanted incantations, moving around the couple faster and faster until she suddenly stepped through, grabbed their entwined hands and thrust them high.

'I declare you joined together before the tribes of Coritani and Catuvellauni. May your bloods mingle and bring health, prosperity and longevity to your shared peoples. May you sustain each other, share with each other, and support each other. May the earth grow green beneath your fingers and may peace blossom under your protection. May you bring wisdom, strength and joy to this your land for many moons to come. Regan and Aledus, we bless you.'

'We bless you!' the crowd echoed.

'We salute you.'

'We salute you!'

'We welcome you.'

'We welcome you!'

Voices carried from the flat hilltop out across the tribal lands, filling the air with joy in the match. Regan looked near to tears as Aledus gathered her in his arms and kissed her and everyone whooped in delight. Well, nearly everyone. Goneril stood stiff as a newly honed plank in the midst of the leaping crowd and Cordelia could not resist tugging on her sister's beautiful scarlet tunic to encourage her to join in.

'Don't, Dee,' she griped, pushing her off.

'Why not? It's fun. Just enjoy the day. It'll be your turn soon enough.'

Goneril sniffed.

'I'm the heiress, Cordelia. I cannot just go marrying anyone who lands in my fortress.'

'Aledus isn't just "anyone", Goneril. He's a prince.'

'Oh, I don't want a prince.'

Cordelia stopped jumping and looked at her.

'You looked like you wanted him when you first met him.'

Goneril glowered.

'Nonsense, Dee. I was just being welcoming. As Heiress. As ruler-to-be. And as such, I have authority enough of my own and will find a husband to suit my own ends.'

She glared at Cordelia who smiled.

'I'm glad to hear it, Gee, and would expect nothing less of you.' She straightened her blue-green tunic, askew from her celebrations, and gave her grumpy sister a quick kiss on the cheek. 'Now, if you don't mind, I shall go and offer my congratulations to our sister who looks very happy.'

Goneril looked over to Regan, who was chattering away to Mavelle, quite unlike her usual self.

'She does,' she conceded. 'And, after all, she and Aledus will be very useful to me – to the tribe – out here in the east. I shall do all I can to help them thrive.' With that she swept forward in front of Cordelia. 'Regan! Aledus! Congratulations! This is such a glorious day. I'm so proud. So very happy for you both, for us all. Aledus, you're a very lucky man and I trust you will look after my dear little sister well.'

Both bride and groom looked stunned but Aledus rallied first.

'Of course I will, Goneril, for she is very precious to me.'

'As she is to me.' She hugged Regan tight, pulling Cordelia in with them in a show of royal togetherness. The crowd sighed delightedly. 'A gift, Sister.'

Taking the heiress' golden torc from her neck, she moved to place it around Regan's instead but her sister put up a hand to stop her.

'I can't, Gee. It's yours.'

'Not today. Today it is yours, for today is *your* day.'

Regan flushed in delight as her big sister squeezed it firmly shut around her neck. She touched her fingers to it in awe and gazed up at Goneril. The crowd had fallen back as tall torches were lit in a wide circle around them and the three royal daughters stood alone at their centre.

'I'm honoured,' Regan stuttered.

'You're treasured,' Goneril replied, at her most unctuous, and kissed her as the crowd sighed again.

Cordelia could take no more and slipped away from their pretty tableau. Even when she was supposedly handing first place to someone else, Goneril seemed somehow to command everyone's attention and Cordelia was glad to step beyond the ring of light.

'Your sister shines.'

Suddenly there he was, Taran, looking so very tall and broad before her.

'Which one?'

'Both, though one perhaps from a deeper place.'

'And the other like sunset on water?'

'Sorry?'

'That's what you said of Goneril.'

'Did I?' He considered. 'It is a good description. I didn't know I was so poetic.'

He gave a funny little grin and Cordelia felt her heart beat faster, not this time with nerves but with a sort of eager recognition. She took a few more steps away from the circle of light and he followed.

'You should, perhaps, be a druid not a smith, Taran?'

He chuckled.

'I have much to learn of ironwork but even so I think I am far less likely to wreak damage on the world with metal than with words.'

'You shaped those words well.'

'Those, perhaps, but that was a mere lucky strike. Others I would mangle, believe me, and words, you know, cannot be stuck back in the fire and reformed. Once they have been spoken they are out there, to wound or praise as the receiver chooses.' He shuddered. 'No, give me a forge any day. It is far, far simpler than poetry.'

'Or conversation?'

'That depends with whom you are conversing. With some people it is torture, with others joy.' Behind them musicians were striking up a pretty tune and the crowd were cheering as Aledus led Regan out, but Taran's eyes stayed fixed on Cordelia. 'I have missed *our* conversations.'

She held his gaze.

'And I.'

He seemed to have nothing further to add and she could think of no clever addition herself so they stood there in the shadows without speaking. Cordelia glanced back to see Regan beaming in her husband's arms and remembered her lying in the dust of the training area, talking of the very thing they were here to celebrate today: *You should try marriage, Cordelia.* She straightened her spine.

'I am glad you are back, Taran.'

'You are?'

She stepped closer, turning her face up to his.

'Unlike you, I am not poetic enough to find the words to explain how much but this will, perhaps, suffice.'

Then she put her hands on his shoulders, reached up and gently pressed her lips to his. He responded instantly, kissing her gently at first but then with more passion as he gathered her in against his strong body. Eventually she broke free and, taking his hand, tugged him urgently up and over the rampart. They were tumbling to the ground together before they had even reached the bottom. It seemed she would be muddy after all but, Danu help her, she cared not one jot.

Chapter Eleven

Two days later

Cordelia felt certain that everyone must know what Taran and she now were to each other. The passion they had shared was surely dyed into every part of her skin for all to see? But no one seemed even to notice, still less care. Which made what she had to do next easier.

She started her campaign on the journey home. Those of the Coritani who were not staying at Breedon with the newly-weds rode east together. They would call at Beacon first, then the inhabitants of Burrough would move on the next day and Cordelia intended Taran to be among the second group. If she was to consider him as her consort, she needed time to get to know him and that wasn't going to happen if he had to stay at the heartland fortress.

They were not long out of Breedon when she manoeuvred her horse up next to Leir's.

'An excellent celebration, wasn't it, Father?'

He looked sideways at her.

'Excellent, Daughter, yes.'

'And such a good alliance for the tribe, is it not?'

'What do you want, Cordelia?'

'Nothing! I was actually thinking more of what you might want.'

She forced herself to ride on ahead. Her father caught her up.

'In what way?'

'Remember how you've been talking about forging a plough that can cut through the hardest ground?'

'Yes.'

'Well, I was just thinking – this might be your chance.'

He frowned.

'You're talking in riddles, Cordelia. What do you mean?'

'Just that with Taran here amongst the Coritani we may have the skills to develop it at last.'

'That's true. But Taran is with our tribe to make wings.'

Cordelia tossed her hair.

'Surely that cannot take up all his time, Father?' She leaned in closer. 'We want to make *real* use of him as well, do we not?'

'You do not think flying is real, Dee?'

'I think it *might* be. One day. I think Olwen and Mavelle believe it is, and if anyone can make it happen they can.'

'And Taran.'

'And maybe Taran but it cannot be all he does. The tribe has need of a good smith on the ground as well as in the air. Dubus has been wanting an apprentice for years.'

'As has Ollocus.'

'True, but it was you, after all, who bought Taran's apprenticeship, Father, so surely you deserve to have the use of him? And, besides, we all know where the real innovation is taking place, don't we? Burrough is the finest fort in the land. Even Gleva and Map say so and they have seen hundreds. And that's down to you.'

'Nonsense,' Leir protested, but he was colouring promisingly.

'And of course the forge at Burrough is so much bigger than at Beacon, so much better equipped, so much safer. The Beacon forge even lies outside the fortress walls – anyone could get at the wings at night. Imagine if, after all that work, they were stolen.'

'Imagine,' Leir agreed thoughtfully.

Cordelia rode on, feeling pleased with herself, but shortly afterwards, as if the air spirits had seen her pride and chosen to teach her a lesson, clouds obscured Lugh's face, grew rapidly blacker and finally, with a sort of eager spite, threw rain down on them in pailfuls. So heavy and so sudden was the storm that even in the time it took to stop beneath a cluster of trees and retrieve waxed leather cloaks from the packs, Cordelia's plaid tunic was soaked through. As they took to the road again, she had the curious sensation of it steaming beneath the sealed outer garment.

'Fine weather for water-fowl,' Mavelle said cheerily, coming up at her side.

'I'm not a water-fowl,' she told her grandmother tersely.

'You should have put your leather cloak on when we set out, Dee, like some of us did.'

She flapped her own cloak triumphantly and Cordelia groaned.

'It was hot then.'

'It was. Then.'

Her grandmother looked unbearably smug. But here, at least, was an opportunity for Cordelia.

'Sadly, Grandmother, I am not as wise as you.'

'Not yet, Dee, but it will come. You did well to find us that smith.'

Cordelia jumped. Perfect.

'Thank you, though he is Father's smith now, I believe. I hope you will be able to make the most of him at Beacon.'

'Of course we will.' Her grandmother peered more closely at her. 'Why would we not?'

'It's just your forge, that's all – is it a wingspan wide?'

Mavelle gaped at her.

'The workshop is.'

'That's true. Perhaps, then, it will be fine. As long as the pieces can be assembled away from the fire.'

'That's what Ollocus did.'

'And his wings are good, are they?'

107

Mavelle shifted in her saddle.

'They are as I asked. Just too heavy, that's all. Olwen!' The druidess steered her white horse over to join them. 'Did Ollocus' wings have joins?'

'They did. Big ones. It was one of the problems.'

'Was it?' Cordelia asked. 'That's a shame.'

And she rode forward again, no longer feeling anywhere near so wet and cold. The rain, however, battered on and soon there were grumbles up and down the group of riders, none louder than from Goneril.

'We'll have the life washed out of all of us if we don't find somewhere to shelter,' she protested. 'And then where will the Coritani be?'

'In Regan's hands,' Cordelia suggested, gaining herself a vicious glare.

'Well, you may not care about our great chieftainess' welfare, Cordelia, but I do. Mavelle is old, our father too.'

'Not so old,' Leir protested.

'Your eyebrows have gone white, Father, and very long. You really should get them trimmed.' Leir tugged bemusedly at them but Goneril was not to be deflected. 'I shall wait with Mavelle under these trees until proper shelter can be found.'

She turned imperiously into the woods but Olwen stopped her.

'No need, Goneril, for it has been found already. Look!'

The druidess pointed to where Anghus had diverted off the path and was sniffing at the entrance to a cave a short way up the rise to one side of the road. Goneril looked at it disdainfully.

'Is it safe?'

'More importantly,' Leir said, 'is it dry? Only one way to find out.'

He led the party forward as Anghus plunged into the gaping entrance. Cordelia watched nervously but her hound reappeared, bouncing eagerly back to them with nothing more threatening than an old bone in his mouth. Cordelia examined it. Free from flesh and bleached clean, whatever spirit had lived within it had long moved on and with the rain still throwing itself viciously upon them, they all scrambled inside.

The cave was thankfully large but, as a result, nearly dark and the group huddled together whilst two men battled as near to the opening as possible to light a fire. There were sticks and leaves within, presumably blown in last Lughnasad and now nicely dried out, and as soon as one of the men drew a spark from his flint they caught. The pile was hastily raked backwards as others pulled stray rocks into a circle to contain it. A handful of brave souls went out to find logs dry enough to stand a chance of burning and someone took off his cloak and folded it into a cushion, setting it at Cordelia's feet with a flourish.

'Sit, Princess, please.'

He looked very pleased with his gallantry so she sank down with a smile of thanks. Goneril was already seated on a fur she'd had laid out on a rock "for Mavelle", who was perched on the far side, but Cordelia felt stupid down there whilst the others all stood around, the flames casting shadows twice their size against the rocky walls. Spotting Taran's big frame a few steps away, she leaned back and tugged on his trews. He jumped as if she were a creature on the attack then gave the lopsided smile she was growing to love and crouched down at her side.

'Is all well, Princess?'

'Cordelia! And no, it is not. I feel silly down here on my own. Join me.'

'Me?'

He looked round a little awkwardly but now Olwen swooped in.

'Why not, Taran? We're all equal here.'

Cordelia glanced to her sister, unsure Goneril would agree, but Mavelle was waving everyone to join them around the makeshift hearth and the heiress could do little but smile her assent. The log fetchers returned with branches that spat indignantly then caught. Leir sneaked one and began contentedly whittling it with the tools he kept in his belt, and someone set up a low tune. A skin of ale was passed around and within moments the whole place had taken on the feel of a roundhouse before dinner.

Anghus crept in under Cordelia's legs, watching the still spitting flames warily, and she felt a strange contentment rise within her. She dared to lean sideways and felt Taran's shoulder supporting her, strong and firm. All the light was on their faces so she reached for his hand and slid it round her waist, thanking the air spirits for the blessing of this sudden storm.

'Anghus did well to find us shelter,' Taran said.

'He's a clever dog,' Olwen agreed.

'He's a *crazy* dog,' Cordelia corrected, but at that Leir reached over and patted her knee.

'We're all a little crazy when we're young but he is calming already and will make a good sire. You have done well, Dee.' He glanced towards the chieftainess. 'Mavelle and I are aware that your pups have brought the tribe riches.'

'I am glad, Father.'

'And we think that you should see some of that treasure.'

Mavelle nodded keenly and leaned over to pat Cordelia's shoulder. 'Is there something you would like, Dee? Clothes? Jewels?'

Cordelia did not even need to think.

'A doghouse.'

'Sorry?'

She stroked Anghus.

'If possible, I would like a doghouse with room for at least two whelping boxes and space for pups as they grow. I would like it to have a secure cage within so they cannot escape and food bowls bolted to the posts so that they cannot knock them over and—'

'Stop, Daughter, stop!' Leir's deep voice echoed around the cave but he was laughing. 'You have thought of this in some detail!'

'It would make breeding so much easier. And with more dams of my own, I could create a purer strain of hound than by using everyone else's. And it would, you know, spare others from having them in the house and—'

'Enough. I'm convinced. Mavelle?'

The chieftainess laughed.

'If you have the resources to build it, Leir, then Cordelia should certainly have her doghouse.'

'I should? Truly?'

She looked delightedly at Taran and felt his hand squeeze her waist.

'I could help design it,' he offered. 'The bowls, for example – if you fix them to the post you won't be able to wash them but if you had a hook that fitted into a hole in the bowls it would hold them firm when you needed and release them when you did not.'

'That would be perfect.'

'And you could have hooks higher up as well to hang the bedding from to dry it.'

'Yes! And maybe even build two cages because if litters overlapped, the younger ones would need peace.'

'I can do that. Would you want a gate?'

'Could I have one?'

'Of course. That is, if your father is happy for me to make it?'

Leir laughed again.

'I am happy.' He gave a little cough and then went on, 'But we will, you know, need you at Burrough to build all that.'

Cordelia saw Olwen tense.

'At Burrough? Taran is coming to work on the chieftainess's wings, is he not, Mavelle?'

'He is,' she agreed then glanced at Cordelia who held her breath. 'But you know, Olwen, the forge at Beacon is not very big.'

'What?' The druidess looked furious.

'It is not a wingspan across. Not the wingspan of a human bird at least.'

'Whereas at Burrough it is easily big enough,' Leir said. 'And then Taran can also help with the doghouse and, perhaps, a few other small projects.'

'But the wings!' Olwen protested furiously and Cordelia felt Taran gulp next to her.

'I will willingly go wherever you wish me to,' he stuttered. Cordelia dug her nails into his palm.

He jumped and everyone looked at him curiously.

'The doghouse will not take up much of Taran's time,' Cordelia said smoothly. 'I'm sure the wings can be a priority, can they not, Father?'

'A priority? Oh, yes, of course. And we have Dubus who is, you know, skilled in his own right and can assist Taran, who is young yet. He is still an apprentice, remember – *my* apprentice – and this will be the best way for him to develop as a smith, do you not think, Mavelle?'

Olwen glared at the chieftainess who winced but stood her ground.

'I do think so,' she said, 'for now. But things may change.'

Things may indeed, Cordelia thought, and relaxed against Taran again as the flames flared brightly, blocking out the dankness of the weather beyond. Already she was yearning to feel his skin against hers again but for now they could take their time and get to know each other. All being well, the Coritani would have another wedding to celebrate before the year was out.

Chapter Twelve

BEACON HILL

Semiuisonns; Bright days (June)

Olwen lifted the knife and then hesitated. She hated this bit. Even though she was desperate to see inside the little bird, making the first cut into its perfect shell always felt like a desecration. She bent her head and murmured a prayer of thanks to the Mother for the gift of this beautiful creature's life and the even greater one of the knowledge it might offer her. She had dissected hundreds of birds and still the magic of flight eluded her, but every time she hoped it would be the one that unlocked their precious secrets.

She stroked a slim finger down its soft, brown chest and then, with a small sigh, ran the blade fast and hard along its abdomen. Once the decision was made, it was best not to shrink from it. To do so was to dishonour the subject. It was the same with a sacrifice. To die by the holy knife was an honour but it was a suffering too and should not be prolonged. Olwen could still remember the long hours of being taught the exact point at which to plunge in the blade to get straight to the heart. She could picture the bodies on the slabs, all different shapes and sizes and all with the heart marked out in woad.

No one wanted to see a sacrifice writhe and gurgle beneath a bungled strike and no one wanted to be the druid who bungled it. For years, every time Olwen had met someone new, she had found herself assessing exactly where their heart lay. She'd had to train her mind to stop; it wasn't good to size up every new friend as a potential sacrifice. But even now, five years since her graduation as a full druidess, she found herself twitching her arm to check the angle required to correctly position a knife, especially if it was someone whose dimensions were off the ordinary scale.

The smith, for example, Taran. He was a big man and strong too. His chest would be solid muscle and therefore far harder to penetrate than the thin flesh of a long-held prisoner. Not that she'd want to see that one sent to the Otherworld. He was the craftsman they'd been seeking, she knew it. The fire spirits danced with him and he had an eye, besides, for the natural shapes of the world. With him, they might finally send Mavelle into the skies. It was irritating that Leir had managed to whisk him away to Burrough but Olwen would not let that get in her way for long.

Carefully she peeled back the flesh of the bird and bent to peer inside. It grew dark and she pulled two torches closer, adjusting their stands to give the greatest light. Up in the fortress she could hear the sounds of people damping down their fires, calling their goodnights and closing up their doors. She heard the creak as the big gates were wound shut but didn't let it distract her. The guards would always let her in and she could sleep here if need be, roosting with the living birds once she'd finished learning from this dead one. Would Goneril come to find her? For once Olwen hoped not, for there was much to do.

She spent a while probing the joints between the wings and body but that was not something they would surely ever be able to recreate and eventually, with only a little reluctance, she cut both wings away. Moving to the scales she had built last Imbolc, she placed the wings in one pan and the body in the other. The wings, as she'd observed many times before, were heavier and yet she also knew from previous studies just how light the bones were. She'd cut numerous examples open and found them hollow within where humans had a rich, dense marrow. Feathers she also knew were heavier than the skeleton but there were feathers on both body and wings so that left only one difference – muscle.

The flesh on the wing, although thin, was dense and taut, with the upper muscle greater than that on the underside – the force of the downstroke, then, was key to flight. The muscle across the creature's rigid chest was pronounced too, presumably so that the flap of the wings did not tear it apart. She shivered. Mavelle had little muscle and with the wingspan required to carry her cumbersome human body she stood little chance of creating the force needed for lift. Olwen sighed. Her eyes stung in the smoky light and her neck ached from hunching over. Stretching out, she looked up into the rafters and then back to the now broken corpse before her.

'Maybe,' she whispered to it, 'we just aren't meant to know your secrets. Maybe it's not curiosity in me, but arrogance. Maybe . . . '

'Maybe you're beautiful when you're concentrating.'

Olwen nearly jumped out of her skin as a pair of arms wrapped around her from behind.

'Goneril! I never heard you come in.'

'I know. I've been here ages watching you muttering to yourself. What's wrong, Olwen?'

Olwen sighed.

'I can't work out what makes flight possible, Gee.'

Goneril dropped a kiss on the side of her neck then came around next to her to look down on the table. 'Studying birds again?'

'Again, yes. Is it foolish?'

'Foolish? No! You are many things, my flame, but not foolish. Never foolish.'

Her vehemence was comforting but it wasn't that simple.

'But if I am not *inherently* foolish, then perhaps it is worse to be devoting my mind to impossibilities. Should I not be turning my talents to other things? Things that can be of real benefit to the tribe.'

'Such as?'

Olwen shrugged.

'I don't know.'

Goneril smiled and took her face in her hands.

'You are tired, Olwen. It is late and you work too hard. Flight is a truly amazing aim and of course it will be a struggle to achieve, but if anyone can do it, it is you.'

'And Mavelle.'

'She has the desire, yes, and the power to command, but it is you, my flame, who have the knowledge.'

'And Taran, perhaps, the skills.'

'Taran? Oh, the young smith. Perhaps, if we can keep him from Father's ploughs long enough.'

Olwen groaned.

'Ploughs are of real benefit to the tribe, Gee.'

Now Goneril laughed. She came closer, so close that her breath blew across Olwen's face, warm and scented with spiced mead.

'Do you think, Olwen, that the men and women who invented the cart did it in a day? Do you think they didn't break and stick and grind their rough wheels endlessly into the mud? But now you and I can speed across the tribal lands in style. And the boatbuilders – do you think they didn't end up floundering in cold water again and again, cursing their own foolishness for ever thinking they could do it? Yet now Gleva and Map sail the seas all the time.'

At that, Olwen had to smile.

'You speak true.'

'Of course I do. I'm no fool either.'

'*That* I know.'

'So, tell me – what can I do to help?'

'You want to help?'

'Of course. What do you think I am, Olwen? I will rule this tribe one day and if I can do it from the skies so much the better.' Goneril kissed her. 'I want to help you, my flame. So, what can I do?'

'We need a forge.'

'A forge?'

'Yes.' Olwen grabbed for her hands. 'We need a bigger, better, newer forge, like they have at Burrough. Whilst Taran is working there and I am working here we cannot progress as fast as I would like.'

Goneril nodded slowly.

'You want me to build you a forge, Druidess?'

'I want you,' Olwen corrected, 'to release the wood and the stone and the craftsmen to build me a forge.'

'And in this forge you will work magic?'

'Taran will.'

Goneril looked at her curiously.

'You like him?'

Olwen looked to the ceiling. The birds had settled quietly in their cages and moonlight shone through the gaps in the thatch and danced in the dusty air, as if claiming it. As if telling her something. She looked to the Coritani heiress.

'I like what he can do. I like his skill, his vision, his strength. He augurs well for the tribe.'

'I see. You think we should bind him more closely to us, Olwen?'

She drew in a breath and looked again at the moonlight, which seemed to dance more brightly than before. The Goddess was talking to her and she must listen.

'You want a man, Gee. A husband.'

Goneril squinted at her.

'The smith?'

'Maybe. You say you do not want a prince who might seek to control you.'

'Like any man could!'

'So why not have a craftsman to help you control the whole

world?' She took Goneril's hands and looked into her green eyes. It would be so hard for her to give up this woman but the prosperity of the tribe was worth more than her own petty gratification. 'The fire spirits are with you, Gee, and they are with Taran too; it seems a perfect match. And iron is the future. Worked with skill, it can give us the best tools and the fastest vehicles; the safest homes and the cleverest cooking devices; the sharpest ploughs and—'

'The most lethal swords.'

Olwen shook her head at that.

'Better a plough than a sword, Gee. The best tools make the best tribes.'

'And the best blades make the strongest ones.'

'But—'

'Hush, Olwen. We can have both can we not? We can have everything, you and I. If you wish it, I will order a forge. Tomorrow. First thing.'

'You will?'

'Of course. We will have a forge and then we will have a smith. If iron is, as you say, the future, then let us seize it. Let us, indeed, seize him.'

With a wicked grin, Goneril pulled her into her arms. Olwen sunk into her kisses and tried to ignore the thought of Goneril taking Taran to her bed, though she feared that now she had planted the idea in her fiery lover's head, she would pursue it with all her usual haste. She must make the most of her royal lover whilst she still had her for the lowly smith would, surely, never refuse such an honour.

Chapter Thirteen

BURROUGH HILL

Semiuisonns; Bright days (June)

'Here.'

Taran stood behind Cordelia, his body strong against hers as his powerful arms reached around to show her how to hold the hammer. The heat of the forge fire was fierce against her face but not as great as the heat of his touch and she had to force herself to concentrate. She came to his pallet most nights now and was deliciously used to his arms around her but this was different. Her lover's hammer was his most prized possession and he did her great honour letting her work with it.

'Like this.'

He adjusted her fingers on the handle. He had wrapped them with infinite care in linen before they started but it was thin enough that she could feel the delicious roughness of his fingers over hers and the worn-smooth leather of the handle. Her hands were far smaller than his and sat awkwardly across the letters of his name slashed in the hide but she liked it. She could almost feel the hours of work he'd put in pulsing beneath her skin, showing her what to do.

'And like this.'

Now he was wrapping her other hand around the tongs used to grip the iron bar sitting in the fire pit. This was no sophisticated piece of ironwork. Her only task was to draw out the iron by hammering the rounded bar flat, but she felt the thrill of bending it to her will all the same and listened carefully as Taran told her how to pull it from the burning heart of the coals and position it on the block.

'Now?' she asked, glancing back over her shoulder.

He shook his head.

'Just a little longer, if you can bear it?'

'I can bear it,' she said, gritting her teeth.

'Good. That's good. Count to three and – now!'

Cordelia tightened her grip on the bar and drew it from the coals. It glowed angrily as it hit the air, as if daring her to touch it. She laid it on the block, gripping the tongs tightly. The rest of the forge seemed to recede into shadows as she focused on the already darkening bar and even Taran faded from her consciousness as she lifted the hammer and, biting her lip, brought it down, hard and true on the centre of the iron.

'Yes!' she heard him cry but his pleasure was muted by the pain juddering up her arm. Danu help her, that hurt!

'Again,' Taran was urging. 'Again and again whilst it is still hot enough. Beat it into submission, Dee!'

Blinking back a droplet of moisture that had run into her eyes – and taking a moment to be grateful Taran couldn't see her pink, sweating face – she did as instructed. Again she hit, again the pain ricocheted up her arm. Four more times she did it, her vision blurring with the effort.

'That's amazing!' Taran cried.

She lifted her arm once more, feeling it shake like new leaves in the Quitos winds, and had rarely been more grateful than when she heard him say, 'Best put it in the fire again now.'

Slowly she lowered her arm and held the bar over the fire to examine her handiwork. She could have wept.

'I've not even dented it!'

'You have.' His hands closed around hers and she felt their raw strength. 'See – here. You have definitely flattened it here.'

She leaned as close in as she dared and saw a very slight disruption to the curve of the iron – surely visible only to someone blinded by love. She shook her head.

'I thought my dog tags were amazingly thin before but now I know what it takes to get them that way I am even more impressed. How will you do that for a whole pair of wings?'

Taran flushed.

'I'm not sure but I really do need to get on with making an attempt. Dubus thinks they're foolish or, to quote him, "bloody bonkers", and he's always finding me other things to do. Like bowls and cages for the doghouse.'

She reached up and kissed his nose.

'In which case, I'm with Dubus.'

Taran grinned. 'Then that's all that matters. Look – your iron is hot again.'

She glanced down at the glowing bar and stretched out her arm nervously.

'You do it, Taran.'

'No. It's yours.'

'But it hurts.'

'Hurts!' Instantly he took both the iron and the hammer from her and spun her round to look into her face. Damn! But he didn't seem to care how dishevelled she was, just wiped his big fingers, oh, so softly across her damp forehead and bent to press his lips to hers. 'I don't want it to hurt you. I don't want anything to hurt you.'

She laughed.

'It's only a little judder in my arm, Taran. Although, actually, that is making it feel a lot better.'

She pushed herself up on her toes to kiss him again, revelling in the feel of him. She'd loved his gentle strength from the start but now she saw how effective it truly was – he'd have had that bar totally flat in four hammer strikes. She pressed herself tighter against him and his kiss deepened.

'Oi! You two – this forge is hot enough already, thank you very much.'

They scrambled apart as Dubus came lumbering in. Anghus, stretched out on the doorstep in the sun, dragged himself to his feet and lolloped in after him.

'Some guard dog you are,' Cordelia told him. She would have blushed if her face wasn't scarlet enough already.

'I thought you were out collecting ore,' Taran stuttered.

Dubus grinned broadly.

'So I see.'

'I was just showing the Princess how to draw out iron.'

'Is that what you call it?' the older smith chuckled, clearly loving every moment of their discomfiture. 'Well, I'm afraid the Princess has visitors and will have to leave your iron bar for another day.'

He winked lewdly, pleased with his wordplay, and Cordelia groaned.

'Visitors? Who is it, Dubus? I'm a mess.'

'Fret not. It's just Gleva and Map.' Cordelia smiled at that. 'Oh, and some foreign dignitary come all the way from over the seas to talk to you about dog breeding.'

'What?' Cordelia shot to the door and peered out. 'Where are they?'

'Your father had them taken into the ceremonial house. I was on my way out for the ore and offered to fetch you.'

'How did you know I'd be here?'

Dubus shook his head.

'Princess, you are always here.'

'There's been a lot of work to do on the doghouse,' she started but, really, what was the point? She cut herself off and smiled at him. 'Thank you, Dubus. I'm glad it was you who came to find me.'

'Drawing out Taran's iron bar?'

Oh, yes, he was very pleased with his wordplay. She turned back to Taran.

'You will come with me? Gleva and Map will be pleased to see you.'

'I think I'm a little rough for foreign dignitaries, don't you?'

'No,' Cordelia said simply. 'I don't. Now tidy yourself up and I'll meet you outside.'

And with that she made a run for the royal house, to wash and tidy herself and go to meet this mysterious dignitary.

'Prince Lucius at your service, Princess.'

The man bowed low as Cordelia scrambled into the ceremonial house a short time later with Taran at her shoulder. The visitor was tall and slim with cropped blond hair and wore a fine-woven tunic of subtle green checks that made him look very elegant – until Anghus went bounding up to him, all-but knocking him over. Cordelia gulped and leaped forward but Lucius just laughed and bent to the dog.

'And who are you, fella? You're a handsome one, aren't you?' Anghus rubbed his head against the prince's thigh in rapt agreement and Lucius fondled his ears. 'A strong back,' he commented, 'and fine haunches.'

Anghus gave a little rumble of pleasure and Cordelia went forward.

'He was a runt, you know.'

'No!'

'Yes. A lucky ninth pup. We thought his dam was all done and then out he came – small and pale and not even breathing.'

'What did you do?'

'Cleared the birthing sac and blew on him.'

The prince nodded sagely.

'I've seen that work.'

'You have?'

'Several times. My tribe breed a lot of hounds and I've always been gripped by the process. When I was just two, my poor mother lost me one night and after what I am told was an increasingly frantic search by considerable numbers of the tribe, they found me curled up in a whelping box with a new litter. I was, apparently, most aggrieved to be returned to my own bed.'

Cordelia laughed.

'A man after my own heart.' There was an awkward pause and Cordelia turned hastily to Taran. 'This is Taran our smith. He knows Gleva and Map well.'

'Indeed,' Gleva agreed, hurrying forward and hugging them. 'It's so good to see you both.'

'And you. Where have you been?'

Gleva shrugged.

'Oh, you know us – here, there and everywhere. We have been further north than ever before this Beltane and seen great mountains, purple-coated with heather and snow-topped even now. We have brought your father horn from the huge deer that roam their sides.'

She nodded to Leir who proudly held up a vast pair of antlers.

'Fine drinking horns, hey? Perhaps, Taran, you can forge me some holders?'

'Of course, Chief. It would be my pleasure. It must be an amazing country.'

'Oh, it is,' Map agreed, hugging them too. 'And we met a man who told us that there are great seas not far beyond. He claimed that these lands of ours are an island.'

'An island?' Leir queried.

'A large one, to be sure, but totally encircled by seas to the north, south, east and west.'

'Is that possible?'

Map looked around them all.

'There is a cartograph of it, I am told, though it is somewhere in the Grecian lands so it could be nonsense. One day, perhaps, Gleva and I will follow the coast and see if it takes us all the way around.'

Cordelia stared. She could not picture one sea, let alone a circle of them.

'How far do you think the world must stretch?' she asked.

Gleva and Map looked at each other.

'Who knows, Dee? Every time we travel a little further, we meet people for whom that new boundary is but the start of their own lands. Maybe it stretches forever? We have heard tell of lands locked in ice all year round and others permanently kissed by Lugh's fiercest heat. We have heard of mountains far bigger than the heather-coated peaks north of here and plains that stretch further even than the Coritani ones. We have heard of white bears and giant cats, of snakes bigger than men and of beasts with necks stretching into the sky or noses so long they touch the ground.'

Cordelia's mouth was open, she knew.

'And of places,' Prince Lucius said quietly, 'with perfectly formed hounds.'

She looked at him gratefully.

'And where are you from, Prince?'

'Lucius, please. I am from the Belgae, sent by my mother, Chieftainess Sophia, to commend you on the hounds we bought at Imbolc and to offer you, if we may, a gift.'

'A gift?' Cordelia heard Taran's voice echo her own but had no time to look at him for now a man was coming forward, bringing with him a slim, rangy hound. 'Oh!' Cordelia ran to her. 'Oh, Lucius, she's beautiful. Is she not beautiful, Father?'

'Beautiful,' Leir agreed obediently.

The hound was wary but when Cordelia offered her hand for the bitch to sniff, she seemed to approve and hugged in against her leg. Cordelia ran a hand along her side.

'Such a splendid colour.'

The dog was not brindled like Anghus or Keir, but russet, like a wild fox.

'She was the only one of the litter to come out like this,' Lucius said. 'We don't know why.'

Cordelia considered.

'No one does, Prince. I have asked Olwen about it before but even she does not have the answers.'

'Olwen?'

'Our high druidess. She is an expert on animals. Well, birds mainly but all of the Mother's creatures fascinate her. We think it most likely that an ancestor – her dam's dam perhaps – was this colour and some part of that lives in the blood, to come out when the spirits choose.'

'Lives in the blood?' Lucius nodded thoughtfully. 'I can see that. So if this one breeds, she might have russet pups?'

'Or her pups' pups might, yes. It is one of the things I am looking into.'

'Then I hope you will accept her as a gift?'

Cordelia looked up at him.

'Truly?' He smiled. 'Then of course I will.' She bent and hugged the slim hound. 'I shall call her Endellion – "fire" in the tongue of the ancients – and you, Prince Lucius, will have the first of her pups.'

'I would be honoured.'

Anghus, momentarily distracted by a lamb bone he'd sniffed out in a corner, had now spotted Endellion and came bounding across, tail wagging so hard it swiped a wine goblet off a nearby table. Lucius deftly caught it.

'It seems he likes his new friend,' he laughed.

'That,' Cordelia said drily, 'would be helpful.' She grabbed Anghus, trying to contain his enthusiasm. 'The prince has brought you a lady-love, Anghus.'

'It is an excellent match,' Leir pronounced, coming forward.

'I do hope so,' Lucius said.

There was a loaded pause.

'Dinner?' Cordelia squeaked.

'Most welcome,' Map agreed, rubbing his stomach. 'Taran?'

But the smith was edging away.

'Not for me, thank you. I have iron to draw out.'

Cordelia spun around but he was gone before she could stop him and she was left to sit down with the Belgic prince and his gift of a hound.

Silly man, she thought crossly, but then Lucius was asking her more questions about dog breeding and she had little chance to fret further.

Chapter Fourteen

Burrough Hill

Semiuisonns; Bright days (June)

Taran pumped harder and harder at the bellows until the fire rose so high that Dubus roared at him to stop.

'You'll have the thatch alight, lad. Calm it down!' Taran grunted and Dubus came over and put a hand on his arm. 'What's up with you? The princess not drawing out your iron?'

Taran threw him off.

'She's not coming anywhere near me these days. She's too busy talking dog breeding with that damned foreign prince.'

Dubus shook his head.

'And if it was a foreign princess?'

Taran shrugged.

'That would be different, wouldn't it?'

'It wouldn't. She's just found someone who shares her interest, that's all. It would be like you meeting another expert smith. You'd have things you wanted to discuss, styles to compare, techniques to show each other.'

'I don't want him showing her his bloody techniques.'

'Then you're an idiot. Jealousy is an ugly emotion, Taran.'

'Jealousy?'

'Yes. Come on, man, he's just a slip of a dog breeder. Why would she want him when she can have a strong, lusty smith?'

Dubus jokingly squeezed his bicep and Taran had to laugh. He was being an idiot, he knew, but it was hard. This Lucius was a prince. As Leir himself had suggested, he would be an excellent match for the third Coritani daughter and if he "shared her interests" then maybe it would be a good match for her too.

'Has she given you any reason to doubt her, lad?' Dubus probed. Reluctantly Taran shook his head. Cordelia had been busy with Lucius in the day but most nights she snuck to his pallet in the forge and made love to him with all her usual fervour. 'Well then. It will only annoy her if you go moping around like a fool. Be as strong in your thick head as you are in your arm and the prince will soon be gone.'

'You're right, Dubus.'

'Of course I am. Now – we have a plough to craft so stop punishing those bellows and get hammering.'

'Yes, Dubus.'

He picked up his hammer, stroking his hand across the soft handle and, for a delicious moment, remembering Cordelia's fingers wrapped around it, but then a voice called, 'Taran? Taran are you in there?' and Leir came striding into the forge with a tall, slim figure in his wake.

'Druidess! This is an honour indeed.'

Olwen smiled as Dubus lumbered forward, bowing low, and Taran joined him, trying desperately to wipe the soot and sweat from his hands. She waved them up immediately.

'Mavelle is keen to know how her wings are getting on, Taran.'

'Of course, of course.' He flushed and looked to Dubus, who refused to meet his eye. 'I have been very busy, Druidess.'

'As I knew would happen.'

She looked sternly at Leir who gave an easy shrug.

'Fields need ploughing, Olwen.'

'Fields will always need ploughing, Leir,' she said witheringly, 'but we are running out of time to send Mavelle into the skies.'

At that, Leir gave a sombre nod.

'You speak true, Olwen. I apologise. Taran, clear all other tasks for your chieftainess wants her wings. Dubus, your help would be much appreciated. Taran is a man of talent, but you are a man of experience.'

'Not when it comes to making wings, Chief.'

'No, well, the same could be said of all of us but we must try, mustn't we?'

'Yes, Chief. Of course, Chief. It would be an honour.'

If Leir detected sarcasm he chose to ignore it.

'Good, good. Get on then. Olwen will wait with us at Burrough. Prince Lucius is keen to discuss animal breeding with her.'

'Of course he is,' Taran muttered.

'Sorry, Taran?'

'Nothing, Chief.'

'Good. She will escort you to Beacon with them as soon as possible.'

'Perhaps,' Dubus said, 'if we perfect the wings, Taran could fly there?'

This time Leir did not ignore the smith's jibe. He stepped up to him, his blue eyes hardening to iron grey.

'You will apply yourself to this task, Dubus, to the very best of your considerable ability. Yours is the execution of the machinery; leave the rest to others better versed in the ways of nature than yourself.'

Big Dubus cowered.

'Yes, Chief. Of course, Chief.'

'Good.' Leir stepped back. 'Thank you.'

And then he was gone, taking Olwen with him. Taran tried not to imagine her locked in discussion with Lucius and Cordelia about dog blood, or with his dear Gleva and Map about the width of the world. They were all too clever for him, he knew it.

'Is it possible?' Dubus asked suddenly and Taran looked up from his dark thoughts to see that his boss had followed Leir to the door and was peering out into the skies where Lugh was shining brightly down.

He went to join him and they both watched a flock of sparrows swooping in and out of the hedgerow with a light agility of which humans could surely only dream. He glanced back to the fires and felt a quiver of excitement. He might not know about dogs but he certainly knew about iron.

'I'm not sure,' he said. 'But what *is* possible is to craft a wing.'

Dubus looked at him and gave a wry smile.

'Then that, lad, is what we shall do. I hope those arms of yours are strong indeed, because it's going to be a long, hot day at the fire.'

It *was* a long day and the next one too. Taran and Dubus barely left the forge, even eating their meals in the doorway, seeking the minimal relief of the shadows between Lugh's heat and their own fire. Olwen flitted in and out, checking, questioning, measuring, checking again. It was hard but Taran was glad of the distraction and by the end of the second day the two men stepped back and looked down on their creation.

'It's kind of magnificent,' Dubus said carefully.

'It is,' Taran agreed, feeling himself swell with pride.

He had laboured to hammer the strips of iron as thin as it was possible to get them without breaking. Plenty had done so, causing him to curse and hammer more than he should and then, with a sigh, start over again. The result was both light and flexible, too much so for the long top strips so they had created an interlocking web to keep the wings semi-rigid. The spaces between would need to be covered with fabric but that was someone else's concern. The ironworkers had done their jobs and now they clasped forearms, both more emotional than they cared to show.

'Ale,' Dubus grunted. 'We deserve Nairina's finest ale.'

'Lots of it,' Taran agreed, 'but first we must show Olwen.'

He sent a boy to fetch the druidess and she came eagerly, Leir in her wake. Lugh was dipping over the horizon but the fire was still high and Dubus lit torches around the edges of the forge to better show off their work. The light caught in the iron at every angle, making it glimmer, and Olwen gasped gratifyingly as she stepped inside.

'They're magnificent,' she cried. 'Look, Leir – are they not magnificent?'

She knelt down, stroking them reverently.

'Magnificent,' he confirmed, and strode outside again to boom out to all those nearby, 'Come and see. Come and see this now!'

Taran and Dubus looked at each other, both gratified at his pleasure and terrified for their precious structure. Taran had a fleeting memory of Cordelia's face, made startlingly beautiful by her fear for her new pups when they'd all stumbled in to see them on his very first day in Burrough, and felt a piercing longing for her but stamped it down.

'Take care,' he cautioned the people as they filed in. 'They are fragile.'

'Not too fragile, I hope,' Leir countered, 'if they are to carry our great chieftainess into the skies.'

'The skies,' Olwen said, standing up and joining the smiths in front of their creation, 'are kinder than the earth – or than men.'

She glared repressively at the people and they fanned out obediently in a wide circle around the wings.

'Will they work?' someone asked.

Taran shrugged.

'They might. It is in the hands of the air spirits.'

'How do they flap?'

Taran looked at Dubus and grimaced. They had tried to

configure the wings separately so that the action of the wearer's arms could move them but it had proved impossible, for without the solidity of the cross-bar the wings simply collapsed. This had worried them greatly and they had spent long hours discussing it with Olwen. She had been researching muscle power and had discovered that the larger birds had proportionately less developed wing-muscles than the smaller ones. She put it down to one thing – the ability to catch the upward currents of air to do the job for them.

'They do not flap,' he said now. 'They are for gliding.'

'Gliding?'

Dubus glared at the enquirer.

'If you took time to watch the birds as our honoured high druidess has, you would see that the more majestic of them rarely flap. They are very sparing with their movements.'

The man frowned.

'They flap to take off though.'

Again Taran looked to Dubus. This had been the subject of more long discussion with the druidess and in the end they'd had to admit that Mavelle had attempted the only solution at Imbolc – it just needed a little refinement.

'The wearer will have to take off from a high spot. The ramparts of a hill fort for example would be perfect for the human bird.'

'Human bird!' The words were passed around the circle, half in derision, half in awe, and Taran found himself desperately hoping that Mavelle did it – that she proved to them all she was not going mad but was a visionary, an inspiration, proof that humans could conquer nature. Or, rather, mimic it to their own benefit. And proof, too, of their own skill as smiths. Plus, of course, if he did not succeed – if, Danu forbid, Chieftainess Mavelle plunged to her death – they would certainly be made to take the blame and would be lucky to keep not just their jobs but their lives. He swallowed nervously but just then someone slipped into the forge – a slight figure with long, dark hair. Irritatingly, Cordelia was followed by the young prince. He couldn't take his eyes off her as she wriggled to the front of the crowd.

'Oh!' she cried. 'Aren't they marvellous?' She bent and very, very carefully touched the nearest section. 'So thin! So light! Oh, Taran, Mavelle will soar!' She looked up at him and then, seeing the crowd around them, coloured. 'Great work, Smith. You too, Dubus. Really. Grandmother will be delighted!'

And with that, at least, the crowd could agree. They all cheered and Leir thankfully ushered them out. The dinner hour was close and with the smell of food wafting on the evening air they went readily enough. Cordelia, however, stayed firmly put. She was gazing up at Taran who longed to sweep her into his arms as if there were no one else around but Prince Lucius was still here.

'Are they wings?'

Leir shared a worried look with Olwen at the realisation that he had let a foreigner in on the tribal secret. He slid hastily round to the prince's side.

'Just a little piece of fun, Lucius. Chieftainess Mavelle loves birds so we thought to, er, mark her birth date, we would make her a giant pair.'

'To fly with?' Lucius paced around the wings curiously.

'As a statue,' Taran said hastily.

'Yes, that's right,' Leir agreed, 'as a statue.'

'In iron?'

Leir patted his arm. 'I prefer wood myself but I am told we must move with the times. They are to be nailed to the Beacon, to mark the Coritani out as lovers of birds.'

Lucius bent down and ran a finger along one edge.

'They look a little flimsy. Will the winds not break them?'

Leir coughed. Taran squared his shoulders.

'They are not meant to be permanent, Prince. With fabric on them it is hoped that the winds will indeed move them, like the living creatures they represent.'

'I see. Curious. Not as much use as ploughs perhaps?'

'Not at all,' Leir agreed loudly, 'but sometimes rulers must be indulged, must they not, Olwen?'

'Absolutely. And there is surely room, Prince, for beauty as well as utility in this world.'

'Of course, Druidess.'

They all shuffled around the wings, glinting now with more menace than promise.

'Heavens, Cordelia,' Leir said eventually, 'is it Anghus making all that noise?'

Everyone listened to the conspicuously quiet compound beyond.

'I'm not sure, Father,' Cordelia said, 'but I'll go and check. Perhaps it was Endellion. She is still a little unsettled in her new home. Will you come, Lucius?'

The prince went straight to her side and together they left the forge.

'Thank Danu for that!' Leir said.

Taran could understand his relief but for himself it was little consolation to have the Belgic noble so easily distracted by Cordelia. *Taran's* Cordelia.

Jealousy is an ugly emotion, he reminded himself, but wasn't sure that made it any less real.

'Well done, Taran,' Olwen said warmly. 'We should have been more careful. I'm sure Lucius means well but we do not want those Belgae beating us into the skies – and especially not off the back of all *our* work. We must press on. How do we get them to Beacon?'

They all looked uncertainly at the great span of the wings.

'Do they close up?' Leir asked hopefully.

Taran and Dubus shook their heads.

'I see. It seems, then, that your next job will be to modify a cart, does it not?'

Dubus groaned and Taran had to bite his lip to check his own disapproval. Normally he liked nothing more than working his forge but with Lucius fawning around Cordelia it had lost some of its appeal.

'You could come to Beacon with me,' he dared to suggest when she stole into his bed later. 'See your sister.'

'Enticing,' she laughed. 'But Father would never forgive me if I left whilst we are entertaining a—'

'Royal dignitary,' Taran finished grumpily.

She laughed again and sat up, straddling him.

'Are you jealous, Taran the Smith?'

'No! Well, actually, yes.'

She leaned over and kissed him, long and hard.

'Well, don't be. You do your job with Olwen and the wings and I will do my job with Lucius and the pups, and soon both will be done and we will be together again.'

'He wants to marry you,' he said darkly.

'Nonsense. He talks often of his home and family over the seas. His mother, Chieftainess Sophia, suffers from a wasting disease, poor woman, and his twin sisters are but twelve years old. His father needs him there.'

Taran grunted.

'I'm not sure Lucius would be too worried about what his father needs if you were to propose.'

She groaned.

'I'm not going to.'

'You won't marry him whilst I'm away, then?'

'I won't marry him whilst you're alive on this earth, Taran,' she shot back. 'Now shut up grumbling and kiss me.'

What could he do but obey?

Chapter Fifteen

BEACON HILL

Semiuisonns; Bright days (June)

It was a long, slow journey to Beacon with the wings strapped to a carefully extended cart and an escort of six guards walking alongside but they could not afford to rush for fear of bending the wings on the rougher parts of the road. Olwen walked with them, leading her horse behind her, and would not be persuaded to mount.

'It is good to take the time to enjoy the tribal lands more slowly than usual,' she said calmly. 'There is so much to see. Look!' She leaped forward and plucked a handful of bright green leaves from the side of the track. 'Garlic,' she told Taran proudly, 'very good for problems of the heart and blood. There's a fine crop here.'

'Shall we pause the cart?' he asked but she waved him on.

'No, no. I'll catch you up.'

A little later they paused in the shade of an oak to eat bread and cheese and Olwen laughed to see daisies in the grass.

'We used to make chains of these while we were being taught druid lore,' she said, plucking one and pushing her nail gently through the stem to thread the next one into it. 'We'd put them on our heads and pretend they were our druidic garlands. We felt very important.'

Taran looked sideways at her.

'How long were you away?'

'Two years.'

'You were quite young to leave home, were you not?'

Olwen tipped her head on one side, considering.

'I was eleven so I suppose so, but I didn't feel young. I was desperate to learn about the world and so immersed in all the teachers had to show me that I didn't really think about much else. Sometimes I think I'd like to be there still, with no responsibility to anyone but myself, but life is not like that, is it? The tribe sent me to learn and I owe it to them to bring that learning back for their benefit.'

Taran squirmed.

'I have never been back to my tribe.'

'But you have made a new one. The Goddess sent you to us, Taran, I'm sure. The wings prove it.'

'We'll see.'

'We will. Did you always want to be a smith?'

He felt his cheeks flare and plucked self-consciously at one of the daisies.

'From the moment I saw the flame spirits dance,' he admitted. 'They drew me to them and showed me what they could do and I knew it was where I was meant to be. Working with iron brings joy to my soul.' He flushed even darker at the words that had somehow tumbled out of him. 'Not soul,' he corrected swiftly.

'Why not?' Olwen asked.

'It sounds too grand.'

'Not at all. All things have a soul, Taran, though only the wisest are aware of it. Besides, why not be grand, or, rather, great?'

He plucked at another daisy, feeling exposed. Was she under instruction to probe his association with Cordelia?

'Oh, I wouldn't begin to presume to greatness.'

'All are equal in the Goddess' sight; all can make of themselves what they will.'

Uncomfortable, he looked at the wings. 'A human bird perhaps?'

She laughed and followed his lead. 'Perhaps.' But still he had the sense that she was assessing him in some way and was glad when they came within sight of Beacon and she finally mounted her beautiful horse to ride on and announce their arrival to Chieftainess Mavelle.

It was nearing darkness when they finally trundled in through the gates and the men's heavy footfall beat time to the rumble of their poor stomachs. Taran knew how they felt and was grateful when Olwen directed her druids to take the cart down to the workshop and showed them into the royal house. Something delicious was steaming in a pot and they all pressed eagerly forward. There was no sign of Mavelle but Goneril was seated on her high-backed chair on the far side of the fire and smiled as they all bowed before her.

'Please, be seated. Eat.'

She waved them to the benches around the hearth and herself rose to dish out bowlfuls of broth. Taran had just taken a delicious mouthful of dumpling when Goneril spoke to him.

'You have had a long journey, Smith.'

He fought to swallow the dumpling but it was very hot. He nodded furiously and, thankfully, she smiled.

'You are hungry. Don't let me stop you.' Taran chewed gratefully but within moments the heiress was speaking again. 'I am glad you are here. The wings have arrived safely?'

'They have,' he managed through the remnants of the dumpling.

'Good, good. Olwen has been so keen to see them. Mavelle even more so.' She leaned forward. 'My grandmother grows old.'

'Not so old,' Taran protested automatically.

'Not *so* old,' Goneril agreed, the emphasis strong. Then, just as he thought it safe to take another mouthful, she said, 'We have building works going on at the moment, you know?'

'You do, Heiress?'

'We do. Do you want to know what we're building?'

In truth Taran wanted to eat his dinner but he could hardly say so.

'Yes, please.'

'We are building a new forge.'

He spluttered out a mouthful of broth. It hit the fire, sizzling madly, and Goneril laughed.

'You are pleased?'

He was, if anything, shocked. Why was she building a new forge? What did it mean? But again he knew what the answer had to be.

'Delighted, Heiress.'

'I thought you would be. I will show it to you after dinner.'

'After we have revealed the wings to Mavelle,' corrected Olwen, taking a seat next to Goneril.

'She will not come to dinner?'

'She says she is too excited for food. We shouldn't linger.'

Taran needed no second urging. Gladly taking the druidess' lead, he applied himself to his food and within a short time his bowl was empty and he could rise and follow her down to Mavelle's workshop. The chieftainess was sitting on a bench in the evening sun and came leaping forward as soon as she spotted them, greeting Taran as if he were a spirit made man.

'Smith! At last! I cannot wait to see your creation.'

She pointed and Taran saw the cart parked next to the workshop, still covered over. Mavelle had obviously been waiting for him to unveil it like a good child waiting for a birthing day gift and he felt a rush of tenderness for the old lady.

'I hope you like it, Chieftainess. It is only the frame, you understand. It needs fabric yet to harness the air and—'

'Just show it to me, lad, and we can move on from there.'

Taran nodded and began to untie the cover, praying the wings were intact beneath. Olwen rushed to help and the two of them carefully unveiled the structure which caught the last of the light and sparkled obligingly.

'Oh!' Mavelle gasped. She stood there, hands to her mouth, for a moment not daring to approach. 'Oh, it's marvellous. Bladdud would have loved it.'

'See, Chieftainess.' Taran took her arm and guided her forward, noticing as he did so how frail and thin she was now. It would at least, he thought guiltily, make her lighter to lift. 'The frame is held by this big cross-bar and the rest, the "wings", are a lattice to combine lightness with strength.'

'I see. I see. Olwen, do you see?!'

She smiled.

'They seemed promising, Chieftainess.'

Mavelle bent and gently lifted one wingtip.

'Light,' she said approvingly, then walked around and around them, touching the joints and stroking the longer strips as if feeling for their spirit. Taran prayed she found it. 'It's rigid,' she said eventually.

'It is, Chieftainess. We tried to make the wings mobile but the structure loses all integrity without the cross-bar.'

Mavelle considered this. Taran held his breath but finally she nodded.

'You are right, I think. Do you not, Olwen?'

'I do. We talked about it for a long time before the smiths forged the cross-beams, but it seems the only way. You will be more eagle than robin, Mavelle.'

She grinned.

'I like that. It's very clever, Taran. Indeed, it may even be the reason why we have failed so far.' Taran started to stutter his thanks but the great chieftainess fixed him with her pale eyes and asked, 'But will it work?'

Taran swallowed. Out of the corner of his eye, he could see Goneril, watching intently. Now was not the time for hesitation.

'I believe it will, Chieftainess, given a high launch point, the right winds and the favour of the air spirits.'

Mavelle looked up, raised her hands to the skies and closed her eyes. Olwen bowed her head and Taran followed her lead. Behind them Goneril gave a little moan of impatience but Taran could wait. Mavelle, however old and slow, was in touch with the elements and they would need that. Finally the great lady gave a low sigh of satisfaction and came back to them.

'The spirits are pleased.'

'That is good, Chieftainess.'

'Good?' Goneril cried, swooping in on them. 'It is wonderful. If you succeed, Grandmother, you will bring great honour to the tribe. People will travel from all over to see your miracle.'

'Not miracle,' Olwen said. 'Science.'

Goneril was not to be put off.

'Even better, for if it is science we can do it again and again. Who knows? Within just a few years people could be flying to visit each other all the time, and all because of us.'

'Us?'

Mavelle arched an eyebrow and Goneril pouted.

'Have I not supported you, Grandmother? Have I not encouraged your experiments and sought out the finest druids to increase our knowledge and found this genius smith to craft your wings?'

Mavelle frowned and Taran willed her to tell her self-obsessed granddaughter what he knew to be true: that no one could have discouraged Mavelle from her passionate experiments; that it was Olwen who had pushed for them to work on the project; and Cordelia, his own dear Cordelia, who had introduced Taran in the first place. But Goneril's certainty was beguiling and she swept them all with her as she called people over to have the wings taken down from the cart. It was growing dark and suddenly he longed for a bed but the heiress had turned to him now and he would not yet, it seemed, be allowed to rest.

'You have done fine work here, Taran.'

'Thank you, Heiress.'

'You must be an excellent smith.'

'Dubus helped me.'

She waved this away as of no consequence.

'Very strong too.'

'Well, I . . . '

'Very fit.'

'It is all the time at the hammer and bellows, Heiress.'

'And such finesse for one so young.'

He saw her send a look in Olwen's direction but could not quite interpret what it meant. It made him uncomfortable and perhaps Olwen saw for she took his arm and led him towards the workshop.

'Let's go inside. Look – the other druids are coming to see and it is far too dark out here for them to appreciate the wings.'

Taran looked back to the fortress and saw a small group of white-clad figures coming down the path. At the head of them was a young woman, so slight as to look little more than a stripling in the fading light, but as she drew close he could see the womanly curves of her body through her light tunic. She fixed a pair of the most luminous violet eyes upon him.

'So, this is the man who will send us into the skies,' she said in a lilting voice.

'No, no,' he corrected her hastily. He had no desire to claim either the credit or the responsibility. 'Mine is the arm not the brains.'

She gave a tinkling laugh.

'How sweet. Come on then, show me what this arm of yours has made for us.'

She ushered him inside and he went self-consciously, already wondering what on earth it would be like when – if – the wings were shown to the whole tribe. Suddenly he wished Dubus were here for he felt very out of his depth as the druids crowded in, assessing their creation and throwing around ideas like juggling balls so it was all he could do to keep up.

The young woman was introduced as Caireen and spoke with a low, charged energy that made her impossible to ignore. She had apparently joined the tribe last year and was, it seemed, keen to make an impression.

'We do not need feathers,' she said confidently as Mavelle spoke of bribing children with honey to collect them.

The chieftainess squinted at her.

'The wings will be useless without them. There must be a covering to catch the air.'

'Of course, Chieftainess,' she agreed, 'but a far simpler fabric will suffice. Birds need feathers to stay warm and to keep the rain out. They need them for fine movements, especially at take-off and landing, and whilst that might be desirable a little further into this amazing experiment, I think for now the key is to work out how to glide, is it not?'

She looked to Taran who nodded. That, at least, he understood.

'These wings are rigid so designed only for gliding. They must be launched from a high point and simply held steady on landing.'

'So, feathers are a sophistication too far at this point.'

Olwen sucked in her breath at this.

'Can we have a sophistication too far?'

'Not eventually,' Mavelle allowed, 'but this young woman is right that we should take the experiment in steps. What fabric would you recommend?'

Caireen paced around, considering. Clearly, she knew where to find the best fabrics for her tunic was astonishingly thin and fine and it was hard, as she passed each torch, not to look through it to her alluring outline beneath. Taran imagined Cordelia in a similar tunic and was momentarily lost.

'You need something solid enough to hold the air behind it,' he heard Caireen say, as if from afar, 'but not so heavy as to drag the human bird down. It seems to me that we should learn from the boatbuilders.' She looked around expectantly and Taran dragged his mind back to the discussion, but the Coritani lands were far from the seas and everyone was mystified by this reference. 'You have not been on the seas?' Caireen sounded astonished. 'Not even you, Olwen?'

Olwen drew herself up tall.

'I have had no need. Here amongst the Coritani we prefer to draw knowledge to ourselves than to go chasing it across wild waters.'

Caireen hid a smile, though not very well.

'Then I shall have to explain. Boats are, on the whole, powered by oars – as you may have seen on rivers?' Several people nodded keenly at this. 'But out on the seas, the winds blow fiercely and if you can harness them, they will propel you far faster than any measly man-power.'

'Harness them?' Olwen asked, casting the slight aside and moving closer to her young apprentice. She seemed, to Taran, to be a woman who thirsted for new knowledge as others for fine ale.

'They use a sail – a square of linen coated with beeswax to make it hold back both air and water, much like feathers. We could surely use that too? Sewn tight to the frame, I believe it would create the wing we are looking for.'

'Waxed linen?' Olwen repeated. 'I have seen it used to cover goods but never for propulsion. That is clever, Caireen. Good work.'

The girl glowed.

'I am glad to do anything in my humble power to help you fly.' Mavelle beamed.

'That's settled then. Looks like we won't need the bees' honey but their wax. Taran – can you work with Caireen on the best way to attach the fabric to the frame?'

Taran jumped.

'Me, Chieftainess?'

'Is that a problem?'

Taran stared at Mavelle. It seemed she envisioned him staying at Beacon but no one had spoken of that. Indeed, Leir wanted him working on his plough and Cordelia – well, Cordelia just wanted him. Plus, the sooner he got back to keep that Belgic prince away, the better.

'I have no expertise in stitching, Chieftainess,' he said hastily.

'We do not yet know if stitching will be the best way,' Olwen retorted. 'Nails might be more effective. I take it you know about nails?'

Taran inclined his head.

'Of course, Druidess, as does Ollocus.'

'You would trust someone else to hammer nails into your creation?'

'It is not my creation, Druidess, but *ours*. The genius was yours; I simply made what I was instructed.'

She laughed.

'So modest, Taran. That is not true. Yours was the vision for the gliding frame, yours was the shaping of the tips, and yours, above all, the skill to make them as light as possible. We cannot risk all that effort with substandard nails.'

'Stitches would be lighter.'

Olwen frowned at him.

'Possibly. But surely you wish to see? Surely you wish to be a part of getting your wings off the ground?'

Taran put up his hands.

'I am, of course, keen to see the wings launched, but there is much to do before that can happen and none of it, as far as I can see, will need the skills of a smith. I would be wasted here.'

She came closer, studying him as she might a creature on her dissecting table.

'But do you not,' she repeated, 'wish to be part of it?'

He shrugged awkwardly, remembering the intimacy of their conversation on the road.

'I admire your passion for the project, Druidess, as I admire your knowledge and skill, but I am just a simple ironworker.'

'We are building a new forge,' she told him.

'And when it is ready, I would be honoured to work in it.'

She shook her head disbelievingly.

'You truly will not stay?'

Taran looked nervously at Mavelle.

'I will, of course, if it is commanded of me, but I believe I will serve the Coritani best at the moment by returning to Burrough.'

'If that is what you wish,' Mavelle said easily. 'But you are here for now, so come, what does everyone think the best launching points will be?'

The druids were, as before, keen to voice their ideas and Taran sat back and marvelled at them. Olwen, though, was quiet. When he tried to catch her eye in apology, she would not look his way and he felt that he had in some way failed her.

Chapter Sixteen

'Why?' Olwen paced Goneril's beautiful chamber. 'I can't understand it. I'm offering him a brand new forge, high status within the tribe and the chance to work with, with . . . '

'With one of the best minds beneath Danu's skies?' Goneril suggested.

'I'm not looking for praise, Gee.'

'I know that.'

'Just to understand him.'

'Maybe he's not as clever as you thought?'

'Oh, I believe he is. Those wings are a marvel. If we can get the covering right – and it seems young Caireen may have the solution there – then we might really stand a chance.'

'Caireen?' Goneril asked, sitting up on her cushion-bed.

'My new apprentice. A sparky child but potentially brilliant. With her help we've made good progress today. We might really fly!'

'As I always said you would.'

'You did.' Olwen looked at her gratefully. 'You did, Gee, but there's much more to do if Mavelle wishes to fly at Samhain and Taran can be a part of that, so why would he not wish to?'

Goneril shrugged.

'Fear?'

'Of me?'

'You are pretty intimidating, my flame.' Goneril made a grab for her hand and pulled her down next to her. 'I remember the first time I saw you perform a sacrifice. I was awe-inspired.'

Olwen flushed.

'It's just an act, Gee, part of the ceremony. Young druids are instructed in all the tricks of it.'

'Maybe, but they can't teach you how to have a commanding presence. You are the closest thing we have to the Goddess, Olwen.'

'No!' She couldn't have that. 'No, Goneril, I am nothing like the Goddess. No woman is, nor man either. The Mother's knowledge is infinite and I could never hope to come even close to—'

Goneril covered Olwen's mouth with her own and kissed her into silence.

'You are too humble, Olwen,' she said when finally she was still beneath her caresses.

'You can never be too humble.' Goneril rolled her eyes. Olwen stopped. 'It's just the . . .'

'Wings, I know. Don't fret, Olwen. Leave Taran to me.'

'To you?' Goneril gave Olwen a wicked grin and her heart turned over. 'You will seduce him?'

'I will *propose* to him.' She laughed at her shock. 'You said I should make him my husband, Olwen, and I trust your judgement. A Lughnasad wedding would be a fine thing for the tribe, would it not? And perhaps that will be the encouragement he needs to stay here with us.'

'Perhaps? Come, Gee, what man could refuse you?'

She said it lightly but every word felt heavy enough to drag the edges of her heart down into her very gut. She did not want Goneril to marry and, yet, it must happen. A life must follow its inevitable cycle and Goneril's cycle must include a husband. How else would she birth the next heiress for the Coritani?

'Goneril,' she asked softly, 'have you been with a man?'

The younger woman blushed.

'You know I have not, Olwen. But you have initiated me well and I am willing to try. Taran seems very well formed.'

Olwen's skin prickled with an unfamiliar emotion. Was this jealousy? It was not a feeling she approved of; people were not put on Danu's glorious earth to possess her gifts.

'You may find,' she said carefully, 'that men lack the finesse of women.'

'Finesse?' Goneril considered this. 'Surely a craftsman's hands must have finesse?'

Olwen pictured Taran's hands. They were big and strong and already bore the inevitable ravages of the forge fires, but his fingers were long and surprisingly fine and he was undoubtedly light of touch. Her skin prickled again.

'It is not so much his hands I was thinking of,' she shot at her lover.

'Ah! It is his other weapon? I shall be curious to see what it can do.'

Goneril was teasing now and Olwen wasn't going to rise.

'Then I hope it impresses you,' she said, extricating herself from the heiress' arms and heading for the ladder.

'And I hope it secures him for *you*,' she said softly. Olwen froze, looked back. Goneril blew her a kiss. 'Anything for science, my flame.'

Olwen was back in her arms in a moment.

Taran spent the whole of the next day in the workshop with the eager druids and finally returned to the royal house for dinner, weary but excited. The atmosphere at Beacon was different from Burrough. It felt charged, like the skies before a storm. Was it something to do with the age of the ancient fortress? The ramparts here seemed less to enclose the craggy land than to encircle it like a decorative torc. Or was it simply the heiress' fierce energy infusing her people? It was invigorating but exhausting too and Taran had no idea how anyone lived here all the time.

'You are tired, Smith?'

He looked round to see Goneril herself had come in after him.

'A little.'

'Would you like to rest?' He looked uncertainly at her and she laughed. 'Have you seen my chamber?'

'*Your* chamber?'

'Yes. It is up here.'

She indicated the carved ladder to one side of the communal area.

'In the skies?' Taran suggested nervously.

'Exactly that. Come and see.'

He didn't want to but she was waving him forward so there was little he could do but follow. Then, when he stepped into the upper room, he was glad he had, for he had never seen such a place, filled with rich fabrics, twined with purple vines and glowing from the firelight below, like a very Elysium.

'It's beautiful.'

'You think so? I'm glad. No iron here.'

'I am not only interested in iron, Heiress.'

'No? No, I see that. You seem like a man of very fine tastes.'

'I am learning.'

'Fast.' She paced around him then suddenly grabbed at his wrists. 'I did wonder about some hooks up here.' She pushed one of his hands up hard against a roof beam. 'And here.' Now the other, so that he was pinned like an insect before her. Her body was up close to his as she stretched to match his height and he fought to breathe.

'I can make hooks if you'd like them, Heiress.'

Her grip tightened.

'Oh, I would like them, yes. The question is, Smith, would you?'

'I'm sorry – I don't understand?'

'I want you, Taran.'

151

He looked around in panic. Why had he come up here? Why had he come to Beacon at all?

'But you are the heiress,' he stuttered. 'You cannot lower yourself to my level.'

She gave a slow smile.

'Oh, I do not believe I will be lowering myself. I believe you will suit me well.'

'You do?'

Below them Taran could hear others arriving for the evening meal but Goneril still had him pinned to the roof of her magic bower.

'I do. We are children of the fire spirits, you and I – a perfect match. You will put fine babes inside me.'

'Babes? But, Heiress, you must marry.'

'I know.'

He stared in disbelief.

'You are ... are ... ?'

'Asking you to marry me, yes.'

Worse and worse. Goneril was looking at him keenly with her piercing green eyes but all he could think of were Cordelia's soft blue ones. He remembered asking her not to marry Lucius whilst he was gone. She had laughed at him but now it seemed *he* was the one being propositioned.

'But I am a mere apprentice,' he objected.

'So? I like a man who knows how to obey.'

Goneril pushed his hands harder against the wood so that it ground into his skin, then leaned in and nipped suddenly at his neck. His body pulsed and he fought it.

'I am owned, Heiress, by Leir, your father.'

'I will gladly buy you from him.'

'No!'

'No?'

Her eyes went cold and she dropped his hands. He flexed them nervously.

'I mean, no, I don't wish to be bought. I wish to be free.'

'Free?' She considered this as if it were a natural curiosity. 'Oh, I don't want you *free*. I want you as my own. I will, you know, treat you very well.'

Her hand stroked his chest and his damned body responded instantly. She smiled and ran her tongue over her lips.

'But,' he stuttered, 'you need a prince. A man of high blood.'

Goneril tossed her head.

'I do not. Such a man would only interfere. Try to take command, to control me.'

'He would not dare.'

'No, Smith, *you* would not dare. That is why I want you. Oh, and for your glorious body, of course. And your seed. Above all, your seed.'

'You want me as a stud?'

Goneril clapped delightedly.

'Exactly! As a stud for the tribe. Is a hound not honoured for his seed?' Her eyes narrowed even further. 'What I am asking you *is*, you know, an honour.'

'I know. Oh, Heiress, I do know, and I am, of course, honoured. Of course.'

'Good.'

Her hand reached down and closed around his groin and, Danu help his treacherous body but it rose irresistibly to her touch. Her eyes turned darkest green, the gold flecks within them seeming to glow like fire. *Sunset on water.* His own words came back to him, spoken in Cordelia's soft tones, and he yanked away.

'What are you doing?' she snapped.

'I cannot, Heiress.'

'What?!'

It came out as a shriek, driving deep into Taran's ears, but he had to resist her fury.

'I cannot marry you. It would not be right, not fitting.'

'*I* decide what is fitting.'

'Even so, I could not debase you with my unworthy body.'

153

Her eyes narrowed dangerously.

'Oh, I would be quite happy to be debased by your body, Taran. You can take me however you wish for I am open to all nature's delights.'

Taran knew his mouth was gaping but could not find the will to close it.

'That is very, very generous, Heiress. But I . . .'

'What is it, Smith? You don't wish to be kept in luxury? You don't wish for your pick of fine food and fine clothes and fine women? You don't want to bed me, the Coritani heiress, and make babes for the tribe, to carry your bloodline down all time?'

Taran hesitated. Put like that, it was hard to voice his own objections. But Goneril's ripe body was attuned only to the ferocity of her own desires and ambitions, and that terrified him.

'No, I . . .'

He could see that she could not believe his continued defiance. He could read it in every line of her and now she advanced on him, crushing him back against the rafters so that the twining vines seemed almost to reach out and bind him. He knew that was what would happen if he said yes to her. She would wind him up in her wiles until he was subsumed by them – a stud, like Anghus, only far less loved.

The thought of the shaggy hound tore at his heart and suddenly he wanted nothing more than to run out of here and all the way back to Burrough, to throw sticks for Cordelia's hound in the open meadows. All he had said to Goneril was true. He did not believe himself a worthy husband for a royal daughter, but if Danu were ever to bless him with such an honour it would not be the woman before him he would choose to wed.

'I don't want to,' he said firmly. 'Thank you.'

'You don't want to marry me? Are you mad?'

'Maybe.'

'So what then, Smith, *do* you want?'

Her voice dripped poison but even so an answer came readily from him.

154

'I want Cordelia.'

'Cordelia?' The name came out like a tortured scream. Taran heard the people below freeze and then cries of alarm. He moved fast.

'Help the heiress!' he cried, making for the ladder. 'Come quick. I think she is unwell.'

He made it to the bottom as people pounded into the round-house. Olwen was first and stared at Taran with a dark fury that told him instantly that she had known what Goneril was going to ask of him and had expected his eager compliance. But he wasn't theirs to command and he darted out of the royal roundhouse as it began to fill. He could sense Goneril's anger filling the air like a black cloud and knew he must move fast before it poured down its poisonous rain.

'We are leaving,' he told the first of his men he saw, yanking him from his dinner.

'Now? It's almost dark. I don't want . . . '

'Now! Fetch the others – fast.'

'But the cart . . . '

'The cart stays here. Now move!'

The guard looked furious but he had been placed under Taran's direct command and thankfully did as instructed. Within a very short time all six Burrough men were gathered at the gate, moaning furiously but ready to leave. Taran led them hastily down the east road, moving sideways into the woods as soon as they were out of sight of the bemused sentries on Beacon's gates.

'What have you done?' the men asked him in something like awe.

'I don't know,' Taran said fearfully, leading them further into the darkness. 'I really don't know.'

Chapter Seventeen

'Why?' Goneril was raging and Olwen could find no way to calm her. 'I mean, how dare he? A smith. Nay, an *under*smith. A poor young man of no family or repute. A wanderer, brought into the Coritani tribe by our charity. How dare he refuse me? I am the heiress! I am, I am . . . ' She was angry – hurt and embarrassed and angry, like a wild cat trapped in a place she did not recognise and spitting and scratching to get out. 'Kill him!' she screamed suddenly.

Olwen tried to put her arms around her. She'd managed to dismiss everyone from the chamber but many would still be able to hear them.

'Goneril, please,' she hissed. 'You cannot kill a man for refusing to marry you.'

The heiress' green eyes narrowed.

'Why not?'

'It would be wrong.'

'For whom?'

'For all of us. You cannot take away a life bestowed by the Mother, save to gift it back to her.'

'I can,' Goneril spat.

'Maybe you *can*,' Olwen allowed, 'but you must not. It would be an abuse of your power. And besides, it runs counter to nature.'

'Not to *my* nature.'

Olwen grabbed at her hands. She was delirious, confused.

'Hush, Gee. Please. This is not you speaking. This is hurt pride, no more.'

'Justified pride. I am heiress here, Olwen.'

'I know it. Are you sure he said no?'

'Do you think I'm stupid?'

Olwen's mind raced. This was a blow. The smith was truly a strange young man. What rational person would turn down marriage to the heiress of a great tribe? It made no sense.

'Did he say why?' she asked, but that just set Goneril off again, shouting incoherent things about her royal sisters.

She flung herself down on her cushions, squirming as if trying to burrow deep into them, and Olwen was relieved when Caireen appeared with a steaming beaker.

'What is it?' she asked her apprentice.

'Honey and herbs – chamomile and valerian and poppy seed. It will calm her.'

'Fast?'

Caireen looked down at the writhing Goneril.

'Maybe not fast enough, but we can try.' She dropped down next to Goneril. 'A drink, Heiress?'

Goneril stilled momentarily and glared at the beaker.

'Is it his blood?' she snarled.

Olwen stepped forward to hush her but Caireen put up her hand to deter her.

'Would that it were, Heiress, but there are subtler ways of wounding a man than with a knife.'

'Caireen!' Olwen protested, but Goneril's eyes were fixed on the girl and she took the beaker.

'And there are more ways of owning one than marriage,' Caireen went on, her voice seductively soft.

'Caireen, enough!' Olwen strode forward and yanked her young apprentice away. 'No one owns anyone else. You know that.'

'Yes. Of course. Sorry, Olwen.' She dropped her violet gaze. 'I was just trying to console the heiress,' she whispered.

'Well, you are going about it the wrong way.'

'Sorry, Olwen,' she said again, but Goneril was sitting up now and observing the apprentice girl.

'You're Caireen, aren't you? The new druidess?'

'I am, Heiress. It is an honour to serve you.'

Goneril nodded graciously.

'You're the expert in fabrics?'

'Not an *expert*, Heiress, merely lucky enough to have had some experience.'

'And with potions too?' Goneril took a cautious sip and winced. 'What's in this?'

'Just herbs, Heiress, soothing herbs. They will make things feel easier.'

Goneril's brow knitted.

'I don't want things to feel easier, Caireen, I want them to *be* easier. How dare he refuse me? How dare—'

'Men are fickle,' Olwen consoled her. The potion was definitely not working fast enough. 'They are weak and sometimes don't know what's good for them. We will find someone better for you, Gee. Someone more appreciative.'

'Who?'

'I don't know yet. These things take time.'

'I don't want to take time. I want to take a husband. I want the ceremony at Lughnasad. We've discussed it, planned it. I'm ready.'

'That was when we thought Tar—'

Olwen cut herself off on the name but Goneril caught it anyway.

'Taran is a fool and I won't marry a fool. Find me someone else.'

'I will, Gee, but it takes—'

'Time! Why?'

'It is an important role. We must let the Goddess guide us.'

'As she guided us to Taran?'

'I still think he was a wise choice. Perhaps I can talk to him, Gee. Perhaps—'

'No! He is gone. And I don't want him now. I am Heiress. I deserve a man who will beg for me.'

'You deserve a man who can stand as your support and—'

'Yes, yes, all that too.' Her eyelids were drooping, perhaps Caireen's potion was hitting its mark. Olwen knelt down and put her arms around her, pushing her gently back on the cushions. 'Find me someone, Olwen,' she whimpered.

'I will, I promise. But there is no rush.'

Goneril snorted but with little energy. She was calming at last. But then Caireen said, 'I know a man,' and she sat up instantly.

'Who?'

'Caireen,' Olwen warned, but Goneril was beckoning her forward and the girl slid smoothly past. She was clever that one; perhaps too clever.

'Who?' Goneril demanded again.

'He lives in a homestead near here.'

'A farmer?' Goneril spat.

Olwen hid a smile at her disgust but Caireen wasn't done yet.

'Nay, he is Lugh made flesh and living amongst farmers.'

Olwen sprang forward.

'Caireen! That's enough. No man can be Lugh.'

'Beg pardon, but you haven't seen *this* one!' She must have noted Olwen's furious face for she put up her hand in apology. 'I jest, Olwen. Is that not allowed? Of course he is not a god but he has a magical form for sure. Tall and strong with broad shoulders, a small waist, a tight arse and the biggest—'

'Caireen!' Olwen snapped. She was wearing out the damn' girl's name but this was too much. 'You do your calling great dishonour. Goneril is heiress to the Coritani. She is above mere considerations of the flesh. She needs a consort, not a plaything.'

Again Caireen's eyes dipped, though not before Olwen had seen them flash blue fire at Goneril.

'Apologies, Druidess. I am but a humble apprentice. Forget my foolishness.'

Olwen was certain there was nothing humble about this recruit. She was like an unbroken colt, all energy and pace. She had potential but would need to be kept on a very tight rein if Olwen were to harness her to the service of the tribe.

'Your enthusiasm is appreciated, Caireen, but you know nothing of the complications of this matter. Goneril's marriage is of the utmost importance to the tribe and we must choose very carefully.'

'But this young man might be worth a look,' Goneril said. 'This . . . '

'Maedoc,' Caireen supplied.

Olwen glared at her apprentice again and she dived for the ladder but as she scrambled down Goneril called after her, 'Have him brought to me.' Caireen paused, just her pretty head showing. 'Tomorrow,' Goneril added.

'Yes, Heiress.'

She was gone before Olwen could intervene.

'Goneril, really?'

She gave a lopsided smile.

'Oh, come, Olwen, don't be angry.' Goneril grabbed for her tunic, pulling her down so she fell on top of her. 'Let's see this god of Caireen's.'

'Goneril! She should not have said that. It goes against all druidic code. No man can—'

'Be Lugh. I know, my flame, I know. She is a silly girl and he will doubtless be a silly man but that is all the better for us.' Olwen frowned and Goneril kissed her. 'Think about it. If I can find some stupid stud to put in my bed and parade at ceremonies, then we – you and I, Olwen – can truly run the tribe.'

Olwen tried to pull back but, although the potion had made Goneril loose and relaxed, it had not in any way diminished her strength and she held on tight.

'I am a druidess, Goneril,' she protested. 'It is not my place to run a tribe, but to guide it in the ways of justice and ceremony and progress.'

'But, Olwen, that's why it's so perfect – I can rule, and you can guide me.'

'I can?'

'You do already, you know you do. I'd be half the woman I am without you at my side.' Goneril pulled her into a deeper embrace, so close that their bodies seemed to meld together. 'See!'

Olwen felt the heat of the heiress pouring into her at every point, fusing them more powerfully than any smith could ever manage.

'I see,' she murmured.

It was not the way she had seen things going but fate ran in spirals and if hers had just turned an unexpected way, she was surely flexible enough to turn with it. Goneril was impulsive, yes, but perhaps Olwen was too naturally cautious. Perhaps she, too, was half the woman she could be without the energetic, exciting, fiery Heiress at her side. Let the spiral turn!

Chapter Eighteen

BURROUGH HILL

Equos; Horse days (July)

Cordelia made for the forge, her heart beating fast; she was never sure if she'd be welcome there these days. Ever since he'd come back from Beacon, Taran had been surly and distanced. He'd eschewed her bed, claiming tiredness and pressure of work, and she could find no way to lure him back. It couldn't be jealousy of Lucius for he was gone and under no illusions about his position with her.

'It has been a great pleasure working with you, Princess,' he'd said as she'd seen him to his horse before he set back for the lands of the Belgae. 'A great pleasure *being* with you.'

He'd stared at her pointedly and she'd looked around for someone to interrupt them and spare her confusion but Leir had disappeared and no one else would presume to interrupt a princess' private conversation.

'You have been very welcome,' she'd managed.

'I would like to visit you again. If you would have me?'

She'd swallowed.

'Did you not say that you could not leave your homelands until your sisters are older?'

Lucius had shifted uncomfortably.

'I did, yes, but I don't think it would really matter if . . . That is, it would be good, I think, for our two tribes to make an . . . alliance.'

Cordelia had felt sick with the weight of his delicate hopes but that was as far, thankfully, as he'd dared to go. It was not his place to propose and he'd been far too polite to break rank. The heavy hints, however, had been excruciating.

'Thank you for Endellion,' she'd said, trying to edge him towards his horse. 'I will send you a pup when her first litter is born.'

'You could, perhaps, bring it yourself?'

Cordelia had taken a deep breath. She'd remembered Taran checking that she wouldn't marry whilst he was away. She'd thought he was being absurd but had not realised quite how far advanced Lucius' hopes were. It wasn't fair on him not to tell him of her own intentions.

'Lucius,' she'd said gently, 'I expect to marry soon so I don't think that would be advisable.'

He'd visibly paled.

'Marry? Marry whom?'

'That matters little.' She'd drawn in a deep breath. 'I apologise, Prince, if I have led you to believe otherwise, but my heart is already given.'

The Belgic prince had looked horribly wounded, though to her relief his natural graciousness had not failed him.

'His gain is my loss,' he'd said stiffly. 'I wish you both well. I say only that if anything should change . . . '

'Change?'

' . . . if ever you find yourself free again, or . . . or in need, you can find me at Braquemont.'

'Over the seas?'

'Over the seas, yes. But perhaps one day you will wish to cross them and, when you do, seek me out.'

She'd promised she would but had meant not a word and had been desperate to see Taran and laugh with him over it. He'd been back more than seven days now, though, and had largely avoided her. It unsettled her more than she cared to admit, not so much the fact of him pulling away as her own reaction to it. She felt abandoned, slighted, embarrassed, enraged. The tangle of emotion had come on her as suddenly and blackly as the storm on their way back from Breedon and she had no idea how to defend herself against it. Today, though, she had news that would surely interest even Taran and, taking a deep breath, she entered the forge.

'Goneril is to marry.'

Both smiths looked up from their work. Dubus gave a little snort but Taran visibly started.

'To ... to marry?' He stared at Cordelia, his brown eyes wide. 'Who is the groom?'

'We're not sure. Some nobody. Father isn't happy at all. He met someone at the horse fair who could line her up with an Iceni prince and Father was very keen on that idea. Something about it offering us a port, whatever a port is.'

Still Taran stared at her and she saw strange shadows passing across his face before suddenly he let out a huge breath and his face broke into the lopsided smile she hadn't seen for far too long.

'Truly, Cordelia? Truly Goneril is to marry?'

'Why would I make it up?'

'No reason. Sorry. It's just a surprise.' He put down his tools and came over to her, closer than he'd been since he'd left for Beacon. Then suddenly the shadow was back over his face. 'Do you have a name for the lucky man?'

'The messenger said he was called Maedoc, I think.'

'Maedoc! Lovely. Excellent.'

She looked at him, confused.

'Are you well, Taran?'

'Very well. Very well indeed. Maedoc. Lovely.'

'Does the name matter so much?'

'No. No, I merely thought maybe she'd sent a . . . a command.'

'A command? Taran are you *sure* you're well?'

She'd hoped the news would interest him but it seemed to have done far more than that for he was wiping sweat from his brow. At her question, however, he gave an exaggerated shrug and went back to the curved blade he'd been polishing when she'd entered.

'That's a fine bit of work,' she said, hoping to get him talking again.

'I hope so.'

'What is it?'

He gave a smile, faint but there all the same.

'It's the plough blade your father's been wanting, Cordelia – a new design, especially for hard soil. I was expecting him to come down to see it this morning but if he's had news that would explain his absence.'

'Yes. He is a little . . . distracted by it all.'

'He is not a prince, then, this Maedoc?'

Taran's voice was casual but she couldn't help noticing that his hands polished harder at the blade than she was sure was necessary. Why was he so concerned about her sister's marriage? Had something happened between them? Her heart squeezed, as if her very ribs were pushing in on it, and she had to force herself to breathe normally.

'He is not a prince, no, but the messenger said that Goneril divined him in the stars so who's to argue with that?' Taran gave a strange snort; he really was behaving very oddly. 'Why not come and hear all the details? It's almost dinnertime.'

'Is it?' Dubus looked up hopefully. 'Good. I'm starving.'

'You're always starving,' Taran told him. He looked back to Cordelia. 'Who brought the news?'

'Olwen's apprentice druidess. The young girl. Caitlin, is it? Coleen?'

'Caireen?'

'That's it! Striking-looking and wearing a very interesting dress. Very thin.'

'Thin?' Dubus' eyes gleamed. 'Then I'm definitely coming. Come on, Taran, leave the damn' plough and let's go and hear more about the heiress' mysterious new husband.' Taran, however, polished so hard that he caught his finger on the sharp edge. Blood spurted forth and Dubus laughed. 'Beginner's error, lad. You should be ashamed.'

'I am,' he growled, sucking on the wound so fiercely that Cordelia took a few steps back to the doorway.

'I'll, er, go to dinner then,' she said. 'Magunna has made lamb pastries and they smell good. Will you come, Taran?'

'I should bind my hand.'

'I could do that.'

He looked over to her and she saw so much sudden longing in his dark eyes that her heart turned over, but then he looked away again.

'I'll sort it. Thank you. It wouldn't do to bleed on Chieftain Leir.'

'Or his lovely guest.' Dubus rubbed his big hands together. 'I'll come with you, Princess. I love a lamb pastry. Let grumpy-guts here catch us up when he's ready.'

It wasn't what Cordelia wanted to hear but Taran had retreated to the back of the forge and it seemed she had little choice but to accompany Dubus. Ah, but . . .

'I've just remembered, I was sent to tell you that Goneril wants a sword making for her chosen husband – the finest, sharpest one possible. She's specifically requested that you, Taran, make it.'

His head snapped up again.

'Me? But Dubus is far better at making swords than I am.'

'I am,' Dubus agreed.

Cordelia looked at him apologetically.

'The druidess said something about Goneril wanting the blade infused with the power of youth.'

'The power of what?!' Dubus stared at her incredulously then caught himself. 'Ah, well, who cares? It will mean a big bonus if we make it well, Taran.'

'But I've barely made a weapon before and certainly not a fancy one. I can't do it.'

He looked so worried, so unlike his usual self, Cordelia moved cautiously towards him.

'Of course you can do it, Taran. Look at the beautiful blade you've just completed.'

'It's a plough, Cordelia.'

'It's a *blade*, Taran. It's surely much the same in the making?'

She looked to Dubus for support and he nodded readily.

'You're more than up to it, lad. Why not make a practice one first?'

That reminded Cordelia of something else.

'You can,' she said. 'Twenty, in fact. According to the druidess, Regan is asking for swords too, more workaday ones, so you'll have plenty to try your hand on.'

'Why does Regan want swords?'

Cordelia shrugged.

'Regan always wants swords and now she has the means to order them. Goneril is very keen on the idea and is providing the funds herself.'

'She is?'

'Oh, yes. She says Regan is guarding the west and must be supported. The Setantii may have been defeated once but they'll come again.'

'I suppose so.'

Dubus went over and grabbed his arm, pulling him out of his corner.

'Come on, lad, cheer up. This is good news all round – a wedding feast and a ton of new work. You can forget that plough; it's finer blades for us now.'

'I'm not sure swords are finer than ploughs,' Taran said, and

Cordelia had to agree, but he did at least summon up a smile and allow Dubus to pull him over to the door. 'Is the druidess staying to eat?'

'Bloody well hope so,' Dubus said. 'I want to see this dress – or rather, what's beneath it.'

'Dubus!' Taran snapped, and the old smith looked over at Cordelia and flushed.

'Sorry, Princess. I'm just starved of female, er, companionship.'

Cordelia waved it away but Taran surged off in front of them, muttering something like 'female companionship is overrated', and her heart sank again. For a moment or two it had seemed that maybe the old Taran would reappear, but he'd retreated again and as his long legs strode out to the royal house, she was left with nothing to do but take Dubus' gallantly offered arm and follow in his shadow.

'Truly, Chief, this match is carved in the moon.'

Cordelia heard the voice, clear and pure, as she approached the royal house and she paused in the doorway to study the young druidess unobserved. She'd seen the girl a few times at Beacon, following Olwen around, but hadn't paid her much attention so far. She was a tiny creature and very slight, but somehow still ripe with the curves of womanhood. She must be from somewhere far away for her hair was not dark like Coritani girls' but the colour of the corn currently ripening in the fields. She had plaited it in some clever way to pull it off her pretty face but still allow it to fall in soft curls down her back and Cordelia found herself wondering how it would feel to run her hands through it. She shook the wanton thought away.

'Glorious,' Dubus breathed behind her, and she stepped hastily inside.

A lot of people seemed to have been drawn to the royal hearth this dinnertime and many eyes turned their way, including those of the young druidess. They were a deep blue, almost violet, and Cordelia found it strangely hard to tear her own gaze away.

'Princess.'

Caireen swept into a low bow, offering a glimpse of the swell of her breasts that made Cordelia flush and had Dubus groaning like a man in exquisite pain.

'Druidess,' she said stiffly. 'These are our smiths, Dubus and—'

'Taran, yes. I worked with him at Beacon. He's very skilled. Made quite an impression on us all, the heiress included. Are you well, Taran?'

Her violet eyes seemed to drill into his and Taran's reply was a mumble, begrudgingly given. His strong frame had hunched like a boy's before their visitor and Cordelia wondered what had passed between them. The young druidess was very beautiful and clearly free with that beauty. Jealousy washed over Cordelia like ice-water and she forced her shoulders back and moved to stand by her father.

'I have told the smiths of their commission,' she said and Leir blinked at her, as dazed by their visitor as the rest of the men – and indeed women – in the room. Had this Caireen dulled all their senses? 'The swords,' Cordelia prompted.

'Oh, the swords! Yes. Marvellous. Can you do it, Dubus?'

'Taran,' the young druidess corrected. Her voice was every bit as clear and pure as before but it rang with ferocious determination. Leir looked at her in surprise. 'Taran must make Maedoc's ceremonial sword. Goneril asked for him especially,' Caireen explained.

She looked at Taran, her violet eyes suddenly shadowed to black, and Cordelia flinched.

'And why is that?' she asked.

Caireen turned back to her and gave a little tinkle of laughter.

'I do not know, Princess. I am but the messenger.' Cordelia doubted that very much. 'It is perhaps because she was impressed by his work on the chieftainess' wings. They are very fine.'

'They are,' Cordelia agreed, 'and made by both Taran and Dubus, his teacher.'

Her answer sounded strident, she knew, and she was not surprised when Leir stepped forward to silence her, but Caireen put the lightest of hands on his arm and he spoke not a word.

'Cordelia is right to defend the senior smith. Dubus, is it?' He bustled forward and bowed before her. 'You must be a very skilled teacher, Dubus.'

'I do my humble best, Druidess.'

'You look to be a strong man.'

She let her eyes travel up and down his ageing frame and Dubus swelled with pride.

'I work hard,' he said.

'Commendable. I am sure, then, that you can aid your charge in his endeavours.'

'Of course, Druidess.'

'Caireen, please. We are all friends here, are we not? All Coritani.'

That, Cordelia thought bitterly, wasn't true. Caireen had been brought into the tribe by Olwen from one of the centres of druid learning beyond the Coritani lands. Presumably the High Druidess thought she had talent. She certainly had confidence.

'Where do you come from, Caireen?' Cordelia asked lightly, reaching out to touch her blonde hair.

'Does it matter?' the girl shot back. 'I am here now.'

'And very welcome,' Leir said, glaring at her. 'Shall we eat?'

Caireen turned instantly to him.

'Thank you. I'm so hungry.'

'Here, please be seated.'

Cordelia watched her father usher the young woman onto the bench at his side and took a seat as far across the fire as she could. It was only Magunna, bringing round pastries with an eyebrow arched in Cordelia's direction, that made the situation bearable. That and Taran sliding in at her side. Her skin flared at his closeness but she refused to show it.

'You do not wish to converse with the druidess?' she asked him stiffly.

'I do not.'

The reply was pleasingly vehement.

'She is very charming.'

'Dangerously so.'

Cordelia turned to face him.

'How do you know that? Have you . . . ' she swallowed but forced herself on ' . . . experienced her charms?'

'Caireen's? No!'

Again his vehemence was comforting, though the question less so.

'Or those of her fellow druidesses perhaps?'

'No, Cordelia, truly. No druidesses.'

His eyes locked with hers and for the first time since he'd ridden to Beacon, Cordelia felt he was truly looking at her. She leaned closer.

'Why will you not come to my bed, Taran?'

At that, though, he looked down. Conversation buzzed merrily all around but between the two of them there was dark silence. Cordelia forced herself to wait and eventually he spoke.

'I do not feel worthy of you, Cordelia.'

'Worthy? Taran, that's ridiculous.' He said nothing more and her heart pounded. 'Why? What's happened? What have you done?'

'Nothing. That is—' He looked up suddenly, as if he had made a decision. 'I will tell you, but not here.'

His eyes were wild and he looked nervously around the round-house but all were eating merrily and no one was paying them any attention.

'Where then?'

In reply he nodded at the door. She wasn't sure if she was more scared now that he was promising her an explanation than she had been trying to guess. Battling to stop her legs from shaking, she got up and calmly left as if heading for the latrine pits. Outside, she leaned against the thatch and waited for him to join her. It did not take long.

'Taran, what's wrong?'

'Not here. Please, come out of the compound with me.'

Now he was frightening her.

'I'm not sure I should.'

Her father had always instructed her not to leave the safety of the fort alone at night, but this was Taran, so she let him tug her to the back gate. The guards looked at her uncertainly but she waved them to open up and with a fearful glance at each other they complied.

'Here?' she asked but Taran tugged her on.

'Not much further, Cordelia. Please. For me.'

His voice carried a tremor she'd never heard before so she resisted no further and just held tight to his hand as he pulled her under the trees. Up above them she could hear the sounds of people happily enjoying dinner but down here there was only the rustle of woodland creatures settling for the night. The moon was rising and silver light dappled through the leaves so that Taran suddenly looked more spirit than man.

'What is it?' she asked again. 'What have you done?'

'Nothing,' he promised. 'That is ... something. But I pulled away, I swear it. As soon as I could, I pulled away.'

'From what? Who?'

He swallowed.

'From Goneril.'

'Goneril!' Cordelia thought of her eldest sister with a sudden hatred that shocked the breath out of her. When they'd been young, Goneril had always coveted anything she or Regan had had but this wasn't poppets or honey treats; this was a man. *Her* man. 'Goneril seduced you?' she choked out.

'No! That is ... ' Taran put a hand to the nearest tree, digging his fingers into the bark, then finished on a rush: 'She asked me to marry her.'

'She what?!'

Cordelia hadn't thought it was possible to be any more shocked; she'd been wrong.

'When I was in Burrough. She asked – nay, commanded – me to be her husband.'

'But you're . . . '

'A nothing, I know.'

'Not a nothing, Taran, never that. But not . . . '

'A prince. Exactly. I said that. I said it over and over but she doesn't want a prince. She wants to rule alone, or rather with Olwen. She only needs a husband as a . . . a stud.'

'And that is what she has found in this Maedoc?'

But at that Taran shrugged.

'I don't know. I don't remember him at Beacon. She must have found him since, Danu knows how.'

Cordelia grimaced.

'When Goneril wants something, she moves fast to secure it.'

'I know! She said we were both children of the fire spirits, Dee.'

'Did you . . . ?'

'No!'

The protest was vehement but even in the moonlight Cordelia could see him blush.

'Truly?'

'Truly, Cordelia. I did not bed her, though she . . . she tried.'

Cordelia stared at him, further astounded.

'You said no to my sister?'

'I did.'

'My sister the heiress?'

He nodded.

'I did not want to marry her, Cordelia.'

'But why not? You'd be rich. You'd be prized. You'd be free.'

He shuddered.

'I would *not* be free. Her fire is not my fire, Cordelia. She is ruthless – ruthless and conniving and cold. I didn't want to marry her because none of the riches or the power she offers would be worth it. And because . . . because I'm in love with you.'

She stared up at him. He met her eyes and she saw in them such sincerity, such trust, such fear that her heart melted. She didn't know exactly what had happened at Beacon but she knew what was happening now.

'And I with you,' she said simply. 'I told Prince Lucius as much.'

'You did?'

'Of course I did. Marry me, Taran.'

Tears glistened in his eyes.

'I would love to, Dee, my Dee. I would love nothing more.'

She stepped closer and he clasped her tight, as if he would enfold her right into his very self.

'Husband,' she whispered against his chest.

'Wife,' he whispered back.

Cordelia gave a small laugh. It seemed to release something in her and before she knew it, she was laughing harder, clutching at Taran's chest as it shook blissfully through her.

'Dee? Are you well?'

'I am well, Taran. I thought you didn't like me anymore! I thought you were bored here at Burrough and missing Beacon and whatever excitement you had met with there.'

He shook his head so vehemently they both nearly fell over and had to lean against the tree trunk to steady themselves.

'Never. I was embarrassed by what had passed between Goneril and me. And I was scared – scared she would send for me or look to punish me for my temerity. And even more scared that she would look to punish *you*. And that you might have to run away to the Belgae to avoid her.'

Cordelia laughed again.

'Never, Taran. I told you – you're the only man I want to marry. And now I shall make it happen.'

He kissed her long and hard until, finally, he pulled back.

'I cannot wait. But we should perhaps, my love, keep this between ourselves for now.'

She stared up at him.

'Why?'

'Because Goneril's marriage has just been announced and she would never forgive you if you stole even a morsel of the attention she believes to be her right.'

Cordelia laughed again.

'True, Taran. That is true. Let her enjoy her Lughnasad wedding, and then – then, I promise you, it will be our time.'

LUGHNASAD

Autumn

Chapter Nineteen

BEACON HILL

Elembiuios; Claim days (August)

'All hail, Danu – Spirit, Goddess, Mother Earth!'

Cordelia watched, entranced, as the curtain fell back from the wooden stage below the Guardian rock and revealed Goneril to the large crowd below. The fat Lughnasad moon, high in the clear night sky, cast her glow onto the Coritani heiress and the silver effect was enhanced by a row of tiny torches set around the edge of the stage. They lit her cleverly from below, sending her shapely shadow up onto the craggy visage of the Guardian so it was as if two of her stood before them all.

Dressed for the Lughnasad celebrations as the Goddess, she wore a long, flowing robe, cut high on both sides to allow glimpses of her shapely thighs. In place of her usual fiery colours, she was dressed in simple whites and greens and around her neck, instead of her golden torc, was a circlet woven from simple barley, though threaded with gems that winked enticingly in the clever lighting.

She wore her auburn hair loose down her back and, to complete the natural picture, held a cornucopia filled with nuts and fruits.

The crowd sighed its appreciation and now Olwen, stunning in a gauzy robe elaborately draped with vines to match the bride's, led a line of children from around the rock. They, too, were dressed in white and carrying fruits, vegetables, flowers and loaves, which they deposited in a circle around Goneril until everything grown on Coritani lands was surrounding her.

'Goneril and Olwen are very good at putting on a show,' Cordelia whispered to Taran.

He nodded grimly and moved a little closer and she was glad of his reassuring bulk to root her in the airy atmosphere of Beacon. They had been here for three days, to attend the annual claims-court, and it had become very clear that Goneril was now in charge. She had invited Regan and Cordelia to join her before the plaintiffs and they had sat as the three royal daughters with their triskele amulets gleaming at their throats. Goneril, however, striking in red and amber plaid, had made sure that she was on the highest chair, her darker-tunicked sisters safely in her shadow. And she had consulted only with Olwen, standing at her shoulder, on any of the few matters on which she did not immediately pronounce judgement.

Mavelle had been seated to one side with the elders, apparently snoozing, though she had interrupted her granddaughter on several occasions, to her clear annoyance. Tonight, too, she was at the front of the crowd in a magnificent cloak sewn all over with feathers – apparently the work of the wonderful Caireen – but Goneril was doing her best to keep herself centre stage.

It's her wedding, Cordelia reminded herself. *She's meant to be central*. But this was not a blushing Regan marrying her prince. This was a woman in full command of her tribe, her ceremony and her husband-to-be.

'Behold!' Olwen's voice drew Cordelia back to the scene before her. 'Lugh the sun, bringer of light, bringer of warmth, bringer of fire!'

From around the rock came a man, naked save for a burning hoop suspended from a harness around his waist. The crowd gasped as he stepped slowly onto the stage, his flaming belt lighting up the rippling muscles of his oiled body. Maedoc.

Cordelia gaped. At her side someone snorted and she looked around to see Map. He and Gleva had ridden in just in time for the ceremony but didn't seem impressed.

'Looks like a suckling pig if you ask me,' he muttered.

'Map!' Gleva reprimanded him, though Cordelia saw her ample bosom shaking with amusement and bit down, too late, on her own laughter. Taran looked over at them.

'What are you three giggling at?' he hissed.

Cordelia repeated the joke and the four of them shook with amusement, then had to look hastily down before anyone else noticed. It would not do to disrespect Goneril's ceremony. The hoop was burning itself out now and two of Olwen's druids came forward to loose the cords that held it from Maedoc's outstretched arms. One was obviously tied too tight and there was some unseemly fumbling that set Goneril frowning in a most ungoddesslike way. Cordelia, Taran and the traders bit harder at their lips but Olwen swept forward to slash it away with her knife and the mysticism held.

'Is it not beautiful?' Cordelia heard a soft voice say, and saw Caireen leaning in to talk into Leir's ear just in front of her. 'Mother Earth is joining with Lugh to bring fertility and prosperity to the tribe.'

'Beautiful,' Leir agreed, though as far as Cordelia could tell he'd been looking at the druidess the entire time. And no wonder.

It had taken Olwen's apprentice one night at Burrough to get into Leir's bed and so rapturous had the encounter been that Cordelia had fled the royal house. Thanking Danu that her doghouse was all but finished she'd dived inside, rolled herself up in her cloak and slept in peace with the far less disturbing snuffles and snorts of Anghus, Keira and Endellion. And so it had gone on every night since, though she had at least been able to invite Taran to join her. Her husband-to-be kept her warm far more effectively than her hounds.

'Caireen is winding herself around him like ivy,' she'd told him, one night as they'd lain together.

'Poison ivy,' he'd agreed. 'She is not to be trusted, Cordelia.'

Cordelia had considered this.

'Perhaps we are being unfair, Taran. Perhaps she truly likes my father. He is, you know, a good man.'

'Far too good for her.'

'But if he loves her?'

'Then he is in trouble for she will not love anyone, save perhaps Goneril. Caireen is her creature, Cordelia.'

It made her uneasy but, really, what was to be done? Leir was free to choose who he took to his bed and if he chose Caireen then Cordelia should respect that choice. She pulled her eyes away from them as Maedoc approached his wife-to-be in her circle of fruitfulness.

'Kneel, Lugh,' Olwen commanded. 'And look upon your goddess.'

Maedoc did so instantly. Cordelia had no idea where Goneril – or perhaps Olwen – had found him but she had picked well. He was a handsome man, his features as sharply chiselled as the Guardian's and his body a perfectly defined triangle from his broad shoulders down to his arrogantly impressive manhood.

'Rise, Lugh!'

Goneril held out her hand to him and he snatched at it and let her pull him over the circle of goodness and into its centre. With a flourish, she presented him with a sword, shining bright and patterned all over with intricate leaves.

'You made it beautifully, Taran,' Cordelia breathed. 'Are those vines?'

'Ivy,' Taran growled. 'And it may be beautiful but it would shatter like ice before a half-decent enemy.'

'Taran!'

He gave her a dark grin before looking hastily back to the royal couple. Goneril was making her own oblations to the Goddess, offering the fruits and nuts to a fire burning in a bronze bowl behind them, but she did not linger in private prayer. Pulling Maedoc to her side she stood, radiant before her adoring crowd, as the druids set up their song and Olwen circled them.

Cordelia looked around the gathered tribe and saw awe upon every face. Even Gleva and Map were drawn in now and as Olwen lifted the couple's hands to the skies and proclaimed them joined, the cheers of the crowd shook the very stars. Cordelia wondered if she was the only one immune to their carefully orchestrated charm and if, therefore, she was wrong, but a glance at Taran showed her that his face, too, was rigid with distaste.

The feast that followed was a sensory parade. The fattened Imbolc lamb turned succulently on the fire, myriad smaller dishes circulated, and copious fruit wine flowed cleverly from a specially built fountain. Cordelia tried to enjoy these delights but Goneril had insisted, against all tradition of one big, communal circle, on arranging the seating so she was in a small group with Regan, Aledus, Leir and Caireen and seeing the girl forever whispering in her father's ear killed her appetite.

'Do you not find it a little intense here these days?' she asked Regan, trying to keep her voice too low for Caireen's sharp ears.

'Oh, I do,' her sister agreed earnestly. 'I've spoken to Goneril about it and she says I should allow my spirit to roam more freely.'

'You should?'

'Oh, yes. I am too rigid, apparently, too keen on order and training and . . . and the use of the body as a weapon.' These were certainly not her own words and Cordelia opened her mouth to say as much but her sister rushed on: 'It is what you have always told me, Dee.'

'Is it?'

'That I must relax, push myself less.'

'Well, yes, but not *change*. Your spirit is fine as it is, Regan. More than fine.'

'Oh, I know, but we can all learn, can we not? Goneril has taught me the value of ceremony as a way of drawing the community together. I can try and use that on my return to Breedon – though I doubt I will be anywhere near as good at it as she is.'

They both looked to their elder sister, shining above them.

'You can do it your own way, Ree,' Cordelia said quietly. 'You should run Breedon as you see fit. Father entrusted it to you as a fighter and he was right to do so.'

Regan shifted uncomfortably.

'Thank you. I, er, will run it my own way. Of course I will.'

'Good.'

Cordelia looked longingly across to where Taran and Dubus sat with Gleva and Map. She could hear them laughing and couldn't wait to be released to join them but when finally the food was finished, Mavelle rose to speak and she was still trapped with the royals.

'Granddaughter!' said the chieftainess, beaming at Goneril. 'We are blessed tonight in your glorious union and I wish to honour you with a gift.'

Regan turned to Aledus and Cordelia was sure they were thinking the same as she was – what could they give the heiress that she did not already have?

'You may ask for anything you wish,' was the chieftainess' proclamation, her thin arms flung wide for emphasis.

'Anything, Grandmother?'

'Anything. It is your wedding day.'

Goneril seemed to consider. Her green-gold eyes swung in every direction and Cordelia swore they fell on her for a moment before she gave a beatific smile and said, 'I do not ask for much.'

'Anything.'

'Then I confess that it has long been my wish to breed hounds as my dear little sister does. So perhaps, to start my own humble endeavours, I can ask for a stud?'

'No,' Cordelia choked.

'For Anghus.'

'No!' Cordelia was on her feet instantly. 'Anghus is not Mavelle's to give, Goneril. He is mine.'

Goneril looked at her.

'He is the *tribe's*, Cordelia.'

'But he lives with me. He *must* live with me.'

'Or?'

'Or he will not thrive.'

'Really? You estimate your care highly, Sister. He is just a dog.'

'Then he will not matter all that much to you. I will breed you a hound, Goneril, I promise. I will breed you ten hounds if you wish but Anghus stays with me.'

Goneril looked to Mavelle, who turned in confusion to Leir. Their father stood up at her side.

'We can get you a better hound than Anghus, Goneril,' he said.

Cordelia nearly opened her mouth to say there wasn't any better hound than Anghus then remembered herself.

'But I like him, Father,' Goneril said. 'He reminds me of Maedoc.' All eyes turned to Goneril's new husband. The smooth, muscled man looked as little like a hound as it was possible to imagine. 'It is the eyes,' Goneril said irrepressibly. Then, 'You did say *anything*, Grandmother.'

Mavelle frowned.

'The hound stays with its mistress, Goneril. Choose something else and you will not be refused.'

Goneril gave a dramatic sigh but bowed.

'Very well then, but the hound was all I wanted for myself so I shall ask something for you instead, Grandmother.'

'For me?'

'For you and for Olwen, our most treasured high druidess, who infuses this whole tribe with wisdom and strength.' Olwen coloured almost shyly – most unlike her usual self – and Goneril beamed down at her. 'They have both worked with brilliance on a project that may set this, our glorious tribe of the Coritani, high above all the others, as high, indeed, as the very skies. Therefore I ask my Father to grant them the full-time service of their creator – Taran the Smith.'

'No!'

This time the cry came from Taran, echoed by a shaken Dubus.

'We have built a new forge here at Beacon,' Goneril pushed on. 'A fine forge where he can work with our chieftainess and high druidess.'

She beamed again on Mavelle who glanced excitedly to Olwen, then turned to Leir.

'The smith is your apprentice, Leir – the final say is yours.'

Cordelia looked desperately at her father but he was helpless before the seemingly humble bridal request.

'Of course,' he said with a bow. ''Tis a fitting choice for the boon of the whole tribe. Smith, here!'

Leir beckoned Taran forward, leaving him no choice but to step up and join him. He walked within touching distance of Cordelia but all she could do was watch, horrified, while his fate was decreed.

'Taran,' Goneril said, rolling his name around her tongue. 'Not a bad second prize. You are mine now, Smith. Welcome to Beacon.'

Taran tried to smile but it came out more like a grimace and as Cordelia watched her sister pace around him, she feared that the smith had been exactly the prize she'd been after all along.

Chapter Twenty

BEACON HILL

Cantlos: Song days (October)

'We need to test them,' Taran said, looking down at the wings, which now had fabric tautly sewn across the iron frame.

'You mean *fly* them,' Mavelle said, flexing her thin arms in anticipation.

'I mean test them without a person so that if they go wrong no one will be hurt.'

'But without a person how will they be safely steered? They'll just crash and be lost to us. Such a test, surely, is doomed to failure?'

Taran grimaced. The chieftainess had a point. Her eyes might have faded but her wits were as bright as ever. 'We just need to do it, Taran,' she went on. 'The first moon of Samhain – that's the time. The dead will be in the skies and they'll carry me. All I need do is get up onto the ramparts and jump.'

She gave a little skipping motion, like a girl at play, and Taran had to admire her spirit. In the few weeks he'd been at Beacon, he'd come to love Mavelle dearly. Working with her and the passionate Olwen was the only thing that made his life in this brooding fortress worthwhile. Even the new forge, although very well appointed, lacked the spirit of Dubus' one at Burrough – or perhaps just the joy of visits from Cordelia.

Watching her ride for Burrough without him had been more painful than Taran had thought possible. Gleva and Map had stayed to keep him company at Beacon for a time, but they had goods to sell and soon took the road north again. He missed Cordelia's easy company so much. He missed her teasing and her laughter and the way her brow crinkled when she was explaining something about her beloved dogs.

And it wasn't just her. He missed Leir's interest in new tools and inventions. He missed Dubus' rough jokes and Nairina's sweet ale and Magunna's cooking and chivvying. He missed the ease and communality of life at Burrough, for everything in the heartland fortress seemed tense in comparison. But what could they do? Now that Goneril had so cleverly claimed his apprenticeship, he would need her permission to marry so Cordelia and he must bide their time and pray that the heiress lost interest in what could surely only be petty revenge.

Goneril had set herself up very grandly with her new husband but treated him more as a pet than a consort, keeping him largely in her chamber, oiled and ready for her pleasure. It was Olwen who sat with her when she heard pleas, Olwen who rode out with her to inspect the tribal lands, and Olwen who controlled the vital grain stores. Maedoc did not seem to care and, when he was allowed out, wandered the compound with a smug smile on his handsome face, sneering contentedly at those who actually had to work for a living. Taran assumed he was meant to be jealous but in truth he thanked the Goddess every single day for sparing him such a fate. He'd far rather the fires of the forge than those of the heiress.

'Mavelle,' he said now, 'I cannot launch you into the skies without knowing if you at least stand a chance of landing safely.'

'Why not?'

'You are precious to the tribe.'

The old lady waved this away and two sparrows flew off her shoulder and circled around above them.

'I am not precious, Taran. I could slide into the realm of the Samhain dead and no one would even notice for days.'

'*I* would,' Olwen protested, looking up from her minute studies of a bird's foot to one side of the cluttered workshop.

'Thank you, my dear. But I mean more that my granddaughter has full charge of the tribe now.'

'That's not true,' the druidess protested hotly.

Mavelle smiled at her.

'You're right, it is not. You, Olwen, are a great help to her.'

'I meant—'

'Which is a great comfort to me.' Mavelle wandered over and patted Olwen's shoulder. 'Truly. All is well here, Druidess, so why should I not give myself to the skies? If the air spirits drop me, I will know it is my time and will go gladly.'

'But you'd break the wings doing so,' Taran objected and Mavelle laughed.

'I would, lad, I would. But they are no use, you know, lying prettily on the ground.'

She put her arms out and made a swooping motion that set her birds flying again. Olwen laughed and Taran was glad to hear it. She'd seemed tense lately and must be worn out with all the time she put in with Goneril and then in the workshop. Often he saw her burning torches late into the night.

'You work too hard, Olwen,' he said as she came over to join them.

She looked at him in surprise.

'I work as much as I wish to and on those things that interest me most. I am truly lucky, Taran, for I am fed by the grain others bring in, kept warm by the wood others chop, and clothed in fabrics others weave.'

Taran considered.

'I suppose that is true. I, too, work mainly as I wish.' He took his turn at the cooking pot and with the tidying of the roundhouses and, of course, in the fields at planting and harvest, but most of the time he was free to do what he did best. He stared at Olwen. 'I had not thought of it like that.'

Mavelle chuckled.

'You are both gifted. The tribe would be foolish to waste your talents.'

'Right now,' Taran said bluntly, 'it is your life, Chieftainess, that I do not wish to waste.'

Olwen laughed.

'Ever practical, Smith. But you are right, we should test the wings. We might only have one chance at this so we should get it right.'

'True,' Mavelle agreed reluctantly. 'So, what do you suggest?'

Olwen looked awkwardly to Taran; they had no suggestions. One of the druids had offered to make a model from straw, weighted with stones to mimic the chieftainess, but as Mavelle had just pointed out, the wings relied on their wearer steering their course by tugging the cross-bar and no straw figure could manage that. Taran cast his eyes to the rafters and saw Olwen's perfect bird skeleton flapping lazily in the breeze filtering in through the thatch.

'We need a model,' he cried. 'If we replicate the frame in miniature, and add a tiny straw woman, we can launch it as a test.'

'That's it!' Olwen agreed eagerly. 'It won't be perfect but it will give us an idea how the wings might bear up.'

Mavelle looked at them impatiently.

'But how long will that take? I want to fly on the first Samhain moon before all the tribe.'

Taran quivered. 'All the tribe' meant Cordelia and he could not wait to see her again. He missed her as if she had been physically hollowed out of his chest and had stamped the number of days to Samhain on a strip of iron so he could cross them off every morning as he lit up the forge fire. There were forty to go, which felt like forever, but at least now he would have something to focus on.

'Just a few days,' he assured Mavelle. 'I'll get onto it straight away, I promise – it's not as if I have anything else to do.'

But there he was to be proved wrong.

'We need swords.'

Goneril had summoned him to the royal house at almost exactly the moment he'd got the fires high enough to heat the iron into strips. He'd longed to say that he could not attend her, but there was no refusing the heiress' summons so he'd had to leave his hard-won charcoal and report to her. He'd found her in the damned bedchamber in which she had proposed to him, reclining across her cushions with Maedoc at her feet, stroking his hands up and down her thighs. Taran tried not to look.

'Swords, Heiress? *More* swords?'

'More swords,' she agreed imperiously. 'Breedon is all but completed and Regan needs them for the builders.'

'Swords for builders? Why?'

Goneril sat up suddenly, sending her husband tipping sideways.

'It does not matter to you why, Smith. It matters simply that I have ordered them.' She looked down at her husband. 'How dare he question me?'

In response, Maedoc ran his hand higher still until it disappeared beneath the hem of her short tunic.

'See, Smith, this is a man who knows how to please his mistress.' She smiled and moved her legs apart to allow him easier access, keeping her eyes drilled onto Taran. 'Twenty more swords. Normal ones, for normal men, not like Maedoc's special one.' His hand moved faster and Goneril gave a low moan. Taran prayed to be released but the heiress had no intention of letting him go yet.

'Now, Maedoc,' she commanded, flinging herself back on the cushions.

Taran bit his lip and prayed for patience as Maedoc obediently drove himself straight into her. It was noisy and rough and Goneril did not take her forest-dark eyes off Taran until she climaxed with a wild bucking motion. He longed to turn aside from her ostentatious lust but refused to give her the satisfaction so stood there, legs steady and fingers clenched so hard into his palms that he made them bleed, until finally she waved Maedoc away.

'So sorry, Smith,' she drawled, 'but if the spirits call, I must obey. I have a line to propagate.'

'And you do so most assiduously, Heiress.' Her eyes narrowed and he hastened on. 'Swords. Of course. It will be my pleasure. When for?'

'Samhain.'

He blinked, picturing the forty days marked on his strip of iron.

'That's one every two days, Heiress.'

'So? You chose to be a smith, after all.' Her lip curled and she added, 'You should take Maedoc's work ethic as your example.'

Maedoc fixed Taran challengingly with dark eyes.

'I see he is tireless in his efforts, Heiress,' Taran said. 'But I have promised Chieftainess Mavelle a set of wings and they will take all my time.'

'Another set?'

'A miniature, Heiress, to test the flight. Olwen thinks it best.'

For a moment Goneril hesitated but then Maedoc's hand stroked lightly across her ankle and her back straightened.

'Olwen, bless her, does not always have the full benefits of the tribe in her sights as I do.'

Taran bit his lip.

'Of course, Heiress, but you would not, I'm sure, wish to launch the head of the Coritani into the skies if there is a risk to her life?'

Goneril simply looked at him with a slow smile and said, 'Twenty swords, Smith, by the first moon of Samhain,' and all that was left for him to do was to bow his agreement and flee for the ladder as, once again, Maedoc's hand crept up his royal wife's robe.

Two days later Taran found out a little more. He had sent word to Goneril that he could not make her sister's swords without ore and a vast heap of it had been dumped at the door of his smart new forge. It had taken him half the morning to lift it inside and it would all need smelting before he could even begin to start fashioning the blades.

Ollocus, the old smith, was canny enough to have spotted Goneril's interest in Taran and was now more often to be found 'advising' Beacon's brewers than working the forge, so Taran could see no way to complete the commission bar working through the night. He began to pump his flames higher, but was interrupted almost immediately by a surprise visitor.

'Prince Aledus!'

He rushed to bow to the newcomer but Aledus gave him a nudge that almost toppled him over.

'Just plain Aledus, Taran, please. I need a little time off from royal duty.'

Taran looked at him curiously.

'Do you not like it?'

'Oh, I do, very much. Breedon is a prize indeed but, Lugh knows, it brings responsibilities. Everyone always praises Burrough to the skies so how are we meant to match up?'

Taran shrugged.

'You're not. Yours is an outpost, a means of controlling the border, at least for now. Such a fort need not be as sophisticated as Burrough.'

'You're saying my fortress lacks sophistication?' Aledus retorted indignantly.

Taran laughed.

'I am saying it is a practical place – as surely suits you? Why are you here, Aledus?'

'Goneril asked Regan to some meeting, which thankfully I'm excused. The heiress surrounds herself with a group of friends whose only interest is fawning on her and I cannot bear their company.'

Taran didn't blame him. Goneril was quietly edging the elders aside, replacing them with obsequious youngsters and they seemed a tedious bunch to him too. He reached for the jug he kept ready.

'Ale?'

'Goodness, yes.' Aledus grabbed cups and Taran filled one for each of them. 'May the Goddess smile on you!'

They clinked cups then Aledus sank onto a bench and Taran joined him. He should not with so much to do, but it was a relief to talk to someone familiar and he settled his head gladly against the sloping roof.

'Decisions,' Aledus said into his ale cup. 'That's one of the big problems of rule, Taran – decisions. Regan makes most of them, obviously, but she's kind enough to ask my advice and I feel that as a good consort I should be able to give it. Should we, for example, build a forge?'

'Yes!' Taran said instantly.

'Why?'

'So *I* don't have to make all your swords.'

'You?' Aledus looked at him curiously. 'Goneril said she'd buy them in for us.'

'Does it look like she's doing that?'

Taran indicated the pile of ore in the corner and Aledus ambled over to feel one of the misshapen lumps.

'Is this how it comes out of the earth?'

'This is how Danu offers it up to us, yes. Then it is a simple matter of heating it, over and over, to draw the pure iron free.'

'It must take time.'

'Too much. It keeps me from working on the wings. Perhaps, Aledus, you could ask Goneril to send half the commission to

Dubus at Burrough? He will love the work and is faster at it than I am.'

'Of course, of course. We need them quickly.'

'You do? Are we in danger?'

Aledus shrugged.

'Not yet but Goneril says there will be war.'

'War?' Taran did not know this word.

'War, yes – many battles on a grand scale.'

'Why?'

Aledus shifted on the bench.

'There is a feeling that if one tribe is strong it could maybe, in time, rule another.'

'Rule another tribe? Why?'

Aledus shifted.

'Why not? It gives you more people, more resources, more land.'

Taran pushed himself up and went to the door of the new forge. It faced upwards to the fortress but just a few steps aside and he had an uninterrupted view across the vast Coritani lands. Even Breedon in the west and Burrough in the east could not be seen and there was more land beyond them both. He turned to Aledus who had followed him out.

'Is this not enough? We would have to have fifty children each, and they fifty more, ever to scatter houses across the plains.'

'That's true, I suppose,' Aledus agreed awkwardly. 'Goneril said it would be glorious to defeat another tribe and I didn't look much beyond that. The Setantii are worthless people after all.'

'All of them?'

Aledus rubbed at his nose.

'Probably not,' he conceded. 'I don't know, Taran. I don't understand it all. I'm but a humble husband – I leave the ruling to the women and just do as I'm told.'

'Which is?'

'Training fighters. Or, rather, warriors.'

'Warriors?'

'It sounds more refined, does it not? And now most of our building projects are completed, we do not need so many men so it is a new trade for them.'

'The trade of war?' The word sounded odd coming out of Taran's mouth but Aledus nodded and shuffled back inside the forge. Taran took a last look around the peaceful plains and followed him. 'Well, I think it's a bad idea.'

'Perhaps but Goneril says it will work out well if we are better equipped to win than the other tribe. And equipped to supply men to others. That's Regan's plan. We train fighters and then sell them to chieftainesses who need them.'

Taran sat cautiously down.

'What if they don't want to be sold?'

'Why would they not? We will share the profit with them – half for us for their keep and training and half to them for their skills and hard work. It is how trade works, Taran.'

'Save that at the end of it, you are free and they are not.'

'Save that at the end of it, we are still as we were and they have a way of earning a far better living than as a humble builder. They will be kept in style by their new tribe in return for doing what they do best.'

'Fighting this war of yours?'

'Not of mine, Taran. The world is changing and we cannot just ignore that. Chieftainesses pay well for good fighters – as they do for good smiths. Did Gleva and Map not, after all, sell you?'

Taran flinched. Gleva and Map *had* sold him. They'd sold him to Enica, who had sold him to Leir, who had gifted him to bloody Goneril.

'They did,' he snapped, 'which is how I know the true price of the transaction.'

'I suppose. But you like being a smith, do you not?'

Taran drank deep of his ale before he replied.

'I do, Aledus. Truly, I do. And when I think what might have become of me, I can only be grateful that I reached the Coritani. But it's hard, sometimes, not to want a little more.'

Aledus patted him on the back.

'True, Taran, very true. Some days I watch Regan drilling all those men and women and I thank Danu for sending her to me. A year ago I was kicking around Raven's Hill in my sister's shadow – and now look at me!'

'Still skulking in the forge drinking my ale,' Taran teased and Aledus gave a soft laugh.

'It's very good ale.'

He held out his tankard and Taran poured them both more and tried not to look to the ore or the swords it would become. He did not like this build-up of fighters and could only pray that all would go well when Mavelle launched herself beneath the first Samhain moon, for if not he might, Danu forfend, need one of the wretched weapons himself.

SAMHAIN

Winter

Chapter Twenty-one

BEACON HILL

Samonios; Seed-fall days (November)

At last the first moon of Samhain was rising. Cordelia had been so desperate to come to Beacon her skin had physically itched but finally she was approaching and it looked glorious. The fortress, on the great craggy hill above them, was lit up with what must have been two hundred torches and shone like Lugh brought to earth. No wonder Goneril had asked that they didn't arrive until tonight. She had wanted them to see the glory of the ancient fortress from afar – and Cordelia had to admire her showmanship.

Their procession ground to a halt as several of their party dropped to their knees to thank Danu for this vision and Cordelia looked at them impatiently. Any further delay, especially this close to her destination, was agonising.

'A fortress of purest bronze,' a gruff voice said at her side, and she turned to see Dubus looking up at Beacon with a cynical eye.

'You do not like it, Dubus?'

'I've never been a man for bronze, Princess. It's pretty all right, but too malleable to be of any true use. Give me iron any day – solid, reliable, dependable.'

He reached out a big hand and for a moment Cordelia thought he was going to pat her on the back but he pulled it away and instead added, "Course I'm just a rough smith so what do I know?'

'I like rough smiths,' she said and this time he did pat her back – a swift touch but welcome. All her life Cordelia had been used to receiving easy hugs and smiles from Leir, but since Caireen had come to Burrough he'd been too preoccupied with her to pay much attention to his remaining daughter. It had somehow made Taran's absence even harder to bear.

'You have the swords?' she asked Dubus.

'I do and I bet they're better than Taran's crappy ones.'

Cordelia managed a smile. She'd been delighted when Aledus had ridden in with the commission and had joined him in the forge to grill him for information on events at Beacon.

'Oh, everyone just gets on with their business,' he'd said airily.

'Right. How's, er, Taran?'

'Taran? He's fine. A bit overworked. That Ollocus is a lazy old sod and Taran cannot make all these swords alone. Will you help, Dubus? With Leir's approval?'

"Course I will. Anything to get the lad in my debt, hey?'

Cordelia had been grateful for the men's commonsense attitude and told herself to stop fretting. If Ollocus was so useless then Goneril had been very sensible to commandeer Taran's talents for her new forge. And yet, Cordelia had seen the fear in Taran's eyes when he'd told her of Goneril's proposal back at Lughnasad and she suspected that her sister had more than one iron in his fire.

'How are the wings?' she'd asked Aledus.

'Marvellous, truly.' His eyes had lit up. 'Taran made a small version complete with poppet woman. He, Mavelle and Olwen launched it off the ramparts onto the dusk breezes and, oh,

Cordelia, it flew for ages. Swooped and turned like a true bird. We all watched and willed it to stay up there and it did. It really did.'

'But it's not still up there?'

'Oh, no. Of course not. It had to come down eventually. It was quite funny actually. Landed on a cow. Made the poor thing bolt, mooing all the way. The whole herd went after it, kicking up their hooves like mad things whilst we clapped them on.'

'What happened to the wings?'

Aledus had sobered.

'They were trampled beyond recognition.'

'And the poppet?'

'Trampled too.'

He'd lapsed into silence while Cordelia had tried desperately not to picture her grandmother trampled into the Otherworld by terrified beasts.

'What did Mavelle say?' she'd asked eventually.

'Oh, she was delighted. Says they are ready and she will fly under the Samhain moon.'

'And land under it too?'

'Of course. A woman, you see, can steer as a poppet cannot.'

'Steer free of a herd of charging cows?'

Aledus had visibly swallowed

'Let's hope so,' was all he'd managed.

Dubus had provided a little more encouragement. 'Your grandmother is one with the air spirits, Princess, and when the first Samhain moon rises, the dead fill the air. Your mother will be beneath one wing and your grandfather the other. Our chieftainess will not fail.'

She'd smiled at him gratefully and now, looking into the air shimmering above Beacon, she prayed Branwen and Bladdud were up there waiting to catch Mavelle when she made her leap. Cordelia's heart beat faster and she turned to Leir.

'We should go on, Father. The druids will be waiting for us.'

That got him moving. Caireen had returned to Beacon some

days before to aid Olwen with the important preparations for the arrival of Samhain, and he'd been moping ever since.

'Ride on!' he called and everyone leaped to obey.

Cordelia kicked her horse into a gallop and Leir followed her lead. Inside the gates, Beacon was every bit as dazzling as without. Samhain was the time of the new fire, drawn out of wood afresh for the year ahead and taken into every individual hearth to keep the community warm. This year, though, Goneril had ordered five Samhain fires so that the whole compound was as light and as warm as a Beltane day. Even Gleva's poor bones would have been warm enough here, Cordelia thought, but her trader friends had long since gone south. She would be able to tell them of Mavelle's flight on their return at Imbolc and prayed the tale would be a happy one. She looked eagerly around for Taran as they entered the compound but druids were throwing herbs onto the fires, filling the air with a musky smoke that made it hard to see anything.

'Cordelia!' She turned eagerly but it was Goneril swooping down on her. 'My darling sister, welcome. Regan – come quickly, let all the royal daughters be reunited at last.' Regan came hurrying across and Goneril embraced them both ostentatiously. 'Doesn't Beacon look well? Isn't Olwen clever? How did it appear from the road?'

'As if Lugh were resting here in person,' Cordelia assured her.

'Perfect!' Goneril clapped her hands like a child. 'Oh, it's all so perfect!' She turned to Leir. 'Father! I'm so happy to see you and I won't be the only one either. I swear poor Caireen has been wasting away, sighing to the moon and barely touching her food. What have you done to her?'

'Or she to me,' Leir said, sounding as shy as a man half his age.

The beautiful druidess had seen them then and Cordelia watched her detach herself from a group to hurry over and jump into Leir's arms, wrapping her legs around his waist and covering him in kisses. Like all the druids, she was cloaked in a cow hide, flayed from the animals they had slaughtered in the sacred grove

204

earlier to feed the tribe through the cold Samhain months, and it had tainted her slim arms a blood-red that made Cordelia's flesh crawl. Goneril, however, had no such qualms.

'Isn't it lovely to see them?' she said as the pair kissed deeply. 'Poor Father has been so lonely for so long, it melts my heart he has finally found someone to love.'

Cordelia looked at Goneril and back to Leir. She supposed the girl's bloody arms *were* holding their father kindly and she felt suddenly mean. He had been without his dear wife for fourteen years and deserved happiness. But something about this match still felt wrong.

'Isn't he a little old for her?' she asked.

Goneril laughed.

'Oh, Dee, you're so naïve. Isn't she, Regan?' She gave their middle sister no time to reply. 'Age is no boundary to love. And, besides, she has made him younger.' Cordelia looked to their father. His hair was more white than grey now and she could swear he was shrinking, but his blue eyes were certainly bright so maybe Goneril was right. 'You wait,' she went on, 'one day you will find someone special, as your sisters have.'

Cordelia ground her teeth.

'And when I do, Gee, you will be glad to see me happy?'

'Of course, little sister. Why would I not be?'

Cordelia dared to hold her eye as Regan fidgeted beside them both.

'Where is Taran, Gee?' Cordelia asked.

'Taran? Oh, the smith. I'm not sure. Why?'

'You know why.'

'I do not.'

'Oh, I think you do. I am not as naïve as you believe, big sister.'

'Really?' Goneril arched one eyebrow. 'Lucky you!'

She was crackling with energy tonight and it was never a good idea to provoke her when she was like this. Anyway, here was Taran, moving agonisingly slowly towards them with Mavelle on his arm. The chieftainess looked tiny and so thin she reminded Cordelia for one terrible moment of the rotting skeleton in the sacrificial pit at Breedon, but even that distraction could not keep her gaze from Taran. As their eyes locked, she saw her own joy reflected in his and stepped forward to embrace him, but he swiftly looked down and she checked herself.

'Grandmother!' Cordelia cried loudly instead. 'It's so wonderful to see you!'

'It is?' Mavelle looked at her in surprise.

'Of course it is.'

'But we have not long been talking, Regan.'

Cordelia started and glanced around for her sister but she had melted away into the crowd.

'I am Cordelia, Grandmother.'

'Are you?' She peered at her. 'Damnation, so you are. It's this wretched smoke. Fills my eyes up and my nostrils too. Olwen says the herbs will summon the dead, but if you ask me, the stink will keep them well away. My Bladdud was never one for heavy scents.'

Cordelia laughed, mirth fuelled by relief. Mavelle was not losing her wits, just her sight, and it *was* very smoky. The myriad guests were barely visible for the haze as the flames burned higher but that, at least, meant she could take Taran's spare hand and dare to kiss his cheek, just a finger's width from his lips.

'I have missed you,' she said softly – though not, it seemed, softly enough.

'Have you indeed?' Mavelle asked. 'Interesting.' She looked at Cordelia so intently that she feared for a moment her grandmother, like her sister, would disapprove, but then she smiled. 'You have made a fine choice, Dee. Perhaps the finest of the three of you, though Aledus is a decent man and Olwen is, of course, quite brilliant.'

'Olwen?'

Mavelle just smiled again.

'I am old, Dee, not stupid. Now, I must go and find Leir. We have much to talk of as, I'm sure, do you two.'

With a quick pat of Cordelia's hand, she released Taran and limped off into the smoke. Cordelia watched her go.

'She looks frail, Taran.'

'Not in spirit. She is ready to fly.'

'And will she?'

'I believe so. The test went well.'

'Until the cows?'

He looked sheepish.

'You heard?'

'Aledus told me when he came about the swords.'

'Of course. The cows were ... unfortunate. But Mavelle would have more sense than to steer herself into a herd.'

'And good enough sight to spot them? At night?'

She looked up at the black sky above the great fires and Taran sighed.

'It is the first moon of Samhain, Cordelia, and the spirits are abroad. It is her best chance of flying.'

'And of landing safely?'

Taran glanced around but no one was looking their way and he pulled Cordelia close in against him.

'That I cannot say. I offered to wear them in her stead but she will not have it. This was a royal project for years, Dee, and Mavelle's passion since Bladdud's sad death. She is ready.'

'And the wings?'

'They are ready too. Look.'

He turned her gently and pointed up to the southern ramparts where she saw them set on a stand between two large torches, a monument to the air spirits. The moon swelled behind, as if calling them to her, and the smoke, thinner up on the ramparts, wisped around them like a blessing. Cordelia drank in the sight. They were big – as wide on each side as a person lying down – and the iron lattice she'd seen leave Burrough with Taran had now been covered with a fine fabric dyed in a swirling pattern of browns and golds like a mystical eagle. She shook her head in awe.

'They make *me* want to fly.'

Taran dropped a kiss on the back of her neck, light as one of the feathers on Mavelle's magnificent robe but still somehow strong enough to run round every stretch of her body. She leaned back against him.

'Are you safe here, Taran?'

'I am. Not happy, Dee, but safe. And Goneril will tire of me, I'm sure. Already she torments me less. She has been all over Maedoc recently and not just for his seed. It is almost as if she is growing to like him.'

'I hope so.'

'Me too. A happy Goneril is an easy Goneril.'

Cordelia sighed.

'It has always been so.'

'But look, here she comes.'

They sprang guiltily apart but the heiress swept past them, Maedoc in tow. As they reached the wooden steps set below the wings all eyes turned their way and Goneril took her handsome husband's arm and began to climb. She took her time, moving slowly so that all had a chance to admire her costume. Woven in reds and ambers, fading into icy blue around the bottom, the clinging sheath dress turned her into a living flame as she moved to stand, perfectly positioned in the centre of the wings.

'Coritani, welcome!' She flung her arms wide and the crowd roared their delight. 'Tonight is a glorious night – a night of celebration, a night of commemoration and a night of inauguration. For tonight, Coritani, it will not just be our ancestors who fill the sacred skies above this our most ancient fortress but our own living chieftainess.'

The crowd roared loudly. Somewhere beneath the smoke a drum started playing, low and insistent, like a tribal heartbeat. Cordelia felt the ground pulse with it as Olwen began to slowly escort Mavelle up the steps, the rest of the white-clad druids following respectfully behind. Goneril did not speak as her grandmother climbed and all held their breath as she tentatively took each step, cut just a little too high for her old legs. When, finally, she reached the top, Goneril rushed forward and took both her hands, drawing her to stand in place at the centre of the wings. Mavelle was a scrawny figure in comparison but her granddaughter clapped her wildly and the crowd obediently followed her example.

'She doesn't look up to it,' Cordelia whispered urgently to Taran.

'It's easier in the air. It's more forgiving.'

'But look at her, Taran. She's so frail. Please, stop her.'

'I cannot, Dee. She's determined.'

'She's mad.'

'No.' The word was low but firm. 'No, Dee, she is not mad. She is brilliant. This could be a huge advance for us all.'

'Or a huge last for *her*.'

'Believe, Dee.'

The word came out in a hushed whisper and she looked at him. 'Believe?'

'Yes. Believe in her. Love her and believe in her.'

'You would will her into the clouds?'

'I would. I have to – for who else do you think Goneril will blame if she does not reach them?'

Cordelia looked at him in horror.

'You? Oh, Taran, no, you should not—'

'Hush, Dee.' He kissed her quiet. 'I've checked them over and over. If Mavelle does it right, they will carry her, I am sure of it.'

'Then I am sure too.'

She looked back to the ramparts to see that Olwen was very gently removing the chieftainess's glorious bird-cloak. For a moment the pair were silhouetted against their precious wings and Cordelia's heart thrilled for them as they stepped up to attach her to their joint creation. Before Olwen could lift the first strap, however, Goneril made a grab for her hand, drawing her to her side and waving Caireen and Maedoc to do it in her stead.

'Take a bow, Druidess,' she urged, and Olwen did so, looking confused but pleased.

'Olwen is getting all the credit,' Cordelia objected.

'That suits me fine,' Taran said. 'And, besides, she has worked on this far longer than I have.'

Cordelia nodded. She knew she had to calm down but the drum was beating louder and the fires were burning higher and the smoke was swirling faster and she felt giddy with it all, nauseously giddy.

'I have news!' Goneril announced suddenly. 'Happy news with which to send my dear grandmother into the skies.' She paused then beckoned Maedoc back, forcing Olwen to move down a step. A whisper of anticipation shot through the crowd and Goneril let it run. 'Yes!' she cried finally. 'We are blessed indeed, for I am honoured to tell you in this Samonios month of seed-sowing, the best seed of all has taken root within your heiress – a new daughter to carry the Coritani forward into the future.'

She placed one hand on her belly and the other on Maedoc's arm. He was wearing a tunic to match hers and his ceremonial sword slung across his shoulder and together they looked magnificent – the tribal future, perfectly presented and glowing with life and power. The people's cheers rang up into the fire-lit skies, over and over, and Goneril stood smiling modestly before finally waving them to silence.

'But that is for tomorrow. Tonight is for Chieftainess Mavelle!'

She stepped aside to reveal her grandmother, even more skeletal in a plain white tunic, her arms strapped to the wings as if she were a sacrifice for the air spirits. Cordelia's heart turned over but when she looked more closely, she could see that Mavelle was smiling broadly and that, at least, gave her hope.

'Please, my royal sisters and my dear father – come up and join us.'

Taran nudged at Cordelia.

'That's you.'

'I don't want to.'

But even as she said it, she knew that what she wanted had nothing to do with this. She was joined to Goneril as surely as the spirals on her amulet, threaded forever around and around each other, and there was nothing for it but to release Taran's hand and go. It was crowded on the steps so Regan bounded up the grassy slope and Cordelia reluctantly followed, but the crowd cheered to see them standing there, together, and she waved as graciously as she could.

'All well, Grandmother?' she asked.

'Couldn't be better, Dee-Dee. I am sky-bound.'

Her eyes were already fixed on the stars, as if she could see her husband and daughter beckoning.

'Exciting, isn't it?' Regan whispered.

'Terrifying more like.'

'Oh, come on, Dee, where's your sense of adventure? Mavelle is going to fly!'

'And then what?'

'And then she'll land and be escorted back up here and we'll give her a hero's welcome.'

'Escorted?'

'Oh, yes. I've stationed my guards all around the plain. Olwen has told us where the winds are likely to carry Grandmother and it's not as if she will be hard to spot, is it?'

'No. No, it's not.'

Cordelia felt relief flood through her. Olwen really had thought this all through and maybe, just maybe, it would work. She looked for the high druidess but she was still down the steps with the other druids, kept from Mavelle's side by the royal couple above her. She did not look very happy about it but her work was done. It was all down to Mavelle now.

'Cows?' Cordelia dared to ask her sister.

'All chased away! Grandmother is free to fly.'

Cordelia supposed she must also ready herself but Goneril had one last surprise for them.

'And finally,' she announced, 'I must call to this little stage of ours, the most important person of this glorious night – after our great Mavelle, of course.' She paused dramatically and everyone looked at each other as if they might mysteriously be summoned to her side. 'I speak, of course, of the man who made this possible, the maker of Mavelle's wings – the talented worker, Smith Taran! Come forth, Taran, and take the praise of the tribe.'

Cordelia watched, astonished, as Goneril pointed him out. He advanced, wide-eyed, and Cordelia saw a tiny smile tug sideways at his dear lips and felt a rush of gratitude to her sister. It was good of her to credit him so graciously and Cordelia cheered as loudly as the rest as he dazedly climbed the slope and took his place on the ceremonial platform. He moved towards Mavelle and the wings but Goneril put up a hand.

'Not now, Smith. It is time. My grandmother is ready to fly.'

'I just thought I'd check . . . '

'All done.'

'But I could—'

'Do you not trust us?'

'Of course. Yes. I—I'm sorry. It is a little overwhelming.'

Goneril beamed at him.

'Oh, don't apologise. I forget, as I'm so used to it. Maedoc too. Here, stand next to Cordelia so that you can see as our chieftainess takes to the skies.'

She ushered him into the line of royals and he glanced in disbelief at Cordelia. She dared not reach for his hand in front of the whole tribe but gave him a smile and a silent nod. Perhaps this was the start of a new acceptance towards him? Perhaps, if this went well, she could ask for him as her husband? Perhaps . . .

'Ready?' Goneril demanded loudly of Mavelle and Cordelia was reminded guiltily that her own concerns were of little matter on this weighty day.

'I am ready,' Mavelle agreed, her voice strong and sure. Then, to Goneril's barely hidden astonishment, she addressed the crowd below. 'I thank you, my people of the Coritani, for bearing witness to this great day and ask you to send your prayers into the skies with me. Above us, in the circle of this glorious Samhain moon, Chieftain Bladdud and Heiress Branwen await to carry me forth, the first person ever to fly.'

Cordelia noticed Goneril look almost uneasily to the skies as if afraid her mother and grandfather might indeed descend, but if they were there, they were content to wait for Mavelle and Goneril's smile lit up her face again. She tried to get close enough to nudge her grandmother on, but the wings prevented her and the chieftainess continued to speak.

'I thank all those who have worked on this with me. In particular, Olwen, my treasured daughter-in-science, and our new recruit, Taran the Smith. But if it does not work, it is the fault of no one but myself.'

'Well now,' Goneril started, but Mavelle swung around to see who had interrupted and the wing knocked her granddaughter sideways.

Goneril's brow tightened and she said no more but she did not need to. Mavelle was ready.

'Enough talking. People of the Coritani – watch me fly!'

Then she turned, stepped as nimbly as if she were a young woman again to the edge of the platform, and, without a moment's pause, launched herself off it.

Cordelia caught her breath. All this build-up and the actual moment of flight was so quiet, so unassuming, so very Mavelle. She rushed to the edge of the platform as the crowds poured up the ramparts and there she was, Chieftainess Mavelle, gliding across the night sky like a giant bird.

'It's working!'

Cordelia's cry was echoed all around as the Coritani watched their chieftainess hover on the night air.

'Yes!' Olwen cried. 'She's flying. We did it. She's flying!'

Goneril rolled her eyes at the high druidess' uncontained joy but Cordelia was glad to see it.

'It's amazing, Taran,' she said. 'Look at her! She's a bird ... just like a bird.' The winged figure turned to the east and a sound drifted back to them on the air – a whoop of ecstasy. Cordelia laughed. 'And listen to her!'

Taran shook his head in awe.

'You know what this means, Dee – this means the wings work. This means we can make more, better, can learn how to really apply them. One day I might be able to launch myself from here and land at your feet in Burrough, with no rutted roads or high streams or exhausted horses to stop me. I could ...'

A strange noise cut him off, not so much a crack as a sort of pop, like a log bursting on a fire. Then came an odd tearing sound. It wasn't loud but it carried and the gasps of excitement died in the throats of every one of the Coritani as the wings, with Mavelle tied helplessly to them, spun wildly and plummeted at sickening speed towards the ground.

'No!' It was Goneril's cry, shrill and piercing. 'Grandmother, no!'

But even the command of the heiress could not stop Mavelle now. The spinning shape swung back towards the fortress, lurched wildly to the left and smashed, with a crunch of iron, rock and bone, into the side of Beacon Hill.

'No!' Goneril cried again, on an echoing sob.

She buried her beautiful moon-face in her hands and wept as, below, Regan's guards raced to the wreckage. Cordelia raced with them, shooting down the steps and running for the gate to scramble on down the hillside. It was dark out of the light of Goneril's myriad torches but the guards each held one and they had clustered in a chaotic pattern around what must, surely, be Mavelle.

'Grandmother!'

Cordelia forced her way through but it was instantly obvious that she was too late. This was not, then, to be a happy tale. One half of the wings had bent upwards, taking the old lady's tied arms with it, and she put her hands to her mouth at the sight of the ripped and bleeding sockets from which they had been wrenched.

She forced herself to look at Mavelle's face. It was turned upwards and, although blood was pooling where it had struck the jagged rocks beneath, her eyes were still open to the skies and to Cordelia's astonishment, a smile of purest joy had settled on her face.

She threw herself to her knees and kissed her, not caring that her blood smeared her tunic. A frightened guard tried to pull her away but out of the corner of her eye she saw Regan stopping him and felt her sister stand, strong at her back. Someone knelt beside her and she sensed Taran's solid presence but he did not try to stop her either. Instead, he scrabbled at the wings, beckoning one of the guards to bring him light.

'Where is she?' Goneril's voice demanded as she came rather more officially down the hill. 'Danu help us, where is she?'

Taran moved faster and Cordelia tore her eyes from Mavelle to watch him. His fingers fixed on a part of the wing and he leaned in, running his hand across it. Blood spurted from his fingers and Cordelia gasped but Taran did not even flinch.

'What is it?' Cordelia demanded. 'What happened?'

His reply was curt but pointed: 'The iron has been cut.'

Cordelia stared at him in horror.

'Cut?' someone else asked and she looked up to see Olwen. The druidess threw herself down next to Mavelle, reaching out to caress her face with infinite tenderness, before looking back to Taran. 'What could have cut it in the skies?'

This time his voice was even curter: 'Nothing.'

Olwen stared at him, visibly shaking, but now Goneril was upon them, hands on imperious hips.

'Where is he?' she demanded. 'Where is the man who made the wings that killed Chieftainess Mavelle?'

And before Cordelia could do anything, guards had yanked Taran away and the heiress had flung herself, sobbing majestically, across her grandmother's body. Olwen sat there watching, wild-eyed and weeping, her hand reaching out to the woman with whom she had worked for so long.

'I cannot bear it!' Goneril cried as the rest of the tribe crept closer.

'You must,' came Maedoc's voice, unusually sure and commanding across the chaos. 'She would want you to, Heiress – Chieftainess.'

The elders mumbled gruff approval of this title and around them the crowd fell to their knees. Goneril allowed herself to be prised off Mavelle's grisly form, tugging at Olwen's sleeve as she did so. The druidess looked up at her, utterly lost, but allowed herself to be pulled to her feet. Goneril kept her close as she turned to her people, Regan stumbling to gather her guards around her elder sister in a circle of light, clear and ordered. Goneril drew in a deep breath.

'It is a sad, sad day,' she said, her voice low but sure. 'But my grandmother died doing what she loved and I will do my duty by her and by my tribe.'

The crowd roared their approval. Maedoc led Goneril back into the compound, Olwen in their wake, and the people keen to follow their vibrant new leader away from the broken remains of their last. Regan looked to Cordelia.

'Are you coming, Dee?' Cordelia shook her head. Regan shifted awkwardly. 'You will be needed for the inauguration. You are a royal daughter.'

'And a royal granddaughter,' Cordelia snapped. 'There is no rush.'

'There is always a rush with Goneril.'

'Then she can rush alone. You go, Ree.'

'You will follow?'

Cordelia touched her amulet and looked over to where Taran was being manhandled up the hill ahead of their gesticulating sister.

'I will definitely follow.' She forced herself to her feet and turned to Leir, standing with his head bowed at Mavelle's feet. 'Father, we must talk.'

He looked at her, blue eyes hazed with sadness.

'It so nearly worked, Dee.'

She took his arm.

'It *did* work. Taran said the iron was cut.'

Leir's eyes sharpened.

'Did he?'

'He examined it, Father. He knows iron.'

'That he does.'

'This was not his fault.'

They both looked up the hill to the captured smith. Leir set his shoulders.

'I will do all I can to defend him, Dee, but I am not in charge. Goneril rules the Coritani now and we are all in her hands.'

It was a stark, cold truth. With Goneril at the top of the hill, herself at the bottom and Regan stuck in the middle, the triskele was surely starting to unravel and as Cordelia watched her elder sister marching faster and faster towards the fortress that was now her own, she feared for them all.

Chapter Twenty-two

'This was not Taran's fault, Goneril.'

Olwen looked at the newly proclaimed chieftainess and saw sorrow pooling prettily in her green eyes. Was that real emotion? They were alone in her chamber at last but somehow her royal lover was still wearing her public persona.

'Would that were true, Olwen,' Goneril said on an exaggerated sigh.

Olwen's mind was spinning as sharply as Mavelle had fallen from the sky. She pictured the Coritani chieftainess' skinny body plummeting to earth, taking all that wonderful energy and enthusiasm with it. They had failed her and now they had lost her and she felt as fogged and iced-over as a winter's morning.

She had watched Goneril weep before the tribe, watched her order her five Samhain fires doused, and watched her take the chieftainess' chair with a show of reluctance. She had watched her demand justice and known it was what she felt was expected of her as new ruler, but surely now they were alone Goneril could let her guard down.

'Taran was just one part of the project,' she insisted.

'The critical part.'

'I don't think so. He said the frame was cut.'

'Cut? Did you see it?'

'No. I mean, there was no time, and I couldn't take my eyes off Mavelle, poor, dear Mavelle, and . . . and . . . '

Words failed Olwen then and she buried her head in her hands, shocked at herself. Mavelle would want her to be strong, rational. She sucked in a deep breath, feeling her foolish body shaking. A small part of her wondered why that was but then she pictured her mother-in-science falling from the dark skies once more and could not bring herself to care. A sob racked her and then, at last, Goneril's arms were around her and she leaned gratefully against her lover's strong body.

'Who on earth would cut the frame, Olwen?' Goneril asked softly.

'I don't know!'

'Because it's quite a specialised job cutting iron, isn't it? It takes certain skills, certain tools.'

Olwen pulled back and looked up at her.

'Not iron that thin, Gee. One stroke of a sword would do it.'

Goneril's eyes narrowed.

'What are you suggesting? Regan is good with a sword. Are you saying my sister might have had something to do with this?'

'Regan? No!'

'Aledus perhaps?'

'No. Why would he? And, besides, he had no chance.' Something stirred in her stricken mind – a memory from amongst the confusion of this terrible Samhain. 'Who strapped Mavelle into the wings, Goneril?'

'Maedoc?!' Goneril's voice rose in shock and she took a step back. Olwen felt her absence like a rush of ice against her skin. 'You would accuse my husband of this crime? Oh, Olwen.' She shook her head slowly. 'You are jealous.'

'No!' Olwen closed her eyes. 'It is not that, Gee. I don't believe in jealousy. I don't believe in ownership.' She drew in a deep breath. 'This is not about Maedoc. It is not about you or me. It is about justice. You cannot condemn one man for this tragedy.'

Goneril's lip curled miserably.

'I can. Taran does not deserve to live.'

She said it like a chorus, an incantation. Olwen shook her head.

'Taran does not deserve to die, Goneril, and you know it.' She fought to think what Mavelle would have done were she here, but could see only her frail arms ripped from their sockets by her precious wings. 'Please, Goneril, you cannot do this.'

Goneril gave her a sad smile.

'I must put him on trial before the elders, Olwen, as I have publicly declared.'

'With whom standing as judge?' Goneril gave a low sigh. 'You?'

'It is a hard task but I cannot shirk my duty.'

Something in her tone prickled across Olwen's raw body. It was that public persona again. She needed it, perhaps, as chieftainess, but not here, not with her. She drew herself up, though every fibre of her seemed to ache.

'If you put Taran on trial you should try me too.'

A dangerous smile curved the lips Olwen had so many times covered with her own.

'You are claiming guilt, High Druidess?'

'I am claiming a degree of culpability, Chieftainess, yes, alongside Taran and Caireen and Dubus and even Mavelle herself.'

Goneril drew herself up too. She was not as tall as Olwen but the ruler's circlet, newly placed on her auburn hair, seemed to have made her a far more imposing figure.

'You would put my dead grandmother on the stand, Druidess?'

Olwen looked up at her through a fog of grief.

'If Mavelle could, she would most certainly put herself on it,' she shot back.

A sharp slap stung her cheek and Olwen flinched back and fell to her knees. She put her hand to her face as her mind spun, faster and faster. What was going on here? Why was Goneril being like this? But now the other woman was on her knees too.

'I'm sorry. Oh, Olwen, I'm so sorry. It's the grief. The shock.

Forgive me.' She held out her arms. 'We must not let this tear us apart, my flame. We must grieve together.'

Her eyes sparkled with tears and Olwen saw herself reflected in them, weak and pathetic. Slowly she nodded and then Goneril was clutching at her, drawing her in against her, there on the hard wooden floor.

'I understand your plea,' she said into her hair. 'I do. You are a noble woman, Druidess. And that is how we will make this work.'

'This?'

'Rule. Our shared rule.'

Olwen shivered.

'Druidesses don't rule.'

'But they guide.'

She looked up at the word. Nodded slowly. She must guide. And to guide she must think, must apply all the logic she had been taught.

'We should examine the wings,' she said.

Goneril lifted her chin and kissed her, slowly and infinitely gently.

'I have had them cast into the last of the fires where they belong. They do not matter now, my flame.'

'But—'

'*You* are what matters now. To me at least. You and the tribe. Is Taran all he seems?'

'What?'

'He was quick to suggest iron for the wings.'

'Was it him?' Olwen fought to remember but still the fog clung to her brain, making it slow and foolish.

'Of course, with his drawings and his ideas about gliding and his damned cross-bar – the cross-bar that meant Mavelle was helpless to do anything to save herself when the wretched thing broke.'

Again, Olwen saw Mavelle's torn arm sockets, the blood seeping freely into the earth as if chasing ahead of her soul to the Otherworld.

'It was he who took the wing manufacture to Burrough where he could do it unseen. And he who was so keen to scurry back there that I had to claim him as my wedding gift, to bring him to us here, at the heart of the tribe. Why, Olwen? You could not understand it yourself at the time but perhaps it was to shirk blame?' Olwen stared at Goneril. All she said seemed to make a sort of horrific sense. 'Perhaps that's why he turned down my proposal. Perhaps his agenda is bigger than we can tell, Olwen. He comes from the Catuvellauni, remember.'

'As does Aledus.'

Goneril dismissed this.

'Perhaps he wanted Mavelle dead to weaken our tribe.'

Olwen stared at her. She was tired, so tired. She didn't want this to be true, any of it, but that did not mean she did not have a duty to consider it. If only her mind would work properly.

'Well, if that's what he wanted,' she managed, 'he failed, for no one is as strong as you, Goneril.'

Goneril smiled.

'Too right, my flame,' she agreed. 'Too right.'

And then she drew Olwen into her arms again and kissed her until fogged seemed the only bearable way to be.

Chapter Twenty-three

Three days later

Cordelia crept into the sacred grove at the base of Beacon Hill behind Regan, forcing one foot in front of the other and trying to stop trembling before Goneril and the rest of the tribe. Or, rather, those of the tribe Goneril had chosen to allow here today. She had said that the grove was too small to accommodate everyone and publicly nominated those permitted to attend Mavelle's farewell ceremony.

Cordelia's name had been on the list but she found no honour in it. This felt secretive, underhand, wrong. Even Magunna had been excluded, despite serving the family like a mother for so many years, and Cordelia did not like that. Mavelle had been ruler of all the Coritani and all should be allowed to mourn her, not just the elders and royals. The grove was the same size as it had always been and it had never been considered too small to contain everyone before; they had all crowded in under the trees surrounding the great willow, content with half a view and free to pay their respects as they wished once the formal ceremony was over.

'All are invited to the party,' Goneril had said when Cordelia had objected, as if that was what counted. 'But Mavelle deserves a distinguished ceremony.'

Mavelle deserves a loving ceremony, Cordelia had wanted to retort, but had not dared rile Goneril further whilst she had Taran under guard. Not that it had helped.

She kept her eyes firmly trained on the muddy ground, refusing to grant Goneril the satisfaction of seeing her distress, but she knew Taran was there, strapped to one of the wooden legs of the high platform on which Mavelle had been laid out for the spirits. Despite an eloquent defence from Leir, he had been proclaimed guilty of causing her death in a court presided over by Goneril as her first "painful" duty as chieftainess, and had chosen, in a bold voice that had pierced Cordelia's already broken heart, to die at Mavelle's feet so as to escort her safely to the Otherworld.

Cordelia had not been allowed to see him. He was, Goneril had told her, "preparing his spirit for its new journey".

'But surely part of preparing for a journey is saying goodbye to those you will leave behind?' Cordelia had protested.

'A royal daughter should not taint herself by contact with a criminal,' had been the pious reply.

'A royal daughter should have mercy for all,' Cordelia had shot back, but it had done no good.

They had kept Taran under such close guard that even in the dead of night she had not been able to get close enough to whisper words of comfort and love to him. And now she must watch him die. She must, at least, do him that service.

She forced herself to look up, knowing her eyes were red from crying. It mattered little. Anyone looking at her would assume she was mourning Mavelle, but she had made peace with her grandmother's death the moment she had seen the smile on her forever-stilled face. Cordelia's grief was all for the young man Goneril would callously send after her. And there he was – dressed in a simple white loincloth, his strong body displayed before her so that she ached to touch it and cursed her shyness for not publicly choosing him as husband the very first night she had taken him as a lover. Regan had not been so slow to claim Aledus, nor Goneril Maedoc. What sort of a royal daughter was she to bow so easily to the demands of others? Well, no more.

She planted her feet more firmly in the mud and thanked the spirits of the air for the unpleasant drizzle that was running down the willow branches like tears. Taran's eyes were closed but she knew they would open at some point and when they did, she would be there for him, *with* him. Everyone was gathered now and Olwen, her own eyes nearly as red as Cordelia's, banged three times on the ground with her staff of office and began the slow procession sun-wise around Mavelle's platform. She had been installed there this morning and already the birds were pecking at her. She'd have liked that, Cordelia thought, for every time one of them took to the skies they'd carry a little bit of her with them.

Olwen set up a mournful chanting and Caireen joined in, higher and sweeter, as if Mavelle's spirit were soaring upwards. The hand-picked crowd gave a whisper of approval but Cordelia stayed silent, her eyes fixed on Taran. And now, as if sensing her, his eyes did open and looked into hers and it was as if they were somewhere else – as if they were talking in the forge or kissing beneath the trees or sharing water at a babbling spring. *I love you*, she mouthed, saw his body relax in its bonds, and willed herself to think of happy times, of teasing and sharing and loving, not of blame and anger and death.

She looked around for her father but he was nowhere to be seen. He was angry about the verdict, she knew, but surely he would not miss saying goodbye to Mavelle? She searched amongst the subdued crowd standing between the willow branches. But now Olwen had completed her three turns and as the chanting died down, Goneril stepped forward. For a moment Olwen stood in her way, as if she might stop the ceremony or as if, perhaps, she had forgotten where she should be. Then Goneril leaned in and kissed her softly, moving her gently aside and taking centre stage herself.

No, a voice moaned within Cordelia, but she hushed it; there was no room for weakness now. She glanced to Mavelle, beseeching her grandmother to take Taran with her into the Otherworld and perhaps, if his time in this earthly cycle was done, on to Elysium. Her eyes fell on a scrap of red checked fabric tied to one of the branches behind her. It seemed to mean something but she was too distraught to remember what and could only see it as Taran's poor heart exposed before them all. Sobs racked her body but she forced them deep inside so her core vibrated with sadness. Her feet stayed firm in the mud as Goneril came forward, beautiful in mourning white.

'Tonight we must bid farewell to our dearest and most loved Chieftainess Mavelle,' she proclaimed, her voice wavering touchingly. Cordelia was not fooled. 'Tonight we send her to the Otherworld with our blessing and our prayers for her most deserved rest and safe onward journey. May we meet her again one day.'

I'm sure she'll have a few things to say if you do, Cordelia thought bitterly but she crushed that thought inside her too. She was here for Taran; she would weep later.

'But she will not go alone.'

Later, Cordelia urged herself, though unshed tears seemed to fill her to the brim. She looked urgently around for Leir but still could not see him anywhere.

'For this noble smith, Taran, mindful of his own culpability in our chieftainess's death ... ' Goneril paused as if willing Cordelia to protest but she clutched it deep inside, ' ... has volunteered to escort her to the Otherworld.' The crowd shifted, murmured uneasy appreciation. 'It will be a comfort to my grandmother not to travel alone.'

Goneril lifted her hand and a knife, long and thin, flashed before them all. She turned to Taran and Cordelia kept her eyes on his. Let all who wished, see. She would not deny him her love in his last brave moments. She saw his body quiver, his heart almost leap against his skin, as if imploring to be left there, but, unwavering,

Goneril raised the dagger high. Cordelia felt Regan put a supportive hand under her elbow, but although it held her body firm, her head swirled and her heart screamed. Someone cried out, Olwen perhaps, but it was too late as Goneril brought the dagger down, fierce and hard.

But then, at the last moment, Leir stepped from under the platform with Mavelle's own hawk held on a short chain around his arm and the dagger found its target in the creature's breast. It gave a single, piercing shriek, cast its wings wide so that it momentarily obscured Taran's face, and died. Goneril blinked uncertainly, but Leir was reaching up and laying the great bird reverently at Mavelle's feet and the small crowd were sighing in joy and calling blessings on the new chieftainess. She looked slowly around them all, her eyes simmering with fury at their weakness. Olwen was on her knees and behind her Maedoc and Caireen looked at each other in astonishment and then back to Goneril. For a moment longer the chieftainess hesitated and then, ever the show-woman, she dropped the bloodied dagger and turned to kiss Taran loudly on the lips.

'Smith,' she declared, 'I pardon you. I wish to start my reign of my beloved Coritani with an act of mercy. With peace and forgiveness, joy and optimism. Unbind him!'

A druid freed Taran who collapsed to his knees. He gazed up at the platform, hands raised to the hawk who had taken his place at Mavelle's feet, and Cordelia, too, looked to her grandmother, sure her soul would be happy for her beloved smith to live on. The wind was rising and the dead ruler's cloak seemed to flap a little, as if she and her hawk were leaving.

Cordelia smiled and then something hardened in her mind and she swung around to look from Mavelle's torn cloak to the scrap of red material still hanging on the willow. Goneril's Imbolc wish. Cordelia had suspected the fabric had been cut from the chieftainess' cloak and now she was sure of it – the eldest daughter of the Coritani had been set on taking her place at the head of the tribe at the start of this year and had dared to ask the Goddess' help to secure it. But, ever impatient, had she then taken the matter into her own hands? Fearfully, Cordelia's eyes slid to her elder sister. Goneril had been prepared to engineer Taran's death for turning down her proposal; had she engineered Mavelle's also?

It was a thought too wicked to countenance and Cordelia shook it away to dwell on later. For now, she should have only one concern – Taran's safety. Every fibre of Leir's body was taut with the success of his action and as he met her eyes she knew what she had to do. She, too, had a hawk to offer her lover at this critical time.

She stepped forward.

'Chieftainess, you do the smith great kindness.' Goneril forced a gracious smile onto her face. 'And I, learning from your example, and working as your sister and fellow royal in the service of this, our beloved tribe, will match that kindness.' Goneril frowned. Cordelia pushed swiftly on. 'To bind this pardoned man to the service of the Coritani, I, Princess Cordelia, will take him as my husband.'

A gasp ran around the elders and then the cheers came again, even louder than before. Goneril's eyes blazed pure fire but she was stranded before her people, as Taran had been when she had claimed him at her wedding. Cordelia dropped to her knees before her sister.

'I beg your blessing, Chieftainess, on this match.'

She bowed her head, staring at the ground. Inside, she was quaking, but she had been too slow to act before and could not be so again. Taran had met his apparent fate with bravery and she must support him. The people quieted as everyone looked expectantly to Goneril. She put her hand on her sister's head and Cordelia felt it pushing down on her hard, as if she would drive her into the mud right there before them all. But not even Goneril could do that.

'I grant your request,' she said.

Cordelia heard her teeth grind on the words but the sound was drowned out by the renewed cheers and now Leir was sweeping her up into his arms and kissing her and linking her hand with Taran's before the people, and somehow, some blessed how, she had turned a funeral into a wedding. She only prayed it had not earned her Goneril's eternal hatred.

Chapter Twenty-four

The next day

'Cordelia, little sister, welcome.' Goneril came sweeping forward as Cordelia entered the royal house the next morning. Uneasily, Cordelia took her proffered hands and let her sister kiss both her cheeks. 'Did you sleep well?'

In truth, she had barely slept at all. She had tumbled into bed with Taran when the strange wake had finally danced itself out, tangling tightly up with him to feel the pulse of his lifeblood against every possible part of her. He was alive. And he would be her husband. She had won.

'I slept feeling blessed in your approval of my wedding,' she said cautiously.

'Good. Good. It is time you married, Dee, time you stepped up as a woman.'

'Stepped up?'

'Though you were, perhaps, a little precipitate asking me in front of everyone at such a time.'

Cordelia looked uncomfortably around the royal house. Maedoc was reclining on a pile of cushions by the fire, Olwen was huddled on a stool to one side and Regan was doing one of her strange stretches on the other. They all avoided looking at her. Only Leir, standing with his legs planted wide by the door, gave her a smile of encouragement.

'I thought you would appreciate the ceremony, Goneril,' she said carefully. 'And the way you spared Taran inspired me so.'

'Hmm. That was not me, you know, but our father.'

'Then I must thank him.'

Goneril shot a glance of pure loathing in Leir's direction.

'Thank him for undermining his chieftainess? Thank him for killing a good hawk? Thank him for disrupting the careful ceremony our own anointed high druidess had planned?'

For answer Leir planted his feet a little wider, defiant before his eldest daughter, but his hands were whittling away at a small chunk of wood and Cordelia suspected this confrontation was costing him far more than he was prepared to show. She glanced to Olwen, huddled on her stool as if trying to hold herself together.

'I hope the high druidess will forgive me but it seems that at least now we can bring forth joy from sorrow.'

Olwen looked up and stared at her, wild-eyed.

'You are confident in your choice of husband, Cordelia?'

Her voice was harsh and Cordelia frowned.

'Confident?'

'In his integrity?

'Of course. Taran is the most honest man I know.'

'Sweet.' Goneril rose and came over to Cordelia, leaning in to drop a kiss on her forehead. 'But it is best, I think, if we are all sure – for your own safety.'

Cordelia drew herself up straight.

'I *will* marry him, Goneril.'

Goneril gave a little laugh.

'Of course you will, Dee-Dee. Of course you will. At Rantaranos.'

'Rantaranos?!' Cordelia was horrified. Rantaranos was the extra moon-turn added every three years to keep the lunar calendar aligned with the turning of the seasons. The Coritani honoured it as a sacred gift of extra time but it was a long way off. 'Rantaranos is not until Imbolc.'

'Correct, Dee-Dee. Imbolc – your favourite watery ceremony. A time of renewal, when the dark days of Samhain are over and we are done mourning our beloved Mavelle. And her hawk.'

She glared at Leir who paid her no attention.

'It's not a bad idea, Dee,' Regan said, getting up and coming over. 'Rantaranos is special so will call great blessings on the match. And it is not, you know, so far away.'

'The time will fly,' Goneril agreed airily. 'You can breed us some more hounds and I can keep an eye on Taran to be sure he is . . . fit for you.'

'He *is* fit, I swear it on my royal blood.'

She touched her hand to her triskele amulet. Goneril did not mirror her.

'Sweet,' she said again. 'But as your chieftainess, I would rather take extra care. And, besides, he can help us to prepare for the feast.'

Cordelia frowned.

'What can Taran do towards a feast?'

Goneril gave a sly grin.

'I want a new beacon stand.'

'A new beacon?' Olwen's head snapped up and she fixed red eyes on Goneril. 'But the beacon was planted in the earth by the ancestors and has shone a light on the Coritani forever. It cannot be replaced.'

Goneril gave a strange little smile.

'Maedoc said you would say that. He says druids are . . . what is it, Maedoc?'

'Such traditionalists,' he drawled.

'Not all of them,' Caireen said.

'Not all of them,' he allowed with a small smile. 'But most.'

'Of course we are traditionalists,' Olwen said, leaping up with

232

something, at last, of her old energy. 'And with good reason. A tribe has its roots in the past.'

'And its eyes on the future,' Goneril said calmly. 'Fret not, Olwen, I have thought about this. A smith with Taran's talents can easily rework the metal from the existing beacon into the new one so that continuity is maintained. We can grow out of our past.' She beamed at the crumpled druidess. 'Change is not always bad, my flame – we must be able to move, must we not?'

'Move?' Cordelia asked in alarm. 'You want to move the tribe, Goneril?'

'No, Dee. Goodness, you are almost as literal as Olwen. I have ideas, big ideas to take the tribe forward and extend our influence further. Maybe even our rule.'

'Our rule?'

Goneril waved her quiet.

'It is progress, little sister, like Grandmother wanting to fly.'

'That was not progress.'

'But it could be. In time. Then she would not have died in vain. Grandmother was a woman of great enthusiasms and interests and we did our best to harness those. It ended in tragedy but it was, nonetheless, the right thing to do. We must allow our more talented tribal members to exploit their own talents, must we not, Olwen?'

Olwen nodded slowly and her misted eyes seemed to regain a little focus.

'We must. All people should be allowed to concentrate on those tasks that suit them best. Some are seekers, made to look for new truths and ways of doing things. This we know, yes?' Leir gave a grudging nod and Olwen rushed on. 'Some, like Princess Cordelia, have abilities with animals. Others, like Princess Regan, are fighters.'

'Warriors,' Goneril put in.

'Warriors?' Leir questioned.

'It is a more apt word, Father. Warriors are fit and fierce and clever with a sword. Regan is using her skills to develop our training school at Breedon and people are coming from far and wide to join us.'

'From other tribes?' Leir asked sharply, looking to Regan.

'Yes, Father,' she said nervously. 'We train young men and women from all over.'

'Like who?'

'Like the Iceni and the Catuvellauni, the Brigantes and the Setantii.'

'The Setantii?! You are training our enemies to fight?'

Regan looked nervously at Goneril.

'To fight *for* us, Father,' she said smoothly.

'But why would they do that?'

Goneril gave an exaggerated sigh.

'I've told you – because we are the better tribe. Because *I* am the better ruler so they would choose *me*.'

'Over their own tribe?'

'Oh, Father, can you not see beyond your own boundaries?'

'It sounds as if I need to look to those boundaries if you are sending trained fighters over them.'

Goneril shook her head pityingly.

'If they wish to go – and most do not – we sell them on to others. They are like grain.'

'Grain, Goneril?'

'Or hounds if you prefer – a commodity, a way of increasing both our wealth and our reputation. We are, of course, keeping the best warriors for ourselves. We are not stupid, Father.'

'No, you are not stupid, but Goneril—'

'Hear me out, please. Some are breeders, here to bring strong new talent to the tribe, and they must be protected.'

'All, surely, are breeders?'

'Perhaps. But perhaps some are better off without that burden to distract them from what they do best.'

At her side, Regan shifted awkwardly. Cordelia leaned towards her but before she could ask what was wrong, Leir was talking again.

'So you see our tribe members simply as seekers, fighters or breeders, Goneril?'

'And farmers,' she said with a smooth smile. 'Obviously, we need farmers – men and women to grow the grain and harvest it.'

'We *all* harvest the grain.'

'We do now,' she agreed with exaggerated patience. 'But it need not be that way. Let those who are less – that is, those who have a talent for getting the most from the fields – work them.'

'So that the seekers can sit on their arses looking at the birds and the stars?'

'So that everyone can do what they do best.'

'Right.' Leir paced around the edge of the communal area, running his hand around the willow walls as he went. 'So take me, under-chieftain of the tribe for many long years in your dear mother's stead, creator of Burrough and now Breedon, breeder of you and your royal sisters, fighter in defence of our borders, seeker of new ways of ploughing and building and trading . . . and, yes, farmer with the rest in the rich fields that we all share. You would reduce me, all of us, to single jobs when we are capable of so much more?'

'It's not like that, Father. It's about making the best use of people's different talents.'

'It's about status, Goneril. And it is wrong. You cannot restrict someone into only one part of him or herself. If this is your vision, Daughter, then I want no part of it.'

'But, Father—'

'No part!' Leir strode to the door. 'And the elders will feel the same.'

'The problem with elders,' Goneril said lightly, 'is that they are old.'

Leir spun back, glaring at her.

'They are experienced, knowledgeable, wise. You ignore that at your peril, Daughter.'

'Or at theirs.'

Leir threw his hands in the air.

'Danu help us, I thought you were foolish when you tried to take the life of the best smith we've ever had. Now I think you are actually insane. I am going to spend some time alone, honouring our lost chieftainess, and then I am going back to Burrough. There is work to be done to clear the fields for the dark days and I, for one, wish to be with my people to do it. Anyone who wishes to join me is very welcome.'

He shot a look at Cordelia and then yanked the door open, letting a cloud of icy cold inside, and disappeared. Cordelia turned nervously back to Goneril. The chieftainess was glaring after Leir, copper fire burning in her green eyes. Caireen was fidgeting by Leir's vacated stool, Regan was staring hard at the floor and Olwen just stood, frozen. Only Maedoc looked relaxed and, as his hand quietly caressed Goneril's neck, she closed her eyes for a moment. When she opened them again she was smiling. She patted the cushions next to her and Cordelia went nervously forward.

'Poor Father grows old,' Goneril said, her voice silky soft.

Cordelia looked at her in alarm.

'Not that old.'

Goneril patted her hand.

'You will not see it, Dee, as you are with him every day, but since I have moved to Beacon it has become sadly clear to me. To you also, I am sure, Regan?' She held out her other hand and Regan joined them on the cushions.

'He looks shakier than he used to,' she admitted.

'He is not shakier. He—'

'Hush, Dee,' Goneril soothed. 'Don't fret. I am not saying the Otherworld is calling him. It is simply that it can be hard for those with their feet planted so firmly in the past to see the possibilities in the future.'

'A way in which people are tied to doing only one thing in life?'

'A way in which people are liberated from having to do things they are less good at so they can excel at those that suit them best.

It is hard, perhaps, for us to truly understand, being royal. We are privileged enough already to be allowed to do what suits us. Consider, Dee, if you were in one of the lesser households you would still have to cook and clean, to tend the crops and milk the cow, to weave and sew. Under those conditions you would, I think, be far less effective at breeding dogs, would you not?'

Cordelia fought to consider this. There was a certain logic to Goneril's words. She was terrible with a weaving frame and after just a few painful days of tying herself and everyone else up in tearful knots, she had been allowed to stop. Royals could order their clothes to be made by someone else but in other households that was not a possibility, not unless you used Goneril's system in which those with a talent for weaving made cloth for all, and those with a talent for, say, fighting, honed that to protect them in return.

'I sort of see it,' she said cautiously.

'I knew you would. Women are much more naturally astute.' Goneril leaned forward suddenly, touching her fingers to her amulet. '*We* are the royal daughters; *we* should be in charge. Our father has done his best since Mother died and should be praised for that, but maybe he has reached his limits. Men are best kept to battle and bed – are they not, Regan?'

Regan gave a small smile.

'Battle and bed,' she echoed.

'And Father, surely, grows too old for either.'

'He does not,' Cordelia protested hotly, 'ask Caireen.'

Goneril looked to the tiny druidess who blushed prettily.

'He is lusty enough in *intent*,' she said slyly.

Goneril shook her head.

'Poor Father. We must take care of him. Perhaps, Olwen, you have some herbs that could help him?'

'Herbs, Goneril?' Olwen looked confused again but Caireen leaped up.

'I have some herbal knowledge, Chieftainess. Nothing like Olwen's, of course, but the high druidess is grieving for her

237

mother-in-science and does not need to be bothered with this. Let me see to it.'

She bowed lowed before Goneril and Cordelia saw her sister's eyes travel up and down the pretty young woman. It looked, for a moment, as if Caireen peered up at her through her long lashes, but she surely would not dare?

'Yes,' Goneril said decisively. 'Yes, that would be very good. Very kind. Is that not kind, Olwen?'

The high druidess looked at her but said nothing.

'Very kind,' Maedoc agreed loudly. 'You do great service to the Coritani, Caireen.'

Caireen straightened, smiled around at them all.

'It will be my honour and my pleasure. I'll go and find him now. I know how to soothe him.'

'He's not a baby,' Cordelia snapped.

Caireen turned beautiful violet eyes her way.

'Oh, I know that, Cordelia. But we all, do you not think, need soothing sometimes? A quiet Samhain with me will soon sort him out.'

'But—'

'And then it will be Rantaranos, Cordelia,' Goneril said. 'And your wedding. We will all three be married. Royal daughters together, as was intended, and the men there to serve us and not to meddle.'

Her eyes followed Caireen out of the door and hardened to purest, darkest gold. Cordelia could only pray that Taran would be safe here until the seasons turned and brought him, finally, to her side.

Chapter Twenty-five

BURROUGH HILL

Dumannios; Dark days (December)

'Princess! Please, Princess, you must come. It's your father. He's not well.'

'My father?'

Cordelia leaped up from Endellion's side and stared at Solinus in horror. The Belgic hound had recently been impregnated by an enthusiastic Anghus and Cordelia had just been feeling the pups move inside her belly. The shift from coming life to possible death was impossible to comprehend.

'He was fine at dinner,' she stuttered foolishly.

'He is not fine now,' was the dark reply. 'Please come.'

'Of course.'

She leaped up and rushed after him, but when she pulled open the doghouse door she saw the snow swirling around as if chased by demons and flinched back. It had been snowing lightly for several days now, coating the world in purest white, but this was a new level of fury from the ice spirits.

'Sorry, Princess,' Solinus said, and she realised the poor man was standing there in the storm while she hesitated in the doorway.

'Not at all.'

She reached for her cloak, on the hook by the door, and clutching it tightly around her, followed him out into the gale. Anghus seemed to think it a great joke and capered happily around with the whirling flakes but Cordelia kept her head low and was grateful when she reached the shelter of the royal roundhouse. The fire was high and she moved instinctively towards it before a deep groan from Leir's bedchamber at the back caught her attention and she ran to his side. Her poor father was thrashing on his bed, clutching at his stomach and groaning as if someone were sticking knives into every part of him. Magunna was trying valiantly to hold him down but his fever seemed to have given him god-like strength.

'What happened?' Cordelia demanded.

'I don't know,' Magunna stuttered. 'It was so fast. He said he felt a little sick when he went to bed. Caireen made him a potion and it seemed to help but then I was woken by his raging and found him on fire.'

She looked desperately at Cordelia as if she might have the solution but she was no medicine-woman.

'Where's Caireen?'

'She's gone.'

'Gone!'

'Gone to Beacon at all speed to fetch medicines from Olwen. She told us to keep him cool and try and get water down him but I don't think it's going to be enough. That's why I sent for you, Dee. I . . . I'm scared.'

She looked to Solinus who was as pale as the snow-covered compound outside and Cordelia drew them both close.

'We must do all we can and trust to the Goddess to pull him through.'

All night they sat at Leir's side, mopping his brow with cool cloths and talking away to him with no idea whether he could hear them or not. The water was fresh from the spring and laced with ice but it did little to cool his burning skin. He cried out constantly, contorting his body into terrible shapes as he did battle with whatever evil spirit was crawling within, but as dawn crept, cold and thin, across the snowy land he fell quiet. It was some relief and Cordelia could only pray that it did not mean he was hovering on the brink of the Otherworld.

'What would we do without him?' she asked Magunna.

The older lady wiped away a tear and looked at Cordelia.

'You would rule Burrough, Dee – and rule it well.'

Cordelia shook her head.

'No. I'm too young. I'm not ready to rule.'

'Is anyone ever ready to rule?'

'Goneril was.'

'Goneril *thought* she was; it does not mean she was right.' Solinus gave an alarmed cough and Magunna caught herself. 'I talk too much. Ignore me. I'm sure Goneril will be a fine ruler – but you will be better.'

'Magunna! That's nonsense.'

The older lady folded her hands over her bosom, as she had done so many times throughout their childhood. Anghus laid his chin on Cordelia's knee and whimpered and she knew exactly how he felt. Beyond the roundhouse she could hear the wind whipping the snow around the compound, cutting them fiercely off from the rest of the world. The others were looking to her, as the royal daughter, to lead them through this and she would – she must – but she longed for Taran's support.

'I just want my father to get better,' she said, replacing the cloth on Leir's forehead. 'I want him to get better and the snows to stop and Imbolc to come and . . .'

'And us all to stand at the Rantaranos altar?' Solinus suggested.

Cordelia nodded miserably and Magunna drew her into her arms.

'Patience, child. Good things are worth waiting for. Like pups, they take time to form and grow to readiness.'

Cordelia grunted.

'I find that I am getting less patient as I grow older.'

'Older!' Magunna let out a rough laugh. 'Cordelia, you are but sixteen years old.'

'It is enough.'

'It is.'

'So what do I do?'

Magunna shrugged.

'You wait. This delay will seem as nothing once you are wed.'

Cordelia ground her teeth. Waiting was so hard. So much time with Taran already seemed to have been wasted and Samhain stretched before her like the darkest forest.

'I pray you are right.'

'I know I am. Think of Gleva and Map.'

Cordelia frowned at her.

'What of them?'

'They had to wait years to marry.'

'They did not!' Cordelia said indignantly. 'He's told me the story a hundred times. He came to Gleva's village when she was gathering the grain in the fields and she brought him water and her smile was so soft and her eyes so kind and her breasts so ripe that he knew immediately he must make her his.'

Magunna laughed softly.

'He always tells it well. And then what, pray?'

'And then he took the cup and drank the water and when she reached out her hand to take it back, he seized it and said, "I want to spend the rest of my life with you." Where's the waiting in that?'

Magunna laughed again.

'As I said, he tells it well but not, perhaps, as fully as he might. Gleva told me the true version once.'

Cordelia stared at her.

'The true version?'

The old woman glanced to Solinus who nodded her on.

'The true version,' she confirmed, 'in which Gleva's reply was, "Don't be ridiculous, I'm getting married beneath the Lughnasad moon".'

'What?' Cordelia looked from Magunna to Solinus, astonished. 'So what happened then?'

'Map had to move on and Gleva stayed in her village and the Lughnasad moon rose.'

'And Map rode in and challenged her groom?'

'No.'

'Gleva told the groom her heart had been stolen and came to Map?'

'No. She married the man.'

'What?!'

'She had no choice,' Magunna said easily. 'It was all arranged. And she told me he was a nice person who did not deserve to be ditched for "some chancer with fire in his eyes and far too much cheek".'

That certainly sounded like something Gleva would say but still Cordelia could not take it in.

'So how, then, did they end up together?'

'Simple – time. Map travelled far and wide but always made sure his road crossed back through Gleva's village. They talked. Often.'

'Talked?'

'Just talked, yes.'

'And then?'

Magunna shrugged.

'And then one day, about two years later, her husband died.'

Cordelia stared.

'That's it? He just died?'

'People do, Dee.'

'It's not much of a story!'

243

'Which is why Map never tells it that way.' Magunna smiled and pressed a warm hand over Cordelia's. 'He did nothing grand or brave or skilful, Dee, but he did persist. He travelled that road time and again and one day when he rode in, he found her alone. And again he said—'

'Now can I spend the rest of my life with you?' Cordelia suggested.

Magunna grinned.

'Exactly. Simple. Sometimes the only way is to wait.'

Cordelia sighed.

'It's a very dull way.'

The old lady leaned over and dropped a kiss on her forehead.

'It is. But learn from Map, sweet one – one day when you look back, it won't even be worth including in your story.'

Cordelia nodded slowly, praying her dear friend was right. She would wait and one day she would surely marry the man she loved.

'Thank you Magunna,' she said but at that moment Leir gave a low moan and she was jerked back into her present concerns.

'Father? Father, are you well?'

She leaned over him, willing him to respond, but there was nothing more.

'Is he dying?' she asked, finally daring to speak the word out loud.

But at that Leir shook his head so wildly that the cloth fell off and landed with a splat across Anghus's muzzle. The dog leaped back, shaking his big head furiously, and a laugh burst out of Cordelia. She lifted the cloth off the poor hound and leaned closer in to Leir.

'Can you hear me, Father?'

He gave a grunt, then said: 'Not dying. Too busy for dying.'

Tears sprang to Cordelia's eyes and without thinking she pressed the cloth to them. It was cold with ice-crystals and itchy with dog hair but she welcomed the sensations. They made her feel alive, aware, hopeful.

'The fever may be breaking,' Magunna said. 'Give him water if you can.'

That, however, elicited another shake of the head from Leir.

'Ale,' he grunted. Then opened his eyes and looked straight at Cordelia. 'Ale, Daughter. I'm parched.'

Cordelia smiled down at him as Solinus went running to fetch ale from Nairina. They might not have whatever fancy medicines Caireen had ridden into the night to fetch but it seemed their own everyday brews might just do the trick. And, indeed, when Solinus returned, his cloak coated with snow, Leir sat up, fully alert.

'It snows?' Solinus nodded grimly, brushing the white coating off his cloak.

'Badly?'

'It is up over the lower edge of the roofs, Chief.'

'Then why is everyone not in here, keeping warm together?'

Cordelia looked to the others and back to Leir.

'You were so ill, Father.'

He gave a little snort.

'I am but one man, Dee. No point saving me and losing everyone else. Call the tribe inside immediately – and fetch me more of that ale.'

He had, it seemed, shaken off his fever completely and Cordelia ran gladly to do his bidding. The wind had finally died down and the rising sun was casting a pretty pink blush across the land but the reality was not so benign. The snows could be fatal to anyone without sufficient fuel or food and it was important to gather the tribe – those within the compound, and especially those without – into the royal house to weather the storm together. Already she could hear people gathering beyond the gates and she rushed to tell the guards to let them in.

Had Caireen really ridden out in this? she wondered as she welcomed the bedraggled group of people who'd trekked to them from the open farmsteads on the plains. Looking to the west, she sent up a prayer to Danu that she was safe. She did not like the young druidess but certainly did not wish her frozen into the earth. And then, as the sun tipped over the horizon and turned the snow to flames, she sent up another prayer that Taran's forge fires would keep him warm through these dark days until Rantaranos came and she could do the job herself.

Chapter Twenty-six

BEACON HILL

Dumannios; Dark days (December)

Taran tumbled through the door of the forge, snow thick on his cloak and only a frozen-solid hare to show for his harsh trek into the forest. He switched his cloak for a blanket – thin but at least dry – and stoked up the fire. With the cold biting a moon-turn back, Goneril had set him to sharpening axe blades to hack wood from the forest and he'd asked to live in the forge to better complete the task. It put him outside the compound at night but no one would attack in this bitter weather and if sometimes he feared whatever beasts might threaten out here, they were nothing to those within the fortress.

At least he had his work. He looked to the iron beacon stand, set in the corner of his fancy new forge awaiting installation when the snows cleared. Though he hated all it stood for, he was proud of it too. He had worked the iron from the old one into thin vine patterns to trail from the base up and around the solid stem to the sturdy basket. It gave the beacon the look of having grown up out of the ancient Coritani heartlands, but it also, more privately, symbolised the love that Cordelia had twined around him and that, if he could just get through these dark days, would be his forever.

He wrapped his arms around himself, desperately trying to pretend they were Cordelia's, but his imagination was a poor substitute for her living body and he turned his attention to the hare instead. He was just setting it at the hearth to thaw when a knock sounded at the door. He started. No one had been out of the compound for days. The lucky few were shut up inside Beacon's big walls, protected by Goneril's guards and no doubt enjoying the plentiful grain still in the royal stores.

The only movement had been three days ago when Caireen had come riding up Beacon Hill at dawn, hallooing the guards imperiously. They had scrambled from their brazier but snow had backed up against the gate and it had taken the help of numerous people dragged blearily from their beds to crank it open wide enough to let her slide through. By then she had been cursing like one of Regan's coarsest warriors and Taran had hurried to find out what was going on.

'It's poor Leir,' she'd said. 'He's raging with fever. I have come to fetch medicines to bring him back to us.'

Her violet eyes had been rimmed with red, though possibly as much from the harsh ride as from sorrow for she had disappeared into the royal house and not, as far as he'd seen, come out again since. He'd worried that Goneril had ruled it was too dangerous for her to ride back to Burrough and had gone to offer to take the medicines himself, but had been told it was all in hand and sent back to his axe heads. He had considered going anyway, to help Leir and to support Cordelia if, Danu forbid, anything happened to her dear father, but Goneril had sent a guard to 'help him' and, besides, the snows had kept falling, making it near impossible to track ten strides into the woods, let alone all the way to Burrough.

Now he hastened to the door to find, to his astonishment, Aledus outside.

'Prince! Come in, come in. What are you doing at Beacon?'

Aledus slid inside and shook the snow from his clothes.

'Regan thought it would be good training for the troops to do a snow march.'

'And was it?'

He shrugged.

'We survived so I suppose it was, but I've never been gladder to see Beacon. Not that Goneril was exactly welcoming. They've got a lovely set-up in the ceremonial house, you know. I've never seen so many blankets and furs but they weren't keen to share them with our frozen warriors . . . well, except for that violet-eyed druidess.'

'Caireen? She's still here then?'

'Where else would she be?'

'Taking medicine to Leir – her lover.'

'Well, he's not her lover at the moment, believe me, though even she can't fit them all in her bed and there's been much grumbling. Goneril says she needs space because of her pregnancy but really, Taran, how much room does one slightly swollen belly take up? Too much for me so I thought I'd come and see this new beacon.' He drew a jug from behind his back. 'I brought wine.'

Taran seized on it. Fetching two goblets, he poured them both generous measures and, taking an iron from the fire, plunged it into each in turn to set the rich wine steaming. Even the scent of the drink set his head whirling wonderfully and he held a cup out to his royal friend.

'To you, Aledus – a beacon of light in the darkness.'

Aledus laughed.

'Why not go into the royal house yourself and then you can have this all the time?'

Taran raised an eyebrow and prodded at the hare, which was starting to sizzle gently as the flames rose.

'Is that your dinner?'

'Afraid so.'

'A feast.' The two men pulled up a bench and drank deeply. 'I haven't had a chance to congratulate you on your upcoming marriage.'

'Is it upcoming?' Taran asked gloomily. 'At the moment it feels as if these dark days will never end.'

'Oh, they will. They always do.' Aledus set his boots on the edge of the hearth. 'Patience, man, it will all be worth it.'

'Just a glimpse of Cordelia would be worth it right now.'

'Oh, dear, like that, is it? Does she love you too?'

'I believe so.'

'Lucky man. To be loved by a princess is a blessing.'

'Maybe, if you're a prince.' Taran didn't feel lucky, just fed up.

'Oh, there are limitations for princes too.'

Taran squinted at him.

'Limitations?'

Aledus leaned in, not that there was anyone to hear him out here in the wilds beyond the compound.

'I am not permitted to . . . to plant my seed within her.'

'What?!'

'Hush, Taran. It is for good reason. Goneril has brought twenty of our best men and women to Beacon for her own guard, so we need to build up more. Regan is too valuable to the training school to be wasted on childbirth.'

'Wasted?' Taran breathed. 'How can furthering the royal line ever be a waste?'

'That's what I said. And I also said, who would know? But Regan pointed out that if she falls pregnant it will be obvious to Goneril straight away.'

'And yet it would be too late for her to do anything about it.'

Aledus just looked at him and Taran grimaced. In his head a hawk shrieked. It was never too late for Goneril to act and the thought of what she might do with her new "guard" didn't bear considering.

'So can you not ... you know?'

'Oh, we can. We do. Goneril encourages it. It is good for us to be in touch with our bodies. It is divine.'

'It certainly is.'

Aledus allowed himself a gruff laugh.

'Too divine sometimes. I have to ... withdraw. Spill my seed on the ground, not in the princess.'

'Oh.'

Taran fought to take this in but even as he did so another knock sounded out and both men leaped so violently that they knocked the bench over.

'Who the hell is that?' Aledus asked, rushing to the window. 'Is someone spying on us?'

'Of course not,' Taran said but his heart was beating hard as he went to the door.

He opened it a crack. Standing on the doorstep was no spy but a shivering woman with a child on her hip and three more tangled about her legs.

'Please, Smith,' she said, her voice trembling, 'could we possibly come into your forge for a time? Our wood is gone and the children will freeze if they have to endure another night without a fire.'

'Of course.' He ushered her in instantly, recognising her from one of the homesteads nearby. 'Danu bless you, of course you can. Please. But have you not been up to the compound to ask for shelter?'

She looked nervously at Aledus as the children ran to the fire, stretching little hands eagerly towards its warmth. The prince gave her a smile and went to supervise them and, reassured, she turned back to Taran.

'We went there first but were told there is no room.'

'No room?!'

'The heiress needs space – because of her pregnancy.'

Taran looked down at the woman, whose own belly was swollen far further than Goneril's, and his heart raged at the chieftainess' cruelty. She'd had the gates cranked open for Caireen, not to mention for Regan's warriors, but she'd turned this poor starving woman away? She did not need his rage, however, but his charity, such as it was.

'I have little food, I'm afraid, but the fire is high and all are welcome.'

'All?' she asked, a note of hope entering her voice.

He nodded firmly.

'All.'

The eldest child, once sufficiently warmed, ran back out to pass on the word and as the remains of the iron-grey day unfolded, people from the outlying homesteads began arriving in small groups, bringing whatever food they had. By nightfall there were near thirty people and they filled the big new forge with thanks and chatter and even laughter.

Aledus had reluctantly left for fear of Regan worrying about him but had promised to send food and, true to his word, two guards arrived with bread, meat and even a handful of sweet pastries, presumably sneaked from the bulging royal table. Taran's impromptu guests made short work of them all, then someone pulled out a pipe and music filled the forge.

'You, Taran, know better how to feed the people than the high-born folks up in the compound,' a burly man called Bardo said to him as the fire burned high and the ale sunk low.

Taran put up his hands.

'Not me! I'm taking charity the same as you.'

'But sharing it out equally.'

'Well, of course,' Taran said. 'It's the Coritani way.'

'Not anymore,' Bardo said darkly. 'What you eat up there now depends on where you sit at the table.'

'Table?'

'Goneril has brought the side tables into the centre of the round-house and we all have to sit at them in set places,' someone supplied.

'With her and her cronies at the top.'

'Top?' Taran queried. 'What do you mean, the top?'

He had not eaten in the compound for many days but how could it have changed so much, so quickly?

'The heiress has her table at one end, set higher than the others.'

'With the elders?'

Bardo shifted uncomfortably from one foot to the other.

'She has granted the elders a rest.'

'A rest?'

'She says they have worked hard and deserve to see out their days in ease. Which is true, I suppose.'

'And has ever been so,' Taran agreed. 'But counselling the chieftainess takes little strength and the elders, surely, hold the wisdom of the tribe.'

Bardo shrugged uncomfortably.

'Goneril says it is more important to look forward than back. She says we need energy and vision to lead us forward. That's why she sits up high at dinner, so all can see her if we have need of her – yet no one can get close for the guards all around.'

Taran frowned; this was sounding worse and worse. He'd known Goneril had him under close watch but had not realised she was doing the same to all the tribespeople.

'Guards – at dinner?'

'Guards at everything,' Bardo shot back. 'Including in the fields. They are there to check we are doing things right.'

'But surely you must know what is "right" better than they do?'

'Apparently not. Apparently they think we can do it better than we have before – produce more grain.'

'Have you, then, gone short?'

'No! Not of grain, nor wood, nor fuel but Goneril wants more of them all.'

'I suppose,' someone put in nervously, 'more fuel would be good right now.'

Taran looked around at the people huddled around his big fire.

'But have we not found a solution?' he said. 'Together? No guard called this gathering, just a struggling mother. Yet here we are.'

'That's true.'

All were listening now and he felt self-conscious before them but this was important.

'What will happen if we grow more grain?' he asked. They all looked at him curiously. 'Where will the extra go?'

'Into the grain pits.'

'And then?'

'And then to, to trade.'

'For what?'

'For luxuries,' one woman said. 'For better wool and softer beds and stronger fire-dogs.'

'For whom?'

Everyone's eyes slid towards the crumbs of the feast that Aledus had smuggled out of the compound for them.

'So it's all pointless?' Bardo asked and Taran shook himself, suddenly wary of the trusting faces turned his way.

'Oh, I don't know. Don't listen to me, I'm just a humble smith. There may well be a plan I'm too foolish to see that will benefit us all. And there is little we can do about it now. More wood on the fire, hey, and who knows another song?'

The moment passed but two days later, when the snows began to recede and Goneril sent her guards to cast out all the frozen people who were stopping Taran from working, they left, grumbling amongst themselves. Alone again, he could only forge his axes and cook his hares and send his love across the frozen plains to Cordelia and Leir and pray that news would come soon that both were alive and well. The tribe, it seemed, needed them now more than ever.

Chapter Twenty-seven

BURROUGH HILL

Riuiros; Cold days (January)

'Come on, Endellion. Come on, sweetheart. You're doing so well.' Cordelia crouched down in front of the panting hound and clasped her head in her hands, running her fingers over her soft ears to soothe her. 'Only one more to come, I'm sure of it.'

The poor creature looked into her eyes and Cordelia willed her to understand. Endellion did not seem as natural a mother as Keira and looked bewildered by the squirming creatures squeaking in her bed and latching onto her teats, sucking frantically for sustenance. It was a bitterly cold dawn and the pups needed their mother to keep them close, not try and escape.

'I think it's coming,' said Solinus, crouched at the other end of the poor dog.

'Last one,' Cordelia promised her. 'Just a little longer.'

Endellion gave a whimper then dragged herself to her feet, puppies popping indignantly off her teats. She turned in a confused circle and Cordelia had to scramble to stop her treading on her babies, before Solinus grabbed her and held her firm, whispering soothing woods into her ears as the final pup made its appearance. Cordelia helped ease it out and felt it squirm in her hand and nuzzle hopefully at her fingers and her heart burst with love for the little thing.

'She's settling,' Solinus said, his voice low, as Endellion lay down with her pups, licking at the final one as the others scrambled for milk.

'She is.'

'And they look fine pups.'

'They do,' she agreed but, to her horror, her voice cracked and she felt tears brim in her eyes.

'Cordelia? Are you well?'

Solinus edged round the box towards her but she waved him back, wiping frantically at her eyes and busying herself stowing the final placenta in a bowl with the others. She remembered the last litter, almost a year ago, and pictured Leir bringing Aledus and his cronies rolling into her chamber. She could so vividly see dark-eyed Taran standing quietly at the back and her heart ached to have him here for this special moment.

'I'm a little tired,' she managed. 'As you must be. I'll fetch us some food.'

Solinus looked horrified.

'Let me do that, Princess,' he said, but she waved the offer away. She had to get out before these damned tears overwhelmed her.

'I'm happy to go. I must find my father anyway and tell him the good news. You will watch the pups?'

'Of course.'

Cordelia smiled at him and slid out of the door. The icy air hit her, shocking her instantly awake, and she pulled her cloak close and quickly pushed the doghouse door shut to protect the newborns. She had, a long, easy time ago, promised to send one of them to Prince Lucius and intended to honour that. Making a run for the royal house, she was grateful to find Magunna risen and stoking up the fire.

'You're up early, Dee.'

'Not yet abed,' she told her. 'The pups are born.'

'Wonderful! Congratulations.' The older woman came rushing forward and clasped Cordelia's hands. 'Are all well?'

'Seem to be.'

'It's cold for babies. I've a lovely fur, if you'd like it, to keep them snuggled.'

'That's very kind, Mags, but they'd ruin it.'

'Nonsense – nothing a good wash wouldn't sort. That fur came from an animal so it's only right it should nurture another. I'll bring it over later.'

'Thank you.'

Cordelia clasped her hands, tears threatening again, and Magunna chuckled.

'It's an emotional time becoming a new mother, hey?'

Cordelia laughed and the tears spilled out. She wiped at them. 'It seems so.'

'Wait until it's your own babe in your arms and then you'll really weep.' The whole idea seemed so unlikely that Cordelia cried harder. Magunna gathered her into her arms and patted her back. 'There, there, let it all out.'

And it seemed Cordelia was doing so, though she wasn't entirely sure what "it" truly was. Just, perhaps, that the usual easy flow of life seemed so badly iced up at the moment.

'What's all the noise?' A sharp voice cut into her ridiculous sobs and she yanked away from Magunna to see Caireen standing there looking very cross. But as the druidess noticed Cordelia's tears she started forward, real fear in her luminous eyes. 'What is it? What's happened? Is someone ill?'

'Would you care if they were?' Cordelia snapped.

She had not yet forgiven the young druidess for leaving Leir in the grip of his fever and was still finding it hard to believe her claim of a mad dash to fetch medicines, especially as she hadn't returned for ten long days. She could picture her now, coming running into the royal house on her eventual return, flanked by four burly men from Goneril's new guard. She'd been all wide eyes and pretty tears, flinging herself at Leir's bedside and covering him with kisses. He'd resisted at first, but Caireen had never been more persuasive, talking of her grief at being held back by the snows and thanking Danu over and over for his recovery.

'It is not so much Danu you should thank as Cordelia,' Leir had told her stiffly.

'The tribe owes her a great debt of gratitude,' Caireen had agreed, without blinking. 'And will see it paid in the grandest of wedding ceremonies. I am come straight from Goneril with messages of love for you, my dearest Leir, and requests for forgiveness. She did not, she says, pay you enough heed and she is sorry. She wishes, to show her great reverence for you as her father, to honour you with central place at Cordelia's wedding.'

She'd beamed at Cordelia who, despite herself, had felt a little lifting of her heart. It was really happening then? As for Leir, he had reached for his one-time lover's hand.

'A central place?'

'If you are well enough. And you *will* be well enough, Leir. I will make it my own special task – if you will have me?'

She'd looked up through moist lashes and he'd been gone.

'Of course I will have you,' he'd said. 'Of course.'

And with only the smallest of smug smiles in Cordelia's direction, the young druidess had put down a bag, supposedly full of medicines, and clambered neatly into his bed.

Now she drew herself up before Cordelia and demanded, 'What's happened?'

'The pups are born,' Cordelia told her.

Caireen took a step back.

'Is that it? I thought it was something dreadful.'

'No. It's good news.'

'So why cry?'

'I don't know.'

'Oh. How foolish. Try eating something.'

'I will if there is something to eat?' She looked hopefully at Magunna who bustled off to the food area at the rear. 'And now, excuse me, please, I must tell Father.'

'Why?'

'Because it is good news.'

'He's sleeping.'

'Then I will wake him.'

'I'd rather you didn't.'

Cordelia bristled.

'Well, that's not up to you. You're his mistress, Caireen, here to warm his bed, not to run his life.'

'I am here to care for him.'

'As am I. And for the whole tribe besides.'

Caireen's lip curled in a sneer.

'The whole tribe, Cordelia? I thought that was Goneril's job?'

'The whole tribe here in the east.'

'Oh, I see. It would have suited you, then, if Leir had died.'

Cordelia gasped.

'How dare you?! I battled to keep my father alive and what did you do?'

'The snow . . . '

'Has nothing to do with it. I don't even know what you're doing here. You're a druid and, I'm told, a good one. You should be with Olwen, not wasting your time at Burrough.'

'I am not wasting my time. I'm doing important work for Goneril.'

'Sleeping with her father?'

Caireen flushed.

'*Caring for* her father.'

That again. Cordelia was fed up of it and stepped up to the slim girl.

259

'If you care, then you will want him to know that the next litter of Coritani pups are safely here in Burrough. Father!'

She pushed past Caireen into her own chamber and round to her father's at the back. Leir was sitting up in bed, white hair wild around his head and his chest bare and she saw with concern that he looked very thin. She rushed forward.

'Father, it is cold.'

She pulled a blanket up round his shoulders and he looked at her blankly.

'Cordelia?'

'Yes, Father, it's me. Sorry to wake you but I have news.'

'News?'

He seemed to struggle with the word.

'Good news,' Cordelia pushed on. 'The pups are born.'

'Pups?'

He was reduced to an echo. Cordelia sat on his bed.

'Endellion's pups, Father. Anghus's first litter. We have been waiting for them, remember?'

Leir blinked his eyes furiously and Cordelia noticed that they were now so pale as to be barely blue at all and clouded like a misty morning.

'Endellion?' he asked. 'Anghus?'

She had to stop herself from shaking him.

'The hounds, Father, the Coritani hounds. Are you still asleep?'

Leir ran a hand over his face.

'These days, Dee, I think I am always asleep.'

Her heart turned over and she took his hand.

'Soon the snows will melt fully, Father, and there will be much to do repairing the roads and the ramparts and readying the grain pits. Then it will be Imbolc and all will feel easier.'

'Imbolc?'

He was an echo again. Cordelia looked to Caireen.

'He does not seem well.'

'I did tell you not to wake him. He is slow in the mornings.'

'He wasn't before.'

Caireen shrugged.

'He grows old, Cordelia. He was ill. It happens.'

'Not usually so fast.'

Another shrug.

'We are all different. I am doing what I can.'

Cordelia looked to the many medicines laid out by the bed. There were potions and lotions and even a bowl in which the druidess burned herbs for Leir to suck up the fumes through a hollow reed.

'I'm not sure that those herbs are working. We should perhaps try him without them for a few days?'

But at that Leir snatched up the reed and glared at her with his misty eyes.

'The herbs are fine. They are good. They help me.'

'You don't know that unless—'

'They help me! Now, what on earth are you doing up before Lugh and in my chamber?'

Cordelia looked closely at him.

'I told you, Father – the pups are born.'

'Pups?'

Cordelia clenched her fists but Caireen sat down and rubbed her hands across Leir's head, smoothing down his hair and massaging his temples.

'You know Cordelia's hounds, Leir. They are very fine beasts. Very sought after. They bring great repute to the Coritani.'

'Hounds?' He stared into her violet eyes as if he'd find the answers in their clear colour. 'Oh, yes, hounds. Of course. Baby hounds!' He looked to Cordelia. 'Born, you say?'

'Just this night, Father.'

'Marvellous, marvellous. Why didn't you say before? This is great news for the tribe. I must rise, see them, proclaim it to all.'

He flung back the covers and leaped naked from the bed and Cordelia saw that it was not just his chest but his whole body that was scrawny and undernourished.

'Is he eating?' she asked Caireen as the girl moved to dress him.

'Not as much as I'd like.'

'I hadn't noticed.'

Cordelia felt ashamed. What point was there in her objecting to the young druidess' influence over her father if she was just leaving his care in the other girl's hands? She vowed to pay more attention and moved to help Caireen get Leir into his clothes but he still managed to bound outside barefoot. Not that he seemed to notice as he strode out along the icy path to the doghouse, Caireen running in his wake with his boots in her hands. Cordelia ducked past to push the doghouse door open and usher him inside where he dropped to his knees by the whelping box.

'Oh, but look at them. Aren't they amazing?' He reached out a slightly wavering finger to stroke them. 'May I hold one, Dee?'

'Of course.'

Cordelia dropped down beside him, remembering again the boisterous Leir of a year ago. Anghus had been just a tiny runt then but as she looked to her dear hound, sitting staunchly to one side of the box, she wondered if her father had changed more in the last year than her dog. Leir, it seemed, had gone from a great hound to a vulnerable pup and it nearly broke her heart to watch him tenderly cradle the little things. But at last Leir's fading eyes were clearing and he looked down at his feet, still bare and turning blue, and shook his head.

'Lugh look at me – I was in such a hurry to see the hounds, I didn't put my boots on. What a fool. Caireen ... Oh, thank you.' He took the boots she held out and slid his feet into them. 'Much better.'

He rubbed his hands and set his shoulders back, looking far more like the father Cordelia knew so well. Perhaps he *was* just a little slow in the mornings now? And who could blame him – it was very early and very cold.

'Let us go and celebrate,' he said. 'When will the pups be ready to leave, Dee?'

Cordelia swallowed. She had counted this out too many times not to know.

'A week after Rantaranos.'

'Perfect! We will get them all little bows for the wedding. Gleva and Map will hopefully be back to celebrate with us and can take them on for trading.' He turned to Caireen. 'We must send to Goneril, find out what preparations she is making. It has been a long hard Samhain. The tribe will need a big party to recover and what better excuse than my third royal daughter's wedding? You promised her a grand ceremony, remember, Caireen?'

'Oh, I remember,' the young druidess agreed, her violet eyes glinting. 'It will be very special, I promise. Very special indeed.'

Chapter Twenty-eight

Burrough Hill

Rantaranos; Extra days

At last it was Rantaranos, the extra moon-turn, the gift from the gods to draw out Imbolc every three precious years. Celebrations were always exuberant but this year would, it seemed, surpass them all. Cordelia was up on the ramparts with Leir, waiting for her grand entrance as bride, and could see all across the fort as a drum beat out and the people gathered around the sacred oak at the centre where the ceremony would be celebrated. Fires burned high, barrels had already been broached, and all were in party mood.

Regan and Aledus were directing the crowd and as the compound filled Cordelia saw that they were being carefully sorted into circles. The royals and the white-clad druids were closest to the oak with Goneril's guard around them, then the mass beyond with Regan's warriors creating a further circle at their backs. They were being arranged with great precision and she didn't like the hectoring formality.

She looked anxiously for Taran and was relieved to see him standing on the far rampart – her groom, solid, safe, tangible. Cordelia had to keep pinching herself to believe it was truly happening but he had arrived four days ago with Goneril's advance guard, and every moment in his arms made it seem more and more real.

'At last,' she'd said to him as they'd woken up in each other's arms, sunlight filtering through the thatch of the doghouse roof to fall across their tangled bodies. 'At last Samhain is over and Imbolc is come. At last we will marry.'

'And I can come back to Burrough,' Taran had said, his voice shaking with relief.

'Has it been unpleasant at Beacon?' Cordelia had asked, alarmed. 'Have they hurt you?'

'No! No, Dee, no one has hurt me. It is just strange there. Goneril's guards patrol as if the people are in some way criminal and they have odd rules about who can do what. I don't have to do any field work now.'

'Why?'

'Because I am better in the forge than the fields.'

'I suppose that might be true.'

'Maybe, but it means I hardly ever get out to see anyone and they're all too busy to come and visit me. It has been lonely.' He'd sighed deeply then pulled her tight against him. 'But it is not lonely anymore, my beautiful wife-to-be, and I will not waste another moment dwelling on it.'

Cordelia had given in easily. Goneril's strange new ways would have to be investigated but not yet, not until she was married and a little more used to the glories of having Taran always with her.

Goneril had ridden in on her fancy chariot the day after Taran with Maedoc at her shoulder and her belly as full as the Rantaranos moon and ever since then the compound had been awhirl with preparations. Her train had been vast. A cart full of cured meats and cheeses had been followed by one with three boars penned in and hurling themselves furiously against the bars. The next had held barrels of ale and wines and all had been guarded by smartly drilled warriors led by Regan and Aledus. It had been an impressive sight that had had the people from the homesteads running across the fields to cry welcome.

'I hope they see the feast,' Taran had said to Cordelia and she'd looked at him curiously.

'Why would they not?'

He'd visibly shaken himself.

'Why indeed? Ignore me. I'm still unsettled.'

Cordelia didn't blame him. It was the perfect term for how she'd been feeling herself since Caireen's ominous promises about her wedding, but here they were, with the Rantaranos moon rising and the celebrations about to begin. Nothing, surely, could stop it now? Taran was there, ready to step up and take her hand, and he had thickset Dubus next to him. He had asked for Aledus as his attendant but Goneril had said the prince was needed to help keep order. Cordelia had pointed out that there had never been a problem with order before but Goneril had just sighed and called her naïve.

'We are growing, Cordelia. Look at all these people. We must be careful.'

Cordelia supposed that was true but most of the increase in numbers was accounted for by the warriors who were meant to be keeping order, so the logic seemed flawed. Taran had happily taken Dubus as his right-hand man, however, so it had seemed foolish to start an argument.

The people, she could tell from her vantage point, were struggling to see the oak. Several of them tried to climb the sloping ramparts but were pushed back by warriors. Some enterprising children had scaled the thatch of the houses for a better view but spoilsport guards were now calling them down. Cordelia wanted to shout out to let them be but it would hardly be dignified. She noted those who had tramped in from Beacon and Breedon talking indignantly to their Burrough counterparts, buzzing with something more than the usual celebratory excitement, and looked to Leir.

'The mood feels a little dark.'

'Dark?'

Leir looked around him but his eyes were as hazed as they always seemed to be these days and now Olwen had started up a chant and was circling the oak with a procession of druids behind her. She and Goneril had prepared layer upon layer of ceremony and Caireen had been coaching Leir in his role for days.

'You know what to do, Father?' Cordelia asked him now.

'Of course. I am to walk down the slope with you when the pipes sound and lead you up the road to the oak. I am to take my place behind Goneril for the sacrifice and ready my knife when the music stops. I am not to plunge it into the man's heart until Olwen's prayers are ended. She will draw a circle across his chest to mark the spot where his spirit will go to the Goddess, and when she stands back, I am to step forward in her stead and kill him swiftly and with ... with style.'

He spoke as if by rote, more in Caireen's voice than his own, and his fingers twitched, perhaps for the reed he'd been smoking all morning. Cordelia could only nod for she had not been party to that part of the plans. She cared little how Goneril wished to play the celebrations as long as Olwen bound her hand with Taran's before the tribe – those who could see – and made them woman and husband at last.

'Do you love Taran?' Leir asked her suddenly as druids lit fires in a circle around the oak.

She turned to him, surprised.

'I really do, Father.'

'Hmmm. I loved Branwen.' He looked to the skies as the sacred smoke began to drift upwards across them. 'She is a star now. That makes me sad.'

Cordelia swallowed.

'But you were happy when she was here.'

'Too happy perhaps.'

'Father! That is not possible.'

'Oh, it is, Dee. Not at the time but afterwards. The higher you rise, the further you have to fall.'

Cordelia pictured Mavelle soaring through the skies only to crash to the ground. She remembered her cry and the splintering crunch of her landing and suddenly recalled Taran's voice as they'd disentangled the chieftainess from her iron wings: *They've been cut.* Mavelle hadn't fallen from the skies, she'd been cut from them, cut by the people now preparing Cordelia's own elaborate wedding celebrations. She felt a shiver of dread and looked for her husband-to-be. He was still there, still solid, though his outline was fading as Lugh sank below the earth and the druidic fires took his place, shining on Goneril – all on Goneril.

This is your wedding night, Cordelia reminded herself. Magunna had strewn her bed with early flowers, and if she could just get through her sister's grand performance, she could tumble back into it with Taran and forget the fancy ceremonies and the power plays, forget the mass of warriors and the rumbles of the humbler people. *Not long,* she told herself.

She scanned the crowd and, to her relief, spotted Gleva and Map up near the front with the druids. Gleva waved and smiled and Cordelia drew her friends' encouragement into her like warm wine. She'd been delighted when they'd ridden into Burrough a few days ago and somehow telling them the sad tale of Mavelle's broken flight and the long Samhain that had followed had taken a little of the sting out of it. After all, it was water-blessed Imbolc now, Cordelia's favourite festival, cele-brating growth and renewal. At Imbolc, shy life began to rise from the hard earth once more, making it the perfect time for a wedding. *Her* wedding.

She squeezed herself tight, running her hands down her bridal gown. It was the cornflower blue of her eyes with silver plaiting around the hem, sleeves and scooped neck. Gleva had dressed her in it this morning and Magunna had placed a circlet of Imbolc flowers on her head and plaited fragrant water-grasses through her dark curls. Her sisters had been too busy to help, Goneril with final preparations for the ceremony and Regan with drilling her troops, but Cordelia hadn't minded. The older women's clucking had soothed her as her ever-active sisters could never have done and it was a relief to see Gleva and Map now.

Goneril had vetoed Leir's idea of having the pups at the ceremony but Anghus stood with the traders and it made Cordelia calmer to know he was there. Not fully calm though. The air was too charged, the people too excitable, the performers too grand. This was not the quiet Imbolc that she loved and she felt a sudden rush of panic.

'Taran!' she cried, but the drums were beating louder and a young man was being led out.

'The sacrifice,' Leir breathed.

Cordelia watched, confused. He did not look like a sacrifice. Normally they were naked, stripped back before Danu, their hands bound with soft cords, their hair oiled and bodies washed clean. This man wore a white tunic and a golden belt. Around his shoulders he had a short cloak, also of gold, and he wore a magnificent headdress that marked him out as Lugh's representative. No one, surely, would sacrifice Lugh; that would be to bring darkness and hunger on the tribe.

'Father,' Cordelia said urgently to Leir, 'are you sure you are to kill that man?'

'Oh, yes,' Leir said. 'Here is the special dagger.'

He half drew it from the scabbard at his belt.

'That is *your* dagger, Father.'

'No, it is not. Caireen ordered Taran – your Taran – to make it especially. See how it shines.'

He pulled it right out and lifted it to the rising moon. It did indeed shine for it had been highly polished but it was not new.

'Don't kill him, Father.'

'Why on earth not? He's a sacrifice, a Setantii from our glorious victory over the bastard raiders last year.'

'How do you know?'

'Caireen told me.'

'And how does Caireen know?'

'I'm not sure, Dee. I suppose Olwen told her. Or Goneril. What does it matter? He is there to die for the prosperity of the tribe. He is the sacrifice. It is right.'

'Does he look like a sacrifice?'

Leir peered down at the oak but the fires were high now and the smoke so thick it was hard to see anything.

'I know what to do, Dee,' he said crossly, though his voice sounded thin. 'Walk down the slope, take my place, ready my knife, wait until Olwen draws the circle and then strike.'

'Why you, Father?'

'Because, Cordelia, some people here still honour me.'

'*I* honour you. That's why I'm warning you. Don't . . . '

But the pipes cut across her words, high and clear. Below them Regan and her troops pushed the onlookers back to create a pathway and all eyes turned to Cordelia and Leir. On the far side Aledus was doing the same for Taran and Dubus and there was nothing for it but to head to the oak as Olwen pronounced blessings on their imminent union.

Cordelia forced her feet down the steps carved especially into the earth and along the road to the sacred oak. Caireen stood at Olwen's side beneath it, and Cordelia saw Leir's eyes lock onto hers as he tugged Cordelia onward, faster and faster.

'Steady, Father. Let the people see us.'

And let me delay as long as possible, she thought, desperately trying to work out what was going on. But now Caireen was stepping forward at the supposed sacrifice's side and a glorious white headdress was being placed upon her head as Olwen proclaimed them Moon and Sun. Leir hesitated but Caireen gave him a beaming smile and he moved forward again. They reached the triangle around the oak and Cordelia saw Taran take his place on the far side and felt reassured.

'Danu bless us!' Olwen called. 'For we, the Coritani, meet tonight to celebrate two glorious unions – that of Moon and Sun joined in alignment in this blessed gift of time, and of bride and groom linked in earthly union. May Danu bless us all and accept us as we are – humble women and men beneath Her great glory.'

She stepped up in front of Caireen and the sacrifice and in one dramatic movement ripped their tunics apart down the middle. Caireen stood, breasts glowing in the moonlight, and Leir could look nowhere but at her. Cordelia saw her mouth 'Ready the knife' at him and he reached for his belt.

'No,' Cordelia protested, but now Maedoc had hold of her and was pulling her away from Leir to stand behind Caireen as Taran was placed behind Lugh. Goneril's guards seemed to be all around and Cordelia had no idea how anyone could see the rites. She looked desperately to her husband-to-be.

'This isn't right, Taran.'

He reached for her hand.

'All is well. Let Goneril have her ceremony.'

'But—'

'Step forward, Leir!' Olwen called, her voice echoing around the compound. 'Revered Chieftain, father of our beloved chieftainess. Step forward to do homage to the skies.'

'Homage?' Leir looked even more confused now but for Cordelia the picture was finally as clear as the sacred stream where she had wanted to hold the ceremony.

At her wedding she should have made sacrifice to her own element of water, not to the skies, but Goneril had said there was not enough room beneath the willows and reminded her that it was Rantaranos as well. She had bowed to her elder sister, little caring for the rituals as long as the marriage took place, but she had been foolish to do so. This was not her ceremony but Goneril's and it was all wrong. Her father's eyes were glazed and he was fumbling the knife at his belt. Cordelia tried to reach him but Maedoc had a tight hold on her arm and now Olwen produced a charcoal stick and held it high.

'Danu bless the turning of the moon to keep the skies above us.' She drew a bold line around Caireen's ripe breasts in one smooth motion and then led it across to Lugh's big chest. 'And the rising of the sun to bring us all life.'

The stick moved on across Lugh's chest as Olwen curved a perfect circle over his heart. Cordelia pushed around Goneril in time to see Leir, all obedience, lift his knife high.

'No!' she screamed. 'Father, no!'

But Leir had his instructions and his fuddled mind was holding to them tightly. Taran dived forward but he was too late and all he could do was to knock the 'sacrifice' aside so that Leir's eager knife plunged not into his heart but his arm. The man roared in pain and Olwen caught him and pulled him away, horror and confusion writ clear across her face. The crowd pushed forward, aghast. Lugh writhed dramatically in Olwen's arms and guards leaped up and, on Caireen's screamed command, seized Leir.

'You killed Lugh!' Her voice rang with fury and a clever touch of dismay.

'He did not,' Cordelia objected loudly, pointing to the whimpering figure.

'He tried to. I can't believe it ... I thought I knew you, Leir. I thought you were a good man. I am betrayed. And you too, Princess, for your intended husband helped him.'

'Taran? He did not. He stopped my father making a bad mistake. Taran's a hero.'

'He held Lugh as he tried to escape the blade.'

'That's not true.' Cordelia looked to Taran but guards had hold of him and she couldn't reach him. 'None of this is true.' She ran up to Leir. 'Tell them, Father. Tell the people what your instructions were, instructions given to you by this very woman now accusing you of carrying them out.'

'Kill the sacrifice,' Leir said.

'Louder, Father.'

'Kill the sacrifice!'

Olwen looked up from where she was cradling the whimpering Lugh and spoke in a voice quivering with emotion: 'Is *this* a sacrifice, Chief?'

Lugh's headdress was askew but still glowing in the firelight. Leir blinked, dazed. He staggered a little.

'Kill the sacrifice,' he said again, but less certainly.

Olwen handed the wounded man over and rose to face Leir. She examined him closely.

'The chieftain must be ill. His mind wanders.'

'No!' Cordelia said again. 'No, this is all wrong.' She faced the crowd. 'Father is not ill but drugged. He raised his knife as instructed. It was the instructions that were wrong – and deliberately so.'

'How can you say that?' Caireen demanded. 'This ceremony has been arranged by the chieftainess herself.'

Olwen looked from her to Cordelia. 'You would call the chieftainess a traitor, Princess?'

Too late, Cordelia realised her mistake.

'No. I—'

Olwen snatched the dagger from Leir's now-limp hand.

'Is it she who has brought a knife to the sacred ceremony?'

'No, but—'

'Is it she who sought to kill Lugh and snuff out prosperity for the whole tribe gathered here to celebrate his glorious light?'

'No,' Cordelia said, but she'd had enough now. Enough pressure, enough anger, enough lies. It was all suddenly horribly clear what was happening here and she was not going to let them push her aside again. 'But it is she who has long campaigned for control at any cost. Ask her, Olwen – ask her about the red fabric in the willow tree. Ask her where it came from. Or ask yourself, for I think you know, and if you do not, you need only visit Mavelle on her funeral platform and look carefully at her cloak. Goneril wanted her to die.'

'Treason!' Goneril screamed. The crowd were pulsing now, pushing in tighter and tighter, and Cordelia felt the press of their anger. Olwen was staring at her in confusion but Goneril swept a royal arm around the druidess. 'This is the chaos we have been reduced to,' she pronounced. 'This is what the rule of old women and men has done. I seek to bring us back to the Goddess' favour and look how I am repaid – with treachery from my own family. From my father and from my would-be brother-by-marriage and now from my own sister.' She pointed a finger at Cordelia. 'Seize this one too!'

Goneril looked for a guard and found Regan. For a moment it was the three of them, the elemental royal daughters, bound like the triskele they all wore around their necks. Regan hesitated.

'Goneril . . . '

'Seize her!'

Tears in her eyes Regan reached out to Cordelia, but with a roar Taran broke free from his own guards and bundled her aside.

'Go!' he screamed at Cordelia.

'No, Taran!'

'Go! For Danu, for the Coritani, and for me.'

He fought, kicking and punching, as the royal party beneath the sacred oak fell into chaos. Cordelia heard Anghus snapping furiously at those who tried to seize her while Gleva and Map fought to pull her out of the throbbing crowd.

'I cannot leave Taran,' she gasped.

'You cannot help him now, Dee.'

And sure enough, as Cordelia looked back, she saw Maedoc snatch Leir's knife and bring it down upon her oh-so-nearly husband; heard him cry out her name on a gurgle of blood. Maedoc's arm lifted again in bloody slaughter but this time she saw nothing but tears as her old friends dragged her, weeping, away from the carnage and out of the fortress that had been her home for seventeen years.

'I can't go,' she wept.

'You can't stay,' Map said and then they were in the trees and all was darkness.

Chapter Twenty-nine

At sea

Ogronnios; Ice days (March)

The seas seemed to rise up like unknown monsters, crashing in at Cordelia's feet time and again, roaring angrily before breaking themselves into a thousand foaming pieces across the shifting, sucking sands. She stared at them, stunned. She had always been at one with Danu's waters, but she had never seen them in this furious form and it questioned all she knew about herself. She stood, frozen, her feet sinking in as if the sea spirits were trying to tug her down into the Otherworld. She wished that they would. It would be a relief to escape both the fierce waves ahead of her and the even fiercer torments of her own heart.

Taran was dead.

She still couldn't quite work out what had happened. One minute she'd been stood across the compound of her dear Burrough, waiting proudly to become his wife, and the next he'd been hacked down by Maedoc's damned sword and she'd found herself clinging to Map as he galloped her into the darkness.

Taran was dead. And her father seized. What was the point in going on?

At her side Anghus nudged his broad muzzle into the crook of her arm. She crouched down and buried her face in his neck. His rough hair was wet and tasted salty and she let herself cry into it as the sands tugged at her feet and the winds tugged at her hair and she faced what looked very like the end of the world.

Gleva and Map were negotiating with the captain of one of the boats pulled high up on the shore and Cordelia looked at the vessel in disbelief. It was flat-bottomed, built up high at both ends and secured with some sort of cross-beam, like the rafters in a round-house. The outside was coated with a shiny substance and in the middle, on a stout pole, was a waxed linen square that reminded her all too vividly of the fabric of Mavelle's doomed wings. Cordelia could not believe this thing capable of staying afloat and feared she had ridden all this way in constant terror simply to be tipped into the dark water and disappear forever.

But now Map was coming back and she had to stand and face him. He and Gleva had risked their lives to carry her away and she must be grateful.

'We sail when the tide turns,' he told her.

'Tide?'

He smiled.

'The seas move.'

'I can see that.'

The water before her was vast and dark and the surface seemed to leap and turn in all directions. There must be fearsome spirits within it but Map dismissed her worries with a laugh.

'Not the waves. I mean, the whole body of water. The moon pulls it this way for a half-day and then pushes it the other. If you launch when it is pushing, your boat will carry you away from the shore faster.'

'And that's a good thing?'

'Very because it means you will reach the other shore sooner.'

'Oh, I see. How soon?'

'We're taking the longer crossing to Braquemont so it will be a full day. And we might have to ride out the night, depending on the winds.'

'A whole day and night out there? In that?!'

Cordelia looked in disbelief from the slim vessel to the roaring seas. As if hearing her disgust, the spirits sent an especially big swell that reared up and smashed water around her legs. Cordelia squealed and tried to leap back but the sands were holding onto her ankles and she fell on the wet sand, pinned down ready to be sucked under by their next attack. Anghus barked madly at the vicious waters but Map just laughed, put his hands under her armpits and pulled her out with a loud sucking noise.

'It'll be easier once we get over the breakers, you'll see. Trust the water, Dee. And when we are off these shores you will be safe.'

He glanced anxiously back to the plains behind the beach but there were no pursuers. Either they had ridden a fast and clever route to evade them or Goneril had not bothered sending anyone after her sister. And why would she? Cordelia was hardly a threat.

I am a royal daughter, she reminded herself, but that was all the more reason why Goneril would be glad to see her disappear. One less to challenge her plans. Two less if you counted Taran.

Cordelia saw again, as stark and clear as the spray coming off the seas, Taran's gorgeous face cut through with agony as the knife was driven into him. He'd done nothing bar try to stop Leir being ensnared in Goneril's cleverly prepared trap and had paid for that with his life. Goneril had used the wedding to rid herself of Leir and his opposition to her plans for the tribe and had been quite happy to sacrifice Taran to that aim, and with him all Cordelia's happiness.

On a rush of fury, Cordelia reached for the amulet around her neck and tore it off. She had underestimated her sister. She'd known her to be fierce and determined, self-serving and spiteful, but she hadn't realised the extent of her ambition. Goneril wasn't just ruthless, she was merciless, willing to destroy everything in her path. She had cared not one bit that Cordelia was her sister, had cast aside all their ties of blood and birth and upbringing as easily as Cordelia had just ripped the amulet away. She lifted her hand to sacrifice the wretched triskele into the foaming waters but something stopped her.

She didn't get me.

The thought came to her with a tiny rush of satisfaction and she clutched at it as the only reassurance that was left to her. Goneril had not destroyed her. She'd killed the man she loved but Cordelia was still here, still living and still fighting. Goneril might have broken the ties between the royal daughters but not those between Cordelia and the tribe. There was more to the Coritani than just her sisters and she couldn't let herself be sucked into the Otherworld, for even there she'd find no rest while Goneril was terrorising her people. They had to be her concern now. She looked to Map.

'When does this tide turn?'

'Shortly.'

'And it turns back regularly?'

'Every day and every night. It will be there to carry you home when you are ready to ride it.'

She looked at him, feeling her tears dry against her cheeks. Slowly she opened the leather pocket at her belt and put the amulet inside. Trust the water, he had said, and that was surely something she knew how to do.

'I will be ready, Map.'

'I know it, Princess. I know it.'

It was a petrifying journey, clutching the sides of the bobbing boat as the sea rose and fell endlessly beneath them. The only one more miserable than she was Anghus who cowered in the planked bottom, whimpering, especially when they were blown off course and had to anchor up beneath the night skies. Cordelia tried to sleep rolled in her cloak but with every swell of the sea the vessel felt as if it might toss her into the water and in the end she just lay there, her gaze fixed on the stars, and tried to find the one Leir had assured her was her mother.

Was he with Branwen now? And Mavelle and Bladdud and Taran, her dear Taran? Were they looking down on Cordelia? Could they petition the moon to pull her damned boat to the far shore in safety? And what would they expect of her then? She was the third royal daughter and she was fleeing her sisters; she was hardly worth petitioning for. And yet somehow the moon pulled them onwards anyway and at dawn they were finally eased, with barely a sigh from the seas, onto a long, soft beach overlooked by a fortress set on the impressively straight-edged cliffs above them.

'Braquemont?' she asked Map.

'That's right.'

'Prince Lucius lives here?'

'He does.'

She looked up the line of the stark cliffs and almost wished herself back on the seas. Why should the prince she'd rejected welcome her to his home? He would be more likely to cast her off the precipice. And yet she remembered his voice just before he had left Burrough, cowed but still gracious: *If you need me, I will be at Braquemont.*

She would just have to pray that he'd meant it and at least Anghus was happy again. He had leaped from the boat and was skittering around the beach, digging the sand up with his paws and tossing it into the air as if rejoicing in its solidity. He raced up to the cliffs and began sniffing eagerly at the path cut into them, as he had once sniffed out a safe cave in the rain, and Cordelia could only tell herself to trust him.

'Ready?' Gleva asked, coming up at her side.

'No, but I never will be so let's go.'

Gleva took her arm.

'My heart breaks for you, Dee.'

Cordelia was touched.

'Thank you. Mine feels cracked wide open but somehow it beats on all the same.'

'He was a fine young man.'

Was.

The tense was like a dagger in her flesh but there was no escaping it. Taran was in the Otherworld. One day he would be returned to earth but who knew where or in what form? Meanwhile, Cordelia was still here and the only path to take was upwards to Braquemont and the Belgae.

The fortress was newly stirring and the sentries sleepy and reluctant to leave their fire to learn the business of the new arrivals.

'I am Princess Cordelia of the Coritani, here to pay my respects to Chieftainess Sophia and her people,' Cordelia said formally, pushing her shoulders back and doing her best, despite her travel-stained clothes and bloodshot eyes, to look regal. They didn't seem convinced but one ducked inside to make enquiries and then came rushing back to usher them in with much bowing. He escorted the party to the ceremonial house where they were assured someone would attend them shortly.

Cordelia glanced around the compound as they walked, comforted to see that it was not unlike home. There were the same high ramparts, the same clutch of roundhouses with smoke starting to curl out of their low roofs into the morning air, the same arrangement of workshops, byres and barns. A dog shot out of one of the buildings and bounded over to Anghus, who gave a little yelp of excitement and began chasing it in circles.

Cordelia glanced towards Gleva and Map, daring to imagine this was one of the pups she had sent here with them last year, and felt buoyed by the connection, however slight. But now they were at the royal house and a well-built man in a rich plaid tunic, buckled up with gold, was striding towards them, arms outstretched.

'Princess Cordelia?'

'That's right.'

'I am Prasto, Chieftain of the Belgae.' His accent was thicker than Lucius' and a few of the words were unknown to Cordelia but with concentration she could understand him. 'I am here to welcome you in the stead of my ailing wife, Chieftainess Sophia.'

'As am I,' said a high but determined voice, and Cordelia saw that he had been followed by two girls. One of them had dropped to her knees to stroke a delighted Anghus and the other was now approaching to offer Cordelia her hand. 'Welcome, Princess. I am Ardra, Heiress of the Belgae. We are honoured to see you here at our humble fortress.'

Cordelia took her hand and bowed over it, her thoughts racing. How old had Lucius said his sisters were? Just twelve years she was sure but this girl carried herself like an adult and spoke with welcome clarity.

'I am honoured by your welcome, Heiress.'

Ardra inclined her head and ushered her inside.

'Please, sit. Rest. You must be weary from your travels.'

'A little,' Cordelia agreed warily. 'It is my first time crossing the seas – nay, *seeing* the seas – and they may have had the better of me.'

Gleva and Map chuckled as Ardra peered at her curiously.

'You have no water where you come from?'

'Only rivers and ponds. Nothing so vast as the seas.'

'Magnificent, aren't they? I adore being on the waves.'

'I don't,' said a softer voice and the second girl came up and took Cordelia's hand. 'I'm Bethan.'

Just Bethan, Cordelia noticed. The girl offered no title, nor claim to greatness, only a genuine smile. Her features were identical to her sister's but there was a softness to Bethan's where Ardra's were tight with an awareness of her status. They must have come into the world with just minutes between them but they would tread vastly different paths through life.

'Wine?' Bethan pressed a cup upon her. 'And bread, if your stomach can take it after the rolling of the seas.'

Cordelia accepted both, sipping the wine and taking a cautious nibble of the bread. It was good and she sank onto the rich furs around the hearth. It was a warm day already and with the added heat of the fire she felt her damp clothing start to steam and prayed someone might be able to provide her with something fresh to wear. Her cloak in particular was thick with salt and sitting strangely rigid behind her and she was glad to be able to cast it off as she warmed.

'So,' Ardra said, leaning forward, 'why are you here, Princess?'

Cordelia swallowed and glanced over at Gleva, who nodded her on. Her stomach was rolling indeed now, though not from the motion of the seas.

'I come to you, I admit, as an exile.'

'You do? A royal daughter of the Coritani?'

It sounded so bleak that way. Cordelia felt for the amulet at her throat but it was stashed away in her pocket and her fingers met only skin. Her whole body pulsed painfully at its absence.

'I'm afraid so, Heiress. There has been treachery in my tribe.' It hurt to even speak of it. She swallowed hard. 'When Prince Lucius visited last year, he was kind enough to say that if I ever had need . . . ' Tears choked her and Gleva put a warm hand over hers. Cordelia forced herself on. 'If I ever had need, then I might call on you here at Braquemont.'

'Of course. How very sad. Are you hurt?'

'Not physically.'

'Were others?'

It was a valid question; she was not to know how painful it would be. Gleva's hand squeezed hers and Cordelia nodded.

'I lost my husband-to-be.'

Ardra put her hands over her mouth to cover a gasp of shock.

283

Bethan leaped up and ran to Cordelia, flinging her arms around her in simple sympathy.

'Husband-to-be, Cordelia?'

Cordelia looked around to see Prince Lucius standing in the doorway. He looked exactly as she remembered and she could hardly believe it had been only months since he had last been at Burrough. Mavelle had still been alive then and Goneril had not yet made her advances on Taran. If only Cordelia had spoken out earlier! If only she had gone straight to Leir after Regan's wedding and asked for her own. She had thought there was all the time in the world but it seemed that Goneril had been set on her own path long ago – one that had sucked them all in and ultimately landed her youngest sister here, on a foreign shore, seeking shelter. Cordelia composed herself.

'We were betrayed at our wedding. He was killed and Gleva and Map got me away before I could be seized as well. My sister Goneril wraps a dark fist around the tribe and I fear it will crush us all. I come seeking sanctuary, Lucius.'

'And will, of course, be offered it.'

'I also come seeking your help to return and liberate my tribe.'

He nodded slowly.

'Then you had better come to see Mother.'

Sophia, Chieftainess of the Belgae, lay in a large, luxurious bed set dead centre in a small but elegant roundhouse. She was a tiny lady with fine-drawn features and almost translucently pale skin against the rich cushions and blankets that kept her warm, but her eyes burned with fierce life as Lucius ushered Cordelia inside.

'Thank you for seeing me, Chieftainess.'

'Of course, Princess.' Her voice was calm and clear and Cordelia wondered what sad disease was robbing her body of life whilst her mind was still so strong. 'I am sorry for your distress.'

'My distress, Chieftainess, is mainly for my tribe. And for my father who may be dead or, if not, is certainly in trouble. As are my people.'

'Your tribe has been taken?'

Cordelia shook her head, ashamed.

'Not by anyone from without, Chieftainess, but my sister has lost sight of all that is good and is oppressing our own people. I believe that she arranged for the death of our grandmother, Chieftainess Mavelle, and now plots against our father.'

Sophia frowned.

'You believe? Is there no proof, Princess?'

Cordelia hung her head.

'None bar my word.'

'Which is good enough for me,' Lucius said hotly.

His mother looked at him with something like amusement.

'Is it indeed? What happened, Cordelia?'

Cordelia closed her eyes against the memories but this had to be told; without truth there could be no justice.

'My grandmother sought to fly.'

'Fly?' Ardra gasped.

Lucius looked sideways at Cordelia.

'You said those wings were decorative.'

'I'm sorry. They were a tribal secret. My grandparents spent years exploring the possibility of flight and my grandmother was so close. She flew, truly, for some time but then . . . ' She shuddered at the memory of Mavelle tumbling from the sky to crush her poor thin bones on the unforgiving rocks. 'Someone cut the framework of the wings and I believe it was my sister or done at her command. But she accused my father and my . . . and our young smith.'

Lucius looked at her sharply but she dared not meet his eyes.

'Flight?' Sophia said, sparing her. 'That is bold. They must be remarkable people, your Coritani. And you, Cordelia, are the breeder of hounds my son visited last year, are you not?'

'I am.'

'You made quite an impression on him.'

'Thank you.'

Sophia heaved herself up on her pillows and Bethan ran to help. Prasto and Ardra hovered on her other side and she looked around at them all.

'I am not, as you can see, Princess Cordelia, in a position to help you personally. My days of leading armies are over.'

'I am sorry for it, Chieftainess.'

'As am I. But there are other ways of ruling and my son would be more than capable of leading our troops were I to decide that was the right thing for him to do.'

Her spirit was still purest iron; strong and hard and true. Cordelia appreciated her honesty.

'I will do all I can to convince you of it.'

Sophia smiled.

'I look forward to that. You are, of course, welcome to stay here for as long as you wish whatever course of action I decide upon. I would be glad to look upon you as my daughter.'

Her eyes drilled into Cordelia, bright with meaning, and little as she wanted to, Cordelia understood her straight away. There was to be a condition to this sanctuary; a condition she had half expected. Now it was her turn to be strong. She met Sophia's stare and gave a slow nod. Her heart was fluttering within her chest but if this woman could rule a tribe from her bed then she could surely speak a few, simple words. She turned to Lucius and drew in a deep breath.

'Prince Lucius, would you do me the honour of taking my hand in marriage?'

His mouth dropped open and Ardra giggled.

'Come, Brother, is this any way to take a proposal?'

'But . . .'

He looked at Cordelia, his eyes searching hers, and in this very public arena all she could do was nod him on.

'I would be honoured if you would consider it, Prince, though I understand that I have little to offer you bar myself – for now.'

'It is enough, Cordelia. Truly.'

'And Anghus, of course.'

'Doubly blessed. I consider myself a very lucky man.'

His simple acceptance was a balm to her broken spirit. This was so very far from the wedding she had spent Samhain anticipating and her head was reeling as if she were still being tossed on the crazy seas, but it was a sanctuary of sorts and she had never needed one more.

'You are too good,' she said.

They looked awkwardly at one another until Bethan stepped forward and grabbed her brother's arm.

'Oh, Lucius, how wonderful. This beautiful girl has sailed across the seas for the very first time to ask for you.'

He looked to his younger sister and smiled suddenly.

'It *is* wonderful,' he agreed, 'so wonderful that I was momentarily stunned. I apologise, Princess.' He set his shoulders and came to Cordelia, taking her hands in his. 'If you mean it, then I would be delighted to accept.'

She looked into Sophia's iron eyes and found courage there.

'I mean it.'

'Then, yes. Yes, please. Let us marry immediately.'

He laughed and, before his family, Cordelia tried to join in.

'Kiss her, Lucius,' Bethan cried, clapping her hands.

He looked questioningly at Cordelia but she could hardly refuse and she closed her eyes as his lips softly touched hers.

Forgive me, Taran, she breathed to the skies but Taran was dead and she must, somehow, find the strength to go on without him.

Chapter Thirty

BURROUGH HILL

Ogronnios; Ice days (March)

Taran lay on the rough bed and tried to work out what hurt most –
the throbbing knife wound in his shoulder, the red-raw chain welt
on his ankle or the torment in his heart. There was no contest – he'd
take ten times as much physical pain if he could only know that
Cordelia was safe and well.

Go! he'd shouted to her. It had been an instinct, a burning need to
get her away from this travesty of a marriage ceremony that had so
swiftly turned into a disaster, a disaster of Goneril's clever crafting.
Or perhaps not so clever. He would be dead now if it hadn't been
for the urgent fury of the people Goneril had so carefully confined
to the outer circle. She'd underestimated them. No one, however
lowly, liked to be pushed aside. And no one, however insignificant,
liked to witness injustice.

It had been Bardo, the man who had questioned Taran in his
forge on that snowy night in Samhain, who had led the charge,

pushing through the startled warriors and shouting that he'd seen Taran try to save Lugh. Others had poured after him – big strong men and fierce, vocal women who'd somehow turned Maedoc's knife from his heart. One of the children of that first mother who'd come to the forge had latched onto Goneril's leg, tugging her away from Taran, and even Goneril had not been arrogant enough to turn on an infant in front of the tribe. Instead she'd ordered Taran and Leir to be taken away and the ceremony abandoned.

The next day she'd sent bread and honey out amongst the still grumbling masses and most of them had been appeased and had returned to their homesteads confused rather than angry. Goneril would charm them with Beltane gifts as well, Taran was sure, and hoped that if nothing else came of this sorry night, the chieftainess had at least learned that her people must be treated well.

It was small comfort. It had been put out that Taran and Leir were being kept securely until they were well enough to stand trial before the tribe but Taran was certain they would never get the chance to defend themselves. His wound would, he was sure, spread its poison to his broken heart and kill him first. And if it did not, a knife in the dark would do so just as well. Goneril was biding her time until the tribe settled but she would see him dispatched one way or another – unless he escaped first.

Taran pushed himself up and looked across to his companion in imprisonment. Leir was in an even worse way. Physically he had suffered no more than scratching and bruising in the melee but he was tormenting himself with guilt. Without Caireen or, more vitally, the herbs she had been so carefully smoking into him, his understanding had started to return and it was no gift.

'I'm such a fool,' he railed endlessly to Taran, pacing his cell. 'Such an ignorant, randy old fool.'

Taran had tried to soothe him but Leir was bent on his own punishment and Taran feared he would soon save Goneril a job by dashing his head against the bars of his cage. They were being kept in adjacent pens in Cordelia's doghouse, behind the bars that Taran himself had crafted to keep litters of precious pups apart. Endellion's babies had been sent for trade, though not with Gleva and Map. Taran's dear friends had disappeared on the dread night of Rantaranos and it was his urgent hope that they had taken Cordelia with them. Anghus too, he'd heard tell, had fled the compound and that hound only followed one person. If his so-nearly-wife had gone with those three she might just be safe and he prayed to Danu dawn and night that it was so.

Leir turned in his bed, muttering and flinging his arms wide, not able to find rest even in sleep. Soon he would truly drive himself insane and what use would that be? If they were to escape, they had to work together.

'Psst. Taran!'

He started in surprise at the whisper, suppressing a cry of pain as the chain around his ankle caught at the already worn flesh. Goneril was taking no chances and Taran was secured not just by his own bars but his own chains as well. He had sworn his service to iron back in happier times but now was starting to hate it as much as almost everything else in the world.

'Solinus?'

The man was outside the doghouse by the small hole he and Taran had managed to laboriously cut into the earth beneath the side wall. It had had to be done bit by excruciating bit when the guards – Goneril's third line of security – had been distracted. At present it was only the size of a hand but the moment, last night, when Taran had reached down and felt Solinus' fingers close on his, had been a triumphant one. He could have held on all night to the desperately needed token of friendship but that would hardly have been practical.

Instead, he'd reluctantly let go and accepted the fresh bread and sausage Solinus had pushed through. Eaten beneath his blanket in the dark, it had tasted like the nectar of Elysium after the thin gruel Goneril had been providing and he felt much stronger for it today.

He glanced to the guard but the man was at the doorway looking outwards to the morning sun so he knelt quickly down at the wall.

'I'm here.'

'Cheese from Magunna.'

A package appeared and he seized it.

'Danu bless you.'

'And ointment from Dubus for your wounds.'

'You're a miracle worker.'

'Just a normal worker, Taran, as are we all. Our efforts are poor but we do our best.'

'I'm so grateful.'

'Stay strong. Oh! I have . . . '

To go, Taran finished in his head as he heard a scrabble of something outside, whatever Solinus was using to cover the hole, he presumed. He carefully draped his own blanket over the end of his pallet bed to cover it and shoved the cheese and ointment beneath as the guard turned in.

'Awake, hey?'

'I'm awake, yes.'

'It's all right for some, lazing around all the time. Bet you can't wait to spend another day as a valued member of society, hey?'

The man was a weasel. His name was Mikah and he was one of the Setantii tribesmen that Aledus and Regan had brought into their training school. Having been a prisoner himself not so long ago, Taran had hoped he might be sympathetic to his charges but the reverse was true. Mikah liked nothing better than to torment them.

'The first Beltane moon will rise soon, Smith. Time for a sacrifice. Who on earth could the chieftainess choose for such an honoured role, do you think?'

'Some cocky git of a guard?' Taran suggested.

'Oh, no. The chieftainess loves cocky gits.' That much was true. 'Hungry, Smith? Oh, look, here's breakfast – a nice juicy ham hock. Delicious.'

Mikah took the meat from someone at the door and brought it inside where its pervasive scent curled tantalisingly around the doghouse. Despite himself, Taran drooled. Mikah came right up to the bars and bit into it, chewing with his mouth wide open and letting the rich juices run down his chin so it was all Taran could do not to lean forward and lick them off. He thought of the cheese stowed beneath his covers and turned away to sit on his bed. Mikah gave a low laugh.

'There's news come with the meat too. Do you want to hear it?'

Taran shrugged. He didn't care for tribal gossip. There was only one person of whom he wished to hear.

'It's about the Princess Cordelia.' And that was her. Taran leaped up. The chain bit at his ankle but he barely noticed it. 'Ooh,' Mikah crowed. 'That's got you, hasn't it? Want to know about the traitor princess, do you?'

'She isn't a traitor.'

'Then why did she run?'

'Because no one here listens to reason anymore.'

'Or maybe because she'd changed her mind and was looking to escape marrying you, Smith.'

'Not Cordelia.'

'You seem very sure, especially when she hasn't exactly been pining for you.'

'What do you mean? Where is she?'

But Mikah gave a sly smile and took a seat to continue his blatant chomping on the ham. And now Leir was awake.

'Cordelia! Did he say Cordelia?'

Leir leaned forwards. The chains that held them were just short enough to ensure they were deprived of even the passing comfort of touching through the bars but even so Leir strained towards him. Taran saw blood drip from his thin old ankle and hated the sight. Later he could throw him the ointment but not with Mikah watching them.

'He did,' Taran confirmed. 'She must be well.'

Mikah paused in his chewing.

'Oh, she's very well. Forgotten you already, Smith, and I can't say I blame her. You stink.'

He did but that was hardly his fault. No man could keep clean without water or latrines. He bit his lip to avoid rising but Leir was at the front of his cage now, rattling at the bars.

'What do you know of my daughter, man, my one true daughter?'

Mikah, however, went back to his breakfast. It was now nothing more than a bone but that didn't stop him gnawing loudly on it.

'At least *you* belong in the doghouse,' Taran threw at him furiously.

Mikah tossed the bone aside and came over to the cage.

'Word is, Smith, that your precious bride has found herself a new husband already. Word is that she's with Prince Lucius of the Belgae. He'll be ploughing her now, hey? He'll be filling her up with his big royal cock. He'll . . . '

'Enough!' Leir's deep roar still held the authority of a chieftain and even Mikah cowered to hear it. 'Fetch me my daughter. Now!'

Mikah looked nervously around.

'I cannot leave my post,' he stuttered.

Leir growled, low and sure.

'Then find someone else. And fast!'

Mikah's tiny mind was obviously working hard. Taran he could afford to hurt but Leir might yet be returned to power, and if there was one thing this vicious guard understood it was self-preservation. He turned on his heel and marched to the door and Taran looked to Leir.

'If it is true, Leir, then she is safe.'

The look Leir gave him with his now painfully clear blue eyes was one of such deep sympathy that Taran had to turn away for fear of it breaking him. Kindness, it seemed, was more powerful than cruelty. But if it were true – if Gleva and Map had got Cordelia to Braquemont – then she would be well cared for there, and if the price of sanctuary had been marriage to Lucius then she

293

had been right to pay it. It didn't, he had to admit, feel as good as he had thought it would to know she was alive and well, but it was what he had asked of Danu and he must be grateful.

'She will think you are dead, Taran.' Leir's words, low but clear, penetrated the fug of pain and he looked over. 'Cordelia will think you are dead. *I* thought you were dead and I was standing next to you. She will certainly believe it.'

'Maybe. It matters little.'

'It matters a great deal. You mustn't give up.'

'Give up?'

'I know I've been no use to you. I know I've done little but rage. Danu knows, I've had enough to rage about but I'm done now. If Cordelia is alive – and advantageously positioned – then we have something to aim for. We must get to her.'

'And her new husband?'

'I am sorry, Taran, but yes. There are more lives than our own at stake here.'

Leir gestured to the door where Mikah was barking instructions to a passer-by. Taran thought of Magunna and Solinus, of Bardo and the other workers and knew that Leir spoke true. The chieftain was returning, as Taran had wanted, and this was no time to dwell on personal sorrow.

'Besides,' Leir said softly, 'it will enrage Goneril if we escape.'

It was the flash of humour that did it, bitter perhaps but the clearest glimpse yet of the old Leir, the man who had welcomed Taran to Burrough, who had bought him from Enica and then, reluctantly, gifted him to Goneril. That's when it had all started to go wrong and now, somehow, they must make it right again.

'Are you with me, Taran?' Leir asked him. He held out his hands, palms upward, and although Taran couldn't reach them, he held up his own and swore he felt the warmth of his touch.

'I'm with you.'

'Father?'

They both spun around guiltily to see a figure in the doorway, silhouetted against the sharp sliver of morning sun coming tanta-lisingly through from outside. Leir squinted at her.

'Goneril?' The figure took two steps into the house, a hound at her side. 'Regan!'

'You wanted to see me?'

'I wanted to see the chieftainess. I must talk with her.'

'Goneril is gone back to Beacon but I have brought Olwen.'

'Olwen!' Leir rushed to the front of his cage as the high druidess came in behind Regan.

Taran watched her curiously. She held herself as tall as usual but the lines of her slim body were taut and her eyes strangely wary.

'The chieftainess' time draws near,' she told them stiffly, 'and she must rest and gather herself to bring the new heiress into the world.'

'Good news indeed,' Leir said. 'I would like to see my grandchild when it arrives.'

'When *she* arrives.'

'If Danu wills it.'

'Goneril is most certain.'

'Then I would like to see my granddaughter when she arrives. And I would like to be free to hold her before the tribe.'

Olwen did not seem to know what to say to that and it was Regan who spoke up instead.

'You committed a crime, Father.'

He looked straight at her.

'Do you believe that?'

Regan shifted, looked towards Olwen. The high druidess came forward.

'You tried to stab Lugh, Leir.'

He reached his hands through the bars for her.

'I did not, Olwen. I had been told to sacrifice the one on whom you drew a circle.'

'Told by whom?'

'By Caireen, who said she had been told so by you.'

Olwen shook her head.

'There was no sacrifice prepared for Rantaranos. There never is. You know that, Chief.'

Leir sighed.

'I used to know it. And I know it now, but then . . . My mind was fugged. It was the reed.'

Olwen was looking increasingly confused.

'What reed, Leir?'

He glared at her.

'Enough, Olwen! Your reed. *Your* reed filled with *your* herbs that you gathered for me 'specially. There's no point in pretending innocence in all this. It is as much your fault as anyone's that we are incarcerated here now and Cordelia is lost to the tribe.'

Olwen looked distressed.

'I never wanted to harm Cordelia. Or Taran.' She swung around suddenly and pointed at him. 'You should have married our chieftainess, Smith, but you refused. I chose you for her as an artisan, a man of intelligence and insight, not just a means of pleasure and power.'

Taran shook his head.

'You chose Maedoc too, Olwen.'

'I did not!' She spun away, making for the door, but when she got there she turned back, calmer now. 'I did not choose that man for her, but I admit that I failed to stop the marriage and now I no longer know where our path will lead. The future eludes me. Henceforth we must all fight for what we see fit.'

And then she was gone in a whirl of white fabric and dust. Regan looked awkwardly after her.

'Things are difficult at Beacon,' she said.

'And here,' Leir said sharply. 'Why will no one hear me plead my innocence?'

'There is to be a trial, Father.'

'Ah, the trial. Yes. I welcome it, Daughter. When will it be?'

'When you are well enough to stand before the tribe.'

'Oh, I am well enough, as you can see. I am quite lucid now.'

'I am glad of it, though the smith does not look so well.'

'That is because he is offered no medicine,' Leir said fiercely.

Taran thought of the ointment hidden beneath his blanket and said nothing. If it worked the wound would not poison him – that would annoy Goneril too. Olwen's words were spinning round in his head like leaves in the Lughnasad winds: *You should have married her, Smith.* As if he could have done something; as if he could have wielded any influence. The druidess must be as mad as everyone else around here for no one, it seemed to him, could influence Goneril and it was only the thought of her fury at his continued existence that made him believe his poor heart was worth saving.

Regan looked confused and glanced down at her hound, who gave a gentle wag of her tail.

'I suppose I could ask for Magunna to be sent to tend to you both,' she offered.

'That would be a start,' Leir agreed. 'And then the trial.'

Regan looked at him for a long time.

'You do seem improved, Father.'

'And will be more so once I am out from behind these ridiculous bars. I am the Chieftain of Burrough, Regan. I am of royal blood – *your* blood.'

At this, though, she bristled.

'My blood is my mother's. As is Goneril's. It is time for the daughters of Branwen to reclaim our rightful place – in charge.'

'Of course it is,' Leir said. She stared at him suspiciously. 'That is why I worked so hard to bring the three of you up safe and well – to teach Goneril to light up the world with her fire, Cordelia to nurture with water, and you, Regan, to tread the earth with strength. I will be proud to see you all, as women, step up and rule.'

'You will?'

Regan stared at him, confusion swirling in her eyes.

'I will. Why else do you think I gifted you Breedon, Ree?'

The pet name made her start and Taran saw tears spring to her eyes but they would do them no good; Regan hated tears. Sure enough, her whole body went rigid and she glared at her father.

'Silence, prisoner,' she barked and then, with a nod to the swiftly saluting Mikah, she was gone, her hound at her heels.

Later that day Magunna arrived with soup and bandages, but there was no news of a trial and Taran was not sure there ever would be. Somehow, they had to escape.

Chapter Thirty-one

BRAQUEMONT, THE LANDS OF THE BELGAE

Quitos; Windy days (April)

Cordelia gritted her teeth, forced herself to stroke Lucius' back and tried not to sigh her relief too obviously when he gasped and fell still. She had been his wife for a full moon-turn and had accustomed herself to his embraces but his clumsy loving did nothing to assuage the ache inside her for Taran. With him everything had seemed so natural, so easy. They had fitted together with a passion that had overridden the clumsy tangling of limbs that now felt like the main feature of her nights with her royal husband. The only good thing was that Lucius did not seem to notice her discomfiture and was always tenderly grateful afterwards.

'I hope we will have a baby soon, Dee,' he'd say. 'Many babies. We will be a family of our own.'

It seemed to be something he desired greatly, perhaps because of living in Ardra's small but fearsome shadow. His poor mother, for all her ferocious spirit, was clearly dying, but she had the best druids working to keep her alive and Cordelia could see she intended to maintain control until Ardra was old enough for a smooth succession. That meant Lucius was free to leave.

Cordelia was doing her best to fit in here at Braquemont, learning Belgic words and even letting her tongue pick up some of the softer syllables of the overseas tribe, but her heart, when it did not ache for Taran, burned with the need to return to the Coritani. Sophia was sympathetic but cautious. She had sent spies out over the seas to assess the situation but they were not yet back.

Occasionally news came in from traders and Cordelia seized on it. Gleva and Map had headed south, no doubt afraid for their lives after helping her escape, and she could only hope she'd see them again one day, but there were plenty of others to bring word. Leir, Danu be praised, might still be alive but if so he was not in charge of Burrough, which was apparently being run by a 'slip of a beauty' who could only be Caireen. One man told Cordelia that Burrough felt 'angry' these days and every time she thought of her beloved home, ruled by a stranger and ravaged by hatred and confusion, she was filled with anger herself. She had to get back.

Now she stroked Lucius' blond head as he rested it on her chest and spoke carefully.

'I think, Lucius, that I may be with child.'

'Truly?' He raised himself up on his elbow to peer at her. 'Oh, Cordelia, that would be wonderful.'

'The moon has turned and I have not bled.' That much was true, though she knew from talking to other women that it was no sure indication. 'We must wait a while yet but it is certainly possible.'

'That would be wonderful,' he said again, and kissed her.

Cordelia gave him a smile.

'Our own family, Lucius.'

'Yes.'

'But not our own home.'

'What do you mean? Braquemont is our home.'

He sounded cross; she must tread carefully.

'It is an excellent home – for now. But it will one day be ruled by Ardra.'

'Mother is not dead yet.'

'Nor will be, I hope, for some time to come. But I have been speaking to her and she appreciates our position.'

'Which is?'

'Which is, Lucius, that this is not where we belong.'

'How can you say that?'

She thought carefully.

'If our child is a girl, Lucius, what inheritance will she be born into?'

He sat up fully, his back to her.

'The same as mine – royal duty and privilege. We don't have to inherit to be worth something, Cordelia.'

She heard the hurt in his voice and ran a hand down his spine.

'I know that. I'm a third daughter, remember? And it's not a question of worth but of security. Land is security.'

'Was it for you?' It was a low shot and Cordelia gasped. Lucius turned immediately, taking her in his arms. 'Sorry. I'm sorry.'

'You speak true, Lucius, but that's because I had no control. But if we could take Burrough . . .'

'You still wish to invade?'

'Did you think I would stop?'

'I hoped you might, perhaps, be content to stay here.'

She stared at him.

'I am content with *you*, Lucius.' That wasn't strictly true but it was close enough, given the terrible circumstances of her arrival. 'But I cannot be content to stay here. The Coritani are my people. I am a royal daughter, sworn to their protection and service.'

Her hand twitched, as it so often did, to her amulet, which these days lay curled in the bottom of her pocket. The spiral of her fate was no longer, it seemed, caught up with that of her sisters but it was still bound to her tribe. Lucius sighed.

'Is it not dangerous to invade if you are with child?'

She shook her head.

'To me, it feels more dangerous not to. Every turn of the moon will sew Goneril more tightly onto the throne of the Coritani. If we wait the nine turns it will take to birth a babe, she may be impossible to remove.'

Lucius nodded slowly.

'We had better speak again to my mother.'

Sophia gave them audience sitting in her high-backed chair, padded well round with blankets but with her wasted back held straight and her torc of office around her slim neck.

'Are you well enough to be up, Mother?' Lucius asked anxiously.

'Probably not but some things are too important to consider from bed and I have Prasto to carry me as a good consort should.' She glanced fondly at her husband and Lucius visibly squared his shoulders. 'And he will advise me, too, on the wisdom of backing our new daughter.'

Lucius turned his anxious gaze on Cordelia but, as before, she appreciated Sophia's honesty. There was no point in anything less.

'Shall I tell you a little of my tribe?' she suggested.

'Please.'

Ardra, sitting at her mother's feet, leaned eagerly forward and even Bethan looked up from playing with Anghus.

'The Coritani lands are widespread. It is fully three days' ride from the eastern border to the west. Rule is from Beacon Hill in the centre and for many years now we have had a second fortress at Burrough Hill in the west, where until recently I lived. When my middle sister took a husband, we built a new fortress for her in the east. It is a tricky border and Regan is a good fighter.'

'A fighter?' Ardra asked, leaning forward eagerly. 'She wields a sword?'

'Oh, yes. And teaches others to fight too.'

'Why?'

Cordelia shifted uncomfortably.

'The chieftainess has been looking to expand.'

'Expand?'

'Push out a little. The Setantii do not have a strong leader at the moment and I'm told she looks to . . . to draw them into her sphere.'

'She would take over another tribe? That would be astonishing.'

Ardra's eyes glowed with admiration. Cordelia had the feeling she would take to Goneril and prayed the two never met.

'It seems to me,' Sophia said drily, waving her daughter away, 'that she needs to look to her own tribe at the moment. On which side is Regan wielding her sword in the civil conflict from which you've fled?'

Cordelia winced. It was a key question.

'At the moment she has chosen to stay with Goneril – as is her duty. We are three royal daughters, sworn to each other and to our tribe.'

'So you are the one who has broken the bond?'

'No!' Lucius protested for her. 'Cordelia had to flee for her life.'

Sophia gave him a sympathetic smile.

'I understand that, Lucius. But I am trying to grasp how others might see it.'

Cordelia bowed her head.

'All those who were at my wedding will surely know that I was right to flee. I had done nothing wrong and was under threat of my life. Ask Gleva and Map when they return – they will testify for me.'

'Oh, I already have,' Sophia said easily. 'I questioned them in some detail before they left. They bore out your version of events and talked with some vehemence of the poor influence of your chieftainess.'

'They did?'

'They were particularly upset at the slaughter of the young smith – Taran, was it?'

Cordelia flinched and Lucius stared at her.

'Taran was the man you were to marry?'

She nodded. There was no point in pretence.

'He is dead. Hacked down by Goneril's husband.'

'That's so sad,' Bethan cried, and it was all Cordelia could do to keep her composure. She longed to flee the Belgic royals and run to the cliffs to cry her grief into the salt air. But this was no time to show weakness. She looked directly at Sophia.

'Is this a foolish mission, Chieftainess? To set myself up against my sisters? Goneril has always stood as fire, Regan as earth. I am merely water.'

'*Merely* water, Cordelia? You have been on the seas – did you not feel their power? Water can douse fire and move earth.'

Cordelia glanced behind her to the open door and, beyond it, the ever-shifting seas. The chieftainess spoke true.

'I do not know about my sister Regan,' she said, forcing the words out of some iron-hard part at the very centre of her. 'But I believe the people will rise for me, especially if we can find my father. He has led the people of Burrough for many years and they love him dearly. As do I.'

Again the pain of exile seared through her. Sophia held out a hand and Cordelia stumbled forward to take it. The wasted fingers closed around hers, surprisingly warm and tight with understanding. Cordelia looked into the eyes of her mother-by-marriage and felt the tiny woman's strength flow into herself.

Sophia held her grip for a little longer and nodded, satisfied.

'Then we must find Leir,' she said gently.

Cordelia managed a smile.

'We must find my father,' she agreed, though how on Danu's blessed earth they were to do that, she had no idea.

Chapter Thirty-two

Giamonios; Shoots-show days (May)

Olwen burst out of the workshop and round the lower level of
Beacon Hill, past the new forge, taking the winding path down
to the sacred grove. She had left her feet bare and they slid in the
sodden moss around the entrance but she strode on, ignoring the
splatters of mud upon her white tunic.

She reached the grove and there was the platform on which
Mavelle had been laid out for the Mother to reclaim. The chieftainess' flesh was all gone now, carried away by her beloved birds,
and her skeleton lay white and clean upon her chequered red cloak.
Olwen stared up at it. Bones held no fears for her but she shivered
still to see how swiftly the complex mass of a person could be
reduced to such a humble framework.

'I miss you,' she whispered.

She should not. Life was a cycle spun by the Goddess and all
should embrace their place in it without question. Olwen had

always found that belief easy before but these last months of loneliness and misery had clipped at her shield of rational thought and somehow emotion had slipped past her defences and weakened her.

A sob tore at her throat but she would not let it out. She didn't deserve the luxury of grief. For too long she had ducked the truth but she could do so no longer. *Your reed*, Leir had thrown at her, *filled with your herbs that you gathered for me 'specially. There's no point in pretending your innocence in all this.* She *had* been innocent of any such design but had stayed wilfully ignorant of others' misdeeds, and for a high druidess that was indefensible. This situation was surely all her fault. Taran and Leir were shut up at Burrough, kept in cages like hounds, and Goneril seemed happy to leave them there to rot.

This very morning a message had arrived to say that Taran's wound was healing and Olwen had seen a shadow cross the chieftainess' beautiful face and known that she was willing the smith to die. She did not even have the courage to execute him. But then, she'd tried that once before and her father had stopped him. Here, in this very grove, Leir had stepped from behind Mavelle's funeral platform and sacrificed the tribe's best hawk in Taran's place. He was a good man, a brave man, and now he, too, was locked up like a criminal – and on Olwen's own accusations.

She had seen that shadow on Goneril's face before. Many times, perhaps, but one in particular stuck in her mind – the day the messengers had come through the snow with news of Leir fighting off his fever. The fever Caireen had fled. The fever that had been meant to kill him.

No!

Furious suddenly, Olwen threw herself down before the sacred spring. Water splashed across her, its chill shocking.

'Danu, Mother – wash sense into me, I beg of you, for I have stood as High Druidess before all the people of the Coritani and I have failed them. I have been hailed as wise yet been the most foolish of them all. I, who swore myself to You, have been lost in another.'

The water hammered over her head and she stayed beneath it, listening to its patterns, seeking a voice wiser than her own. It would not be difficult to find. And yet still a part of her prayed that she was wrong, that the flame of the Coritani burned pure. She did not want to believe Goneril was as evil as she seemed for if she was, then Olwen had let love – undiscoverable, untraceable love – override logic. She had not just set Goneril on the wrong path, but followed her blindly down it.

Eventually she sat up. This was no good. Mavelle must be laughing at her from above, for the Goddess would not just hand her the answers. Olwen was a seeker so she must seek. The solution to this mystery lay in her own mind. She must somehow peel back the tangles of grief and identify the source of truth.

Olwen surfaced from the water and looked up. It was a grey day, the clouds squatting so low that she might almost touch them. She reached up a hand and it met with the lowest branches of the sacred willow, tickling her skin like the sweetest goodnight kiss. For a moment she was as innocent and awed as a child again, before she had learned the ways of the druids, before her return to the tribe, before she took Goneril into her bed. Or, as had perhaps been the truth of it, Goneril took her.

She wrapped her fingers in the soft new leaves and shook gently, watching as the movement rippled up the sinuous branches. The pale green made patterns against the grey above and Olwen let herself be drawn into them. See how the branches bowed with the breeze, how they dipped to the life-giving water. See how the leaves sprouted and grew, pushing life down the central core much as blood flowed through a body. She should take a knife to one perhaps. She was done experimenting with living creatures. Too many strange things flowed in blood; things beyond analysis. Plants might be simpler.

'What do you say?' she asked the willow. 'Will you deliver up your secrets to me?'

She tugged again at the branch, fearing perhaps her wits were

307

going but not really caring, and as she did so the branch pushed another aside and a flash of darkest red caught her eye. She blinked up at it. It was an Imbolc charm but must be from last year because they had been at Burrough for this season's ill-fated celebrations. She pushed herself up and reached for it. It was frayed at the edges from a year outside but the fabric was unmistakably fine and beautifully chequered. Instantly she heard Cordelia's voice, as clear as if it had been threaded into the fibres clutched in her trembling fingers.

Ask her, Olwen – ask her about the red fabric in the willow tree. Ask her where it came from.

She stretched up to untie it and turned slowly, painfully, to look up at Mavelle above her.

Or ask yourself, for I think you know, and if you do not, you need only visit Mavelle on her funeral platform and look carefully at her cloak.

Stepping beneath the platform, she reached up through the network of hazel twigs to the chieftainess. The rip was still there – a neat triangle, as if it had caught on a nail or, perhaps, the point of a knife. Olwen placed the scrap up against it; it was a perfect fit.

Goneril had wanted Mavelle to die.

Closing her eyes, she pressed her head against the platform, horrified. Goneril had tied a piece of the chieftainess' cloak to the Imbolc tree to wish for leadership over a year ago, back when she'd first asked to come to Beacon, back when she'd first stepped into Olwen's embrace. She had set her sights on it from that moment – but at what cost?

Pushing her wet hair back from her face, Olwen tucked the missing piece into the cloak and sat back against the slim trunk of the willow. Cocooned in its gentle branches, she forced herself to look, not at the leaves or the grey sky or the looming funeral platform, but right through them all to the past – to that terrible Samhain night when they had sent Mavelle into the skies. She pictured it all – the wings silhouetted so magnificently on top of the ramparts, the steps leading up to them, the little launch platform, so crowded with people. What had she said to Mavelle? She remembered removing her feathered cloak and then—

And then Goneril had pulled her away. She'd shown Olwen to the cheering crowd and she had felt the surge of heat Goneril always sent through her. But behind her Maedoc and Caireen had been strapping Mavelle into her wings. They'd have had the opportunity to cut the frame then. Olwen had had no chance to perform a final check because she'd been forced out of the way by Goneril announcing her pregnancy. And Taran . . . Taran had tried. He'd tried harder than she had but he, too, had been blocked.

Don't you trust us, Taran? Goneril had demanded, and he hadn't. He hadn't trusted her from the start. He'd turned down the proposal Olwen had thrust upon him because he'd seen the flaws in the ore from which the eldest royal daughter had been formed. And, of course, because he'd already chosen Cordelia – a wise choice and one that had earned him his cruel imprisonment.

The memories hurt but Olwen was not going to duck them, not now. She gasped as another one hit, fitting into the rest as painfully perfectly as the scrap of material into Mavelle's cloak: her own apprentice's pretty head popping up in Goneril's chamber after Taran had turned down her proposal.

'It's just a little potion of my own – chamomile, valerian and poppy seed. It will soothe her.'

Caireen had soothed Goneril and then she'd soothed Leir – soothed him into a fug worse than Olwen's own self-indulgent grief. Poppy seed could be lethal, Olwen knew that, but she had done nothing to control her own druid. Mavelle had died because Olwen had not performed the vital final checks on her wings; Leir had been drugged into his foolish role in the farce of Rantaranos because of her negligence as a teacher, and now her lowly apprentice was somehow ruling Burrough in his stead. It was unforgivable.

She pushed herself to her feet and reached up to touch one finger to Mavelle's skull. It was too late for the chieftainess now and

Olwen could only pray that she was with Bladdud and Branwen feasting in Elysium, safe in the knowledge that she had flown. It *was* possible and one day someone braver than Olwen would take to the skies again. But it was not too late for Leir. Or for Taran. She would have to be clever but she was high druidess; she was *meant* to be clever.

Pushing herself up, she made her way out of the grove and headed back up the hill, deep in thought. She was barely halfway to the back gate when screams from above told her something was very wrong. She broke into a run.

'Druidess! You must come. Now!'

The sentry looked panicked and Olwen cast around fearfully but could see no threat on the horizon.

'What is it?'

'It is the chieftainess. She is being torn apart.'

'What?'

Surely Danu was not taking her vengeance so directly? Olwen ran for the royal house and stepped into chaos. Goneril was writhing and screaming on her cushions while her attendants stood around, staring down at her in horror.

'Oh, honestly!' Olwen strode forward. 'She is having a baby, fools. It's nothing special.'

'Nothing special?' Goneril shrieked furiously.

Olwen smiled at her.

'I'm afraid not, Gee. In childbirth, all women are equal. Now, get up, walk around, and do as I say!'

The Mother was not, Olwen was guiltily pleased to see, disposed to be kind to Goneril. The Coritani chieftainess laboured for hours, fighting it all the way, calling curses on everyone and proclaiming at every new contraction that she was about to die. As the hours ground on, however, those attending her stopped fearing the truth of her cries and melted away. Maedoc paced uselessly outside, asking endless answerless questions of the women trying to tend his royal wife until one sent him away with a flea in his ear.

'If you want to do something helpful, go and make offerings to Danu, for she is the only one who can help your wife now.'

Olwen had no idea if Maedoc had obeyed – though by the sounds from the ceremonial house, he and his cronies were making their oblations in ale – but it made no difference. Goneril struggled on. Regan rode in, summoned to her royal sister's side, but this was not a battle she was equipped to fight and she could do little bar fidget at the edges of the room.

'Cordelia would know what to do,' she whimpered at the darkest hour as Goneril ripped the thatch apart with her shouting.

Olwen thought of gentle, calm Cordelia and knew Regan was right, but Cordelia was not here and they must somehow cope without her. They had midwives enough but none of their great experience had prepared them for a chieftainess who could not believe she had to endure this suffering.

Finally, somewhere around dawn, sweating and whimpering, Goneril was able to bear down. Olwen crouched with her, looking into her eyes, and saw a scared girl, stripped for the moment of her beauty and her titles, her privileges and her ambitions. Pity washed through her. This was a woman she had loved, a woman she had *adored*, a woman she had believed was the future of the Coritani and a woman who could maybe yet be so. She locked eyes with her.

'Goneril?'

'Olwen, help me. Please.'

'I don't need to. You can do this yourself. You *will* do this yourself. You will birth the heiress. And soon. When the next pain comes you must push, do you hear me?'

Goneril nodded and clasped at her arms. Her face contorted as her body pulsed again but she kept her attention fixed on Olwen and pushed with all her might.

'Good! Again, Gee.' As always, once Goneril had set her mind to something she was determined in its pursuit. Olwen saw the effort in the beads of sweat on her royal brow but within just a few more pushes the baby's head crowned between her legs. 'She's almost here! Last push, Goneril, and you will hold her in your arms.'

Goneril's eyes lit up, the fire finally golden within them again, and she almost smiled. Then, with a final effort, she pushed the baby out. It lay, pink and bloodied, between them. Its little eyes were screwed up tight but as they both looked down, it opened them wide and peered up with bright, open interest. Olwen was transfixed. This was the Mother's greatest blessing, a new life drawing its first precious breaths on earth right here before them.

'Oh, Goneril,' she breathed, all anger forgotten, 'it's a miracle.'

Goneril looked down too.

'Danu have mercy,' she shrieked, 'it's a boy!'

She glared down at the tiny child and if the peace of the fortress had been rocked by her pain, it was ripped apart by her anger.

'A boy!'

She barely waited to have the cord cut before she was scrambling away from the fruit of her labours. The baby let out a wail of its own and Goneril's face contorted.

'It can't be mine.'

No one spoke. They had all watched the child battle its way out of the chieftainess and all cowered as she glared accusingly at them. She did not even attempt to hold her child and it was Olwen who wrapped the little thing in a blanket and tried to shush his helpless cries.

'Let me.' Regan crept forward and held out her arms. Olwen passed the baby to her and she took him as naturally as if it were she who had just brought him into the world. 'You poor boy,' she crooned. 'You poor, poor boy. You must be hungry.' She looked to her sister. 'He's hungry, Goneril.'

Goneril's face twisted again.

'So?'

'So, you must feed him.'

Goneril raised her hands in front of her.

'No! I will not.'

'Only you have the milk.' Goneril was hissing like a wild cat but Regan did not even seem to notice. She advanced on her sister. 'You *must* feed him.'

'I will do as I choose, Regan.'

'But he will starve.'

'Let him.'

Regan gasped and turned to the midwives.

'Find a wet nurse,' she instructed, 'and fast. This child is a royal son of the Coritani and will not starve.'

Goneril's eyes narrowed.

'Those are not your orders to give, Sister. He is my son.'

'Then treat him as such. He has as much right to life as a girl.'

But at that Goneril started up a new wail and, watching her, Olwen wondered what fool's magic had blocked her rational view of this woman. Well, it was blocked no more. Goneril was shouting for Maedoc who, poor fool, came running like the lapdog he was, to find himself battered by a torrent of abuse. His sword was dull, his seed was poison, his whole existence was a curse on the Coritani. She ordered him tied to a post to be lashed and as he fought the ropes, babbling pitifully, Olwen feared for them all. Goneril's anger would rage itself out, she knew, but in the meantime she was a danger to everyone.

'Regan,' she whispered as a young girl with ripe breasts was ushered in to soothe the poor royal baby, 'are you able to ride out?'

'Of course,' she said instantly, though her eyes lingered on her nephew as he latched eagerly onto the girl's nipple.

Olwen grasped at her hands.

'Then go, will you, please?' The first of the lashes cracked out and Maedoc roared in pain. 'Go to Burrough whilst Goneril is . . . distracted.'

'To Burrough?'

'Hush! She will be looking for more than Maedoc to pay for this and I don't think it should be your father, do you?'

Regan looked over to her sister, drinking in Maedoc's pain as if it might assuage her own.

'I don't,' she agreed, and with a last nod to Olwen, she was gone.

Olwen looked down on the baby, sucking contentedly, oblivious to the chaos he had unwittingly brought into the world, and pitied him. Pitied them all. For a moment she considered following Regan but the child would need her protection, and the tribe with him. She had shackled herself to Goneril as surely as Maedoc was shackled to his post and she must ride out the pain at her side and pray for the circle of the Coritani fate to turn.

BELTANE

Summer

Chapter Thirty-three

BURROUGH HILL

Giamonios; Shoots-show days (May)

'You're nearly healed now, Taran. That ointment worked a treat.'

Taran flexed his shoulder and smiled at Magunna.

'It did.'

'I won't ask where you got it from.'

'No.'

'But people are always handing me things for you and Leir. You're popular men.'

'They feel sorry for us.'

'They want you back. Do you know, Caireen is regulating mealtimes now? Goneril announced it at the first Beltane moon. We are only allowed to eat twice a day – it's more efficient, she says.'

'What about the druids?'

'They are given leeway because, it seems, science and songmaking cannot be regulated.'

Taran had to smile at her casual dismissal of the talents of the druids.

'I like songs,' he said.

'I do too, lad, but do we need druids to sing them?'

Taran thought of that snowy night when the people had sung the cold away in his forge. They had not needed anyone special to provide the music, for all had known it.

He looked to the door were Mikah was lounging in the sun. The sentries had sounded the trumpets a little while back and he was looking curiously across at whoever had arrived and paying no attention to the group in the doghouse. He rarely did now. Magunna came in with food twice a day and Mikah spent most of his time in Lugh's heat, hailing others. He barely even found the energy to taunt Taran and Leir. That left them in a strange vacuum – shut away from society but very much within it. Taran still plotted escape but all had become dulled, as if the lessening of his pain and hunger had lessened his desire as well. It was no good.

He stood up.

'We need to do something.'

Leir looked up from the stick he'd been whittling with his eating knife. Deprived of anything else to do, he had turned to his beloved woodwork. The knife was worn but somehow he carved beautiful pictures into the wood, pictures of people dancing and eating and smiling. Magunna took them to the children and they were swapped and shared and treasured. Mikah thought they were silly, which was good because it meant he didn't stop them. He couldn't see that they were evoking happy memories for the people and that these could also inspire dreams of a better future.

'What should we do?' Leir asked.

It was a good question. Escape was in both their minds but although Mikah was bored he was good at his job, as was his night-time equivalent, a burly lad who talked to the moon but kept a sharp eye on his charges. Taran shivered at the memory of Dubus' recent attempt to free them. The big smith had come in the night, hammer in one hand, glowing poker in the other, but the night-guard had howled to his precious moon and he'd been seized in seconds. They had lashed him in front of the whole tribe, right outside the door to the doghouse, and Taran had wept to see his brave, burly friend reduced to a mass of weeping red flesh.

'I don't know,' he said now, 'but we have to do it ourselves.'

They both looked helplessly at their chains but Mikah had stood up, on high alert, and Taran realised there was a buzz running around the compound – a rumble of conversation and a drumming of footsteps, almost like the old days.

'Something's happened.'

They went to the bars in time to see Mikah leap into a salute and Taran's stomach churned as someone strode imperiously into the doghouse. It was Regan and she addressed herself straight to Leir.

'I have brought you news, Father. I thought it best it came from me.'

'News?'

Her back was stiff and Hawksheart was tight against her legs.

'Our chieftainess has had her baby.'

Leir gasped.

'The heiress is born?'

'No.'

Taran looked curiously at Regan. Was that a ghost of a smile on her lips?

'A boy?' Leir said. 'Oh, dear.'

It *was* a smile. Regan bent down to her hound to hide her expression.

'Goneril is not pleased.'

'I can imagine,' Leir said. 'I thought she saw a girl in the stars?'

'The stars lied. Or so she says. She is screaming abuse at all who approach her. And the poor baby . . . ' To Taran's astonishment, Regan softened visibly and stepped closer to Leir. 'She won't even look at him, Father, and he is so sweet. He's small and soft and he has such big blue eyes and they look so confused. I just want . . . ' She shut herself down but Taran saw the longing in her eyes. Aledus had insisted that Regan was happy forsaking motherhood in order to fulfil her role as a warrior, but it seemed that might have changed. 'Boys are not so bad, are they?' she asked Leir, almost plaintively.

Her father spread his hands wide.

'They are as you see. I do not feel I did such a bad job – until recently. Recently I have been useless.'

'Not useless, Father.'

'Well, I'm useless now.' He gave his bars a little shake. 'Will I be allowed to see my grandson?'

'You'll probably have him in here with you for all Goneril wants him. And Maedoc besides. It's all his fault, of course. He's been lashed.'

'Lashed? For what?'

'For his poor seed. Goneril is looking for people to punish.' She drew in a deep breath and dropped her voice. 'People who might not, perhaps, deserve it.'

Leir reached through the bars for her hand and she took it. She was quivering.

'Regan,' he said softly to her, 'you were a baby like that once. I remember it so well. I lifted you up from between your dear mother's legs and held you to the light and you kicked out your little limbs, eager to stride into life. I knew then that you would be a woman of action.'

Regan stared into his eyes and Taran held his breath, but then Mikah came stamping back inside and she jerked away. Hawksheart gave a single, high-pitched bark and Mikah glared at her.

'All well, Princess? The prisoners aren't giving you any trouble, are they? I'll see them whacked if they are.'

'Whacked?' Regan turned slowly to face him. 'You, Setantii, would see Chieftain Leir "whacked"?'

Mikah's eyes widened in horror.

'Only if they are giving you trouble, Princess. Only if—'

Her sword moved so fast that he didn't even have time to cry out. His head bounced to the earth with a dull thud and she shoved his corpse up against the bars with her boot. Blood pumped out of his neck and onto the keys he'd worn on a cord around it.

'I am going to see Caireen,' Regan said stiffly to Leir. 'She will be upset at the news of the boy child, I am sure. I will stay with her, see she is looked after. It may take a while. And I may need all my guard.'

'Danu bless you, Regan,' Leir said.

She looked at him.

'I will need her to. Farewell, Father. And you, Smith.'

And then she and her hound were gone and Taran was on the floor, fumbling for Mikah's bloody keys and freedom.

Chapter Thirty-four

BRAQUEMONT

Semiuisonns; Bright days (June)

Cordelia paced the edge of the sands, toying with the sea spirits, daring them to catch her feet then scrambling away just in time to confound them. With the Goddess' help, she had made her peace with the seawater and was at one with it and eager to sail. Every day she reminded herself of Sophia's words: *Water can douse fire and move earth.* She wished with all her heart that she did not need to but this was the way the spiral of her life had turned and she must follow it. She had a child on the way and a future to secure for it.

The Braquemont midwives said the baby was a good size and her body was swelling fast, perhaps too fast for this new life to be the product of her two-moon-turn marriage to the Belgic prince. If the child was Taran's then that was all the more reason to take it back to the Coritani lands that had brought them together, but it would be difficult. Sophia's spies had reported that Goneril had iron control of the forts, with her guards patrolling every border. She was worried about her sister's return then. Good.

Anghus came racing back along the sands towards her, a strange piece of driftwood in his mouth. Her father would love that, she thought, and with sudden anger took it from her dog and flung it into the waves. Undaunted, Anghus bounded in after it but then he stopped in the shallows, his body rigid, his big head looking intently out to sea. She strained to see what had caught his sharp canine eyes and then spotted it − a dark square against the sky. A sail.

"Tis just a ship, Anghus,' she told the dog. They came all the time, traders running goods between the shores. 'Come. Home time!' He came out of the water but his reluctance was apparent in the dragging of his paws and she stopped and looked again. 'What is it, boy?'

He gave a little whine and nudged against her and when she patted him, he ran back down to the shore. Cordelia followed. Perhaps it was Gleva and Map returning. She prayed so, for it would be good to see her dear friends again. Anghus began to caper, almost puppy-like, and Cordelia felt her heart lift then told herself not to be so stupid. She could see the man at the helm and he was just an ordinary sailor, running an ordinary trader across the waters. Anghus was a dog; what did he know of ships?

Even so, he barked excitedly and someone turned to look shorewards from where they sat huddled in the stern. Cordelia caught a glimpse of long, white hair, a flash of eyes as blue as the sky, and then the figure cried, 'Anghus? Anghus, is that you? And Cordelia, my dearest Cordelia!'

She fell to her knees, not caring that the waves threw themselves over her clothes for look what they were bringing to her.

'Father!'

He was standing now, wobbling precariously as he waved.

'They said you would be here,' he called.

'I am,' she cried foolishly back. 'I am here.'

Then she was up and running into the water as the boat came drifting into shore and Leir was leaping out, his legs as puppyish as Anghus'. Cordelia flung herself into his arms, feeling the blessed familiarity of his broad chest and drawing in the familiar scent of him, still strong over the salt and the weed of Braquemont's shore.

'Father, I cannot believe you're here.'

She could do nothing more than state the obvious it seemed, but the obvious was so glorious. She had Leir, as Sophia had asked. He was safe and well and together they could attack.

'I am,' he agreed. 'And I am not alone.'

And that was when he pulled her back from his chest, turning her to the boat as someone else leaped down from its deck – a tall, broad figure with a flop of dark curls and a lopsided smile that went straight to her heart.

'Taran!'

This was surely a ghost stepping up out of the Otherworld. But, no, he stood before her, his hands outstretched, and when she dared to reach for them, they clasped hers, strong and sure and so wonderfully familiar. He was truly here, truly at her side, and she could do nothing but stare.

'Visitors!' she heard someone say and turned, befuddled, to see Prasto coming down the cliff path, Ardra and Bethan rushing ahead and, behind him, Lucius, her husband.

'Taran,' she said again, but this time her voice cracked on the dear name.

The sea had delivered her the greatest gift she could imagine and she was not free to accept it. If she thought she had felt pain before, it was nothing to this.

That night Sophia had Prasto carry her once again into the ceremonial house to welcome her new guests before the whole tribe of the Belgae. Everyone took food and settled in wide circles around the fire, built up despite the heat of the day, to keep the chieftainess warm. The chatter was of tribes and boats and weapons, with everyone keen to see what news the guests had brought. Cordelia tried to focus but all she could see was Taran across the hearth, being eagerly questioned by Ardra. He was here. He was alive. Her whole body sang with the joy of it until Lucius sat down heavily at her side and the notes choked.

'So,' he said. 'The man you should have married is not dead.'

'No.'

'And yet, you are married to me now.'

'I know!' she snapped, and he flinched. 'Sorry. I'm sorry, Lucius. It's just – a shock.'

'To us both. You are my wife, Cordelia.'

'I know it.'

'And hate it.'

'I did not say that. I am very grateful to you, Lucius.'

'But you love *him*.'

She wanted to deny it for Lucius' sake but it was impossible. And he knew anyway. Had she not turned him down for Taran back in Burrough when it had seemed as if love was enough? But it had not been. She drew in a deep breath.

'I will learn not to. For you, Lucius.'

'I am honoured.'

His voice was petulant. She had to forgive him that for he was hurting but it did little to keep her gaze from the vibrant man across the blazing fire. Taran was listening intently to Ardra but Cordelia knew from the lines of his body that he was every bit as aware of her as she was of him. Her hand went to her belly and Lucius gasped.

'It is his?'

She snatched her hand away and looked back to her Belgic husband. His eyes were dark with fury and for good reason.

'No! No, Lucius, it is not. It cannot be. There has only been you.'

The lies were coming more easily now that they were sharpened by fear and he looked confused. She had done her best on her wedding night to simulate innocence and, indeed, it had felt so awkward and painful to her that it had been only part pretence.

'You swear to Danu?'

'I do.'

'On the life of the child?' She hesitated at that. She could not curse her baby with its mother's mistakes. Not that they'd been mistakes at the time. She'd given herself to Taran freely and in love, and if this baby came from that, it was a glorious creation. Lucius groaned. 'I have been a fool.'

'No, Lucius!'

'You have played me for a fool.'

'I haven't. I thought Taran was dead. Truly. I thought I was free and I gave myself to you gladly.'

'Not gladly, Cordelia, just wisely.'

His voice was a hiss of pain and she looked around nervously but all were wrapped in their own concerns. All bar the chieftainess who snared Cordelia's eyes with hers and beckoned her over. She rose nervously and edged around the hearth to sit at Sophia's feet.

'You summoned me, Chieftainess?'

'Not summoned, Cordelia, no. I couldn't help noticing your . . . debate with my son.' Cordelia hung her head. 'This man who has travelled here with your father is the one you were to marry?'

Cordelia stared into the dust, watching the sparks from the fire hit the trampled earth and fizzle out.

'Is it that obvious?'

'When you cannot move about yourself, you learn to watch the movements of others.'

Cordelia nodded and dared to look up into the wise eyes of her mother-by-marriage.

'I meant no dishonour to your son.'

'I understand that. You thought your suitor dead and chose the only path open to you. You have trodden it well but now, it seems, the path has forked and you must choose again.'

'I am married.'

Sophia gave a little wave of her hand.

'Marriage is a choice made by humans not by the Goddess. She sees far deeper into us than mere ceremonies and words.'

Cordelia stared at her, astounded.

'You are saying I could be free?'

'I am saying you *are* free. We all are. We are bound only by our own choices and our duty is quite simply to make them wise ones.'

Cordelia hung her head.

'Wise for whom?'

Sophia reached out and patted her shoulder.

'Ah, Daughter – that is where it is harder for you than for others, for you have more riding on your choices than most. You may take the hand of this smith with my blessing and head for the south road, carve out a path of your own. You have been through much already and no one would blame you.'

Cordelia looked into the flames and then on through them to Taran, sitting quietly on the other side. His eyes met hers and instantly she could picture them heading into Lugh's light hand in hand, Anghus at their side and their baby ripening within her. She could see them journeying to Gleva and Map's indolent sea where the sun ever shone and the waves rarely rose. She could see them setting up a forge and a doghouse, living the simple life of a normal family, far from the strife that Goneril was inciting across the lands of the Coritani. The picture was bright, colourful, beautiful. But it was as ethereal as the flames between them.

'I cannot do that.' She looked back to Sophia. 'I cannot do that, Chieftainess. I cannot abandon my tribe.'

Sophia's hand tightened on her shoulder.

'You pick the harder path.'

Cordelia shook her head.

'I pick the only path, Chieftainess. I am a daughter of the Coritani and I must return.'

'You are certain?'

Cordelia looked back to Taran and saw flames of sadness in his chestnut eyes. He knew as surely as she did what her choice must be and she locked her eyes onto his even as she nodded assent to renouncing him forever.

'I am certain.' She sat up straighter and, in a louder voice, said, 'It seems the Mother has sent Leir to us, Chieftainess.'

Sophia raised her own voice to match.

'It seems so. She must back your cause, Princess. What think you, Prasto?'

Her husband looked from Leir to Cordelia and then to his wife.

'I think we should give these people our aid. The world is a wide place and alliances stretch further than they used to. So what if these Coritani lands are over the seas? They are rich, it seems, in grain and iron, not to mention fine hounds.' Anghus gave a short, approving bark and the crowd laughed. 'Do you agree, Lucius?'

Cordelia looked to her husband. He rose slowly.

'I think that if my wife wishes to return to her people, it is my duty and honour to accompany her.'

Cordelia looked at him, hard and sure.

'It is my wish, Husband.'

'Then we should waste no time.'

He held out his hand and Cordelia took it and let him help her up at his side. Sophia gave a nod and Prasto joined them, throwing his arms wide to his tribe.

'Men and women of the Belgae – send out word that Chieftainess Sophia seeks brave fighters to help our new daughter, Cordelia, reclaim her land before Samhain is upon us!'

This was greeted with cheers and the pounding of tankards on stools as men and women called out their eagerness to join the expedition. Cordelia looked around, amazed. She had come to this clifftop tribe with nothing and yet here she had been given sanctuary and welcome and now support. Out of the corner of her eye she saw Taran rise and make his way between the cheering crowds towards the door but she had to let him go. However much she yearned to be in his arms, her place, for now, was with her new tribe.

It was only much later, when the moon weighed heavy in the sky and people had danced themselves into happy exhaustion, that Cordelia was able to slip outside and find Taran. She had to speak to him, not to explain for there was nothing here that he would not understand, but somehow to mark the passing of a love that had never had a chance to blossom. Perhaps, like all things, it would one day cycle back around and bless them both, but for now it must return to the earth from whence it had come and they must try to go on without it.

'Taran?'

He was sitting on the clifftop, shoulders hunched, with only the moonlight in his curls to distinguish him from the rocks to either side.

'Cordelia.'

His voice was hoarse with longing, and she felt treacherous tears spring to her eyes. She had to be strong here, for them both.

'I am glad you are alive.'

He looked out towards the dark sea again.

'I am not.'

'Not glad?'

'Not alive. Not truly. I was only ever truly alive when you were at my side.'

She sat down, keeping a careful distance between them.

'That's not true, Taran. You are alive at your anvil. You are alive when you work with the fire spirits to bend iron to your will and shape it into wonders for the world of men.'

He gave her a small smile.

'I thought I was, once, but the spirits have cast me down too many times.'

She ached to touch him, to be with him.

'You know I love you?'

He turned his head, nodded.

'I know. It is both my greatest joy and my darkest hurt. But I was never worthy of you.'

'That's not true!' Her voice rang out in the night air, clear and

329

angry. She forced herself to lower it but could not suppress her anger. 'You must never think like that, Taran. You *were* worthy because you were worth everything to me.'

'Except your tribe.'

'Except that.' Again tears rose, again she fought them back. 'I cannot sacrifice them, Taran.'

'I know it, Dee, and love you even more for it.' His voice caught and he grabbed at her hand. 'But I'm not sure I can bear it.'

'You can,' she told him, squeezing his fingers as if she could force all her love into his body that way. 'You are strong. I remember watching you tied to Mavelle's funeral platform, so firm and stead-fast in the face of death.'

He looked into her eyes.

'But this, Dee, this is worse than death.'

He spoke true and as she looked into his eyes her whole body seemed to pull towards him, as if a thousand spirits were tugging on every part of her. A third time, tears threatened and this time she let them fall as she leaned forward and pressed her lips to his, trying to imprint the taste of him onto herself like a tattoo and already knowing it would not be enough. Heart breaking, she forced herself away.

'We can bear it.'

'I pray so.'

'Who's there?' a voice demanded and they leaped apart, sending a clod of earth scuttering over the clifftop. It crashed onto the rocks below but they were both already up and facing the newcomer.

'Lucius?'

'Cordelia? Taran!'

'We were just saying goodbye.'

He peered at them in the silvery light of the moon.

'Goodbye?'

'Goodbye,' Taran confirmed. 'I am heading south. Tomorrow.'

A protest bubbled up in Cordelia's throat but she choked it down.

'You are?' Lucius asked the other man suspiciously.

'I am. Alone. Cordelia has made it very clear to me that she is your wife now and I respect that.'

Lucius cleared his throat.

'I'm sorry, Taran.'

Taran let out a low, painful laugh.

'It is not your fault, Lucius, truly. You have been nothing but gracious and will make Cordelia a worthy husband.'

Another protest bubbled inside her but now was not the time for quibbling. It was not individuals that mattered here, but their combined force.

'I cannot stand second,' Lucius warned. 'Not again. I have stood second to Ardra from the moment the twins were born. I can stand it as a brother, but not as a husband.'

'You will not be second,' Taran assured him. 'Cordelia has renounced me and I make no claim on her. I will not go near her. Nor she me.'

'You say that now.'

'I swear it. Here, on the moon.'

Lucius laughed.

'What use is the moon? Forever pulling one way and then the other.'

'Then on what?'

Lucius looked straight at him.

'On the life of your child.'

'My . . .'

Cordelia felt Taran look to her but could not meet his eye or she would crumble. Worse than that, she would move forward and tip Lucius off the cliff and be damned forever more.

'On the life of your child, Taran,' she said quietly.

He fell to the grass, clutching at it as if trying to tether himself to the earth.

'This is madness.'

Still Cordelia dared not look at him and it was Lucius who

reached out a hand. Taran let himself be helped up, brushed down his tunic, and looked at them both.

'I will go south,' he repeated. 'There will always be work for a smith.'

But at that Lucius shook his head.

'No. We will need you.'

'Need me?'

He nodded firmly.

'We will need you, Taran, to help us take Beacon.' They both looked at him, astonished. 'Oh, come, I may be hurting, you may be hurting, but this invasion is bigger than our petty concerns, is it not? So, Taran, will you come?'

Taran looked out to the seas for a moment, then turned and clasped Lucius' hand.

'I will come,' he said. 'And once Goneril is beaten and Cordelia installed, I will go south.'

Sounds of laughter and cheer drifted out of the fortress on the wind, teasing Cordelia with their simple joy. Lucius had spoken nobly but Taran was right – it might be too much to bear. She looked to her Belgic husband, standing so close to the sharp cliff. Out here it was dark. He could fall . . .

But if he did so, he would surely take her soul with him.

The two men were turning now, heading back to the cheer of the roundhouse.

'Will you come, Cordelia?' Lucius asked.

'In a moment. I need a little time alone.'

He nodded and left her, Taran in his wake, and Cordelia faced out to the seas once more. Just this morning she had thrown sticks into these waters for Anghus, readying herself for attack, and now she had an army to lead. But at a heavy price. She had thought Taran stolen from her. Now that he was here, she must, instead, throw him away.

She cast her eyes north as if she might see over the flat horizon to the forts of home – craggy Beacon, new-carved Breedon and her own dear Burrough. The seas were dark now, but kissed with silver light and sparkling enticingly. Opening her pocket, she took out her triskele amulet and lifted it to the light of the moon, visible in both sky and sea. The amulet spiralled slowly and, fixing it once more around her neck, Cordelia made a vow to the Goddess.

If she could not have Taran, she would have revenge on Goneril. Her heart would never mend, but she would shore it up with cold, hard iron and use it as her greatest weapon against the sister who had made this dread situation with her greed and malice. Goneril's death would not rob Cordelia of her soul but soothe it in its loss. From now on she would make revenge her sole purpose.

Chapter Thirty-five

BURROUGH HILL

Equos; Horse days (July)

Cordelia looked up the soft curve of the ripe green land to the ramparts of the fortress of Burrough: home. She'd left in fear and panic; now she was hiding in nearby forest preparing to launch an attack to reclaim it. The next rise of the moon would be decisive. She was ready – ready to rule, or ready to die.

They'd been cautious in their approach, breaking their sixty-strong troop into four groups to be led towards the Coritani lands by Leir, Taran, Cordelia and Lucius. In her own, she'd had Ardra and Bethan – the former determined to be part of the action and the latter unwilling to be left. They'd travelled as three women headed for the Equos horse fairs and attracted no more than passing notice. Cordelia had only been able to pray that the others had met with similar disinterest and it seemed that they had for here they all were, reunited in the forest below her beloved Burrough. She could hardly believe she was staring up at her home as an outsider, an invader even. The world had turned upside down indeed.

We are not invaders *here*, she reminded herself, or at least she prayed they would not be. Their target was Beacon but they had headed for Burrough first in the hope of gaining a feel for the mood of the tribe. Taran and a pair of Belgic lads were plodding up to the gate, packs of goods on their backs like any traders, hoping to make it inside and somehow find allies, and she watched them with her heart in her mouth.

Taran had thrown himself into the mission with a restless energy that Cordelia knew too well. She felt sorrow that by her own choices she had forced him – a simple smith, and not even Coritani born – to pour his soul into the defeat of Goneril, but he had his own reasons for wanting her overthrown and they were driving him hard. Now the time had come to make it happen.

Everyone was nervous. Leir had conducted raids before, of course, repelling the Setantii on several occasions, and Prasto had told them tales of running skirmishes with the Germanae to the east of his lands, but no one among them had attacked a fortress. No one had even heard stories of anyone attacking a fortress. Was this Goneril's damned "war"? If so, Cordelia hated it already. Sophia had gifted her a fine sword, made to fit her own small frame but strong and sharp. She had relished the feel of it during training, with leather covering the blade, but now she would have to wield it for real and the thought of taking life went against all her deepest instincts.

'He's in!' Bethan called back to the group.

Cordelia saw the great gates swing open and swallow Taran and his companions in an instant. Now all she could do was wait.

'Taran the smith? Is that you?'

Taran was delighted to see Solinus on guard but put his fingers to his lips as the older man peered at him.

"'Tis me. Is it safe, Solinus?'

'Lugh no! You're an escapee, an outlaw.'

'I know that!'

Taran looked around, taking in the big open compound at Burrough. In many ways it was still the impressive place he'd first encountered on riding through these very gates with Aledus a year and a half ago but it felt different now. The people working around the byres and weaving sheds all had their heads down. They laboured in silence where once there had been calls and laughter and it created an eerie unease. A group of children ran past him and even they went quietly. When he looked closer, Taran saw that they held not hoops or balls but little scythes. Well, he supposed, it was harvest time and all must help, but still it felt strange. He looked nervously to Solinus but he was making no attempt to call for help.

'Is Cordelia with you?' the guard whispered. Taran gave a small nod and a broad smile broke across Solinus' face, quickly smothered. 'She is the finest ware you could ever carry, trader.'

Taran's heart squeezed. Solinus spoke true but Cordelia was no longer his. He pushed the pain aside, as he had been forced to do time and again in these last long days.

'Who is in charge, Solinus?'

'Chief Caireen. But she is not here.'

'No?'

That was a blessing!

'She's gone on to Beacon to consult with the chieftainess before the Lughnasad celebrations.'

'The celebrations will be at Beacon this year?'

'They will.'

'And everyone will go?'

'Everyone in a fit state to walk, yes. We leave in two days but it is a long way on foot and the druids say the rains will come so many may plead illness.' He leaned in closer. 'There is not much appetite for celebration.'

Taran swallowed. This was more good news but he had to tread carefully.

'Who is in charge here at the moment?'

'Goneril's guards,' Solinus growled. 'We are like children, you see, Taran, not trusted to go about our business alone.'

His voice was bitter. Taran chose his next words carefully.

'You would be free?'

Solinus looked at him sharply.

'We would be respected.'

Taran nodded but people were looking over now, drawing closer; he was surely courting danger. He raised his voice a little.

'I wonder if I could, perhaps, take some refreshment? My fellow traders and I are hungry from our travels. Is Magunna still here?'

'She is. She's not well, I'm afraid, but I'm sure she will rouse herself if your goods are worthy. This way.'

Solinus led them, not to the royal house, nor to the ceremonial one, but to the animal byres in the western corner.

'No one lives here, do they?' Taran asked, as they threaded past a stooped man slopping out squealing pigs.

'They do now,' came the dark answer.

Taran tried not to look too obviously around him, though it was hard to miss the one-time elders of the tribe sitting hunched in the doorways of the rough outbuildings, soaking the sun into their frail bodies. He kept his head low and pulled his cloak tight to hide what felt like a drum pounding in his chest.

Solinus knocked at one of the doors and a thin voice called, 'Come in.' Taran edged inside to see an old woman sitting on a stool with a blanket wrapped around her. Chickens filled the room and she was huddled to one side of a makeshift hearth. He moved a little closer.

'Magunna?'

'Who are you?' She waved him closer. 'I know that voice. Come here, boy.'

Taran almost smiled. He'd not been called "boy" for a long time.

But his heart was still beating hard and seeing how frail Magunna had become shocked him. Was this really the woman who had tended him in his imprisonment just two moon-turns ago? Her stout body had dwindled and her ruddy cheeks turned pale from what he could see in the fire's meagre light. Her lively eyes seemed to have sunk into their sockets and her shoulders into her chest as if she had aged ten years overnight. She reached for his hand and tugged him down closer, recognition flaring in her eyes.

'Taran! Is that you, Taran?'

'Shhh.' He bent and kissed her hands where they held his own but already she was standing up, scattering the birds. 'Please don't get up, Magunna.'

'Don't get up! Listen to you. You're back after being who knows where and going through who knows what, the least I can do is heat you some stew.' She found a jar in the makeshift kitchen area at the back, poured broth into a cauldron and set it over the fire, throwing her whole stash of thin sticks beneath to stir up the flames. 'And you'll have some ale? Of course you'll have some ale. It's not as good as Nairina's but it'll wet your lips.'

'It'll do a good sight more than that, Magunna,' Taran said, accepting a cup and drinking deep. 'Danu bless you, that tastes of home.'

She looked closely at him.

'This is not home now, though, is it? They'll kill you if they find you. You're outside the law, boy, so there'll be no protection.'

'Shhh, Mags. You think I don't know that?'

'Sorry. I'm sorry. Oh, Taran, it's good to see you. You don't know how we've sickened here since you left.'

'You do look unwell.'

She banged at her scrawny chest so fiercely Taran feared it might break.

'I'm heart-sick. We all are.'

'Dubus?' Taran dared to ask.

'Dubus lives, as much as it is possible to do around here with everyone slaving all hours. We're not people anymore, Taran, we're animals and I'm sick of it.'

She spat out the last words so vigorously that the chickens squawked and flapped furiously but it was music to Taran's ears. He glanced to the door where Solinus hovered with his two Belgic "traders".

'Do others feel the same?'

'They do, Smith,' he said quietly. 'They do. No one will say it, save in whispers in the dark, but many whispers make a strong sound.'

Taran nodded, beckoned them all in close, glad of the noisy indignation of the birds to cover his words.

'We have men beyond these walls who can raise more than a whisper but not enough of them. We need help.'

Magunna's eyes shone. She glanced to Solinus, who edged closer.

'Taran has Cordelia with him, Mags,' he whispered.

'Cordelia!' The old woman rolled the name around her tongue like a charm. She slid her hand into her pocket-bag and drew out what looked like a small stick. Taran stared at it, puzzled, but as she held it out, he saw that one side was carved with a picture of people eating around a hearth. It was one of Leir's; she had kept it close. She stroked a finger across the raised image then straightened her back. 'Help to do what, Taran?'

He took a deep breath. If the wrong person was listening, or if he'd judged the mood here incorrectly, he was putting himself, the displaced royals and sixty brave Belgae in grave danger. But this was what they'd come for and it was time to act.

'Help to overthrow the chieftainess.'

There was a silence, filled only by the thud of his heart, and then Magunna said, 'I'll help with that.'

'And I,' Solinus said. 'And many more besides.' He also drew a stick out of his pocket, the design showing children racing with bounding dogs. 'We are all but overthrown by Goneril at the moment so we have little to lose.'

Taran's heart slowed. He felt a calm rise within him. Magunna slid her stick back into its hiding place then passed him and his companions stew. He ate hungrily, drawing in the taste of home. This might just work. And even if it did not, they would know, he and Cordelia and Leir, that they had been right to try.

'What would you have us do?' Solinus asked.

Taran cleared his throat.

'You are due to march to Beacon in two days, yes?'

'Yes.'

'Then go a day early. Gather just after daybreak tomorrow. Caireen's guards will have to follow you outside, if only to try and stop you. And when they do, we'll be waiting.'

'You will kill them?'

'If we must. Then I will join you on the road and so—' he took another breath '—will Leir.'

'Leir!' Magunna gasped, and he clapped his hand over her mouth before she could cry the name too loud.

'Sorry, Mags, but we must be careful.'

'Of course. I'll shut my big mouth, don't worry. But Leir! That will cheer the people.'

'They must say nothing.'

'Understood.'

'They must look as usual.'

'Downtrodden and dulled?'

'Perfect. We will look so too. And once inside Beacon, I hope we can recruit more to our cause. Is Bardo still there?'

'As far as we know. News from the other forts is kept for the Upper House.'

'The what?'

'That is what they call the ceremonial house now.'

'Upper?'

Magunna shrugged.

'Stupid. But not for long, hey?'

'Not for long,' Taran agreed. 'I should go.' He handed her his empty bowl and she shuffled over to the table with it, worryingly slow. 'Are you sure you're capable of this, Mags? You look—'

'Heart-sick, I told you. But I am mending fast, for I have the best medicine now – purpose. Thank you, Taran the smith. Thank you so much. We will not let you down, will we, Solinus?'

'We will not,' he agreed. 'Just after daybreak we will be out on the road.'

'If you can.'

'Oh, we can. We can and we will.' He showed the three of them to the gate with some loud grumbling about the state of their supposed wares and kicked them unceremoniously out. 'Try Beacon,' he called after them, 'though I doubt you'll be welcome there!'

'I doubt it too,' Taran said under his breath to his companions as they scrambled down the road and, at last, back under cover of the trees.

The group were waiting, Cordelia first among them, and he saw joy in her eyes as they came into view, before she quickly veiled it. This was how it had to be now, their love living only in the cracks between their duty. It was not how he'd wanted it. None of this was how he'd wanted it but one thing at least he could get right – he could return the Coritani lands to the Coritani.

'We have help,' he said and felt the words ripple like a cooling breeze around the anxious group concealed beneath the trees. 'We have help and tomorrow we strike.'

Chapter Thirty-six

The next day

Cordelia had not thought she would sleep but the exhaustion of the long days of travel and the emotion of seeing Burrough again must have got to her for she did not stir until Lugh sent grey fingers of light through the trees. It was a chill morning, with mist rising around them, but no one dared light a fire so they ate hunks of hard cheese and pieces of stale bread and then traced a careful way through the trees, as close to Burrough as they dared.

Cordelia's spirit soared. There must be upwards of fifty people milling around on the road, all carrying travelling bundles. She made out plump Nairina, thickset Dubus and wiry Solinus with her own dear dogs at his heels. Magunna had done it! She had brought the people of Burrough out for them.

She pictured the old lady pottering around when she, Goneril and Regan had been small, feeding them and cleaning up after them, doing their hair and fitting their tunics and mothering them as best as she could whilst they bickered and played. How had they grown into three young women who would tear themselves apart so terribly that she must now, when she should be resting at the end of her days, march out to an uncertain battle between them? But Cordelia could not dwell on that. Her heart was iron now and she would try, somehow, to make things right for the Coritani. She glanced to Leir, dressed all in brown with a rough, hooded cloak hiding his features.

'You are sure about this, Father?'

'Very sure. I will walk with my people.'

'You will be careful?'

'Of course. As will you?'

'I promise. We will see you at Beacon.'

'We will see you *inside* Beacon.'

She gulped. The plan was for Cordelia and Lucius to lead the Belgae in a stampede up to Beacon and for the Burrough men and women already within to overcome the guards and gain them entry. From there it would be every man and woman for themself so it was less a plan than a thread of hope, but they had come too far to turn from it now.

'You are ready?'

Taran appeared too suddenly for her to shore herself up against him and her whole body pulsed at his nearness. She glanced around, saw Lucius bend to his pack, and shot out a hand to catch Taran's for the briefest of moments.

I love you, she wanted to shout through the trees, so loud it sent the ravens cawing from the tops, but she dared not and could only hope her eyes said it for her. He gave her a smile, lopsided as ever and rich with times shared, and it spread through her as if Lugh had broken from the clouds and shone down.

'Danu be with you,' she choked out, and then he was gone and she was left to clutch at a tree and watch as he made his way agonisingly slowly out onto the road.

Taran, Leir and the four Belgae reached the outlying workers in safety and moved steadily up to the front. Cordelia saw a few heads turn as Leir passed by and noticed people drawing small sticks from their pockets and holding them out to touch his cloak in some ritual of their own. It was quietly done, however, and the guards arguing with Magunna at the front noticed nothing.

Nothing, that is, until the six men sprang, in perfect unison, and cut their throats.

Cordelia watched them fall to the ground, gurgling out fury and fear, and hated it. This was not the dignity of a sacrifice, or the prayer-laden passing of the sick-bed. This was raw, sickening horror and it was only the cry of release that came instinctively from the mass of oppressed people on the road that made it bearable.

Clutching the iron of her duty around her aching heart, she turned to the group she must now lead through the forest and around the back of the Coritani Hills to surprise the enemy – to surprise her sisters. She could only pray Taran and his band would get inside undetected, for upon that the whole flimsy plan depended.

Taran felt ... he wasn't sure what it was. Light, giddy, relaxed – happy. That was it. He felt happy. He had been too long a stranger to the emotion to recognise it at first but that's what it was. Ridiculous, really, to march towards terror and feel happy, but his time left on Danu's precious earth might be too short not to embrace happiness when he found it. He might not have Cordelia's hand but he had her heart, and he had her blessing, and he had her cause to fight for.

He looked around at his fellows as they walked. They were all being cautious, keeping their heads down and their steps slow, but many held Leir's sticks as talismans and he felt purpose rippling through them. At his side, Magunna moved like a new woman – not the shuffle of the servant he had walked in on yesterday, but the march of a leader.

'You walk like a princess, Mags,' he told her, and she laughed.

'I walk *for* a princess, Taran.'

That said it all. Cordelia's bold plan had given them back belief in themselves and he ached to make it work. They had to convince the Beacon guards that they were loyal workers, arrived to worship at the altar of Goneril, eagerly early and minus their guards. It was a risk but a far lesser one than arriving at the same time as Regan and Aledus' highly trained warriors. The people of Burrough carried weapons hidden in their packs but they were mere knives, hammers and plough blades – no match for the swords that he, Taran, had made for the warriors. He shivered and reached into his own pack, fingers closing around the reassuring shape of his hammer. Magunna had handed it to him once the guards were dead.

'I saved it for you,' she'd said simply, and he'd been touched and grateful.

Just holding it in his hands again made him feel more himself. Running his fingers down his own name, carved into the handle by old Vindilus to mark the end of his first apprenticeship as a smith, restored a little of his identity. The path of his life had turned in many unexpected ways since it had been so nearly cut off by the predatory Catto in a market and today's turn was just one more.

Defeating Goneril would do little for his own future but it was vital for the safety of those that he loved, and not just Cordelia. On his other side Dubus walked bravely but his skin was bitterly lined from the lash's bite and his spirit cowed. Taran owed him vengeance. Then there was Gleva and Map, who had so unflinchingly rescued him as a boy and were now on the run for helping Cordelia escape. Today was his chance to make the Coritani lands safe for them once more.

Taran whistled a little tune and felt it taken up by the man behind and then the next until the whole procession was piping out his ditty and he looked to the skies and laughed. Yes, he was happy and he would make the most of it for by the time Lugh reached his peak they would be at Beacon – the heartland fortress of the Coritani.

It did not take long and the party slowed their steps nervously as they saw Goneril's fortress on the horizon. Once inside, they were to put up their tents as usual, cook their rough meals as usual and then wait – very much not as usual – for Cordelia's Belgic troop to attack so they could rise up. The weaker adults had been assigned to keep the children as far from the fighting as possible but other than that there was only one instruction: fight.

They crept closer. There were many workers in the fields outside the fortress still, to Taran's surprise, gathering in the grain that the tribe would bless into the storage pits at the first Lughnasad moon in just two days' time. He scanned them eagerly and, to his delight, picked out Bardo not far from the road. The man seemed to sense him there but had the wit to say nothing so Taran dared to lift his cloak and show his knife. Bardo gave a small, grim nod and Taran could only pray he had understood.

The gates loomed and Taran and Leir had to drop back and leave Magunna and Solinus to face Goneril's guards. It was a big task for humble people but they had insisted they were ready.

'What are you lot doing here?' The sentry's voice rang out, clear and scornful.

'We are here to celebrate the start of Lughnasad with our glorious chieftainess,' Magunna's voice came back.

'You're early.'

'Early?'

'Yes. You're a day early. You're due tomorrow.'

Magunna made a good show of turning to her companions and sending a ripple of apparent shock down the group.

'Beg pardon, sir, we were told to come today.'

'Told by whom? Where are your guards?'

Magunna bowed low.

'They went up into the Black Hills, sir. The Goddess called them. There is a herb Chief Caireen wanted for the ceremony. They'd been unable to find it for her but as we crossed a stream, a single flower from the very plant floated past on the current. It was a sign, sir – a sign that Danu wishes the herb to reach Chieftainess Goneril. They could not turn from it so they sent us on and will follow later.'

The guard squinted at her.

'What is this herb?'

'I know not, sir. I am but a humble farmhand.'

The guard grunted but his companion nudged him and they conferred in low voices for agonising moments. Taran glanced sideways at Leir, his breathing compressed in his chest, but the old man was standing very straight, eyes fixed on the Guardian rock to their left, and suddenly the guard was speaking again.

'It's damned inconvenient so I hope you've brought your own food, but as it happens there's grain still to be got in so we'll make space for you.'

Leir gave a single nod and Taran felt his breathing relax to something like normal. Danu was surely on their side. He certainly hoped so and as the gates ground open to let the people of Burrough trudge silently into the ancient compound they were one step closer to finding out.

Another forest, another fortress. Cordelia looked up at the craggy rise of Beacon Hill and noted Goneril's new beacon, standing tall and bright against the skyline. Her heart twisted. It was a thing of beauty indeed but commissioned by a dark spirit and it seemed to loom arrogantly over the heartland fortress. She swallowed. Here, they had no chance of a friendly welcome.

Lugh was curving high above Goneril's monument, his face veiled behind cloud as if he could not bear to watch. By the time he headed beneath the earth once more, she would either have control of the Coritani or be buried with him. Today she would face the monster her sister had become and either defeat her or be defeated. There was, at least, clarity to that. She looked to Prasto standing at her side.

'No doubts?'

'Many but this is not the time to indulge them.' He smiled at her. 'It's a craggy place this heartland fortress of yours.'

'No cliff, at least, to be thrown from,' Lucius said, coming up on his father's other side.

'I am so grateful to you both for standing with me,' Cordelia told them.

Prasto looked to Lucius and gave him a quiet nod, one man to another. He received a smile in return. Bethan and even Ardra had grown quieter since the slaying of the guards at Burrough but Lucius had led his group with a quiet assurance that had kept them calm and focused.

'Your sisters will stay in the trees?' Cordelia asked him.

'They will. They are too precious to risk in a fight. I have assigned them a guard and they know their place.'

He looked to the twins who nodded meekly. Cordelia saw that they were holding hands – children again at this harsh time – and went to kiss them both.

'You can come in when we win,' she said.

Bethan raised a smile.

'Shall I care for Anghus?'

Cordelia shook her head.

'Anghus comes with me.'

'Into war?'

The new word sounded stark. She'd hoped he would never have to fight but she had trained him for it and needed all the support she could get.

'Into war, yes. He will fight for me like no other.'

'Not quite,' Lucius said, and she kissed him too.

'You are a good man, Lucius. I wish our return here could have been peaceful.'

'It will be, Cordelia. After today it will be. If there is one thing I fear this battle will teach us, it is that we never wish to see another.'

At that, however, Ardra finally spoke.

'You will win.'

They all looked at her.

'You see it in the stars?' Prasto asked eagerly.

She gave a small smile.

'Not in the stars, Father, no, but I do see it in Cordelia's people. They are with you, and if a ruler has their people with them, they will succeed.'

'Wise words.'

She gave a little grimace.

'I have learned much from this strange trip.'

She was sombre, all too aware of her duty. She was not, after all, like Goneril and Cordelia was grateful for it.

'If anything goes wrong, Ardra, you are to flee. You and Bethan are to take your guard and get away. Go home to the Belgae who need you. Promise me.'

'I promise, Cordelia. But I told you – you will win.'

'Pray Danu you are right. And now, it is time.'

She looked to Beacon. On the rise above the ramparts she could see Taran and Leir's workers being organised into a group. It seemed they were to be marched out of the gates again, perhaps to join the others in the fields beyond. It was perfect.

'Ready?' she asked the men and women of her command. And as one they nodded.

Chapter Thirty-seven

They ran with all speed, weapons held high, voices screaming murder. The time for stealth was gone and they must shout their fury to the skies and pray Danu bounced it back onto their enemies. The war-cry ripped from Cordelia as if she were pouring her soul out into the bright Lughnasad air and as she ran, she saw the workers up above take up the roar. The sentries wavered, confused, and were cut down. Then the gates were being wrenched open and she was heading up into the heartland of the Coritani, Anghus at her side and her people at her back.

A man came at her, fury in his face, and she lifted Sophia's sword in readiness, but Anghus was ahead, leaping at his throat and bringing him down with one bite of his big teeth. Cordelia blinked but had no choice but to step over the dying body and push on. Goneril had many guards and the noise as they piled into the fight was immense – shouts of rage and spite, cries of pain and victory, clashes of iron and crunches of bone. A glance back told her that the Beacon field workers were coming running, tools lifted, and she could only pray they were pouring in on her side, though in the melee of people it was hard to see who fought whom.

Cordelia held her own sword nervously aloft, desperately trying to recall the training Prasto had given her with his Belgic troops, but every bit of it had gone from her brain and she would have to rely on the quivering rage pulsing from her heart straight down her sword arm. That and her wits. Eyes darting everywhere for attackers, she threaded her way round the sacred oak to look at the royal house. And there she was – Goneril.

Cordelia hovered in the protection of the great trunk and saw her sister emerge, looking round at the fighting with indignation. Caireen and Maedoc were at her shoulders and Olwen behind, her sharp eyes taking in the horrific scenes around them. The high druidess spotted Cordelia and seemed to give a little nod, as if she had seen them coming in the stars. But if she had, she had not chosen to share that with the chieftainess.

'What are they doing?' Goneril shrieked, pointing a furious finger at a worker attacking one of her guards with a rusty but highly sharpened hoe.

'I think they're trying to rebel,' Caireen said, peering around as if at insects trapped in a dish for study.

'Rebel? Why?'

Cordelia felt all her rage coalesce into sheer hatred for the woman she should have loved above all others. Sunset on water, that's what her sister was, all display with no warmth or kindness, and Cordelia was determined to see that false light extinguished.

'Perhaps,' she said, stepping forward, 'they are sick of your oppression.'

Goneril swung her way.

'You! You would lead these peasants against me, Cordelia?'

'We should have killed her when we had the chance,' Caireen snarled.

'And her bastard smith,' Goneril agreed. 'Is he here?'

'Does it matter?' Cordelia challenged.

Goneril shrugged.

'It won't once he's a corpse, like the rest of you. Kill her!' she shouted at her guards and two of them came forward, but Anghus growled, low and fierce, his big teeth bared, and they hesitated. Goneril laughed.

'It can wait. We can execute her properly when her pathetic little troop has been dispatched. What made you think you could defeat me with this lot, Sister?' She waved scornfully at the hoe-wielder as he was cut down by the swing of a guard's heavy sword. But now Prasto stepped up with five of his finest fighters and her green eyes widened. 'Who ... ?'

'It is best,' Cordelia called, 'to make friends not enemies.'

Goneril's eyes filled with raw, gold-flecked fury.

'Kill her!' she screamed again, but her guards were squaring up to the Belgae and could not break loose to threaten Cordelia.

She glanced around. All over the compound the people were holding their own. The Beacon dwellers were standing side by side with their Burrough counterparts and they vastly outnumbered Goneril's guards. They could do this. They could win. She looked triumphantly back to Goneril but her sister was smiling now – a thin, sly smile.

'Oh, I have friends, Cordelia. Or, at least, subjects.'

She waved a hand to the gates and, glancing over, Cordelia saw the worst possible sight – a mass of warriors marching on Beacon and already quickening their pace as they scented the very thing for which they had been so rigorously trained: war. Cordelia gripped her sword tighter as the first of them ran into the compound. All eyes turned, all faltered. The fight paused as if Danu herself had reached out and frozen it then Regan rode in, Aledus at her right shoulder and Hawksheart on high alert at her left.

'About time, Regan,' Goneril shouted across. 'Kill them!'

'Kill who, Chieftainess?'

'The people.'

'*Our* people?'

Goneril glanced around as the myriad men and women of the Coritani shifted their field weapons and bravely planted their feet more firmly in the ground. Cordelia's heart shook for them.

'Our people,' Goneril said coldly. 'And their leaders too.'

'Leaders?'

The air seemed to tremble and then a man stepped from the midst of the suspended fighting and lifted his helmet.

'I am a leader of our people, Regan.'

Leir's voice was clear and strong as he faced his middle daughter and Cordelia knew immediately what she had to do.

'And I,' she backed him loudly.

One of Goneril's guards came for her but Anghus bared his teeth and he edged back.

'And I.' The voices of Lucius and Taran came out as one and Cordelia quivered to hear it.

Regan's eyes flitted across them uncertainly and still the mass of warriors waited. She held the balance of the battle and Goneril did not like it. The chieftainess moved up to the high ground by the beacon, her guards around her like a magic circle. She peered down at her subjects.

'Regan, order your warriors to serve.'

'To serve whom?'

'Me, of course. To serve *me*.'

'Or,' Cordelia challenged, 'to serve the tribe.'

Regan glanced to Aledus then down to her hound. Hawksheart pressed tight at her side but her eyes were on Anghus, the brother with whom she had tumbled in their whelping box. Regan frowned and looked back to Goneril.

'Where is your son, Chieftainess? Where is the prince?'

Goneril squinted at her.

'What does *he* matter? Do as I tell you, warrior – now!'

Regan gave a shake of her head and looked to Cordelia. Their eyes locked and Cordelia saw confusion and fear and desperate uncertainty in her middle sister's strong face. She put a hand to Anghus' head and saw Regan do the same to Hawksheart. *A hound knows what is important*, her own voice said from a far-off Imbolc dawn when Goneril had first left them to pursue power alone.

Loyalty, love and trust. As if she'd heard it too, Regan gave a quiet nod and raised her hand to those behind her.

'Troops, stand down!'

Her warriors fell back instantly and the people, deprived of an enemy before it had struck, looked at each other in confusion. Goneril's remaining guards retreated to the group around the chieftainess and all eyes turned their way. Regan approached and Goneril stared her down.

'You would desert me, Sister?'

'As you deserted Cordelia.'

'Me? Cordelia left us.'

'No, Goneril. *You* drove her away. *You* broke the triskele.'

'The triskele!' Goneril touched her fingers to her amulet. 'Oh, come, Regan, that was always a joke.' She ripped it from her neck and held it high. The triple spiral spun in the low sun. 'This was never us.'

'It was!' Regan spluttered. 'Three royal daughters. A *Deas Matres* for the Coritani.'

'A pleasing idea, but look at it – three equal spirals? We have never been like that. I am in command, I am on top, I am fire, the greatest of the elements, and that is as it should be. That is why it is better if you do as I say.'

Regan stood, open-mouthed, and Cordelia stepped up at her side.

'Perhaps, Goneril, this unevenness is why the spiral unwound? But we are two now, and you are only one.'

'Yet still chieftainess.'

The word hung in the air, heavy with ancient symbolism. Swords and hoes alike quivered around the compound. Then someone stepped forward, tall and stately in brightest white.

'And, as such, subject to the rule of law.'

'What? Olwen!'

Goneril glared at her high druidess who met her fury calmly.

'I call you, Chieftainess Goneril, to trial for murder.'

'Murder?'

'Murder of Chieftainess Mavelle.' She advanced suddenly, stabbing a finger into Goneril's face. 'You sabotaged her wings, Goneril. You deliberately and cold-heartedly sabotaged her wings to send her to her death so that you could take the throne. You robbed us all of a wonderful invention and, more importantly, a wonderful woman and a wise ruler.'

Goneril shook before Olwen's cold fury.

'It wasn't me,' she stuttered.

'It wasn't you who cut the wings?'

'No! Of course it wasn't.'

'But they were cut?'

Goneril gasped, looked frantically around, and decided, as ever, to save herself.

'It was him. It was Maedoc. It was all his idea. "You'll be a stronger rule, Goneril"; "She's old anyway, Goneril"; "It will be better for everyone, Goneril".'

Olwen did not even glance at the protesting man.

'I see. But you agreed? You sanctioned his act. You, Chieftainess, highest of the Coritani who must be obeyed in all things, agreed to cut Mavelle's wings.'

'No, I . . .'

The druidess shook her head.

'With power comes responsibility, Goneril.'

'Olwen!' Goneril pleaded desperately. '*You* chose Maedoc for me.'

'No,' Olwen said, her voice cold. 'I chose Taran thé smith. And I choose him again for his fire is finer than yours. Cordelia, I stand with you!' And with that she drew a long slim dagger from her belt and lunged at Maedoc. 'For Mavelle!' she cried. 'And for science.'

All watched, open-mouthed as she slashed at his arm. Maedoc winced but drew his sword – his ivy-patterned, ceremonial sword. Lifting the magnificent weapon, he moved to meet Olwen's tiny blade in an easy defensive parry, his shoulder already swinging round to drive on into her flesh. But the moment the blades met, his shattered and fell in pieces at his feet – just as Taran had

355

told Cordelia it would the very day it was presented to Goneril's oiled groom.

The crowd gasped and called on Danu. Olwen staggered but pressed her advantage, plunging her blade deep into his muscled chest and sending him falling at Goneril's feet, blood spurting across her in a bright scarlet arc. Olwen stared, frozen by her own action, and Cordelia wrenched her backwards as Regan's warriors poured past.

'You cannot let them take me,' Goneril screamed at the gang of men and women still clustered tightly around her. 'You are as guilty as I am. Would you see out your lives on their stinking gibbets? Or would you fight for your freedom?'

Terrified, they leaped to her command and the fight began. Cordelia saw Regan drop low and chop across the thigh of one man, sending him sprawling as Lucius ran in at her side, stabbing into the neck of a second. He, too, fell but still they came. Taran and Prasto joined the fight, Leir swift on their heels and Dubus hammering in behind, roaring fury.

One of the guards peeled off and swung out at Cordelia. She ducked aside and felt his blade glance off her shoulder, sending pain juddering through her body. Her vision misted but through it she saw Anghus spring, growling destruction, and the man fall. Wiping her eyes clear, she ran forward. Anghus had taken a cut but was whole and up at her side as the fighting raged on. Regan's warriors outnumbered Goneril's faithful ten to one but the defenders were in a tight circle on the high ground and were hard to break.

'Goneril must die,' someone cried. Taran ducked round next to Cordelia, his gorgeous chestnut eyes dark as a storm and his sword held high. 'It's the only way – Goneril must die.'

She grabbed at his arm.

'Not by your hand, Taran. Whoever attacks her will be cut down straight away.'

'But will take Goneril with them to the Otherworld. It is my final gift to you. Rule well, my love. Rule well.'

He planted a fierce kiss on her lips then pulled away and charged into the fighting, cutting between the battling warriors and making straight for Goneril. The guards were momentarily wrong-footed and he leaped into the circle, bringing his precious smith's hammer down on her royal head in one smooth motion and driving the life from her instantly.

The crowd gasped as her guards turned inward to cut her killer down and it was a matter of moments for Regan's warriors to hack at their backs in turn. Suddenly there was a heap of bodies beneath the beacon with Taran, her own dear Taran, buried in the bloody centre.

Silence fell across the ancient compound. Somewhere in the trees below a hawk cried and in the animal byres behind the bloody fighting, chickens clucked anxiously. A pig snorted, the people shifted and slowly, like a breeze rising up from the Coritani plains, normality blew across the melee. It released Cordelia's feet from the mud and she ran forward, hauling corpses aside to get to the mutilated body of the man who had saved them. Falling to her knees, she cradled him to her, stroking a curl back from his bloodied brow and closing his soft brown eyes forever. So many times in these last desolate moon-turns she had thought she'd lost him and he had been miraculously saved for her but now he truly was gone. Or almost.

Her hand cradled her belly and, as if its father's spirit had passed directly into it, she felt the babe within quicken and kick lightly against her skin. It was a pulse of life amidst the death and Cordelia's iron heart cracked just a little and beat, hard, against her ribs. Goneril was dead and the Coritani were dropping their weapons and drawing close. She tried to stand but her legs buckled and it was left to Regan to haul her up and away from the mangle of death.

Anghus pressed against her leg and she put a hand to his head to steady herself as she looked around. Aledus was coming out of the royal house with Goneril's unwanted baby held safe in his arms.

Dubus was leaning on Bardo, and Olwen was pressing herself against the sacred oak in supplication to the Goddess. Magunna and Solinus were wrapped together like young lovers, the horror of battle overcoming what must have been thirty years of shyness. Cordelia smiled to see it.

'Cordelia?' Lucius came to her, his voice hesitant. 'I'm sorry about Taran.'

She held out her hands to him.

'Do not be. He has gone to the Goddess in glory.'

'And we will honour him for it.'

She smiled at her husband. He was streaked with blood and, as his father came up to join them, she could see him limping. Prasto seemed sprightly enough, however, as he went to welcome Ardra and Bethan who came running in through the gates. They crossed paths with a slim figure in white who fled into the woods, blonde hair streaming behind her. For a moment Cordelia considered sending warriors after Caireen but there had been enough death and she went to welcome the Belgic princesses instead. They looked around in wonder at the craggy heartland fortress of their brother's adopted tribe and Cordelia felt blessed to have this new family with her. But now the people were crowding in and there was no time for personal reflection.

'Long live Chieftainess Cordelia!' Regan cried out.

The tribe joined in as one, their voices echoing from all over the craggy compound, and the music of their shared joy burst Cordelia's heart out of its iron shackles and let pure love flow back in. For too long the Coritani had been lost in darkness but it seemed that light had finally come. Gripping Regan's hand in one of her own and Lucius' in the other, she opened her arms to them all.

Epilogue

We held no funeral for Goneril. We called no mourning, said no prayers, burned no torches. We sent no sacrifice with her to the Otherworld for too many had been made already. Instead, we laid her on a simple platform, not in the sacred grove, but beneath a solitary oak that had grown inexplicably apart from the rest.

For two days and nights we left her there alone. I kept a distant vigil – not for her soul, but for my own that I might never again make such a grievous error – and on the third I saw two women slip out beneath the moon to stand before her. To stand with her.

Without words they took their amulets from around their necks and laid their two triskeles on her breast, along with the third, retrieved from the blood and mud of battle.

'She ripped us apart,' Regan said.

Cordelia shook her head.

'She never truly saw us together. She was not made to be one of three and her fire burned itself out.'

'Leaving earth and water?'

'Yes. But that way we are solid and, remember, we have the cleverest druids in the land – if we need it, we can make fire.'

Regan nodded slowly as they stepped back and looked again upon the rotting remains of their elder sister. She reached for Cordelia's hand and Cordelia clasped it tight.

'Two can be strong,' she said.

Regan looked at her, smiled.

'Two will be strong,' she corrected.

Then together they turned from the corpse and headed back up Beacon Hill with determined step and I knew that, at last, they were ready to serve the Coritani as true rulers.

Acknowledgments

I have really enjoyed both researching and writing *Iron Queen* and owe a big debt of gratitude to so many people for being around for me during the process.

Firstly, my marvellous editor, Anna Boatman, whose insight and encouragement worked marvels on this manuscript. Her intelligent reading of my rather lurid first draft really helped me to hone this novel into something far better than it would have been and I'm eternally grateful. I'd also like to thank the rest of the team at Piatkus, especially Ellie Russell and Jess Gulliver, for all their hard work on my behalf – it's so appreciated.

A big shout out to my fabulous agent, Kate Shaw, who took me on for a contemporary fiction novel thirteen years ago and didn't even bat an eyelid when I said I fancied writing historicals. She's been with me all the way, encouraging me, guiding me, shaping my books and my career. She keeps my wings in the air and my feet on the ground! Thank you so much, Kate.

A really big thank you to my mum, Jenny King, for producing the totally beautiful drawings of a roundhouse and Burrough hillfort for the novel. I was keen for readers to have a visual entry into the world of Iron Age living and was so lucky to have my own talented artist on tap – especially one patient enough to 'add a top floor' and 'move the hearth a little' and 'make that willow panel higher'. Roundhouses fascinate me and I have to thank you, Mum, for bringing mine to life so well.

As always, I must thank my immediate family, perhaps especially for this novel my son, Alec, who was so very unkeen to come and look around Burrough Hill with his enthusing mum but did it anyway. I'm not sure he feels hillforts are a progression from castles but he did his teenage best to show a vague interest. Thanks, too, to Hannah, Emily, Rory and of course Stuart. They keep me happily tethered to the present, allowing me to fly off into the past at will, and I'm so grateful to have them all.

This novel is dedicated to my dad, Will Gibb, and with good reason. For years now he has been the first to read my drafts, always doing so speedily and offering considered and helpful advice. He's also always the first to say that he's 'no great critic' but I want him to know that to me he is and his involvement in my books means a huge amount to me. Thanks, Dad.

Finally, thank you to you – my readers. Without you this novel would just be some meaningless scribbles on a few sheets of paper. Nothing beats a message from a reader to say that they have enjoyed one of my books, so I really hope you enjoyed this one and do get in touch. I love to hear from you.

www.joannacourtney.com
Twitter – @joannacourtney1
Facebook – @joannacourtneyauthor

Historical notes

The Iron Age is a long time ago – far too long for anything as helpful as written records. What we know of this rich period, therefore, has come down to us entirely from artefacts – bodies buried in the land, personal possessions sunk in marshes, and marking on rocks. The only other way that we can access the misty depths of these times is via oral traditions, usually reported to us by writers some centuries after. Whilst they will, therefore, have been adapted, altered and even misunderstood by the writers who finally committed them to paper, there must be cores of truth – or at least of belief – remaining within them and to that tenuous string historians of the ancient past must often cling.

It has been both fascinating and challenging writing a novel set so far back in time. So many aspects of society were different, especially in terms of cultural and religious beliefs and practices. In truth, I have loved breaking through the barrier of Christianity to look at a world still un-infiltrated by the many moral and practical rules that this very rigid religion has imposed on most of western society and hope I have done it justice. The novel will undoubtedly raise questions and these notes might answer a few of them. If you have more, feel free to contact me via Twitter @joannacourtney1, Facebook @joannacourtneyauthor, or my website www.joannacourtney.com.

Matriarchal society

I must be honest – we do not have concrete proof that Celtic society was matriarchal. On the other hand, neither do we have proof that it was not and there are enough hints from the past to believe it's a firm possibility.

We know for sure that there were sufficient female leaders to make it into tales and 'histories'. We have all heard of the famous Icenian Queen Boudica who led a revolt against the Romans, but she is not the only one history records. Queen Cartimandua of the Brigantes rivalled the authority of her estranged husband Venutius and Queen Medb of Connaught was also noted as being far more powerful than her husband Ailill.

The historian Barry Cunliffe states categorically, 'We know that women occupied an extremely powerful position in Celtic society. Many Iron Age tombs reveal rich and revered women.' One such is 'Wetwang woman', found in 2001, buried on a chalk hill in the East Riding with fine clothes, food stuffs and a chariot. Carbon dating tells us she lived around 300 BC and the fine goods with which she was buried indicate her standing. Throughout Celtic Europe, burial sites of similarly high-status women have been discovered proving that, at least in some communities, women were given equal or higher status to men.

Writers like Ammianus Marcellinus commented on the valour, indomitability and physical strength of Gaulish women who were apparently as formidable in war as their husbands. They didn't necessarily fight but were part of the war movement. Queen Medb, for example, was driven around the camp in a chariot before war to exhort the men to fight well. This picture fits with the idea of a matriarchal society.

But what of the bloodline? If you think about it, there is a sense to matriarchal lineage. A baby born to a woman is indisputably hers, in a way that – in the absence of DNA testing – a man could never guarantee. Passing the royal line from mother to mother, therefore, guaranteed its purity.

Irish and Welsh records suggest a female lineage. Mothers feature regularly as 'dynasty founders' and much of the Celtic mythology (designed to reflect real society with exaggerated supernatural features) traces royal lines through women. *The Mabinogion*, for example, denotes the status of Mabon (the divine youth) through his mother, Modron, not his father. Irish and Welsh heroic groups were often named after a mother, and sagas often identify their heroes with reference to female lineage, e.g. Fergus Fer Tlachtga – Tlachtga's husband.

In the Pictish (Brytonic) royal house, although the rulers were – at least in the later period – male, kingship passed to the brother of a king by the same mother or to a sister's son – i.e. down a matrilineal line – and there is evidence that it was the same at Tara in Ireland. Livy, a Roman historian, reports that Ambicatus, a mythic Celtic king, sent his sister's sons (not his own) to found new kingdoms and whilst this is legend rather than history, such tales tend to be rooted in a believable social structure that mimics the experience of the hearers.

All this suggests a Celtic society that placed great importance and significance on the female bloodline, and there is, I feel, an inherent sense to a social structure in which women organise and men operate. It has been the way of domestic households for centuries and that is only now being overturned in favour of a more equal style of domestic rule and task-sharing. I am not trying to suggest that in a matriarchy women did everything, Amazonian style, but rather that there was a sensible division of labour across the community that more closely mimicked that of the nuclear family. And that it was led by chieftainesses.

I love the idea that within this world, Leir having three daughters would be seen a sign of great divine favour, rather than the 'shame' that it had become for monarchs of Shakespeare's time. It has been fascinating to explore a society in which women were honoured for their beauty, their fertility, but above all their leadership and I hope it sets readers thinking about the impositions of the aggressive and often repressive patriarchies that followed and of what might have been without them . . .

The Mother Goddess and the Deas Matres

If we accept the idea of a matriarchal society, it is perhaps no surprise that the Mother Goddess is the underpinning element of the Celtic universe, representing the care and fertility of the natural world. In a time when lives were dominated by the seasons and their patterns of fertility, the nurturing womb – and its plant equivalents – was a vital element of life and it was therefore natural to worship a goddess who could bring forth life.

The Celts were far from unusual in this; most of the ancient cultures worshipped a Mother/Earth Goddess. The Greeks had Gaia, who rose from Chaos to provide a home for mortals and immortals alike. She married Uranus – the sky – and gave birth to Ourea – the mountains – and Pontus – the sea – as well as the first Titans who, in turn, became parents of most of the Olympic gods. The near identical equivalent to Gaia can also be found in the Romans' Terra, the Etruscans' Cel and the Andeans' Pachamama, and core to Hinduism is the female Shakti, the underlying divine power in the universe.

From what we can tell from later sources, Danu was a known name for the Celtic Mother Goddess, seeming to mean 'water from heaven'. Water was seen as a very feminine symbol and historian Peter Berresford Ellis suggests that the River Danube takes its name from the same source and points out that the headwaters of the Danube are where Celtic civilisation is acknowledged to have evolved, so the idea of a goddess intertwined with the lifegiving river is highly possible. In the absence of any more probable name, therefore, I chose to adopt the use of Danu for the Mother Goddess.

Although the Goddess is often worshipped in the singular, there is also a recurrent motif of her in threes – the *deas matres*, or 'goddess mothers'. Three was a sacred number to Celts and there are triadic goddesses everywhere as the Iron Age progresses. Often local goddesses came in threes, for example, the Nemausicae at Nimes and the Treverae at Triers. The water goddess Coventina in Carrawburgh, Yorkshire is also shown as a triple on plaques. Clearly in such a culture, a leader who could produce three daughters – a *deas matres* made flesh – would consider themselves fortunate indeed.

Druids

One of the most enlightening parts of my research into the Iron Age was finding out about druids. Along with most of the population, I had a rather mystical image of druids as wizard-like, 'Merlin' figures, presiding at lurid ceremonies, divining the future and controlling the people in the manner of later priests. What I discovered, at least for this early period, was something far more interesting. The druids seem to have been the intellectuals of the community – the people who were picked out for their brain power and trained to use it for the good of the people.

Both Julius Caesar and Diodorus Siculus, writing in the first century AD, describe the druids as scholars and much of the widespread misunderstanding about them must be set at the door of their compatriot Pliny, a Roman 'historian'. He was fascinated by magic and many of his druidic pictures of oak groves, mistletoe ceremonies and sacrifices are, at the very least, exaggerated. The barbarous rites he portrays so vividly, however, captured the public imagination more than the reality and the seeds of the dark, priestly figures we believe we know today were sewn. But they were wrong.

The original druids were not so much priests as philosophers, judges, educators, historians, doctors, seers, astronomers and astrologers. No classical writer ever refers to them as priests, or to druidism as a religion. That idea came later as druidism was demonised by Christianity. They were, instead, the intellectual heart of their communities. Druidism was not inherited, but learned by those considered worthy (see druid education below) and was practised in three distinct ways, as identified by Strabo, a Greek historian writing around the time of Christ, and as I describe in the novel:

Singers. By which I mean highly skilled musicians and poets, who captured the feelings and events of the community in oral celebrations that could be passed down through the ages. These were the early bards and strolling players of our country and, in a time before writing, were revered as the vital historians of their age.

Augurs. These are perhaps the more 'mystical' of the druids and the ones who held sway in the popular imagination for the longest time. Their job was to try to communicate with the spirits to interpret signs and see into the future. These were the druids who cut open animals to read the fate of the community in their entrails, but this was just the lurid end of their job. Much of what they did would have been about reading natural signs in the land and, in particular, the stars and seeking to give that practical application. It would most likely, for example, have been the augurs who created the highly sophisticated calendar (see below) that managed to balance the lunar and solar cycles to create the seasons that we still understand today.

Scientists. I had never, until I researched druids, thought of them as scientists but the moment I did, it made total sense. These, remember, are the intellectuals of the community and what else would they be doing but looking to understand the world around them and exploit it for human use? They had so much more than us still to learn, but that does not make them less intelligent and it is to them that we owe so much progress in tools, agricultural methods, production of goods, both everyday and luxury, and advances in medicine, fabric and metals. They were the questioners, the thinkers – the ones who, far more practically than the augurs, looked to the future and tried to make the lot of the communities around them better. I knew instantly that this was the sort of druid I wanted Olwen to be and I hope I did her justice. She still had ceremonies to carry out of course – the goddess and the spirits had to be appeased – but her main fascination and drive was natural science.

Evidence tells us that druids included women equally to men but this was skewed because so many of the writings about them are Roman so reflect their own societal norms rather than those they observed. Romans used women for pleasure and child-bearing and were very threatened by powerful Celtic women. Writing them out of history was one way to suppress that threat.

In the Roman world druids were largely gone by AD 100 but we have evidence of them hanging on in the Celtic world. St Patrick in Ireland and missionaries in Scotland were fighting against them as late as the sixth century. By that stage they had become more of the controlling, priestly figures that pervade the public imagination but I hope that this novel takes us back to the true roots of the druids – as serious, intellectual scientists and artists.

Druid Instruction

In the original manuscript of *Iron Queen* I used the term 'druid school' and my editor picked me up on it, assuming I'd been lured into some sort of fantasy creation. It does, perhaps, sound a little bit Harry Potter to the modern ear so we avoided overtly naming the institutions, but they did exist. The early druids went off to learn their trade from dedicated teachers and it is perhaps helpful to think of this more as a university education. The pupils may have gone there young but in a period in which forty was considered a full life, age is relative. The aim seems to have been to have druids in their twenties and thirties fully instructed and working for their communities, as I show with Olwen.

Britain seems to have been renowned for its druidic institutions, suggesting perhaps that they had very early and/or very skilled druids. Our primary source for this is Caesar, who asserts in his *Commentaries on The Gallic War* (about his invasions of Gaul and Britain, 58–50 BC) that the Druidical doctrine was evolved in the Isle of Britain and taken to Gaul from there. He states that: 'those who wish to study it deeply usually go to the island (Britain) and stay there for a time'. Now, Caesar, for all his brilliance, was not a man to trouble himself with in-depth fact-checking but he must have picked the concept up from somewhere and in the absence of any other information, we can tentatively presume it to have roots in reality.

I always believe that we underestimate the brainpower of more primitive cultures in our history. There is little evidence that we have become significantly cleverer than our forebears; we have simply had more learning to build on. It seems to me that any sensible community would make the most of all its talents, not just physical but also intellectual and would do their best to facilitate learning in all areas. Hence druids' 'schools'.

The Celtic Calendar

Despite, as I asserted above, my belief that we often underestimate our ancestors, I confess that I was astonished when I found out the sophisticated way in which Iron Age people could calculate time. When I thought about it, it made perfect sense as this was a culture dominated by the turning of the seasons and with plenty of time to study the heavens it's hardly surprising they were able to work out a pattern. And, let's face it, as far back as 3000 BC when Stonehenge was built, its creators had been able to arrange it so perfectly that the sun fell in a particular place on every solstice (which in itself fascinates me – imagine if you get a cloudy day and have to wait another whole year to test your stone placement!) so it shouldn't be a surprise that 2500 years later, people had an intimate knowledge of the turning of both moon and sun.

What is fascinating, however, is the way in which they chose to adjust the differences between the lunar and solar calendars, to ensure that the 'seasons' and their attendant festivals were always fixed, making it easier to mark the agricultural changes that dictated life. Put extremely simply, the moon completes a 'lunation' (waxes and wains) every 29½ days, making a nominal 'month'. Twelve such months, therefore, take up 354 days, but the earth takes about 365.25 days to orbit the sun, meaning that we are left with a disparity.

In our modern calendar that is handled by having some months as thirty days and some as thirty-one with an added day on 29 February every leap year. The Iron Age people, however, had a slightly different solution. They opted for an extra month every three years, allowing the seasons to slide a little before pulling them firmly back into place with 'Rantaranos' – a word that means something like 'complete'. It seems to have been inserted in spring/summer – an obvious time to bag an extra month – and would obviously have been celebrated with great joy as a form of bonus time.

The key evidence we have for these ancient calculations comes from a wonderful bronze calendar found in Coligny, France, in 1897. Made in Roman Gaul in the early years after Christ, it was found broken into seventy-three pieces, which together form a 5-foot-wide, 3.5-foot-high bronze tablet containing sixteen vertical columns, with sixty-two months distributed over five years. A similar leaden tablet was found in 1983 (the Larzac inscription) written in Latin cursive and dating to the second or first century BC. Then in 1992 a Celtic text written on bronze was found from the second century BC, suggesting the dating system shown on the Coligny calendar stretched back a long time.

The evidence of these artefacts is what I have used to mark out time in the novel, dividing it into the four Celtic seasons:

Samhain from 1 November (the quiet winter time of repairs, making equipment and tending those animals being overwintered)
Imbolc from 1 February (spring lambing and calving)
Beltane from 1 May (animals out to summer pasture)
Lughnasad from 1 August (autumnal harvest and preparation of grain for storage, plus the culling of animals in days leading up to Samhain).

Within this, the months also have names that seem to clearly denote the primary activities considered vital at that point of the year, as shown in the diagram at the start of the novel. The first day (or rather, night, as they were marked by the rising of the new moon) of each period was a festival of the same name and at least two of these still hold sway in some way today – Samhain as Halloween and Beltane as Midsummer.

Celtic Tribes

When it comes to tribal names, we butt up once again against the lack of written record before Roman times. We can only assume, however, that the tribal names the invaders picked up were the ones used by the natives (with perhaps some Latinisation). How far back they had come from we do not know but the presence of hillforts powerfully suggests leaders and a sense of community – i.e. tribes – so in the absence of any other, it seems fair to use the names the

Romans provided us with. Please see the map at the start of the novel for more detail.

The name Coritani first appears in Ptolemy's *Geography* – an early 'atlas' of the Roman Empire written around AD 150, and as they held all the land in modern day Leicestershire, a place associated with Leir (see below) they seemed the correct choice for the novel. It also happens to be the county in which I grew up so I felt especially connected to it.

The other key tribe is that of Lucius' Belgae. In Shakespeare's play – and its far older source – Cordelia escapes over the channel and marries the unspecified King of France, returning with him to fight her sisters, so I wanted to explore that possibility to expand the Celtic world for the reader. This world reached across much of northern Europe, notably Gaul. There is clear archaeological evidence from the second millennium BC of strong trade and interaction between northern France and southern England – a 'Celtic zone'. Excavations in Manche are almost indistinguishable from those in Wessex. British hillforts from early in first millennium are paralleled by ones at Malleville-sur-le-Bec, Eure and Cagny in northern France. Swords, spears and jewellery are also very similar and it is clear that the peoples shared great similarities in culture, beliefs, living styles and language. Tacitus – a Roman historian living c. AD 56–120 – attested that there was no great difference in language between Gaul and Britain even as late as his era and this is why I show Cordelia able to speak relatively freely with the Belgae when she meets them.

The Belgae were less a single tribe than a confederation of tribes, including one group that had settled on the south coast of Britain by Caesar's time. They lived in northern Gaul in the triangle between the Channel, the west bank of the Rhine and the northern bank of the Seine. We do not know where they ruled from – most likely a number of places – but there are clear remains of a hillfort at Braquemont, making it a good choice in which to set Lucius' homelands.

Casear entertainingly noted that of all the tribes of Gaul the Belgae were 'the bravest, because they are furthest from the civilisation and refinement of [our] Province, and merchants least frequently resort to them, and import those things which tend to effeminate the mind; and they are the nearest to the Germans, who dwell beyond the Rhine, with whom they are continually waging war'. I mention 'skirmishes with the Germanae' in the novel but war would mainly have been a preoccupation several hundred years after the period of the novel (see below for more).

Titles

At the risk of sounding like a cracked record, we have no way of knowing what designations the Celtic people used for their leaders. I did not wish to use Queen or King, as they imply the highly autocratic system we know so well from later periods and did not seem appropriate for a society that was so much less hierarchical. I therefore opted for Chieftain and Chieftainess. I felt for some time that it would be better to simply use Chieftain, rather than singling out a female form, as if suggesting that it was in some way different, but in the end using Chieftainess seemed to help the modern reader remember that the novel is set in a time of true female leadership so I kept it.

The appellation Heiress is, I hope, self-explanatory and makes the inheritance structure of the tribe clear. However, I chose, after much deliberation, to retain the anachronistic titles Princess and Prince for the lower royals to convey their status in a way we, as modern readers, can understand.

Hillforts

It was a glorious summer's day two years ago when I first encountered Burrough Hill. I'd parked in a small car park and headed uncertainly up a rough track, so was completely taken unawares when, barely 100 metres up, I came out of trees and there were the great ringed ramparts just above me. The fort is not especially 'preserved'. There are no reconstructions, no visible markings of dwellings, fencing or roads. That day cattle grazed idly amongst the grass and thistles and nothing but a small sign marked out its history, but there was something magical about that, as if Burrough Hill in some way still existed for itself. I walked across the grass and up the side of what would have been the gateway onto the top of the earthen ramparts to look down into the clear remains of an Iron Age hillfort, and could instantly imagine myself back in time.

The land within the giant ring was wide and flat. The ramparts were high and strong – made to last – and the view across the plains was breathtaking. Here a man, or in fact a woman, could truly survey all they commanded and it seemed such a logical, attractive, clever place to choose to live. I felt a thrill run through me and couldn't wait to start writing the novel.

Archaeological evidence suggests that hillforts began being constructed in around 600 BC, often in lofty positions overlooking prime agricultural land. Although to our eyes (coloured by later castles) they look set up for military defence, it seems that this was not their primary function. They were, rather, set on high to survey the surrounding agricultural lands – the community's most valuable asset. One big job of the hillforts seems to have been to store grain in times of plenty as multiple grain pits have been found in all examples. Food was a marker of wealth in this period and belonged largely to the community rather than the individual. Set aside in a pit and sealed with clay the corn didn't germinate so could be kept for at least a year, either to feed the tribe or to trade with – as Goneril latches onto in the novel.

A little later in the Iron Age it appears things got a bit more aggressive and there is evidence of charnel pits for burying mass dead. In the novel I introduce the word 'war' and whilst we do not know when that concept of larger scale battles was invented, it seems it was as the Iron Age progressed and boundaries solidified that the idea of expanding your territories really took hold. Society was moving towards being more territorial and acquisitional with the emergence of clear and ambitious leaders and I enjoyed experimenting with Goneril being at the start of that.

Hillforts are impressive structures. A historian called A. H. A. Hogg calculated that around 12,500–17,500 man-hours would have been needed to build one (i.e. a team of 200 people over 85–115 days) but the results were stunning. When I drove away from my first visit to Burrough I took a route that led me through the valley, from where I could look up and see the fort dominating the sloping landscape. The wooden fencing that likely topped the ramparts is obviously gone, leaving the lines greener and gentler than they would have been, but it sat there, solid and clear, more protective than aggressive.

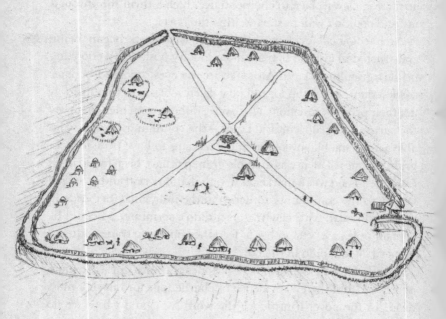

The early Celts were a community people. Almost all discovered hillforts are as round as it is possible for the landscape to allow them to be, suggesting that they were seen as an extension of the roundhouse – a place for all, where some led but all were inherently equal beneath the Goddess' skies. It is an appealing way of living and one that I have tried to show in the novel, highlighting its positive qualities by placing it under threat.

Beacon Hill, Burrough Hill and Breedon Hill

All three of these hillforts can still be visited and I would strongly recommend doing so.

Burrough Hill, as discussed in detail above, sits proudly but very quietly in a field just outside Melton Mowbray and anyone can park and take the easy walk up into its wide confines.

Beacon Hill is on the outskirts of Loughborough and is at the heart of a large and very popular country park, meaning that its ancient lines are less evident than Burrough. It was well known to me as a child and even more so as a teenager as it was where my mates and I went in the sixth form to hang out on summer evenings and drink cider, lager and – Lord help us – Thunderbird wine! However, if you visit it with a clear head, you can just about trace where the lines of the now-lost ramparts would have been and you can certainly stand on the viewing point, where the ancient beacon once was, and look out across the Coritani lands.

Even today the rocks and trees up on Beacon Hill seem to twist out of the landscape, as I describe at the start of the novel, and you can get a sense of how special it must have felt to those so much more in tune with the natural world than we are today. The Guardian rock mentioned in the novel can still be seen in the shape of a face in profile looking out over the plains. It is known these days as the 'Old Man of the Beacon' but I believe that the

Iron Age peoples would have considered it a guardian figure and named it accordingly.

Breedon Hill, not far from Melbourne, Derbyshire, has seen the mark of time more than the other two forts. These days it is topped by the pretty Church of St Mary and St Hardulph, with its attendant graveyard, so it is perhaps harder than with the other two hills to see through to its pagan origins. The area has also been extensively quarried so that it now seems to sit on a far sharper cliff than would have been the case when it was built. Nonetheless, if you dip over the far edge you can see the lines of the ancient ramparts and, as with the other two forts, gain a sense of the commanding position of this most westerly of the Coritani forts. We do not know exactly when Breedon was built but it was almost certainly after Beacon so I took the liberty of pinning down its creation to Leir's time and handing it to his middle daughter who, I feel, got a bit of a rough deal from Shakespeare and deserved a little something back from me.

Roundhouses

There is something wonderful about a roundhouse. They capture the imagination (for me at least) in the same way as a turret (I sooo want a turret!), a tepee or even just a circular window. There is something inherently appealing in the softly curved, inclusive nature of a roundhouse and I suspect it is only really because of the rather boring necessity to 'fit more in' that we ever moved to squares and rectangles.

And yet a roundhouse is not the cramped or primitive dwelling that you might imagine. Far from it. Even a small, 7m diameter, roundhouse offers the equivalent living space to a modern two-bedroom bungalow, with a central living space of about 4m square, a 1.3m wide entrance passage and five sleeping compartments each 1.5m deep, tapering from 4m wide at the outer edge to 2.6m at the inner – not bad at all! The only compromise would be on standing height and this was neatly solved by having bedrooms at the edges where the roof is lowest, as in a modern-day tent.

A 10m roundhouse would equate to a house with three bedrooms, two reception rooms and a kitchen, and archaeology has turned up many as big as 15m in diameter, both within hillforts and in open farms. There is also evidence of upper floors, as shown in the novel. It's impossible to say what they were used for – most likely storage but there is no reason why the enterprising Celt would not think of sleeping up there in peace and warmth.

In the 1970s a group of historians reconstructed a roundhouse based on excavation evidence at Pimperne in Dorset. It was a huge project that told us a great deal about their construction, not the least the materials required. For the 'Pimperne House', of 12.8m diameter, they needed over 200 trees: 36 mature oaks (45–55 years old) for the posts, 65 young oaks (10–20 years) for outer stakes and entrance, 50 hazels for the wattle walls, 55 elm and ash trees for the rafters. They also needed 7 tonnes of straw for a 10cm thick thatch, though the original may have been at least three times that.

The construction of a roundhouse works on the simple principle of building a cylinder in which to live, topped with a conical roof. The cylinder was crafted with two rings of timber posts – a lower outer one and a higher, weight-bearing one about 2m in from the edge. Construction of the cone may have been based around a central pole to which the sloping ones could be bound but once they were in place, resting on the posts and most likely secured with horizontal 'ring beams', the vertical post could be cut away above the upper storey to allow an uninterrupted living area and room for a central hearth. Almost all roundhouses were built with the roof at a 45° angle, still deemed to be the most weatherproof in thatched roofs now, and the Pimperne reconstruction proved remarkably resilient to even extreme conditions.

The hardest part of the reconstruction was the large porch, which breaks the natural physics of the conical roof. There is plenty of evidence of large entrances, supported by four porch posts and wide enough to allow horses or even a chariot to ride inside, presumably for show. However, cutting the porch into the round structure required clever mathematics and fitting the thatch around it without compromising the weather-proofing took great skill. It is no surprise, therefore, that there is evidence of professional architects in the Iron Age, using geometric calculations and even standard measures. The famous Greek mathematician, Pythagoras was born c. 569 BC – some 69 years before the novel is set – and although he was brilliant, he was far from alone in his core abilities so there must have been plenty of men and women who could perfect building calculations.

Inside the roundhouse, a wattle and daub wall would be built between the outside posts. Another one, or a simpler willow screen, could be also built between the inner timber posts to separate off the bedrooms, as shown in the novel. The idea of partitioning and of private space does seem to have been important – perhaps more so than in the much later Anglo-Saxon and Viking great halls – and it would be a mistake, at least for the grander roundhouses, to imagine everyone tumbled in together.

D. W. Harding, one of the leaders in the Pimperne project, was quizzed about the elegance of roundhouses and said, rather brilliantly I think: *'If this sounds too sophisticated for Iron Age building it is only because the image of Iron Age communities as benighted peasants eking out a miserable subsistence existence is so enduring. We have only to examine the sophisticated metalwork of the period ... to appreciate that the supply of raw materials and the skill with which they were worked were of an extremely high technological and aesthetic level. There is no reason to presume that a chief who could command such high-status goods as the Snettisham torcs or the Battersea shield would cower in a draughty shack with the rain leaking through the roof.'*

The Pimperne house was completed in 1976 and stood until 1990. It cannot therefore be seen any more but pictures of the fascinating project are available here – *http://www.butser.org.uk/pimperne.html*.

Historical evidence for Leir and his three daughters.

Needless to say, given all I've discussed above about the lack of written records from this period, there is very little hard evidence for Leir, Goneril, Regan and Cordelia, so I confess to having taken a rather large pencil to join some rather small dots.

The first extant account of Leir is in *The History of the Kings of Britain*, written by Geoffrey of Monmouth in 1135. Geoffrey locates Leir's rule shortly after the reign of King Solomon – so c. 900 BC. However, he has him as a 'King', ruling with 'Dukes' so there are clear anachronisms in his understanding of the social organisation of the Iron Age. He is, nonetheless, our key source and gave me several important features of the story, notably: its Leicestershire location, the family structure, and the idea of flight.

Location

Geoffrey tells us that Leir was a pre-Christian warrior king whose greatest achievement was that he 'built, upon the river Sore a city, called in the British tongue Kaerleir, or in the Saxon, Leircestre'. Now, Geoffrey is not a 'historian' known for his slavish fidelity to the truth, but his stories often have traceable roots into other sources, notably myths, and here these seem to favour a tradition of someone called Leir in that area.

Leir features in a variety of Celtic texts as a water god/spirit. He can be found, for example, in the *Troedd Ynys Prydein* (*Triads of the Isle of Britain* – a group of medieval manuscripts which preserve fragments of Welsh folklore, mythology and traditional history) and is probably linked to Lir, the Irish god of the sea. He is even believed to have had three children, one of whom defeated the other two in a battle to regain their land. Geoffrey of Monmouth reports that an annual festival dedicated to Leir took place in an ancient temple in Leicester and as he is known to have visited the city on a number of occasions, there is little reason to doubt this particular assertion. Although Britain was Christian by his time, many originally pagan festivals lingered all the way up to the seventeenth century and even beyond (note May Day celebrations and many aspects of Christmas).

Archaeologists have turned up evidence of a vast structure in the city centre that may well have been a pagan temple. By Roman times Leicester had become an important city as the *civitas* – capital – of our Coritani and this temple was likely to be one of regional importance, so if it was linked to Leir as Geoffrey suggests, it affirms his importance in the area. It also seems the major river running through the county was originally named after him. In the Domesday Book of 1086, what is now the River Soar is recorded as the Legra, and earlier documents speak of the Leir.

All of this seemed enough, for me, to choose Leir as a chieftain of the Coritani, though once I unearthed the probable fact that the Celts operated in a matriarchy, he had to be downgraded to an underchief.

The Family structure

Bladdud

It is also in Geoffrey's 'history' that I found Chieftain Bladdud, husband of Chieftainess Mavelle, whom he identifies as Leir's father and predecessor as king. This seems odd as Bladdud apparently ruled from Bath – over one hundred miles from Leicester – but such anomalies did not concern Geoffrey. Neither did the niceties of past social structures, which he skewed with his arrogant assumption that it would have been the same as his own patriarchal monarchy. For me, however, the intriguing fact about Bladdud was that he tried to fly (see below for more) and I knew that had to feature in the story.

For a long time in the writing of this novel, Bladdud was the ruling chieftain, but that sat uneasily with the matriarchy I was creating. I explained it away by having him allowed to continue the rule of his dead wife, Chieftainess Mavelle – as Leir holds Burrough for his dead wife, Branwen – but it still felt wrong. It was only when I returned to edit afresh that I realised I had been as guilty as the lurid Geoffrey of applying my own subconscious patriarchal norms to the story and had accepted Bladdud as ruler, when that simply would not have happened. Bladdud had to die and Mavelle, as chieftainess and his fellow experimenter, had to fly. It is a shame that Shakespeare chose to ignore this aspect of his source – and perhaps surprising given his eye for drama and the theatrical device of a trapdoor in 'the Heavens' from which magical spirits could be lowered. Perhaps it sullied the tone of his tragedy, but I certainly wanted Bladdud – or, rather, Mavelle – restored to the story.

Goneril, Regan and Cordelia

Core to Geoffrey's tale are Leir's three daughters, Gonorilla, Regau and Cordeilla, names we know so well from Shakespeare, and, indeed, we find much of the core of the play in this original source. Leir asks his daughters which of them loves him the most. Gonorilla and Regau make extravagant claims to do so whilst Leir's favourite and youngest daughter, Cordeilla, simply says she loves him as a daughter should. She is immediately disinherited and sent abroad to Gaul, while the two flattering sisters get good husbands and half Leir's kingdom. They soon, however, mistreat Leir and he is forced to flee to Gaul himself. Eventually, Cordeilla's Gaulish husband raises an army, Leir defeats his enemies and regains his kingdom, reigning for the next two years, until he dies and is, interestingly, succeeded by Cordeilla.

Geoffrey's twelfth century account of King Leir seems to have suddenly attracted attention in the sixteenth century, spawning several narratives (Holinshed's *Chronicles*, a poetry collection called

The Mirror for Magistrates, and part of Edmund Spenser's *The Faerie Queen*), leading to a play by an apparently anonymous author called *The True Chronicle History of King Leir, and his three daughters, Gonorill, Ragan, and Cordella*. This play was performed twelve years before the first recorded performance of Shakespeare's *King Lear* in 1605, though not published until that same year. It's possible that Shakespeare was somehow involved in this 'first draft' of the now famous play, which shows a more sympathetic Lear and has a happy ending in which Cordeilla triumphs in battle and restores her father to the throne – an ending I chose to partially adopt, though sadly minus my invented character, Taran.

King Lear is a gory and much-loved play which owes many of its core elements to a twelfth century monk but what really fascinated me was to take the story of a ruler and his daughters and put it into the Iron Age in a more believable way, not with dukes and Kings of France, but with tribal leaders, hillforts, roundhouses and a matrilineal succession. I hope the result is, at least, interesting.

Experiments with Flight

The moment I read of Bladdud who, according to Geoffrey of Monmouth, 'finally constructed a pair of wings for himself and tried to fly through the upper air', I was captivated. I always thought of experiments with flight starting with the Wright Brothers in the early 1900s, so to think of people making wings 2400 years before that seemed astonishing. The more I looked into the period and read of the natural scientist druids, however, the more logical it seemed. These were an agricultural people, clearly fascinated by animals, as their art shows. They had time aplenty to study horses, dogs, cattle and, of course, birds. And it would be only natural, having done so, to attempt to mimic all those things that they do best, including flight.

When you start to dig into the archives, it's possible to uncover various reports and legends of flying men. Myths from across the globe are rife with flying chariots and carpets, from the Indian Vimana, the Irish *roth rámach*, and the 'flying throne of Kay Kavus' in Persia. Then there's the wings. The Greek legend of Daedalus and Icarus famously tells of how the father and son pair crafted wings made of feathers held together with wax to try to escape the labyrinth in which King Minos had imprisoned them. The wings worked and they escaped, but sadly Icarus, despite his father's warnings, got overexcited by flight and flew too close to the sun. The wax melted and Icarus fell to his death – a salutary lesson to teenagers throughout history to listen to their parents!

But it isn't all just legend. Eilmer of Malmesbury, an eleventh-century English Benedictine monk, inspired by Daedelus, fixed wings to his hands and feet and launched himself from the top of a tower at Malmesbury Abbey. Reports claim he flew for 'more than a furlong' (about 200m), before he crashed, breaking both his legs and making himself lame forever after. He apparently attributed his failure to not having provided himself with a tail but never attempted the feat again.

There is, sadly, no record of anyone successfully flying – or, at least, landing – but I like to think that others tried and hope that I have worked with the known facts about craftsmen of the period to create a narrative that is credible.

Iron

The Iron Age is usually understood to run from around 800 BC to the arrival of Romans in 43 BC, though iron tools were actually only commonplace from c. 500 BC. It came after the far longer Bronze Age (c. 3000–800 BC), which had seen a move towards taming the landscape, creating surplus goods for trade and improving efficiencies with new tools, but the discovery of a far tougher metal meant all this could be rapidly accelerated.

Clearly in a novel about the Iron Age, smiths were always going to be key and that is why Taran was born – a simple craftsman but one with a high level of skill in working the key material that could consolidate progress for the tribe. Unlike bronze, which was made by secretive professionals and had a mysticism and therefore cachet, iron was an egalitarian material. Ore could be found in most places and anyone with the skills could extract the metal. But it was not easy. Iron has a higher melting point than bronze and would need a lot of hammering to remove the slag. It was also strong, hypnotic work so blacksmiths would have been quietly powerful figures and I wanted to harness that to create a romantic lead for Cordelia.

So how is iron made? It exists naturally within the ground as iron oxide – known as ore, or, at a later stage, rust, for if left unprotected it will revert to the oxide form fairly quickly. The ore appears in rock, sand or peat as a reddish brown, water-born deposit. I'm no chemist, so forgive my over-simple explanation, but the process of turning it into pure iron basically involves:

- Heating it with charcoal in a furnace, usually of clay, to high temperatures, to allow (as we know now) the carbon monoxide released by the burning charcoal to suck out the oxygen, leaving the iron behind.
- Keeping the heat high enough to melt the rock in which the ore is encased, so that it flows to the bottom and out through a hole where it cools to form 'slag'. The remaining iron, usually about the size of a football, is known at this point as the 'bloom', despite looking lumpy, ugly and distinctly unexciting!
- Removing the bloom from the furnace and heating it again, before hammering it to release the melted slag trapped inside to create a pure metal. The purer the iron, the more malleable it will be when shaped into tools.

Clearly to achieve this, the smith needed fires capable of producing high temperatures (around 1500°C, compared to the 1100

°C for bronze) so he had to be strong enough to work hefty bellows to pump air into the fire, and tough enough to withstand the heat. He also needed muscles to hammer the iron into submission, a keen eye and a craftsman's attention to detail. No wonder the good ones were considered valuable – not to mention sexy!

The Geography of Iron Age Britain

As discussed above, Iron Age Britain seems to have been divided into tribal lands that the Romans were, towards the end of the period, able to map with some precision. But how aware were those living at the time of others around them? Was there any sense of being part of a 'country', or were people stuck in their immediate surroundings?

The answer, yet again, is that it is hard to know but we can make some educated guesses. In a time when few travelled at all, the tribe would have been all, and the tribal leader the ultimate authority. Whilst people must have known the tribal leaders in the lands bordering their own, and been increasingly open to alliances (and, sadly, battles) with them, as the Coritani are with the Catuvellauni in the novel, we are a long way off any sort of concept of a wider 'kingdom'. This inherent insularity does not, however, mean that people were unaware of what was out there.

The key is the traders. Archeological evidence shows us that artefacts travelled long distances, suggesting wide-ranging and busy trading routes all across Europe and beyond. Those traders must, therefore, have had an awareness of the basic geography of the lands they travelled and it was a joy to me to introduce Gleva and Map into the novel to expand the horizons of my core characters.

As discussed above, the Coritani lands are at the heart of my own home in the Midlands (a place a friend once told me did not exist, being, apparently, a made-up concept to fudge the gap between North and South!). As such, they are about as far from the sea as it is possible to get and it seemed highly probable to me that Cordelia and her fellows would struggle to grasp what the 'seas' could possibly be. I therefore very much enjoyed giving her, her first (rather horrified) glimpse of the channel.

In the novel, Gleva and Map discuss the possibility that the Coritani lands might be at the heart of an island and I have them mention a 'cartograph somewhere in the Grecian lands'. This is a real document, created by a man called Pytheas, a native of Massalia (Marseille but then a Greek colony), who explored the north-western fringes of Europe and almost certainly circumnavigated Britain. He wrote a book called *On the Ocean*, which is now sadly lost but was quoted by first century writers such as Strabo. He gives a surprisingly accurate account of the Britain we know, including a half decent approximation of distances. He made his journey in around 320 BC, so a little later than the novel, but who knows if he was the first, so I took the liberty of including the idea to show how concepts of the world as a wider entity were starting to take shape.

British dog breeding

Various early historians identified British hunting dogs as being highly prized, so it seemed a good idea to make Cordelia a breeder. Strabo described hunting dogs as 'small, strong, rough-haired, fleet of foot and with a keen sense of smell' and the Roman poet Nemesianus, who wrote a piece called *The Hunt* in the third century AD said that, 'besides the dogs bred in Sparta ... you should also raise the breed which comes from Britain because they are fast and good for our hunting.'

There is archaeological evidence of the popularity of dogs in Britain and the wider Celtic world, with a prevalence of dog bones buried beneath the boundaries of hillforts and their skeletons found in ritual pits all over Europe. Dogs were then, as now, man's friend, but also his hunting and fighting companion and his faithful protector. Someone who could breed strong dogs would soon attract both reputation and money, as Cordelia does in the novel and whilst we may tend to think of selective breeding as a later practice, it seems to me obvious that, as with attempting flight, a people with the time to study the natural world, would soon work out how to breed desirable traits into their animals.

Triskele

Celtic art, reflecting Celtic spirit, revolves around circles. They represent the eternal cycle of the years, the seasons, and the birth-death-rebirth cycle of life. They are perfect and unbroken and are the basis of most Celtic symbols. With three considered a magical number by the Celts, it is easy to see why the unbreakable, eternal triskele, or triple spiral (as illustrated), was so prized. It was, therefore, the obvious symbol for the three Coritani daughters. As amulets were a highly popular form of jewellery, it seemed apt for them to all have a triskele amulet to symbol their eternal bond to each other – a bond that, sadly, is broken in the course of the novel.

Iron Queen is set over a thousand years earlier than any of my other historical novels. I was once told that the Iron Age wasn't a period that women should write about (being, apparently, about very male, rough-and-ready warrior types) and this, more than anything else, piqued my interest! When I discovered the possibility of a matriarchal society, it seemed to me that women were exactly who should be writing about it and I began work on the novel. It has, because of the sparse records of the time, had to be a work of careful consideration to try to create a believable society but archeologists have done wonderful work turning up evidence of buildings and artefacts that go a long way to showing us the gentle, clever, curious people who trod this earth so long before we did and I have loved bringing them to life. I hope my readers enjoy discovering them too.

Shakespeare's queens as you've never seen them before . . .

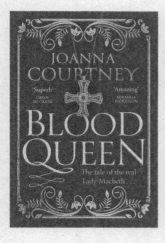 

'Glorious, rich, epic'
Rachael Lucas

Available now from